DATE DUE

N

THE
SUNRISE LANDS

THE
SUNRISE LANDS

S. M. STIRLING

A ROC BOOK

ROC
Published by New American Library, a division of
Penguin Group (USA) Inc., 375 Hudson Street,
New York, New York 10014, USA
Penguin Group (Canada), 90 Eglinton Avenue East, Suite 700, Toronto,
Ontario M4P 2Y3, Canada (a division of Pearson Penguin Canada Inc.)
Penguin Books Ltd., 80 Strand, London WC2R 0RL, England
Penguin Ireland, 25 St. Stephen's Green, Dublin 2,
Ireland (a division of Penguin Books Ltd.)
Penguin Group (Australia), 250 Camberwell Road, Camberwell, Victoria 3124,
Australia (a division of Pearson Australia Group Pty. Ltd.)
Penguin Books India Pvt. Ltd., 11 Community Centre, Panchsheel Park,
New Delhi - 110 017, India
Penguin Group (NZ), 67 Apollo Drive, Rosedale, North Shore 0745,
Auckland, New Zealand (a division of Pearson New Zealand Ltd.)
Penguin Books (South Africa) (Pty.) Ltd., 24 Sturdee Avenue,
Rosebank, Johannesburg 2196, South Africa

Penguin Books Ltd., Registered Offices:
80 Strand, London WC2R 0RL, England

First published by Roc, an imprint of New American Library,
a division of Penguin Group (USA) Inc.

First Printing, September 2007
10 9 8 7 6 5 4 3 2 1

Copyright © S. M. Stirling, 2007
Map by Cortney Skinner
All rights reserved

Ro͞c REGISTERED TRADEMARK—MARCA REGISTRADA

LIBRARY OF CONGRESS CATALOGING-IN-PUBLICATION DATA:

Stirling, S. M.
The sunrise lands / S. M. Stirling.
p. cm.
ISBN: 978-0-451-46170-4
1. Willamette River Valley (Or.)—Fiction. 2. Regression (Civilization)—Fiction. 3. Oregon—Fiction. I. Title.
PS3569.T543S86   2007
813'.54—dc22   2007010000

Set in Weiss
Designed by Ginger Legato

Printed in the United States of America

to Jan, forever and ever

ACKNOWLEDGMENTS

These are getting dense and chewy. Trying to create a world, even in words, is good occupational therapy for lunatics who think they're God, and an excellent argument for polytheism.

Thanks to my first readers:

To Steve Brady, for assistance with dialects and British background, hints on birds, beasts and bugs . . . and spotting some howlers.

Thanks also to Kier Salmon, for once again helping with the beautiful complexities of the Old Religion, and with local details for Oregon, and spotting some howlers, including a six-hour continuity gap. Oopsie! Not God yet!

To Dale Price, help with Catholic organization, theology and praxis, and some excellent suggestions . . . and spotting some howlers.

To all of them for becoming good, if long-distance, friends.

To Melinda Snodgrass, Daniel Abraham, Sage Walker, Emily Mah, Terry England, George R. R. Martin, Walter Jon Williams, Yvonne Coats, Sally Gwylan, Laura Mixon-Gould and Ian Tregellis of Critical Mass, for constant help and advice as the book was under construction, which enabled me to avoid some howlers. And heck, they were already friends.

To John Ringo, for some advice.

Special thanks to Heather Alexander, bard and balladeer, for permission to use the lyrics from her beautiful songs, which can be—and should be!—ordered at www.heatherlands.com. Run, do not walk, to do so. I always do when she's got a new CD out.

Special thanks to Kate West, for her kind words and permission to use her chants.

Special thanks . . . am I overusing the word? . . . to William Pint and Felicia Dale, for permission to use their music, which can be found at http://members.aol.com/pintndale/ and should be, for anyone with an ear and salt water in their veins.

And to Three Weird Sisters—Gwen Knighton, Mary Crowell, Brenda Sutton and Teresa Powell—whose alternately funny and beautiful music can be found at www.threeweirdsisters.com/.

They've not only allowed me to use their music, but to modify it, as for example Gwen's lovely "New Forest," the original lyrics of which can be found at www.gwenknighton.com/lyrics.html.

All mistakes, infelicities (including missed howlers) and errors are, of course, my own.

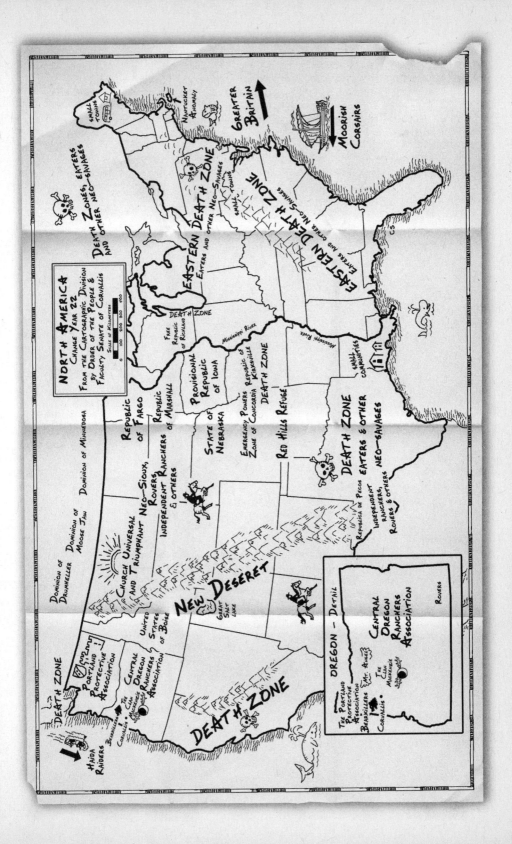

CHAPTER ONE

Ingolf Vogeler slapped his horse affectionately on the neck; he felt a little better now that the rain had stopped, even though it was the tag end of a chilly October day with a ragged sky the color of damp raw wool rolling in from the west. His gloved hand made a wet smack on his mount's mud-spattered coat; its breath smoked in the harsh wet air, and so did his. The hooves beat with a slow *clop-crunch* on the good crushed rock of the road, sending up little spurts of muddy water whitish gray with limestone dust.

He summoned up a little of the old excitement at heading into fresh country as he looked about at the Willamette Valley, inhaling the musky-silty smell of fallen leaves and turned earth, and the faint tang of woodsmoke drifting on the wind.

Riding damp and cold was nothing new to him for all that he'd turned twenty-eight only last summer, but the struggle to get over the High Cascades had been brutal. He'd barely crossed the Santiam Pass alive; the last blizzard would have killed him for sure, if he hadn't had two warm horses, a good sleeping bag covered in oiled bison leather and lined with fleece and stuffed with down, and a lot of experience with cold weather. He hadn't been really dry or warm in the days since either, and he could still feel the storm's white death in his bones, though down here five thousand feet lower things were just uncomfortable.

Look on the bright side, he told himself. *If any of the Prophet's cutters were still on my trail by then, they're surely dead, dead and frozen under twenty feet of snow until spring.*

"Hang in there, Boy."

Boy smelled powerfully of wet horse; but, then, Ingolf smelled of the wet wool of his jacket and pants, and wet leather and oiled metal from his gear and the harness. It had been a good long while since his last bath, too. You didn't, not out alone in the wilds in the cold season; you didn't take off your clothes at all if you could help it.

"That town should be coming up soon, Boy. Good warm stable and oats for you, if it's as fine as those yokels said it was."

The horse snorted and shook its head in what he could have sworn was doubtfulness; the big gelding and he had come a long way together, a lot farther than the remount-cum-packhorse on the end of the leading rein, which looked nearly ready to keel over and die. He'd seen that happen often enough; you could usually follow an army by the bodies of the horses. Past a certain point their hearts broke and they just lay down and gave up.

"You too, Billy."

He stopped to lean over and give the packhorse some hoarded honeycomb; it barely had the energy to lip it off his glove, and Boy didn't even protest.

"Just one hoof ahead of another, that'll do it."

They passed the odd wagon or oxcart, once a flock of sheep whose wet wool smelled a lot worse than his clothes; that had both horses crow-hopping a bit even tired as they were. And plenty of other riders and passersby on foot, now and then a bicyclist; most of the folk wore the funny pleated skirts he'd started seeing as soon as he got down into the valley, men and women both. Ingolf touched a finger to the floppy brim of his leather hat whenever he passed someone, and usually got a wave and a smile back, despite the foul weather; most people seemed to be cheerful and friendly here west of the Cascades, which made sense since they also seemed unusually well fed and clothed.

Wonder just how far it is to Sutterdown? he thought.

Traffic had died down as the sun sank, except for a few hurrying in the same direction he was, probably hoping to get inside before the gates closed. That gave him a good idea of when they were likely to shut . . . and that it would be soon.

"*Uff da,*" he swore mildly.

Most places wouldn't let you in once they'd buttoned up, and the ones that did usually charged a fine for opening a postern after curfew. He touched Boy up with a pressure of his legs. That was hard on him, and even more on Billy . . . but he didn't think Billy would survive a night in the open right now.

There were tall hills to his right—the last stubs of the mountains he'd crossed. The rolling floor of the valley opening westward was divided into small farms, their fields bordered by hedges and rows of trees. Within the enclosures were the green of pasture or new-sown winter wheat just beginning to mist the soil, dark brown of plowland with wind-ruffled puddles between the furrows or the rather messy look of a well-dug potato field, the bare spindly branches of orchards, cherry and apple, pear and peach. Now and then there was a clump of woodlot, oaks and firs, and more thickets along the river. He recognized the crooked stumplike plants on a south-facing hillside as grapevines, still with their spindly branches unpruned, though he hadn't seen their like often before.

I have drunk wine, though, and I wouldn't mind some at all, he thought, and smacked his lips absently. *Though right now something hot would be very good.*

Days like this, as the shadows grew darker and the wind blew colder, even a young man felt how the years would tell on him in another two decades. He coughed to clear his throat and spit aside.

There weren't any buildings in the fields apart from the odd byre and shed. The land was all worked from walled hamlets like the one he'd passed not long ago—they called them duns here. The Sutter River gurgled and chuckled to his left, flowing westward into the valley; the steep hills just north were densely forested, dark green and brooding with tall firs.

Then a scatter of sheds and workshops loomed up to either side of the road out of the misty dimness, showing lamps or furnace light—mostly strong-smelling tanyards and pottery kilns, the sort of trades smart towns didn't leave inside the wall. He heard the splashing and grinding sound of water turning millwheels to his right, and saw the occasional yellow glitter of flame through the branches of thick-planted trees.

His lips shaped a silent whistle when he came through the last fringe of bare-limbed oaks into a clear space and saw the town walls.

"Wouldn't like to have to storm those," he muttered. Even allowing for how the darkness made them seem to loom . . . "No, sir."

Must be thirty feet high, and pretty damned thick, he thought. *And towers every hundred yards, half bowshot apart, and I'd say they're half again as tall. You don't see many things built after the Change that height.*

He'd seen walls that had a bigger circuit—the town couldn't have more than three or four thousand people; Des Moines had thirty times that—but few that looked stronger.

And never *any painted like that.*

The surface looked like pale stucco; along the top below the crenellations was a running design of vines and flowers with . . . He peered through the murk.

Faces. I think. That's a woman's face, isn't it? With vines for hair. And that's a fox or a coyote. And that's . . .

The towers along the wall had pointed conical roofs sheathed in green copper and shaped like a witch's hat, which was appropriate if the wilder rumors he'd heard were true. There were two hills showing above the ramparts, off west to the other side of the town. One was crowned by a huge circular building without walls, just pillars supporting a roof; he could see the outline of it because a great bonfire blazed there, and even at this distance he could catch a hint of eerie music and dancing figures. He crossed himself by conditioned reflex at the sight, but without real fear—he'd never been excessively pious, even before he became a wandering freelance.

Maybe the rumors are true, but nobody said they set on visitors here.

And it didn't smell as bad as some towns did; just woodsmoke and barnyard, mostly. They probably had working sewers.

Four more towers around the gatehouse there . . . right, that's where the bridge leads in.

The town was built in a U formed by the river, which meant a natural moat on three sides; an old but well-kept pre-Change bridge ran to the edge of the gate. A carved and painted statue twice life-size was set into the wall on either side, a beautiful woman with long golden hair standing on a seashell on the left, a naked man holding a bow and crowned with the sun on the right.

As his horse set a hoof on the pavement he heard a thunder of drums

from the gatehouse towers, and a screeching, skirling drone that sent
Boy to tossing his head and snorting, and made the hair rise along the
back of Ingolf's neck. His eyes were still flicking up to the source of that
catamount wail when he halted before the gate guard.

"Never heard bagpipers before, eh?" one of them said with a chuckle.
"It's not someone biting a cat's tail, honest. We're bidding farewell to the
Sun, you see."

Ingolf smiled back and nodded. "Just startled me a bit."

It was always sound common sense to be friendly with armed strangers, and anyway, the one who'd spoken was a good-looking woman about
his own age, with a freckled snub-nosed face and lively brown eyes.
Which was a little odd, but while fighting women weren't numerous, they
weren't so rare that he'd never met one before either. He'd campaigned
with a couple who were pretty good, in fact, and one of them had been
notably better than that.

He took off the hat, slapping it against his knee to shed the water, and
incidentally to let them see his face in the circle of light cast by the big
lamps. Looking him over was their job, and he didn't have anything—
well, not much—to hide.

They'd see a big man, a little over six feet and broad-shouldered, with
a pleasant enough face despite a scar on his forehead and a nose that had
been broken and healed very slightly crooked; his close-cropped beard
and bowl-cut hair were light brown, his eyes dark blue, and his skin had
the ruddy weathered look of someone who spent his time out-of-doors
in all weather.

His gear was likewise plain and serviceable; a thigh-length shirt of
chain mail under his long leather duster, a yard of point-heavy curved
shete hung from his belt, and a ten-inch knife balancing it on the other
side. A horseman's short horn-and-sinew bow was cased at his left knee;
his kettle helmet hung by the right, and a quiver was slung over his back,
covered right now with a round shield painted dark brown with an orange wedge; a tomahawk had its three-foot handle through a loop at the
back of his belt.

There was no glitter of gold or gems on hilt and buckle; unlike some
fighting men he didn't boast by wearing his portable wealth.

While he let them look he studied them in turn. Two of the six guards
were women, in fact. They were dressed like the others, in pleated

knee-length skirts of wool tartan-checked in brown and dark green divided by slivers of dull orange, with boots and knee socks and an odd blanketlike stretch of the same material wrapped diagonally across their torsos and pinned over one shoulder with a brooch. Everyone here seemed to wear their hair shoulder-length or better, braided or loose, and the men sported mustaches; one example dangled down below the chin on either side.

Short swords and bucklers and long daggers rode at their waists. Four had yew longbows in their hands and quivers over their backs, and two held polearms: a seven-foot spear and an ugly thing like a great ax on a six-foot shaft whose blade tapered upward into a point, with a spike-hook on the rear. The man who held it was taller than Ingolf, and broader, and wore a beard the color of rust halfway down his chest. The spear and ax-thing slanted crosswise to bar his way; behind them were the open leaves of massive metal-clad gates, and a raised portcullis. There were murder-holes in the arched ceiling of the gate passage, and another set of gates on the inner side.

"Who are you, stranger? Where from, and what business would you be doing in Sutterdown?" the young woman asked, with her thumb hooked in her sword belt.

Now that she was closer he could see she wore a ring of twisted gold around her neck, the open end over her throat ending in two knobs. She had the same accent he'd noticed in the village—the dun—where he'd stopped to buy bread and cheese and ask a few questions this morning, but stronger. Sort of a rolling lilt, and sometimes a strange choice or order of words; it sounded exotic and musical but not unpleasant, and easier to understand than some dialects that had grown up in out-of-the-way places.

"The name's Ingolf Vogeler," he said, conscious of how his flat hard Badger vowels would sound strange here. "Out of the east—"

"Not Pendleton, I hope," one of the others said.

"Christ, no, and I didn't like what I saw of the place when I passed through," he said honestly.

Several of them laughed, nodding, and Ingolf went on: "I'm from a lot farther east than that. East of the Rockies and the plains."

Best establish that I'm respectable, he thought, and went on: "My father

is . . . was . . . Sheriff of Readstown in the Kickapoo country, in the Free Republic of Richland."

At their blank looks he called up the memory of old maps and books from his brief schooldays and added, "Southern Wisconsin, if that means anything to you."

"East of the Mississippi!" the woman who seemed to be in charge blurted, her eyes growing wide in surprise. "From the sunrise lands! Stranger, you *have* come a long way!"

They all looked impressed. *Natural enough. People would get excited back to home if someone from here showed up. I'm a little impressed they all know where Wisconsin is. A lot of ordinary folks back home couldn't name Oregon to save their lives.*

"Yup," he said. "I wander and do this and that—caravan guard, peace officer, some cowboying, or any honest work—I'm a passable carpenter and blacksmith, and I can handle horses."

He touched the side of his duster, where it covered an inner pocket. "I can pay an entry tax, if you have one."

"No need," the woman said. "All honest travelers and traders are welcome here, but we have a short way with thieves or outland bandits—scourge for the back or Lochaber ax for the neck, as needed—so take warning."

The hulking redhead with the gruesome bladed weapon grinned through his thatch of beard and hefted it, so that must be a Lochaber ax; he looked cheerful rather than menacing, though.

"Fair enough." Ingolf nodded. It was what he'd heard about these Mackenzies along the way. "I'm a peaceable man, when I'm let be."

Her voice took on a formal note as she continued: "Enter then and be welcome, guest within our walls, with the blessing of the Lady and the Lord, who hold dominion here in Sutterdown as the Foam-born Aphrodite and Apollo of the Unconquered Sun."

Wow, he thought. The names were vaguely familiar, but . . . *They are strange here!*

Aloud: "Anywhere I can get food and lodging for myself and my beasts? And I could use a hot bath, by God! I was in Bend four days ago."

The big man with the ax whistled; that was a hundred miles, a lot of it very cold this time of year and very steep in any season.

"You've good horses, then, Ingolf the Wanderer! *And* weather luck in plenty."

"Take my word for it and don't try going back east that way until spring, unless you've got skis."

Just then a voice shouted down from above, where the wild music had been. "Hey, will you be talking through till dawn, then? We can't go home until you close the gate!"

The woman turned and shouted back: "Would you leave a stranger out in the cold, and on the holy eve of—"

He didn't catch the next part; the word wasn't one he'd ever heard before.

"—at that?"

She turned back to him. "I'm Saba Brannigan Mackenzie, Mr. Vogeler; my sept's totem is Elk. And my father keeps an inn here, and you'll be very welcome. I'll show you the way; we're being relieved by the night guard now."

She shook his hand as he dismounted; her brow went up as she felt the heavy swordsman's callus around the inner edge of his thumb and forefinger, and his at the strength of her grip.

They walked through the gatehouse and into streets laid out in a grid, mark of a pre-Change settlement. This one was better kept up and better lit than most and free of sewage stink, the houses neatly repaired and big lanterns on posts where the streets met, the folk looking well fed and prosperous if oddly dressed. But though it was fairly dark—nothing was so dark as a town at night, unless it was a windowless basement—he caught glimpses of things that did look strange.

A terra-cotta of a bearded face over a door with horns growing from its brow; the wood of a shutter carved into leafy tendrils that seemed to be looking at him somehow; a stone post with a head on top and a phallus jutting from its middle, wrought in knotwork; a set of running and laughing children wearing costumes fantastically shaped and painted . . .

He snapped his fingers. "It's Halloween, or nearly!" he said. "Kids wear masks and things back home too, on Halloween."

"Samhain, we call it," she said, and spelled it out for him: she pronounced it *soween*.

He nodded and made a mental note of it; that was the word he'd heard her shout up to the tower. Then she smiled and winked at him and

added, "You'll find we take it, oh, a *wee bit* more seriously than your basic trick-or-treat."

Just then a snatch of song came from another group making its way down the middle of the street, youngsters nearly full-grown dancing amid a cold trilling of panpipes. And singing:

> *As the sun bleeds through the murk*
> *'Tis the last day we shall work*
> *For the Veil is thin and the spirit wild*
> *And the Crone is carrying Harvest's child!*

A girl led them, with a half-mask shaped like a raven's head covering most of her face. Her black-feathered cloak flared in the darkness as she danced a twirling measure and beat a little drum with snake-quick taps of her fingers. Saba made a sign with her forefinger and joined in the chorus:

> *Samhain!*
> *Turn away*
> *Run ye back to the light of day*
> *Samhain!*
> *Hope and pray*
> *All ye meet are the gentle fae.*

Then the raven-masked woman stopped in front of Ingolf, and he had to check to avoid running into her. The dancer's eyes were wide and fixed behind the slits of the mask, holding his locked for a long moment; they were alight with a combination of fear and ecstasy and forgetfulness of self that was not quite like anything he'd ever met before. It made him shiver a little and suppress an impulse to cross himself.

The rest of her group surrounded him, masked as horse and boar, dragon and wolf and elk. She sang again, swaying and beating counterpoint to the words:

> *Stranger, do you have a name?*
> *Tell us all from whence you came!*
> *You seem more like god than man—*
> *Has curse or blessing come to this clan?*

Ingolf wondered for a moment whether he was supposed to answer, and then she danced away again, leading her band with their leaping shadows huge against a wall:

> Samhain!
> *Turn away*
> *Run ye back to the light of day*
> Samhain!
> *Hope and pray*
> *All ye meet are the gentle fae.*

When the band had vanished around a corner Ingolf swore quietly and shook himself. Saba smiled at him.

"Told you," she said merrily.

He asked a few questions; in his experience, that got you further than talking about yourself, at least to start with, and it never hurt to learn. He found that the odd pleated skirts were kilts and the over-the-shoulder blanket things were called plaids; that the ring around her neck was called a torc and that couples exchanged them when they married; that she was a widow with two children, her man killed on the western coast by Haida raiders a year ago; that she took turns with wall and gate duty and practiced with arms, above all with the longbow, as all fit adults did here; and that she was the eldest of three sisters, worked at her father's inn, and kept his books on that and a vineyard and fulling-mill the family owned.

She asked in turn, "What brought you so far from home? We don't hear anything but fourth-hand rumors from that far east."

"I didn't get on well with my elder brother," he said, which covered a good deal of bitterness. "My father died and my brother became Sheriff of Readstown, and we quarreled. So I joined the Bossman's army, when we Richlanders sent men west to help Marshall against the Sioux."

For a moment he fell silent amid a wash of memory: the *shusssh* of arrows over the tilts of the wagons in the dark amid the stale smell of dying campfires, a sudden roaring brabble, thunder of hooves and screams of surprise and pain. The panic-stricken tightness of his grip on the rawhide-wound hilt of his shete as he ran half-naked through the night away from his fallen tent, slashing at figures that seemed to spring out of the ground before him, fighting his way towards the horse lines.

The ugly shock up his arm as the edge cut muscle and cracked bone, the first time and so different from a practice post. Glaring eyes and bared teeth, painted faces and horned headdresses and the long knives in their hands glinting ruddy with the lights of sudden fires. Voices shrieking:

"Hoo'hay! Hoo'hay! It's a good day to die, Lakota! Kye—eeee—Kye! Hoo'hay!"

Then the guttural "Hoon! Hoon!" of the blood call as the blades went in, the sick-making butcher's-cleaver sound of metal hammering home in flesh, the frenzied screaming of a man scalped alive.

"That war took longer than anyone thought it would," he said carefully.

"They usually do," Saba said, with a grim smile.

"And afterwards I couldn't seem to settle down, somehow. Went east and west, north and south—to the dead cities, often, doing salvage."

By then they were in the stables attached to her father's inn; the tavern was a rambling two-story affair seemingly knocked together from several pre-Change buildings, but the stables were newer, made of beam and plank with brick floors. He liked what he saw of the accommodation for the beasts, and he was pickier about that than about where he slept himself. Boy and Billy went into stalls, and he rubbed them down carefully, put on dry blankets and saw to the fodder—good timothy-clover hay without any musty smell, a hot cooked mash of oats and beans, and fresh water.

It looked like the muck was shoveled out regularly, with fresh sawdust and straw laid down; he checked their feet, and made a note to have Bill reshod—the one on his left rear had looked good enough in Bend, but it was a little loose now and definitely getting thin. Pavement wasn't kind to hooves, especially when years of frost and storm had roughened it.

"You boys rest up. You can take it easy for a while," he said, rubbing Boy's forehead as the horse butted at him. "You both earned it."

"You know how to look after horses," Saba said with approval, as she and a teenage boy helped him with the tack and the loads from the packsaddle.

Ingolf grinned. "You have to, if you want the horses to look after you. I had to push these two fellas a lot harder than I liked, but it was that or get stuck in Bend or Sisters for the winter. I got Boy in the Nebraska country and he's the best all-round horse I've ever had."

She nodded, handed him a room key with a number on the wooden tag that dangled from it, and pointed to a door.

"Bathhouse is through there. Bran here will show you the manner of it hereabouts; the stairs on the right past there go to the rooms. Come down those and turn left to get to the main room. See you there—you'll want to wash up before you eat."

He nodded, though in fact he was so hungry that it was a toss-up. But they seemed a cleanly lot here; so was he, when he had a choice, which sometimes you didn't if you were a wandering man. By the time he stowed his gear in the room and finished his bath—they soaped down and scrubbed with buckets of steaming-hot water poured over the head first here, before getting into the tub to soak—and dressed in his good suit of blue denim jacket and pants and roll-necked sweater from the packsaddle, he felt a lot more human and ready to face the Sheaf and Sickle's common room.

And I'm hungry enough to eat an ox, live.

Luckily he'd managed to keep clear of nits despite being on the road for weeks, and didn't need to use the special and very smelly soap provided. That did make him hope the beds would be free of biting company, another thing you had to get used to on the road.

He settled in a booth and Saba brought him a big mug of hot cider, to get the last of the chill out. Her father came with her; he looked formidable still despite the broad streaks of white in his dark beard and the kettle belly under his leather bib apron. His grin showed a full set of teeth and the hairy legs beneath his kilt were like grizzled tree trunks, even though he must have been a man grown and then some at the Change, which was a thing you saw less with every passing year.

The stories said that in those days people had commonly lived to eighty or a hundred or even more . . . but then, those stories said a lot of wild things: flying to the moon, talking-machine servants, sword blades made of fiery light, and islands filled with dinosaurs. Nowadays sixty was *old*, most places he'd seen, and few reached the Bible's threescore-and-ten.

"I hear you're from Wisconsin, Mr. Vogeler," Brannigan said, his voice a deep rumble.

Ingolf noted that he had less of the lilting local accent than his daughter, but there was wonder in his tone as he went on:

"Wisconsin! Haven't seen anyone from that far east since before the Change—wait, no, there *was* one, came all the way from upstate New York on a bicycle that first year. Big guy, went up north and became a knight or something. None since, though."

"We haven't seen many from the West Coast, either, Mr. Mackenzie," Ingolf said.

Brannigan chuckled; he seemed to be one of the jolly plump innkeepers of song and story. Which was lucky; in Ingolf's broad experience they were just as likely to be skinny po-faced tightwads soured on humanity in general and their customers in particular.

"Mackenzie is the Clan name, Mr. Vogeler, and there are going on for sixty thousand others! Just Tom will do, anyway."

"How much do I owe you, Mr. Brannigan . . . Tom?"

"Normally, half a silver dollar a day for a man and two horses, not counting drinks. Today and tomorrow, nothing."

At his puzzlement: "It's Samhain Eve. We set an empty place for a stranger at sunset tonight and tomorrow. A stranger from far away means double luck."

Brannigan's grin got wider. "You could be a god in disguise, after all!"

"I thank you kindly." He sipped the cider, and his brows went up. "And I thank you kindly! This is the best cider I've had since I left the Kickapoo country!"

He smacked his lips meditatively. There were herbs in it, and the scent had a deep fruitiness that was like a memory of September afternoons in the hills of home when the maples blazed. For a moment homesickness seized him, and he was back amid the bee-murmurous orchards in April, looking down from a bluff across fields like rolling snow, with petals blowing in drifts over his father's house and onto the stark blue water of the river. . . .

"Thank you for a taste of home," he said sincerely. "Join me in one? And that I *will* pay for."

He'd directed the invitation to both of them. Brannigan shook his head. "Maybe later. Business to attend to," he said.

A little to Ingolf's surprise, Saba nodded. "I will . . . if we're not too busy, Dad?"

"Nope, it's a slow night, everyone's getting ready for tomorrow," Brannigan said.

Then he made a gesture, index and little finger outstretched, the middle two folded down under the thumb. "Or out defying the fae, the young idiots. See you later, Mr. Vogeler."

She returned with the platters and some cider of her own, and sat across from him. He grinned and clinked his glass mug against hers, happier still when he saw she meant to eat with him. The odd grace she said over the food didn't put him off; you expected to meet strange customs far from home, and nothing here was as weird—or as nasty—as what he'd seen in the Valley of Paradise among the Prophet's folk.

"Your health, Saba," he said.

"And yours, Ingolf. To the Lord, to the Lady, to the Luck of the Clan!"

He was hungry enough that even with a pretty woman smiling at him the plate was the first priority. Everything that went into the food was something he might have had at his family's board—roast pork with cracklin' gravy, potatoes, carrots and cauliflower and broccoli, applesauce on the side, brown bread and butter. The details were different; the outer cuts of the pork were crusted with herbs, chopped dried cherries in the gravy, potatoes whipped creamy with dill and garlic and chives, the vegetables steamed rather than boiled, and a fruity red wine to go with it all when his cider was drained.

Wholly homelike was the wedge of apple pie with whipped cream, and a piece of yellow cheese beside it, sharp and dry and crumbly, just right to cut the rich sweetness of the pie filling and the buttery taste of the crust.

"Now, that's real cheddar," he said, sighing with contentment. "We Richlanders make good cheese; it was famous even before the Change, and this matches it. Is it yours?"

"No," she said. "It's from Tillamook—on the coast northwest of here, in Portland Protective Association country. That's where my man Raen was, trading for it, when the raiders landed."

"Sorry," he said awkwardly.

She smiled and sighed and patted his hand. "It's a year ago now, and he's in the Summerlands, waiting to come back . . . and he helped burn their ships at the water's edge. The Haida carry people off for slaves and steal and burn everything if they get a foothold; the raids are worse every year. . . . Battle luck comes from the Morrigú; a dozen others of our folk were there that day. . . ."

She shook off the thought. "That's an interesting name, Ingolf. It sounds like one of ours."

"It's not usual back on the Kickapoo, either; it's after my grandfather's uncle," Ingolf said. "People used to tease me about it, when I was a kid. What are your children's names, if I may ask? You do have unusual ones here, except for a few like Tom."

"Ioruath's my boy; he's three," she said; her smile grew broader. "And Emer, my girl, she's just one; never saw her father, poor thing."

"Pretty names," he said. "But I haven't heard them before."

"We used to have the same names as most people—some of the older people still do; you know, Tom and John and Mary and David, that kind, like Dad. But a lot of people took other ones after the Change, when we turned back to the Old Religion. Names from the ancient stories that teach us about the Gods. Or they gave names like that to their children—my mother changed to Moira, and she changed me from Sally to Saba."

"I like Saba better," he said.

"So do I," she said, and wrinkled her nose at him. "I like Ingolf . . . and nobody will tease you about it here. It isn't silly, like some of the ones they use up in the Protectorate. *Odard* and *Raoul*, I ask you!"

He took a moment to admire the sight of her. She'd switched to just her kilt and shirt and shoes, and everything he could see was just as he liked it; she was broad in the hips and shoulders and narrow in the waist, long-legged, with strong round arms and the full bosom of a woman who'd borne and nursed children. Ingolf liked her frank eyes too, and the way she returned his interest without being coy about it.

He learned that she wove, and embroidered, and played the guitar, liked to hunt and fish in season. There was a small tattoo above the upper curve of her bosom and below the finials of her torc, a miniature strung bow that also suggested the crescent moon.

"What's that?" he asked, indicating it with his eyes.

She grinned at him. "Never seen a woman's breasts before, you poor man?" she teased, and laughed with him. Then she touched the tattoo. "That's the Warrior's Mark. I got that when I turned eighteen and passed the tests for the First Levy . . . the militia, you'd probably call it."

When she gathered up the empty plates and took them back to the kitchen he watched the sway of her kilt with unfeigned pleasure.

I could stay here awhile, he thought. *I'm not broke by a long shot, and this is where the Voice and the dreams pointed.* His mind tried to turn aside, but he forced it back. *I'll need a base while I look around for . . . whoever it is I'm supposed to find.*

The door to the vestibule opened as he mused, and he looked up with the wariness his wandering years had bred. A group came in, three women and two men, all younger than him but not by that much; they all wore longswords and daggers, which they racked by the door. They moved as if they knew how to use them, too.

He noticed the twin girls first, since they were identical and dressed so alike he guessed they worked at it. Both were tall, five-nine or so, with yellow-blond braids down their backs, dressed in dark trousers and boots rather than kilts; when they took off their jackets, they revealed sleeveless jerkins of black leather over their shirts, blazoned with a white tree and seven stars surmounted by a crown.

The other girl was a year or two older and an inch or so shorter, with brown hair cut shoulder-length and brown eyes and features a little too bold for beauty. She was in pants and a short-sleeved thigh-length tunic of fine-woven wool, forest green, over a full-sleeved shirt of indigo-dyed linen. The tunic had a slit-pupiled eye wreathed in flame on a black shield woven over her chest, and the same device showed on the buckle of her silver-chain belt; it carried a rosary of worked coral and crucifix opposite a dagger.

Saba returned with two small glasses of applejack. Ingolf smiled at her, lifted his and tasted cautiously. It was potent but made from good mash, light-crushed and well strained, and aged a couple of years, just right for sipping liquor.

"Who are those?" he said quietly, nodding to the group as her father bustled over to them.

VIPs, he decided by himself.

Tom Brannigan wasn't in the least servile, but there was an indefinable air of respect. Ingolf's eyes narrowed slightly in professional appraisal.

"The big fella with the bright hair particularly," he said.

One of the men was in a kilt and was about Ingolf's own height, six-one or a little more; a bit lighter than his own one-ninety, he estimated, but not much. Broad-shouldered and long-limbed, well muscled but moving like a racehorse, looking like he was about to leap even when completely still. And strikingly handsome in a way that was almost beautiful without being in the least pretty, down to a cleft in the square chin.

"Oh, that's Rudi Mackenzie," Saba said, with the tolerant tone of a woman towards a younger man she'd known when he was just hitting his teens. "The Chief's kid."

Ingolf's eyes flicked to look at hands and wrists, the way the young man held himself and moved. And at the scars that showed when a sleeve of his saffron yellow shirt of linsey-woolsey fell back from a muscular forearm; there was another along the angle of his jaw. He looked young—probably looked younger than he was; the well-to-do didn't age as fast as ordinary folk—but formidable.

"That's not just a kid," he said. "That's a fighting man. And a very dangerous one, or I miss my bet."

"Well, yes. He fought with Raen . . . and very well, by all accounts. Took that cut on his face pulling my man out of the water with a Haida trying to spear him, but it was too late."

"He's your bossman's son? The heir?"

"Our Chief's a woman," Saba said. "Juniper Mackenzie, herself herself. But he's her son, right enough—and her tanist."

At his inquiring glance: "A tanist is . . . sort of an understudy. His father was Mike Havel—Lord Bear, some called him, the head of the Bearkiller Outfit, over west of the river. The twins are Havel's kids too, Rudi's half sisters; their mother's Signe Havel . . . He fathered Rudi with the Chief before he married Signe."

"Yeah, there's a family resemblance," Ingolf noted.

High cheekbones and slanted eyes; a trace of Injun there, he thought. The man's eyes were a light changeable gray-blue-green, the girls' the bright blue of cornflowers; his hair was worn shoulder-length and there was a strong tinge of copper-red in its yellow curls. He looked as if he laughed a lot; right now he was grinning at the innkeeper.

"Greetings to the Mackenzie!" Brannigan said grandly, then winked and made a sweeping bow. "You honor our humble establishment."

"Hey, Tom, I'm not *the* Mackenzie," the young man—Rudi—said, shaking his hand; that lilting accent of Saba's was stronger still with him. "My mother is *the* Mackenzie. I'm just *a* Mackenzie, like you and the rest, to be sure."

"You're just a clansman, and I'm the Horned Lord come in the flesh," Brannigan said.

"Well, you *are*," Rudi pointed out.

"Only in the Circle," Brannigan said.

Ingolf looked a question over at the innkeeper's daughter. "Dad's High Priest of the Sunhill Coven here," she said casually. "So when he Calls, the God comes to him. Mom's the High Priestess. Lady Juniper is High Priestess of the whole Clan, of course—she's the Goddess-on-Earth. The living vessel of the Mother."

"Oh," Ingolf said. *And I'm not going to ask more about that until I know my way around!* he thought.

"You're not staying at Raven House?" Brannigan went on to . . . *Rudi,* Ingolf thought. *Rudi Mackenzie.*

"Nah, Mom and Sir Nigel and the infants are in, and some guests from overseas, and a whole lot of other people from Dun Juniper, so we just dumped the hunting gear there, said hello, and came on over. You mind putting us all up? The girls can share a room if it's tight, and you can put me and Odard in another."

"You snore, Rudi," the other man in the party said; that must be Odard.

He was dressed like the brown-haired woman in T-tunic, shirt and pants; his were of beautifully woven dark blue cloth embroidered around the neck and hem with gold, but there was a circle on his chest with what looked like a Chinese symbol in it—Ingolf knew enough to recognize them. He went on with the air of a man making a concession:

"You could chivalrously sleep here on the floor by the hearth and give your room to the Princess. It would be more suitable to her state to have one all to herself."

"I'm not sharing with *you,* Odard," the brown-haired woman said, pointing a finger.

"Oh, of course not, Your Highness," the man said smoothly. "I said *all to yourself,* didn't I?"

"Then you'd have to sleep on the floor too, Odard." Rudi grinned. "Which isn't like you. Chivalry or not."

"No, no, *you* sleep in front of the hearth, Rudi, and *I'll* share with the twins."

"And then you wake up, Odard," one of the siblings said.

Her sister just snorted; they both looked down their noses at him—about half-serious, Ingolf thought.

"No, plenty for you and the princess and your friends to have one each," Brannigan said, laughing at the byplay. "Business gets slow after the Horse Fair, and slower after Mabon. Highway 20 won't be open much longer—it may be closed now. They've already had snow up there, though we got one in from over the Santiam Pass just a little while ago—that's him. He's from far back east, way far. East of the Mississippi!"

He nodded towards the booth in a corner; Ingolf raised his glass politely as they nodded at him; they looked in frank curiosity, then gave him what he recognized as the same expert's once-over he'd given Rudi. There was a little more than that in the way the three young women looked at him; they put their heads together and said something in a language he didn't recognize, and giggled for a moment.

Then they went off to their own table, still bickering amiably. *Like pups in a litter,* he thought tolerantly, from the lofty height of twenty-eight, and asked: "Princess?"

"Oh, that's Mathilda Arminger," Saba said. "She comes from up north; her father was the Lord Protector of Portland, and she's his heir, so they call her the princess. Mike Havel and he killed each other in the War of the Eye, eleven years ago—no, sure and I'm lying, it's twelve years the now. By the Sun Lord and the Foam-Born, but the wheel turns faster each time!"

Ingolf felt his brows go up. "Their kids seem awful friendly," he said.

And meant it. He recognized the playful banter, of a style you used only with those you knew well, and it brought a pang of loneliness. He hadn't had the like since the Villains were wiped out last year.

"Long story," Saba said. "Part of the peace agreement was that she'd come here for part of the year, and Rudi . . . Artos . . . would go north."

He nodded thoughtfully; that sort of mutual exchange of hostages was common enough. The Bossmen of Richland and Ellisworth had a similar arrangement back home, which was a big improvement on calling out your farmers and their following of refugees to burn down barns and chop one another up.

"And the other guy is Sir Odard Liu; he's a knight of the Association—the Portland Protective Association, that's what their top people call themselves—who comes down with her. *His* father was a nasty piece of work, too; Lady Eilir and Lady Astrid killed him—"

At his inquiring look she amplified: "Lady Eilir is the Chief's eldest child; Lady Astrid is the twins' aunt, their mother's sister and Mike Havel's sister-in-law, she's the *Hiril* of the Dúnedain Rangers. They're *anamchara,* soul sisters. Astrid's married to Lord Alleyne, the son of the Chief's husband, Sir Nigel. His son by his first wife back in England, that is . . . he and the Chief have two daughters. Sorry to dump all this on you!"

He filed away the unfamiliar names and relationships; family was usually the key to understanding politics, which could mean life and death.

"And Odard?"

"Odard's not bad . . . except that he thinks he's the Lady's own gift to women."

"That's a delusion I've never had," Ingolf said. "I always thought it was more that women are God's gift to an undeserving mankind."

That got him a laugh. He went on: "You've got a mixed lot in here."

"We do," she said pridefully. "The Sheaf and Sickle is famous all through the valley."

She pointed out a few. "Those two are Bearkillers, from over to the west of here; Mike Havel founded their outfit."

A tough-looking pair, with bold challenging eyes.

"See those little blue scars between their brows? That means they're initiates of the A-list—sort of like being knights, but they're a lot less likely to be assholes than the ones from the Protectorate, sure. And that's a monk from Mount Angel. Father Ignatius—if there were more like him, I'd think better of Christians. No offense."

"None taken," Ingolf said, sincerely enough.

The cleric was a spare muscular young man in a black hooded robe; Catholic clergy were still thin on the ground back east, but Ingolf would have pegged him for a fighting man, except for the dress. He read from a small book and told a rosary with his left hand, occasionally taking a sip of wine or a bite of a frugal dinner of bread and cheese and smoked fish.

Ingolf listened as Saba spoke, but found his eyes straying to her more and more often, until she laughed at him and finished her brandy.

"See you around, Ingolf Wanderer."

* * *

He'd barely turned out the lamp in the small tidy sleeping room when the door opened again. He reached for the belt with his weapons where it hung from the bedstead, and heard her quiet chuckle in the dark as the scabbard knocked against the wood.

"I'm not *that* fearsome, am I, Ingolf?" she teased.

"Let's find out," he suggested.

The whiteness of her skin was half glimpsed in the darkness as she slipped out of her robe and under the quilt. Some hours later they lay in a happy tangle, warm while the rain tapped at the west-facing window.

Wow, he thought again. *They're not shy around here, either!*

Suddenly a thought occurred to him. It should have been earlier, but he'd been lulled by the friendly reception. Still, you could never tell. . . .

"Your father isn't going to mind, is he?"

Then he yelped as she tweaked his chest hair, hard. "That's for waiting until now to ask! No, of course not. I'm a grown woman; it's my business who I worship the Goddess with."

He rubbed at his chest and then settled her back on the curve of his shoulder. "Worship is what you call it here? Beats fasting and prayer, I can tell you that!"

" 'All acts of love and pleasure are My rituals,' " she said; it had the sound of someone quoting. Then she chuckled. "And She is well and truly worshipped!"

He smiled himself; that was the oddest compliment a woman had ever given him, but far from the worst.

"And I haven't been with anyone for a year, since Raen died. Time to let him go. You're a strong man, and I think a good one. If you leave, I've had the night and maybe a child—I always wanted more than two. And if you don't leave . . . well, we'll see, shall we?"

She yawned and stretched and settled herself, with a thigh flung across his; he could feel her breathing slowing down to the deep regular rhythm of sleep, and his own followed.

✳ ✳ ✳

Ingolf's dream was the same as always: the screams of his comrades, the terror of the blinding light that pierced hand and eyelid, and the sword, the sword hanging impossibly in the blaze, the Voice tolling in his mind.

When he woke, he thought himself still asleep for an instant, his chest heaving and sweat running down his neck. In a moment more he'd wake to the warm stuffy darkness of the room and find Saba beside him, and they'd go down to breakfast. He'd find what jobs he could do around the inn, or for neighbors, and get to know people before he started asking around. Maybe the Voice would leave him alone for a while.

Then he realized that the long curved dagger raised above him was very real, and threw himself aside with a great hoarse shout. Saba screamed as well, as the razor edge kissed her flank and left a trail of red as it plunged into the quilt and let free a blizzard of goose down.

Thought too swift to notice with his waking mind made him ignore his shete; the long weapon would be deadly awkward in these cramped quarters. Instead he stripped the bowie and tomahawk out of his belt and rolled to the floor, bounding erect with a shoulder roll. There was a full triad of them, three knives glimpsed in the dark, hooded faces covered to the eyes by black half masks. His stones tried to draw up into his belly as the faint light from the window glinted on the sharp metal in their gloved hands. A knife fight was bad enough at any time; knives moved too fast to really see or block well.

A knife fight naked in the dark against three opponents who didn't care if they lived or died . . .

"The Ascended Masters have called your name, apostate," one of them hissed. "Did you think mountains and ice could save you from the Prophet's judgment?"

Then to Saba, as they spread out and approached: "Silence, pagan whore!"

The speaker tried to backhand her out of the way as she struggled free of the tangled sheets. She caught the arm, heaved and twisted to lock it with a speed and skill that would have been a pleasure to see in better circumstances, and swung the elbow wrong-end forward against the bedstead with all the strength of her arms and weight of her body. The joint broke with an ugly crackling crunch of tendon and bone, like a green branch giving way across your knee. Her hawk-shriek overrode the Cutter's scream of outraged pain:

"Scathach! Scathach!"

The knifeman's ululation at the ruin of his arm was cut off as her foot raked up and kicked him under the jaw with explosive power, toes neatly rolled back to present the ball of her foot. She snatched at the knife as it fell from his nerveless hand.

Ingolf roared and lunged himself; the thrust of the bowie in his left hand rammed into a jacket lined with mail—

CHAPTER TWO

Rudi Mackenzie dreamed.

He saw mountains, but not the mountains of home, green and steep where the Cascades rose above Dun Juniper's walls. These were bare save for a scattering of silvery-gray scrub, up great walls of rock and scree to the glaciers floating far above, and he was all alone except for Epona. His senses were sharp; the smell of cold rock and aromatic herbs and old sweat soaked into wool and leather, the rattle of stone under shod hooves, far and faint a baying like wolves, but he knew it was men. The horse's breath came sharp, and there was a sense of overwhelming grief and dread. . . .

* * *

A hoarse shout kicked him into wakefulness. He'd always been one of those who came alert easily; an inner clock told him it was the third hour past midnight, the hour when the Hunter came to lead away the old and sick, the time when sleep guttered closest to death. He swung his feet down and grabbed up sword and buckler and opened the door in the same motion, and went down on one knee to peer out first. Nothing in this short length of corridor—he had good night vision, even in the velvet darkness. The rain was back, and the drumming on the strakes of the roof made a white noise that drowned everything but the sharpest sound.

In the room across, a lantern flared as a door cracked open; that was Odard, always cautious. His head came out at the same level as Rudi's. The twins were on this side and down one; as he watched their door opened too, and Ritva—or Mary—rolled out, coming up in a crouch with longsword in one hand and dirk in the other.

No, it's Mary. She has that little scar over her hip bone. The twins *tried* to look as similar as they could, which was why he was careful about it.

Mathilda was the last door down, and a mirror showed there stuck in the wax on the end of a candle stub. She checked the ground before coming out in her knee-length nightshift, blades ready; the embroidered garment looked a little odd with a sword belt buckled around it.

A faint clash, the sound of metal on metal, and more voices. Their eyes met, and she nodded. The scream had come from around the corner to his left; how far down was hard to tell. The new noise came from the same direction. None of them had their body armor with them, or missile weapons, or any shields besides his buckler. They all had sword and fighting-knife because they'd been reared to put them on as automatically as shoes whenever they went outside their own home-hearth doors.

Not worth taking time to get dressed, he decided. *It would be if we had our war harness, but all clothes do in a fight is comfort you.*

Ritva dashed down to the corner in four deer-swift bounds, then dropped flat to peer around the edge, landing on her fisted hands with the blades still in them.

Rudi called up his knowledge of the Sheaf and Sickle's layout as the rest of them followed. It was chaotic—Brannigan's steading had grown over the years from the original core of the pre-Change tavern and microbrewery, knocking together half a dozen old buildings and modifying them as the business and the number of children and grandchildren and employees and *their* families grew. New doorways and corridors and staircases, and new chimneys for woodstoves and fireplaces . . .

The five of them gathered at the intersection, naturally keeping back where they couldn't be seen from the next stretch of corridor. Odard had brought his bedside lantern, but with his shirt wrapped around it so the light it threw was muffled. The fruity smell of burning alcohol and hot wick melded with the acrid sweat of tension.

Eyes gleamed in the darkness, and teeth showed as bright as the steel; none of them was what you'd call timid, or complete virgins when it came to a fight, but sudden death in a friendly inn wasn't something that happened every day. And they were all of them children of field and farm, river and hill and forest; a town was an alien environment to them, much less fighting in a warren like this building. He could tell they all felt as cramped and out-of-place as he did.

He had his buckler, a little foot-wide roundel of steel shaped like a soup plate, with a hand grip in the hollow boss. As it happened, they also all favored double-edged longswords with cross-guarded hilts. The others were carrying their daggers as parrying weapons; Mathilda tossed strips of woolen blanket to each of the shieldless ones, and they quickly wound them around their left forearms. That wasn't much protection, but it was a lot better than nothing.

Always thinking ahead, that girl, Rudi thought, with a taut grin. *Let's see, half a minute since I heard that first scream . . .*

"Follow me!"

Left down the corridor, bare feet nearly noiseless on the wooden floorboards. More light leaking out from under doors as people woke; one Corvallan merchant opened his, saw warriors naked as the swords in their hands padding by and prudently slammed the door shut again, with a thumping to show he was bracing a chair against it. The sound of fighting was louder now: an unearthly shriek of astonished agony, and a Mackenzie battle shout in a woman's voice:

"*Scathach! Scathach!*"

Someone calling on the Dark Goddess in Her most terrible form. Scathach: She Who Brings Fear. The red work of killing was being done within earshot. You didn't invoke the Devouring Shadow unless you really meant it.

The corridor ended at the door to the kitchens. To their left was a staircase that went through a ninety-degree turn as it rose to the second floor and a row of guest rooms. Mathilda slipped in front of him; she'd brought along her candlestick-and-mirror arrangement, and he nodded as she went up the stairs two at a time. The rest followed in a silent rush that froze for a moment as she reached the top and extended the mirror just up over the lip; they poised, ready to attack if someone peered over the edge. Light spilled from above; someone had lit a lantern, and their dark-adjusted eyes saw the dim flame as brightness.

Then she put down the mirror and spoke in Sign: *Six with shetes and shields. Three facing this way, three the other. One door open between them; the fighting's coming from there.*

Decision flashed through him, and his hands moved, quick and fluent: *Matti, Ritva, Mary, you go back down, through the kitchen and up the other stairs—that's how they're planning on getting away.*

They turned and raced down and around the stairs, leaping recklessly despite the razor-edged steel in both hands, as sure-footed as wildcats. Rudi looked over and met Odard's slanted blue eyes. The other man smiled and shrugged ruefully. Rudi filled his lungs and called on the Crow Goddess in an enormous shout as he leapt:

"*Morrigú! Morrigú!*"

"*Haro, Portland! Face Gervais, face death!*" Odard yelled, the battle shouts of his nation and his House.

You screamed at a time like that to freeze your enemy for a moment. This time the freezing bit didn't work. The men facing him and Odard attacked immediately, the forward pair moving with smooth precision and the one behind alert on the balls of his feet, ready to step in if one of his comrades went down. They were wearing loose mottled gray-brown jackets with hoods and cloth masks that covered all but the eyes, trousers of the same material, and stout boots. It made him feel a little conspicuous in his underdrawers and bare feet, but not nearly so much as did the yard of sharp curved steel slamming towards his face.

Tunnggg!

His buckler shed it with an unmusical crash and a jarring shock to his left hand and arm. His own cut-and-thrust blade darted out, and was deflected in turn by the two-foot circular shield blazoned with a sun disk and three letters—C-U-T.

That was all too appropriate; he jumped as the shete hissed beneath his feet, aimed in a looping, hocking strike at the side of his leg. The man was as good a master of the slashing style as he had ever met, and his shete was a whirling blur like a power-driven saw, but the cramped quarters worked against him—once it nearly caught on the ceiling overhead.

Just then another man dressed like his opponent staggered back out of the door where the first shouts had come from; he had a tomahawk planted in his forehead, the blade sunk deep enough that the shaft was jammed against the bone. The outlander bounced off the opposite wall and fell in a tangle of limbs that twitched like a pithed frog.

A naked man was in the doorway; Ingolf, the stranger from the sunrise lands. He clutched a knife in his left hand, but the limb hung limp and he had a nasty cut down the shoulder and upper arm on that side, with blood that looked black in the poor light glistening in a sheet down his side and dripping on the floor.

"Saba's hurt!" he cried. "Hurt bad!"

"Then get back inside there and look to her!" Rudi shouted.

That seemed to cut through the haze of pain and shock; the big man looked around, saw what was going on, and slammed the door in the face of one of the hooded men. An instant later the blade of the bowie appeared beneath it; the easterner had driven it in as a wedge with a blow of heel to hilt, and the only way to get the door open would be to batter it off its hinges. Two of the hooded killers started trying to do just that, kicking at the stout brown planks and then chopping white splinters out when that didn't work.

As he spoke Rudi cut downward, a savage chopping blow from the wrist, too fast for the movement of the shield to block. It struck, and hard, but the glint of chain mail appeared through the ripped cloth. The armor kept the blade from cutting, but his opponent grunted in pain and the shield dipped lower; Rudi could feel the muffled snap of something giving way up the steel and into the hilt.

"We are the point—"

He chanted the line as he whipped his sword across and caught another shete chop on his own steel; the weapons slid together with a tinging crash and locked at the hilts, and he smashed the buckler into the man's injured shoulder, putting all the power of his hundred and seventy-five pounds into it.

"We are the edge—"

This time bone crumbled audibly, and the power went out of the grip holding his sword locked. The man wailed through his mask, blue eyes flaring open with agony and the despair of imminent death above the dark knit cloth.

"We are the wolves that Hecate fed!"

Rudi threw him backward with a flexing push of both arms and then killed him with a snapping thrust to one eye, a gruesome crunch as the long point of his sword smashed through the thin bone behind the socket and into his brain. Blood and matter spattered the walls as he freed it with a sharp jerk of his arm.

There was motion on the stairs behind him. It had to be friendlies. . . .

"Healer! Get a healer up here, *now!*" he called crisply. "And some more weapons, bows, spears!"

The rear man of the three guarding this end of the corridor stepped into place before Rudi could turn on Odard's opponent. Odard and his man were fully engaged, a flurry of steel moving in blurring arcs, gasping breath, shuffling stamp of feet on the floorboards. The hooded man fought silently, but the knight shouted again:

"Face Gervais, face death!"

His opponent had to be good to keep the young knight off, even with the advantage of a proper shield and a mail-lined coat. He *was* good, and so was the one who'd replaced the first casualty to face Rudi. . . .

What's going on here? There aren't that many folk around who're that good with a blade. It takes too much time away from working to feed your family. These aren't some gang of bandits. They're trained. They're someone's armsmen. Someone with a deep well to pick from.

Two blond heads appeared at the stairs on the other end of this stretch of corridor. The hooded man left on sentry-go there called sharply, and one of the ones hacking at the door left off and raced to join him. The first had to give back a half dozen paces before his comrade was at his side. If they were disconcerted at finding themselves fighting two identical stark-naked amazons, it didn't show. Mathilda followed behind perforce—there wasn't room for more than two with swords to deploy in the strait confines of the corridor.

"Mail under the jackets!" Rudi called.

Steel rang on steel. Even fighting for his life, Rudi grinned at the surprise they were about to get. The twins had been doing *everything* together all their lives, and a lot of that involved swords. Fighting Mary and Ritva together was like taking on a single organism with four hands, and they'd been trained by Astrid Larsson and Alleyne Loring—who were two of the three sparring partners Rudi had left who still beat him as often as not.

He could usually take either of the twins in a straight-up fight, but they'd never lost a pair-against-pair match with *anyone* since they got their full growth.

"*Lacho calad! Drego morn!*" the two screamed as one.

The Dúnedain war cry, known throughout the valley: *Flame light! Flee night!*

"Duck!" Mathilda shouted from behind them, as she wound up.

They both did. The cast-brass candlestick flew over Mary's—or Ritva's—head. It arched over the two hooded men facing the Larsson twins as well, bringing their shields up in reflex. But it blurred past, to go *thunk* into the shoulder blade of the one hacking at the door. He collapsed, sinking to his knees in a scrabbling fall, dropping his weapon and clutching at the battered panels. After an instant he struggled to his feet again and began hacking once more, but his blows were feeble and he held the weapon in his left hand.

Goddess gentle and strong! This bunch are determined! Rudi thought.

Aloud, between panting breaths and the deadly flickering and belling of edged metal:

"Surrender! You've got no way out!"

They didn't even bother to reply. Rudi raised his voice and shouted to the others: "We'll want one alive!"

That *did* bring a reaction, probably because there wasn't any way for them to escape now that the cry was raised; there were shouts and noise all over the Sheaf and Sickle. One of the hooded men barked a single order—Rudi couldn't make out the word, or even if it was in English. Suddenly the pair facing him and Odard leapt backwards, a simultaneous panther bound; then they turned and drove their shetes into each other's throats. The broad points slashed to the spine almost instantaneously.

Rudi was left gaping for an instant as blood fountained out, splashing to the ceiling before the bodies convulsed and went limp. Ritva and Mary were frozen in shock on the other side; their opponents had done the same.

"Get the other one!" Mathilda called, trying to push between them. "Quick!"

Cursing, all five of them did. Rudi managed to grab his right shoulder just as the left arm drove a dagger into his own throat; the body kicked and died. The young Mackenzie forced down an impulse to stand panting and bewildered amid the bodies and the blood that filled the corridor with its copper-iron stink beneath the sickly smell of pierced body cavities.

Instead he and Odard moved as if they'd rehearsed for days; they set their swords point-down in the floor, put their backs against the wall of the corridor across from the wedged door, jumped up and lashed out with their feet.

The planks hit his soles with a hard drumming thump that shocked up through his whole body, leaving him feeling as if he'd been folded too far at the hips. There was a tearing, crunching sound as the upper hinge came half-free of the wood. Both young men dropped crouching to the blood-slick flooring, sprang upward as if driven by springs, and struck again. This time the upper hinge came completely free and the lower twisted three-quarters out. The door fell inward, resting on a body there. Rudi snatched up his sword and jumped through.

The inside was darker than the corridor. It took an instant for his eyes to make sense of what he saw. Two dead men. One half-under the door, with an arm joint bent back in a way not suited to the nature or construction of elbows, a jaw smashed so completely it dangled free within a sack of cloth, and his head back between his shoulder blades. Another was hacked and slashed around the neck and face as if by a bear in a frenzy.

On the bed a woman's body, naked but looking like a glistening black statue with the blood. It couldn't all be hers, but a lot of it was; a long curved knife had been driven into her stomach just above the pubic bone and ripped upwards.

The stranger was trying to hold the obscene wound closed, despite the steady flow of blood from his own gash; his shoulders shook with the harsh sobbing of a man unaccustomed to tears. Astonishingly, the woman still breathed a little. As Rudi watched she seemed to speak—he thought he heard *Raen* in the echoing silence—and went limp. Seconds later the man who held her collapsed.

"Sweet Mother-of-All," Rudi whispered, darting forward.

Saba was beyond help, but the stranger wasn't. And if he lived, he could talk.

CHAPTER THREE

Nigel Loring looked around the great hall of Raven House and arched a wry white brow as Rudi and his friends trooped out to head for the Sheaf and Sickle; people were setting up tables in a long rectangle, leaving a broad patch clear in the center.

"I think my stepson knew more about those visiting diplomats than he said. Otherwise, why dodge dinner here, after a cold day's hunting?"

"Oh, it'll be Saba Brannigan he's thinking of hunting the now," Juniper Mackenzie said. "That she might be out of mourning, you see, and more inclined to look favorably on him now that he's handsome and full-grown. Not that the poor boy has a prayer of getting between her knees; she'll always remember him as the spotty lustful sweaty-palmed fourteen-year-old she looked down on from the lofty height of seventeen. It's a woman's mystery and I know."

They shared a chuckle. *Children do make life more interesting*, he thought.

Juniper had borne a daughter named Eilir long ago, when she was a teenager herself, before the Change. Rudi Mackenzie had been conceived in the first Change Year; and now she had two daughters with Nigel as well, the fruit of their middle-aged marriage. His own son Alleyne Loring had accompanied him to Oregon twelve years ago, and had supplied three grandchildren since with Astrid. . . .

Juniper sighed, looking around. "Though I can't blame the boy for not wanting to sit through a formal dinner at Raven House, when he could be carousing with friends his own age. I have doubts about this place myself, sure and I do."

In theory Raven House was for the use of the local Raven sept's ceremonies. In practice the house was part of Sutterdown's generation-long campaign to get the Chief to spend more time there; they were convinced they could eventually wear her down and/or tempt her enough to get her out of Dun Juniper and into what they considered the Mackenzies' natural capital. Whatever else the Change had wrought in Sutterdown, it hadn't put an end to small-town boosterism.

"I swear, they've gone and made it fancier still," Juniper murmured.

It had been a rich man's house once, a timber baron who'd wrung his wealth out of the Cascade forests around the end of the nineteenth century. The townsfolk had added stables to the rear, and built closed passages to the houses on either hand, and cleared out most of the ground and first floors in the central block to make a single great rectangular room, with galleries overlooking it on two sides. One end held a low dais, with a pair of tall chairs whose backs were worked like the wings of ravens, with the heads looking down as hoods.

Behind it the wall was paneled in lustrous black walnut, polished until it shone with a dark gloss; inlaid in pale birchwood was the Triple Moon, waxing and full and waning, a circle flanked by outward-pointing crescents, the sign of the Threefold Goddess—the Maiden, the Mother and the Hag. If you looked closer you saw what was subtly drawn behind that, barely a suggestion in slivers of rosewood and yew, pear and rowan, a face that might be young or old or ageless. . . .

Down at the other end was the big fireplace where they stood now, crackling with six-foot fir logs and sweet-smelling incense cedar. Above the hearth was another great image inlaid into the wall and towering up to the high ceiling, this time in copper and gold and silver. It showed a wild bearded face with curving horns springing from its brow, forever looking towards the Ever-Changing One.

"I can't really resent it, though," Juniper said, shaking her head. "It's all done from love; and They never turn that away."

"And Sutterdown does have some splendid artists now," Nigel said meditatively, taking a sip from a glass of red wine. "As good as any at home in Dun Juniper. As good as any I've ever seen all my life long."

The image of the Horned God stared down at him, golden locks surrounding it like the rayed Sun, the full sensual lips slightly parted over white teeth. The eyes swallowed the flames until they were like windows into a moonlit forest at night, infinitely deep with rustling mystery, glinting with silvery flickers. Here in the warm well-lit room, within the strong-walled town bowered among tilled fields tamed by the hands of humankind . . . here they still brought the breath of the wildwood, and the lonely sound of pipes heard over hills by moonlight.

"That too." Juniper sighed.

He looked up at the image and murmured a quotation. " 'The face of Power that says: O man, make peace with your mortality—for this, too, is God.' "

Her mouth quirked; she knew he wasn't easily impressed. "Skilled indeed! And who'd have thought we'd breed so many fine makers, with only as many folk as one small city in the old days?"

"Perhaps it's because they *don't* have great cities full of professionals and critics and academics telling them what to like, or television and books to bring it to them. It's like music, in these latter days; if you want it, you have to make your own. Athens itself in its time of greatness was a small place, after all."

"But it all makes me feel *guilty*," Juniper said, looking around. "We're doing well the now, but not so well that we can afford to make all this for an occasional visit by a middle-aged couple and their children."

She gestured helplessly at the rest of the room. It had been done with some cunning and by people who knew Juniper fairly well; the lower parts of the walls held books and pictures and musical instruments on shelves of wood delicately carved with running vines and flowers; above were the brackets that held four great multibranched lamps at the Quarters, and weavings showing the ancient tales—Niall of the Nine Hostages and the Lady of Tara, Ishtar's descent into the Underworld to free her lover, Odin grasping the runes of wisdom below the branches of the World Tree.

Despite the splendor it wasn't a forbidding room; just right for music and dancing, or a ritual gathering, or for children to play in on a winter day and listen to a story, or for simply sitting by the fire reading in the comfortable chairs and sofas that surrounded the hearth, a bowl of hazelnuts and apples at your elbow and a cat curled up on your lap.

"They *do* use it when we're not here, my dear; it's a civic center and doesn't sit empty and sorrowing. And making you feel guilty so you'd come and use it more often was a large part of the intent!"

Just then a sound came from the vestibule that gave on the street door. An apprentice bard named Mabor—he was living with a family at Dun Juniper and studying with Juniper herself, and several others—came in. He was a young man with black hair and eyes and olive-brown skin; his father had been Mexican. Now he cleared his throat and straightened his plaid, face shining with excitement.

"Lady Juniper!" he said.

He was young, just seventeen, but his voice already had a trained singer's resonance. Mackenzies thought highly of bards, not least because Juniper herself had followed that trade before the Change, busking and playing the RenFaire circuit. Every dun wanted one trained at her hearth, and they served as heralds and messengers as well, and their songs nurtured the Craft. A little self-importantly he went on in the formal cadence that for some reason always made Juniper sigh and roll her eyes a little:

"Emissaries from abroad, bringing the word of their king. They ask audience and guesting of the Mackenzie."

"Well, they're welcome," Juniper said. Her brows rose. "Not another cardinal, I hope?"

Nigel hid a grin. The papal nuncio had visited when he came to reestablish contact with Oregon's Catholics, and not so incidentally put an end to the schism of the Portland Protective Association's homegrown antipope. Despite being an American by birth himself, the good cardinal had found it a bit of a strain, since while Juniper was polite to a fault she was as sincere in her fashion as the ecclesiastic was in his. . . .

"No, not a cardinal, lady." Mabor drew another breath, delighted. "I am to herald the right honorable the Count of Azay, ambassador of His Britannic Majesty, William V, called the Great, Defender of the Faith, King of England, Scotland, Wales, Northern Ireland, King of France and Spain and his dominions beyond the seas, Hammer of the Moors, *Rex Britanniae Maioris et Imperator Occidentalis!*"

Nigel's eyebrows shot up. "Good God," he said quietly.

They'd heard *some* news from Europe since he arrived here on a Tasmanian ship, fleeing Mad King Charles and dropping all unknowing into the War of the Eye. But no direct contact . . .

There were two guards in full fig by the entranceway, longbow and quiver over their backs, sword and buckler at belt, and spears with the long heads polished bright in their hands—a mistake by Sutterdown, for while Juniper loved ceremony she hated swank. Now the two snapped to attention and rapped their spear butts on the ground.

Six of the party that entered were guardsmen, one in the full plate of a man-at-arms and the others longbowmen in chain-mail shirts and open-faced sallets. Nigel knew the gear; he'd designed the green-enameled armor himself on the Isle of Wight, that first winter while they were fighting off the hordes of starving refugees and wondering if they'd survive to the next harvest.

A tall man with a limp came through behind the soldiers; he was in riding breeches and a coat of Harris tweed, with a plain sword belt around it and an equally plain longsword whose hilt had sweat-stained rawhide bindings. The man was near Nigel's own mid-sixties, countenance scored by years and turned ruddy by a youth spent under the unmerciful sun of the hot countries. He still had a full thatch of hair, white with some gray, and his hard scarred face was dominated by a great beak of a nose above a wide thin-lipped gash of mouth and a knobby chin; the little finger on his left hand was missing. His eyes were dark green, level and watchful, marksman's eyes.

"Good *God*," Nigel said, still quietly. "Tony Knolles!"

The last time they'd seen each other had been more than a decade ago, over lowered lances. Charles had still been king then, and Knolles still a strong supporter. . . .

"Nigel!"

The aquiline face split in a smile—not much of one, but a great ear-to-ear grin if you knew the man, who made Nigel Loring look like an excitable Latin. Nigel stepped forward, hand outstretched; they gripped with sword-calloused strength and each searched the other man's face. Nigel was suddenly conscious of how he'd gone egg-bald himself except for a fringe and his mustache, and white-haired except for a few fading streaks of yellow. For the rest he was still trim and upright, even if things creaked and moved more slowly nowadays.

"Good God, Tony!" After a moment of struggling to find words: "And a count, no less!"

"His Majesty was badly advised enough to do me that honor."

Nigel shook his head again, hauling his wits together by main force. "My dear, an old friend and comrade in arms, Tony Knolles, who saved my life many times."

"And only tried to kill him once," Knolles said, bowing over her hand. "Lady Juniper."

"My husband has told me a good deal of you, Lord Anthony," she said. With an impish smile: "Both the good and the bad of it, sure."

Two small figures came through the crowd. Nigel went on:

"Our eldest daughter, Maude."

At twelve Maude was already nearly as tall as her mother's five-foot-and-a-bit, slender and all limbs and hands and feet, her hair a darker red, her eyes blue as Nigel's. She curtsied, solemn in her green shirt, silver-buckled shoes, kilt and plaid and feathered Scots bonnet. Knolles winced slightly; Maude had been the name of Nigel's first wife, Alleyne's mother. She'd been killed by the Icelandic mercenaries holding the Lorings prisoner on Charles's orders, during the rescue and escape.

"And Fiorbhinn, our youngest," he said.

"Hello, Lord Anthony." The eight-year-old had her mother's leaf-green eyes; her long hair was the yellow-white color of ripe wheat. She gave the English emissary's hand a confident shake.

"Fiorbhinn means Truesweet," she went on, with a wide white smile. "It's the name of a famous harp. I can play the harp already! And Mom says I have perfect pitch. She knows 'cause she does too."

Nigel smiled, watching Knolles blink, and knowing that that hard-souled man of war was instantly made a slave for life.

The visitor cleared his throat. "And this is my son Robert, Lady Juniper. Robert, your godfather."

The guard commander in the suit of plate slid the visor of his sallet up. The face within was Knolles's own, minus forty-odd years and with the nose shrunk to more human proportions, though paler and freckled and with a lock of raven hair hanging down on the forehead.

Nigel shook his hand after he made his bow to Juniper—carefully, which you had to do when the other man was wearing an articulated steel gauntlet; he marveled a little, remembering the gangly child he'd known. . . . Where did the years go?

Down into the West without returning, he thought, and added aloud, "I hope your mother's well? She was expecting when I . . . ah . . . left England."

"Mother is very well, thank you, Sir Nigel," he said, with a charming smile of his own. "And I have two younger sisters and a brother now. My brother's name is Nigel, by the way."

"Ah . . ." Knolles senior pulled himself together. "My credentials?"

Nigel saved him from embarrassment with a quick flick of the eyes, and he presented the ribbon-bound documents to Juniper.

She took them gravely. "Be welcome here as my guests and the guests of Clan Mackenzie, Lord Count, Lord Robert. Welcome as the voice of your king, and still more for yourself."

Then, raising her voice slightly to take in the whole party and the lookers-on: "Well, if you good people would like to share dinner, there's just time to get freshened up."

She clapped her hands as the watching crowd buzzed. "The Clan has guests from afar, bringing luck beneath our roof on Samhain's holy eve! Rooms for them! Hot water and soap! See to their horses! And tell the cooks dinner is going to be very welcome!"

✳ ✳ ✳

Nigel saw Knolles blink as the bagpipers paced around the inner side of the tables, the wild skirling sound filling the great room. Below, knives flashed as a roast pig—a yearling, with an apple in its mouth—and a smoking side of beef were reduced to manageable proportions. The other dishes came in with a proud procession of polished salvers.

When the musicians had marched out of the room—to shed their instruments and scurry back in for the meal—Juniper Mackenzie rose to her feet and lifted the silver-mouthed horn from its rest before her to make the invocation and libation:

> *Harvest Lord who dies for the ripened grain—*
> *Corn Mother who births the fertile field—*
> *Blessèd be those who share this bounty,*
> *And blessed the mortals who toiled with You*
> *Their hands helping Earth to bring forth life.*

Then she poured out a portion into a bowl and raised the horn high: "To the Lord, to the Lady, to the Luck of the Clan—*drink hail!*"

"*Wassail!*"

Fifty voices roared reply as she drank; Nigel took a sip of his wine. Knolles senior and junior did the same, and then looked down at their glasses with identical surprised respect.

"And to the Clan's guests, come across the sea from the lands of our ancestors—may there always be peace and friendship between us—*drink hail!*"

"*Wassail!*"

As she sat, Knolles leaned close to whisper in Nigel's ear: "Whatever else I expected, it wasn't to find you playing at king of the Picts, old boy."

Nigel looked down at his ruffled shirt, jacket, kilt, plaid pinned at his shoulder with a brooch of silver knotwork and turquoise.

"More the prince consort of the pseudo-Celts, I'm afraid. Make no mistake, Tony, Juniper is the Chief, not I. I'm one of her military advisors—armsmen, we say—in my official capacity, and that's all."

Juniper leaned forward to look around him at the Count of Azay, mock indignation in her tone.

"Pseudo-Celts, is it? I'll have you know my mother was born on Achill Island in the Gaeltacht, no less. And my father was an American of Scots descent . . . mostly Scots. So . . . *nil anon scéal eile agam.*"

Nigel knew that his old friend could understand the Gaelic: *there's no other story,* translated literally. He also knew that Knolles had learned the language for the same reason he had; the Provos had used it as a sort of code.

Both the Englishmen had commanded small and extremely clandestine SAS teams in Ulster during the Troubles, mostly in South Armagh—and occasionally, highly illegally and unofficially, across the Irish border. By her sly grin Juniper was recalling exactly the same thing, and by his snort Knolles had realized that she knew, and knew that he knew.

She went on: "And you're probably wondering—"

Then she dropped impishly into a creditable imitation of the upper-class public-school-cum-officer's-mess drawl that was the native dialect of Nigel and his friend both:

"Are all these people utterly barking mad?"

"Not in the least," Knolles said, obviously lying stoutly.

"The kilts weren't my idea," she said. "Honest. And the rest of it . . . sort of grew, like Topsy."

Nigel saw the other man's reserve crack a little; Juniper had that effect on people. There was a creak of dry amusement in Knolles's voice when he spoke:

"I *did* have thoughts along those lines in Portland . . . those bizarre castles! The titles, and the way they dress and speak! Were they all struck on the head at birth by copies of *Ivanhoe*? Although the regent, Lady Sandra . . . she was disconcerting, to say the least, and impressive, in a rather terrifying way. Still, how *did* all that happen?"

Knolles's voice was a little plaintive by the end. Nigel chuckled.

"The man who founded the Association was a history professor, you see—a medieval specialist—and one of those re-creationist Johnnies, like Alleyne. The most charitable explanation is that the Change sent him mad."

"Or that he was always an evil weasel of a man and the Change gave him the opportunity to show it," Juniper said. "It caused no end of trouble, and it didn't die with him."

"Ah, re-creationists," Knolles said. "Very useful some of them were in England as instructors, as you'll recall, Nigel. Where *is* young Alleyne?"

"Uncle Alleyne is married to Aunt Astrid," Maude Loring said from the other side of her mother.

Juniper amplified: "Astrid is Signe Havel's younger sister, the widow of the Bearkiller lord . . . the people over on the western side of the Willamette, between the Association and Corvallis. Astrid is Lady of the Dúnedain Rangers, with my daughter Eilir."

Maude's grave face suddenly broke out in a smile as she abandoned the struggle to be adult for a moment.

"If you think *we're* weird, Lord Count, you should meet *them*. They live in the woods, and they speak *Elvish* to each other. *All the time*."

Knolles blinked, obviously wondering if his leg was being pulled. Nigel gave him a grave shake of the head: *It's quite true, old chap*. Aloud he added:

"Although Alleyne acts as a moderating influence and so does my stepdaughter Eilir. She's married to John Hordle now. You'll remember Hordle—SAS just before the Change, promoted to battalion sergeant major just before we . . . left . . . England."

"Ah, yes. Big chappie, carried a bastard longsword," Knolles said.

Then he harrumphed diplomatically before going on; Hordle had also put an arrow through one of Knolles's men during Nigel's escape.

"Ah, well, considering all that's gone on back Home, we're not in a position to judge. Have you been following events out there at all, Nigel?"

"In outline; news does travel, if slowly, and Abbot Dmwoski forwards some of the Church's reports to us. I know Charles died—"

"Hallgerda killed him when he finally refused to disinherit his older sons in favor of her brood, though it was never proved," Knolles said flatly.

His knobby fist clenched. "And then tried to seize power herself. Colonel Buttesthorn and I and a few others put a stop to that. And put William on the throne."

"We heard that he'd beaten the Moors. Good show, that."

Though to most here, it didn't matter much more than hearing how Prince Piotr of Belgorod and Hetman Bohdan of the All-Great Kuban Cossack Host defeated the Tartars outside Astrakhan last year, Loring thought. *How one's horizons shrink . . .*

Knolles nodded. "We and a coalition beat them—the Norlanders, the Umbrian League, the Kingdom of Sicily, the Republic of Shannon—we even had ships and men from the Cypriot Greeks. Defeated them at sea off the Canaries, then burned out the nests they'd established along the coast of Morocco, then chased them south and gave them a damned good drubbing at home. There's been the odd dustup with Berber raiders from the Atlas since, but nothing significant."

The fierce hawklike green eyes kindled. "Mind you, about six years ago I was with a party exploring the ruins of Marrakech, and—"

"And we heard that William called a new Parliament," Nigel said dryly.

Knolles flushed; it was for advocating that move that Nigel and his wife, Maude, had been put under arrest by Charles the Mad and his Icelandic ice queen in the first place, while Knolles had still been satisfied with the Emergency Regulations.

"Yes, yes, yes, you were right, you were right, you were bloody well right, Nigel. And we've set up a new House of Lords along the old lines," Knolles went on. "Quite old . . ."

"Not altogether the way our ancestors did it, I hope!" Nigel said.

"Very much in the manner our grandfathers would recognize. Things have worked out quite nicely since. The capital's still in Winchester, the Icelanders and Faeroese are settling in and marrying out, their grandchildren will be English to the bone—"

His son grinned and made a gesture towards his own chest; his mother's name was Dagmar, and she'd come from Torshavn along with a flood of others from the northern isles in the earliest Change Years.

"—and we've resettled Britain—thinly—as far as the Midlands, and made a good start on the Continent."

"That's quick work!" Nigel said.

"Well, you can't move for tripping over the next generation, that's true; everyone's breeding like damned rabbits. And we've been getting a steady trickle of immigrants from the east Baltic, and from Ireland, too— easier since we're all bloody beadsqueezers again. No offense," he said hastily to Juniper.

"None taken," she said, laughing. "I was raised Catholic myself, of course, but"—she waved a hand around—"you might say it didn't entirely take."

"There's understatement of positively English proportions," Nigel said.

"You've corrupted me with your Sassenach ways, my love. Sure, and I can feel my upper lip stiffening the now."

Knolles went on: "And we've agreed to divide things with the Norlanders along the old German border, and with the Umbrian League along the old Italian one . . . that's a trifle theoretical, when all we've got is a few outposts along the coasts and rivers. It'll be centuries before we're back to even the medieval era's numbers."

Nigel nodded. He'd helped develop the initial appraisal and plans, and had led expeditions to feel out that vast eerie wilderness.

"That's where the 'King of Greater Britain' and 'Emperor of the West' come in?"

"The imperial title was the late Pope Benedict's idea," Knolles said. "He and the archbishop sprang it on William at the coronation, after the Moorish War, in 2010."

"Rather the way his predecessor did with Charlemagne?" Nigel mused.

"Precisely. Benedict was there for the Church reunion talks, you see. They both preached a Crusade. . . ."

"And the coronation was with your connivance, Father," Robert Knolles said.

Knolles senior harrumphed and poked his fork at a slice of roast beef, cut a piece, administered horseradish and took a bite. He coughed slightly after that—the sauce was nuclear-strength. Then he continued:

"Ah . . . well, that brings us to the reason for the visit, Nigel. We didn't know your situation here in any detail, you see, except that you and Alleyne had landed on your feet as might be expected of Lorings, and His Majesty is deeply grateful for your saving his life—"

"Several times," Robert Knolles put in, unabashed when his father gave him a quelling glance. "*And* setting up the contacts that put him on the throne instead of his late unlamented stepmother when the time came."

"*Late* unlamented?" Loring asked, with an arched brow.

The elder Knolles continued: "She shuffled off eight months ago, from the effects of house arrest, idleness, curdled venom and lashings of strong drink. And His Majesty has asked me to inform you that it pleases him to offer you . . . well, he's made you an earl, you see. Earl of Bristol. With the estates appertaining thereunto, as well as your family land at Tilford, of course."

Nigel felt his jaw drop, and closed it with an effort of will. "Good God."

"He'd like you to return; earnestly requests it, in fact, and sent a ship we really can't spare all the way here to fetch you. Confidentially, he'd also like you to have ministerial rank with a roving commission, and both Houses concur."

"Father is one of the top nobs of the Tories, these days," Robert added. "And note that His Majesty hasn't given *you* a continental title, godfather, nor the proverbial 'estate in France.' Good English farms, fully tenanted."

At Nigel's raised brow, the young man amplified: "In England 'an estate in France' is a synonym for 'dubious gift,' or 'white elephant,' these days, sir—land that gives you a position in society and then prevents you from keeping it up. Father repented and came over to the side of the righteous, but rather late."

Knolles snorted. "Nonsense. The land at Azay is first-rate; better climate than anywhere in England proper, and there are the vineyards—"

"Bushy, *overgrown* vineyards, half-dead . . ."

"—and the château—"

"The *ruins* of the château."

"Ruins? Nonsense; it never really caught on fire . . . not completely . . . and half the roof was still intact. It just . . . well, it needed a spot of work."

"And still does, I rather think, Father . . . work for *my* grandchildren."

"Silence, whelp. In any case, Nigel, I've got a belt, a sword and an ermine cloak for you, and a bally great parchment to go with it. Thing's festooned with enough seals and ribbons for a publican's license, too."

Nigel began to laugh, quietly at first, then wholeheartedly. Mopping at an eye with his napkin, he replied, "I'm truly sorry to disappoint King William, and you, Tony, but my life is here now. Not to mention my wife, and my daughters; and my son, and *his* children—a grandson and two granddaughters, so far. This is where we'll leave our bones. Give His Majesty my regrets and my best wishes for a long and prosperous reign. I *thought* the lad would turn out well."

He turned his head to meet Juniper's bright green eyes for an instant; they crinkled in the face that loved his line for line, and their hands linked fingers beneath the covering tablecloth.

"Not tempted by the prospect of being Countess Juniper, my dear?"

"Chief's bad enough. I'd scandalize your William's court, that's beyond doubting."

Knolles sighed. "I *thought* that was the reply I'd get, as soon as I walked in. Your stepson warned me; we met outside the gates. Remarkable young fellow, even on brief acquaintance. Usually one feels an impulse to kick a man with good looks of that order, but I didn't this time."

"Remarkable young scamp," Juniper said. "He didn't warn *us* you were here, the creature."

Knolles hesitated. "There is one thing more, Nigel. And Lady Juniper. You haven't had much contact with the Atlantic coast of North America, have you?"

"None at all; we know more about East Asia, or even the Indian Ocean countries," Juniper said. "Scarcely even rumors from east of the Mississippi." She winced slightly. "Just enough to know that it was . . . very bad there. As bad as California, or what Nigel tells of Europe, or mainland Britain."

Knolles nodded somberly. Nobody who had lived through the Change as an adult would ever be quite free of those memories. It had been worst of all in the hyperdeveloped zones.

"On the American mainland, yes, it *was* very bad. But some islands did much better. Prince Edward Island best of all; rather as the Isle of Wight or Orkney did in relation to Britain. After the, ah, after King William came to the throne, they established close ties with the old country—in fact, they've MPs in Parliament at Winchester now, and seats in the Lords."

"William isn't repeating George the Third's mistakes, eh?" Nigel said, savoring the joke.

Though it wasn't like Anthony Knolles to waffle around a subject. The other Englishman cleared his throat.

"Among the places they've landed . . . or tried to . . . is Nantucket."

He shot a glance at them from under shaggy brows to see if the name of the island off southern New England meant anything to them. They both looked back soberly.

"Then the rumors were true?" Juniper asked softly. "I've talked to those who were listening or watching the news services, right at the time of the Change. To some who were listening while they flew a plane over mountains, sure! The reports were of something extraordinary going on there on Nantucket, just before . . ."

All three nodded. The flash of light that wasn't really light—even the blind had seen it—and the intolerable spike of pain felt by every creature on Earth advanced enough to have a spinal cord. And then the world was Changed; explosives no longer exploded, electricity wouldn't flow in metal wires, combustion engines silently died, nuclear reactors sat and glowed below their meltdown temperatures until the isotopes decayed and became inert. A civilization built on high-energy technologies writhed and died as well. There had been little time then for anything but sheer survival, but in all the years since no slightest hint had been found to account for the *why* of it.

Eventually a few scientists had measured the effects with what crude equipment could be cobbled together within the new limits; all they'd found was how eerily the Change was tailored, to make a generator impossible but leave nerves functioning as they always had . . . and that beyond the immediate vicinity of Earth everything seemed to be proceeding as normal. You couldn't even *prove* that the Change hadn't happened before. Prior to gunpowder, who would have known? Most of humanity put it down to the will of God, or gods, or the devil; a stubborn minority held out for inscrutably powerful aliens from outer space or another dimension.

. "A dome of lights miles high and miles across, and the water boiling around the edge of it, yes," Knolles said in a flat matter-of-fact tone. "Multicolored lights, crawling over it like lightning . . . that's quite definite. We've collected hundreds of testimonies, and found some eyewitness records written down right afterwards, even a photograph or two. I do *not* believe it is a coincidence such a thing happened just seconds before the Change."

"So what did they find there, your Bluenose explorers?" Juniper asked.

Nigel could feel the pulse beat faster in the hand he held, and his own matching it. This wasn't just a rumor, that was *proof* . . . though of what, only the Powers could say.

Juniper went on: "Not the dome of lights, still there—that we *would* have heard of. They'd have heard of that in Tibet, sure!"

Knolles turned to his son. The young officer was in the red-coated dress uniform into which he'd changed when he shed his armor, but he'd also brought a small rectangular box pierced with holes from the diplomatic party's baggage. Nigel had assumed it was a gift of some sort.

Now he brought it up from the floor, and folded back the covers around it. A soft *crooo-cruuuu* came from it, and behind wire mesh strutted a bird, cocking its head at the light and looking with interest at a piece of bread nearby.

Juniper's breath was the first to catch. She'd been a student of the wilds all her life, long before the Change, and had read widely then and since about the life of other lands and times.

It was an unremarkable bird at first glance; a long-tailed pigeon with a bluish-gray head, the back and wings mottled gray with black patches, paler underparts blush red at the throat and fading to rosy cream. The only thing startling about it was the bright red eyes. . . .

Juniper made a small choked sound, putting her hand to her torc as if the twisted gold were throttling her. Her eyes went wide as she turned to Nigel.

"Do . . . do you . . ." she stuttered, something he'd never heard before, her eyes so wide the white showed all around the pale green iris.

"Yes, my dear," he said quietly, and pushed a crust into the cage.

Then he began to smile, joy and awe struggling with natural reserve as the bird pecked. "It's a passenger pigeon."

* * *

"What is it, my dear?" Nigel asked sleepily.

"I don't know," Juniper Mackenzie said, sitting up in the bed and reaching for her robe. "But—"

A fist knocked on the door; she turned up the bedside lamp and hurried over. Nigel was on his feet, hand resting inconspicuously on the hilt of the longsword. When she threw open the door a man stood there, white-faced and stuttering.

Nigel's hand closed on the rawhide-and-wire binding of the sword hilt. He knew the signs of raw terror.

"Lady Juniper! Sir Nigel! There's been a fight at the Sheaf and Sickle, terrible bad. Folk hurt and killed!"

* * *

SHEAF AND SICKLE INN, SUTTERDOWN, WILLAMETTE VALLEY, OREGON
SAMHAIN EVE, CY22/2020 A.D.

Juniper Mackenzie pushed through the door into the familiar taproom of the Sheaf and Sickle, the armsmen at her heels; Nigel was outside, seeing to the circuit of the town walls lest any killers still at large try to escape. She let out a quiet breath of relief at the sight of Rudi standing beside a table where a healer worked; the twins and Mathilda and Odard were nearby, and all five were unhurt. The smells of blood and violent death were there, mingling horribly with the familiar homey scent of the place.

"Well?" she said. "It's a slaughter this is, of my people on my land, and I'd know the meaning of it! It's the Morrigú and the Wild Huntsman we're dealing with tonight, and no mistake."

Rudi nodded and gave her an account, succinct and neat as his tutors in the arts of war had taught him; she gasped at his account of Saba's death. His mouth tightened as anger drove the grue of horror out of him. Upstairs Tom and Moira and their close kin were keening their daughter; the muffled sound of the shrieks rose to a crescendo, then died away into rhythmic moans, laden with unutterable grief, before rising again.

"I'm a warrior by trade," Rudi said bitterly. "Saba wasn't. She shouldn't have had to fight her last fight alone. First I couldn't save her husband, and then this. . . . May she forgive me, and speak kindly of me to the Guardians."

"She's with her Raen in the Summerlands, and with all her beloveds," Juniper said quietly, putting an arm around him for a moment.

"I know, Mother. It doesn't make *me* feel any better, much less her children."

"It isn't meant to," Juniper said, a little sternness in her voice. "That's why we keen over the dead; grief is for the living."

He nodded; they couldn't even do that, not being close enough in blood.

"I'm glad we came here, though," he said. "It would have been worse if we'd stayed at Raven House. These dirt were already here, waiting to strike; they might have gotten away over the town wall."

They glanced aside. The healer's lips were pursed in disapproval as she worked at the big dining table; far too many of the inn's guests were milling about and babbling nearby, despite its still being hours to dawn. A stranger was helping her, a monastic in a black Benedictine robe, with the loose sleeves pinned back up to his shoulders.

Most of the rest weren't making themselves useful. Some of the outlanders had even had the nerve to try to demand service from the staff. Rudi looked at Juniper, and she nodded slightly; he made a chopping gesture to his friends.

The twins pushed the crowd back—once by the simple expedient of seizing a man by the elbows and pitching him four feet into the air, to land mostly on his head—and then drew their swords and stood like slender black-and-silver statues with the points resting on an invisible line across the room, and Odard and Mathilda beside them. Nobody stepped over it; after a moment a few neighbors came to stand around them, glowering at the strangers. Some of the wiser foreigners headed back to their rooms.

That gave them space and time to go view the bodies of the assassins, laid out on tarpaulins. Juniper had never become entirely inured to the sight of violent death, but she could make herself ignore the wounds and the tumbled diminished look of a corpse when she must.

"This is a strange thing, and you're right, my darling one; these weren't bandits; they're too well fed and they've the look of trained men."

"They were," he said grimly. "Well trained, at that."

"Nor was this any random killing, despite the wealth yonder stranger has in his baggage. Some ruler is behind this—and not one we're familiar with."

"The Association?" he said reluctantly.

Mathilda was standing out of earshot, her face still white as a sheet beneath her tan.

She handled the fight well, from what Rudi says, Juniper thought. *But she's not as hard-bitten yet as she'd like to pretend, the which is all to the good. Lord and Lady preserve us from rulers who kill without regret or look on it without being shaken. Of which her mother is a horrible example . . .*

Rudi sighed in relief when his mother shook her head.

"Not . . . not quite their style, and those men"—she nodded towards the bodies—"are strangers to this land."

"Lady Sandra's ruthless enough," Rudi said quietly.

"More than ruthless enough, but she has far more sense, and so do Grand Constable Tiphaine and the Count of Odell who's chancellor now. None of them would risk anything while Mathilda is with us. No, this is . . . I feel something moving here. We've had the rest we were promised, after the war with Arminger. Perhaps it's coming to an end, and the Powers sing a new song, with us as instrument and melody both."

Her gaze grew wholly human once more, but harder now and shrewd: she was Chief as well as High Priestess, the woman who'd pulled her friends and kin through the time of madness and the death of a world, and built the Clan from refugees and shards.

"It's best you know. It wasn't just an old friend of Nigel who was calling after you left Raven House and came here, and I don't think it's *entirely* coincidence. We'll have to learn how the threads knit."

CHAPTER FOUR

Father Ignatius, priest, monk and knight-brother of the Order of the Shield of Saint Benedict, stopped and looked around casually as he wiped his quill pen and sharpened it with the little razor built into the writing set that was part of his travel kit. The writing was a combination of letters and numbers that would make no sense to anyone who didn't know the running key—it was based on a medieval Latin version of the Gospel of Mark preserved in the Mount Angel library, and used letters based on their position in the Greek alphabet for numbers under twenty-six—but he didn't want anyone to know it *was* in code.

A balance of risks, he thought. *If I were to write in my room, everyone would assume it was a secret message, since the light and space are so much better here.*

Nobody paid much attention to him, which he'd counted on. Mount Angel, the town and fortress-monastery that held the Mother House of his Order, was only fifty miles north of here, and the Clan and the Benedictines had been allies since the early days after the Change. They'd fought the greatest battle of the War of the Eye together, not far from his parents' little farm. He didn't remember that well—he'd been ten—but relations had stayed friendly, and a traveling cleric wasn't rare enough to be noteworthy in Sutterdown.

And he was nothing remarkable to look at himself, a dark man of middling height, slender save for the broad shoulders and thick wrists of a swordsman.

There weren't many people in the Sheaf and Sickle's common room today in any case; this was the slow season for inns, as well as being a house of grief. He'd offered to move out, but the Brannigans insisted that he stay as long as he wished—and he suspected that they welcomed the prospect of work, as a distraction.

A round dozen guests didn't begin to crowd it, even when half of them were playing darts and the rest sitting, and occasionally singing, over their mugs of cider. A low fire crackled in the big stone hearth, giving off a pleasant smell of fir wood. One of the younger Brannigan daughters came out with a tray bearing his lunch; she looked a little haggard, but the smile was genuine as she set the bowl of stew and platter of cut bread, butter, cheese and radishes down before him.

"Thank you, my child; that smells delicious."

"Sure, and you're welcome, Father," she replied. "Call out if there's anything more you're wanting. We're serving roast beef tonight, and there's dried-cherry pie for after."

If she noticed him moving his arm so that the broad sleeve of his robe covered most of the writing, she didn't give any indication of it.

I like Mackenzies, he thought, not for the first time.

They were a mannerly folk, if less stiff and solemn about it than some would prefer, and for all their free and easy ways they didn't have the magpie inquisitiveness you'd find in one of the Association's towns, or the single-minded pursuit of either Mammon or some academic fad that grated on the nerves in Corvallis. Granted their absurd religion was silly at best and conducive to sin at worst . . .

If only they could be brought to the Truth, what an ornament to the Faith they would be. O Lord, may it be soon! Do not keep Your light from these good folk! Mary pierced with sorrows, intercede for them.

Still, evangelization was not his task, particularly not now; and Mackenzies were a difficult target anyway. Their cheerful eclecticism made ordinary argument about as effective as trying to wrestle with a sheepskin blanket. He signed himself with the cross and murmured a grace over the meal, then began to eat. The stew was mutton with barley and carrots and onions, tangy with herbs—what "savory" really meant, rather than the "dark and salty" which often had to substitute for it. It went down

"Come for a rest from prayer, Father?" a big Mackenzie with a dark beard said, as the cleric stopped to shake out his arm and take a drink of water from the bucket on one of the wooden pillars.

Ignatius laughed. "It's my duty to keep my skills sharp, Cethern," he said; he knew the man, a wagoner by trade. "Prayer is a monk's rest, our joy."

For a moment he was pierced by longing for the beautiful ancient discipline of the hours behind Mount Angel's walls, the sound of chant and bells and silence that was like a singing itself as the mind and heart turned wholly towards God.

Take up your cross, he told himself. *Each of us must. Give me strength, O Lord, that I may carry mine to heaven's gate.*

"Still, any skill can be an offering to God," he said to the clansman. "Care for a bout?"

And physical activity helped the mind relax. It would be some time before he could probe deeper into the dangerous mystery of the stranger from out of the east.

✳ ✳ ✳

DUN JUNIPER, WILLAMETTE VALLEY, OREGON
DECEMBER 1, CY22/2020 A.D.

I'm dreaming, Ingolf Vogeler knew. *By moonlight.*

Three women in dark hooded robes stood at the foot of his bed. The one in the center threw back her cowl; cool light fell across her and touched the silver crescent on her brow and the red hair that tumbled across the shoulders of her robe. She raised her hands, palms open as if to cup the opalescent glow, her lips curved in a smile of infinite compassion. Her voice was soft as she sang; somewhere a bell chimed quietly in time to the tune:

> *Come to me, Lord and Lady*
> *Heal this spirit, heal this soul*
> *Come to me, Lord and Lady*
> *Mind and body shall be whole!*

well on a cold winter day, with rain that was half slush beating against the roof and windows.

As he ate he read: *The assailants were definitely Corwinites and, to a high probability, of the personal troops of the false Prophet, who are often used for special operations. Why the CUT was willing to risk provoking the hostility of the Mackenzies to kill Ingolf Vogeler I have been unable to determine; nor, I believe, do the Mackenzie leaders themselves know. Vogeler has been on the verge of death for many days but is now expected to recover.*

Mackenzie physicians were excellent, and those at Dun Juniper best of all. They added magic and pagan prayers to the drugs and instruments, but that apparently did no harm.

I will attempt to gather further information when he does. My preliminary hypothesis is that he carries information that Corwin is desperately anxious the Western powers should not obtain.

He looked down, wondering if that was a little obvious. The Mother House of his order at Mount Angel had been worried about the Church Universal and Triumphant for some time; they had missions and chapter houses throughout what had once been the Pacific Northwest apart from New Deseret, and of course the Catholic Church as a whole was also concerned. Abbot-Bishop Dmwoski had hoped that as the Prophet sank further into madness the menace would subside, but instead it had grown as his adopted son Sethaz took over more and more of the reins.

The cardinal-archbishop of Portland had been concerned enough to forward their reports to the New Vatican in Badia. Not that the Holy See could do much more than offer advice and comfort and prayer; it was many months' sailing away, across stormy, pirate-ridden oceans and lands often hostile when they weren't empty.

Still, prayer is more powerful than armies, in the end, he thought. *The sword is useless without the heart and will.*

His eyes traveled on through the neat letter combinations:

With respect to my original mission, the Princess Mathilda is still at Dun Juniper, with her retinue. She and they take the Sacraments regularly from her chaplain-confessor. No apparent change has taken place in her relationship to the Mackenzie tanist. I will—

He finished the report and the stew at about the same time, mopped the bowl with a heel of the bread, then folded the pages into the envelope, sealed it, and heated a wafer over the tabletop lantern. That he pressed across the flap—with a cunning hair plucked from his tonsured head concealed beneath it in a certain pattern—and stamped his signet ring into the soft crimson wax. There were ways to lift a wax seal and replace it, but the hair trick hadn't been discovered by anyone yet.

Or at least not that the Order knows of, he thought dryly. Paranoia was an occupational hazard of intelligence work. *Many are the marvels of God's Creation, but none so marvelous as man. Or so cunning, for good and ill.*

"Would you be wanting me to send that down to the station, Father?" the Brannigan girl asked, as she came back to collect the dishes.

He smiled at the musical lilt. The Benedictines still encouraged scholarship, even if their main concerns were more immediately practical these days. One of his courses in the seminary had been on the post-Change evolution of variant forms of English, and the Mackenzies' speech was a fascinating case of the semideliberate formation of a new dialect. The process was continuing in the second generation, and even picking up speed.

"No, thank you, my child," he said, tucking the letter into his sleeve and picking up his sword belt. "I'll take it down myself, and get in some practice."

Outside the dark afternoon was chilly, and the slush had turned to wet snow; even the bright-colored carvings that Mackenzies loved so seemed a little dimmed in the gloom of the Black Months. The warrior-cleric pulled up the hood of his robe and walked briskly, absently telling his rosary with his left hand as he walked and keeping his footing on the slippery sidewalk. Even before he'd joined the Order he'd been no stranger to cold and hard work; his family had a farm not far from Mount Angel, and he'd grown up with chores year-round.

Not many people were out—this was the school season for the Clan's children, and most of the adults in Sutterdown had work indoors, being craftsfolk or artists or merchants. The sounds of labor came through the walls, or opened windows that spilled yellow lamplight; the thump and rattle of looms, the whining hum of treadle-worked machinery, the quick delicate *tap-tap-tap* the hammer of a silversmith made, the clank of a printing press.

Those who passed him were bundled up against the weather; most gave him cheerful greetings. There were a fair number of carts on the streets, loaded with country produce and cut timber and hides and wool

and linen thread and metalwork from the mills and foundry outside the walls. Father Ignatius took the west gate, nodding to the guards who looked cold and miserable and bored as they stood beneath the portals, then walked down to the railroad.

The old Southern Pacific tracks were bare right now; the horse-drawn trains came through only often enough to keep a strip down the center of each metal rail free of rust. The little redbrick train station still stood, though, and several new warehouses near it—full of flax and woolen cloth and huge kegs of Brannigan's famous ale, and Clan handicrafts that were almost as well-known. The letter in his sleeve would go north more swiftly on one of the pedal-driven railcarts that carried mail and high-value goods more quickly than anything else in the Changed world.

One of the warehouses was empty save for a few long bundles of steel rebar against one wall, wired together and waiting to be delivered to some smithy or forge, and an assortment of battered practice weapons hung on hooks. Even here the support columns and rafters had been surface-carved in a design of stylized leaves and branches, with whimsical faces peering out here and there. An elephant-headed godlet sat on a flower in a niche by the door, some protective spirit of commerce.

The dry dirt floor was broad and empty, and a dozen Mackenzies were using it for sparring; this weather was a bit much for even the Clan's long-bowmen to practice their archery outside. Eight men and four women were at work, leaping and shouting in the active, foining Mackenzie blade style as they thrust and cut with short swords of padded wood, battle spears with rubber blades and butt caps. Dull *thunk* sounds echoed as metal bucklers stopped blows, and occasionally a louder *thwack* yelp as one went home.

Ignatius hung up his sword belt, pulled off his robe and drew his sword. Beneath the monastic garment he was dressed in plain tunic of undyed hodden gray wool, a bit chilly in this weather for soaking up sweat.

Then he began a series of forms, slowly at first to stretch muscle and tendon, then faster and faster—singlehanded style derived from old Japanese models, and then with arm. Soon the cloven air was hissing beneath the sharp in glittering arcs, his sharp barking *hai!* cutting through well on a cold winter day, with rain that was half slush beating against the roof and windows.

As he ate he read: *The assailants were definitely Corwinites and, to a high probability, of the personal troops of the false Prophet, who are often used for special operations. Why the CUT was willing to risk provoking the hostility of the Mackenzies to kill Ingolf Vogeler I have been unable to determine; nor, I believe, do the Mackenzie leaders themselves know. Vogeler has been on the verge of death for many days but is now expected to recover.*

Mackenzie physicians were excellent, and those at Dun Juniper best of all. They added magic and pagan prayers to the drugs and instruments, but that apparently did no harm.

I will attempt to gather further information when he does. My preliminary hypothesis is that he carries information that Corwin is desperately anxious the Western powers should not obtain.

He looked down, wondering if that was a little obvious. The Mother House of his order at Mount Angel had been worried about the Church Universal and Triumphant for some time; they had missions and chapter houses throughout what had once been the Pacific Northwest apart from New Deseret, and of course the Catholic Church as a whole was also concerned. Abbot-Bishop Dmwoski had hoped that as the Prophet sank further into madness the menace would subside, but instead it had grown as his adopted son Sethaz took over more and more of the reins.

The cardinal-archbishop of Portland had been concerned enough to forward their reports to the New Vatican in Badia. Not that the Holy See could do much more than offer advice and comfort and prayer; it was many months' sailing away, across stormy, pirate-ridden oceans and lands often hostile when they weren't empty.

Still, prayer is more powerful than armies, in the end, he thought. *The sword is useless without the heart and will.*

His eyes traveled on through the neat letter combinations:

With respect to my original mission, the Princess Mathilda is still at Dun Juniper, with her retinue. She and they take the Sacraments regularly from her chaplain-confessor. No apparent change has taken place in her relationship to the Mackenzie tanist. I will—

He finished the report and the stew at about the same time, mopped the bowl with a heel of the bread, then folded the pages into the envelope, sealed it, and heated a wafer over the tabletop lantern. That he pressed across the flap—with a cunning hair plucked from his tonsured head concealed beneath it in a certain pattern—and stamped his signet ring into the soft crimson wax. There were ways to lift a wax seal and replace it, but the hair trick hadn't been discovered by anyone yet.

Or at least not that the Order knows of, he thought dryly. Paranoia was an occupational hazard of intelligence work. *Many are the marvels of God's Creation, but none so marvelous as man. Or so cunning, for good* and *ill.*

"Would you be wanting me to send that down to the station, Father?" the Brannigan girl asked, as she came back to collect the dishes.

He smiled at the musical lilt. The Benedictines still encouraged scholarship, even if their main concerns were more immediately practical these days. One of his courses in the seminary had been on the post-Change evolution of variant forms of English, and the Mackenzies' speech was a fascinating case of the semideliberate formation of a new dialect. The process was continuing in the second generation, and even picking up speed.

"No, thank you, my child," he said, tucking the letter into his sleeve and picking up his sword belt. "I'll take it down myself, and get in some practice."

Outside the dark afternoon was chilly, and the slush had turned to wet snow; even the bright-colored carvings that Mackenzies loved so seemed a little dimmed in the gloom of the Black Months. The warrior-cleric pulled up the hood of his robe and walked briskly, absently telling his rosary with his left hand as he walked and keeping his footing on the slippery sidewalk. Even before he'd joined the Order he'd been no stranger to cold and hard work; his family had a farm not far from Mount Angel, and he'd grown up with chores year-round.

Not many people were out—this was the school season for the Clan's children, and most of the adults in Sutterdown had work indoors, being craftsfolk or artists or merchants. The sounds of labor came through the walls, or opened windows that spilled yellow lamplight; the thump and rattle of looms, the whining hum of treadle-worked machinery, the quick delicate *tap-tap-tap* the hammer of a silversmith made, the clank of a printing press.

Those who passed him were bundled up against the weather; most gave him cheerful greetings. There were a fair number of carts on the streets, loaded with country produce and cut timber and hides and wool and linen thread and metalwork from the mills and foundry outside the walls. Father Ignatius took the west gate, nodding to the guards who looked cold and miserable and bored as they stood beneath the portals, then walked down to the railroad.

The old Southern Pacific tracks were bare right now; the horse-drawn trains came through only often enough to keep a strip down the center of each metal rail free of rust. The little redbrick train station still stood, though, and several new warehouses near it—full of flax and woolen cloth and huge kegs of Brannigan's famous ale, and Clan handicrafts that were almost as well-known. The letter in his sleeve would go north more swiftly on one of the pedal-driven railcarts that carried mail and high-value goods more quickly than anything else in the Changed world.

One of the warehouses was empty save for a few long bundles of steel rebar against one wall, wired together and waiting to be delivered to some smithy or forge, and an assortment of battered practice weapons hung on hooks. Even here the support columns and rafters had been surface-carved in a design of stylized leaves and branches, with whimsical faces peering out here and there. An elephant-headed godlet sat on a flower in a niche by the door, some protective spirit of commerce.

The dry dirt floor was broad and empty, and a dozen Mackenzies were using it for sparring; this weather was a bit much for even the Clan's longbowmen to practice their archery outside. Eight men and four women were at work, leaping and shouting in the active, foining Mackenzie blade style as they thrust and cut with short swords of padded wood or battle spears with rubber blades and butt caps. Dull *thunk* sounds echoed as metal bucklers stopped blows, and occasionally a louder *thwack* and a yelp as one went home.

Ignatius hung up his sword belt, pulled off his robe and drew his longsword. Beneath the monastic garment he was dressed in plain pants and tunic of undyed hodden gray wool, a bit chilly in this weather, but good for soaking up sweat.

Then he began a series of forms, slowly at first to stretch and warm muscle and tendon, then faster and faster—singlehand, the two-handed style derived from old Japanese models, and then with a shield on his left arm. Soon the cloven air was hissing beneath the sharp steel as it swung in glittering arcs, his sharp barking *hai!* cutting through the clamor.

"Come for a rest from prayer, Father?" a big Mackenzie with a dark beard said, as the cleric stopped to shake out his arm and take a drink of water from the bucket on one of the wooden pillars.

Ignatius laughed. "It's my duty to keep my skills sharp, Cethern," he said; he knew the man, a wagoner by trade. "Prayer is a monk's rest, our joy."

For a moment he was pierced by longing for the beautiful ancient discipline of the hours behind Mount Angel's walls, the sound of chant and bells and silence that was like a singing itself as the mind and heart turned wholly towards God.

Take up your cross, he told himself. *Each of us must. Give me strength, O Lord, that I may carry mine to heaven's gate.*

"Still, any skill can be an offering to God," he said to the clansman. "Care for a bout?"

And physical activity helped the mind relax. It would be some time before he could probe deeper into the dangerous mystery of the stranger from out of the east.

* * *

DUN JUNIPER, WILLAMETTE VALLEY, OREGON
DECEMBER 1, CY22/2020 A.D.

I'm dreaming, Ingolf Vogeler knew. *By moonlight.*
Three women in dark hooded robes stood at the foot of his bed. The one in the center threw back her cowl; cool light fell across her and touched the silver crescent on her brow and the red hair that tumbled across the shoulders of her robe. She raised her hands, palms open as if to cup the opalescent glow, her lips curved in a smile of infinite compassion. Her voice was soft as she sang; somewhere a bell chimed quietly in time to the tune:

> *Come to me, Lord and Lady*
> *Heal this spirit, heal this soul*
> *Come to me, Lord and Lady*
> *Mind and body shall be whole!*

Beast of the burning sunlight
Sear this wound that pain may cease
Mistress of the silver moonlight
Hold us fast and bring us peace—

Come to me, Lord and Lady
Mind and body shall be whole!

"Mom?" he murmured weakly, though he knew she wasn't.

A hand touched his forehead. "Always, my darling one. Sleep now, and heal."

Darkness.

✳ ✳ ✳

DUN JUNIPER, WILLAMETTE VALLEY, OREGON
DECEMBER 6, CY22/2020 A.D.

"Where am I?" Ingolf asked, as his eyes blinked open.

It's been a while, he knew.

There were vague memories of heat and pain and movement, of struggling for each breath as if his lungs were full of hot sticky syrup, of voices and faces and things half-seen in dreams. His head being raised and something salty spooned into his mouth, of voices chanting and more pain, a deep stabbing ache on his left side.

Everything seemed to be very distant and remote, and he was exhausted, as if he'd worked all day rather than just woken up, but he was more himself this time. He looked at his right hand; it was resting on a clean sheet of beige linen, with a checked blanket of soft wool beneath that and a pillow under his head. His arm was thin, thinner than he could ever remember it being, and his whole body felt heavy, as if his skin had been taken off and replaced by lead.

A face leaned over him. A woman's face, with a thick braid of grizzled black hair and a bold beak of a nose in a strong-boned face that had aged well; there was no resemblance in looks, but she reminded him of his mother. Her hair smelled of some herbal wash; the room of soap and warm fir wood and sweet cedarlike incense.

"You're in Dun Juniper," she said. "I'm a healer; my name is Judy Barstow Mackenzie, and I'm looking after you. You've been very sick; your wound became infected when you were moved, and you developed pneumonia as well and nearly died. We've saved the arm and you will heal. Now drink this."

Her hand came behind his head, and he put his lips to the cup she held. It was chicken broth, hot and good but not too hot to swallow, and as he did he could feel how empty he was within.

"I have to . . ." He stopped, embarrassed, conscious of his full bladder, and even more of the implications of the heavy cloth pad around his hips like a giant diaper.

She smiled then. "I'm a mother and a healer and fifty-two years old; there's nothing that'll surprise me, my lad. Here."

She helped him use a bedpan, and then pulled the blankets back up. "Rest now."

* * *

He woke and ate and slept, woke and ate and slept, conscious only of the body's needs.

When he came fully to himself again it was daylight, though dim, and his head was altogether clear, although he still felt no impulse to move. He was in a room not much bigger than the bed; it had a small brick hearth with a little iron door to close on the flame, and a wicker basket of split wood beside it, and a table with jugs and a basin and bottles. Aromatic steam smelling of pine and herbs jetted softly from a kettle on the hearth; a window with four panes of glass let in some light—snow was falling against it, but he was comfortably warm, and streaks of moisture trickled down the fogged glass. Bands of carving ran horizontally across walls of smooth-fitted plank, leaves and sinuous elongated gripping beasts; the floor was brown tile.

There was a consciousness of potential pain in his left arm, but no actual hurt; he spread and closed his hands several times. The hush of snowfall was in the air, but he could hear faint noises—the familiar *thock . . . thock* of an ax splitting wood, the thump of looms, the voices of children playing, the *ting . . . ting . . . ting . . .* of someone beating iron in a smithy. By the noise he judged he was in the second story of a building with thick log walls, and one in a settlement of some size but not a city or even a town.

Right across from him on the wall was a picture, made by carving a slab of wood and then painting to bring out the low relief. It was of a woman robed and mantled in blue, but he didn't think it was the Virgin Mary; for one thing she carried a flame in one hand and a sheaf of wheat in the other, and she was standing on stars and wearing the crescent moon as a crown. The carving was very fine; he could see the tenderness in her smile. . . .

More important, his shete and dagger and tomahawk were standing in a bundle beside the door, wrapped about with his weapons belt, although he couldn't have lifted them to save his life right now. His own rosary and crucifix hung from the bedpost. Whatever he was, he wasn't a prisoner here. There was water on the table, but he couldn't reach it. He croaked out a call, and the door opened and a head came in.

"Hi!"

Another woman, much younger than the one he'd seen, but with a look to her as if she were close kin. Around thirty, he thought, but paler and longer-faced, her abundant braided hair a light brown, with a stocky-strong build but not much spare flesh. She was dressed in a kilt and indigo-blue shirt, knee socks and low buckled shoes, with a stethoscope around her neck; there was the same matter-of-fact competence in the way she helped him drink, listened to his chest, gave him some sharp-tasting medicine in a spoon, then took his temperature with a glass thermometer and compared it to notes on a clipboard at the foot of the bed.

"Perfectly normal, Mr. Vogeler," she said. "For three days now, and the wound's been fully closed for a while. Mother will be pleased; she had to go back in to clean it out, you see. I'm Tamsin Barstow Mackenzie—call me Tamsin. You'll be able to stand a little in a couple of days."

She grinned at him. "And walk as far as the bathroom, with help. Won't that be nice, sure and it will?"

"It will! Could I have something to eat now, Miss Tamsin?" he asked. "Lord, I'm hungry!"

"You *are* getting better the now!"

Then he frowned; the lilting accent reminded him: "Ah . . . there was a lady, her name was Saba. . . ."

She put a hand on his shoulder. "Saba Brannigan? I'm afraid . . . You fought very well, but she was killed. I'm sorry."

Humiliatingly, he felt tears coursing down his cheeks and couldn't stop them, which told him how weak he still was. Tamsin handed him a square of linen handkerchief and left, long enough for him to compose himself.

When she returned her mother was with her, and she carried a tray with a bowl of soup and pieces of fine white wheat bread and butter. The soup was chicken again, but this time with pieces of the meat in it, and carrots and noodles; there were herbs he'd never tasted before for seasoning, and he couldn't remember having anything as good—though that was probably partly because it had been so long. He ate it all, expected to want more, and found that it exactly matched what he could take. While they propped him up by turning a crank under the bed he had a chance to look at his left arm again, knowing what he'd been told.

His eyebrows went up as he really looked at the thick purple scar. Men rarely recovered from such a serious wound if it mortified. He raised the limb and worked it carefully, wincing slightly. There was a tug and pull when he stretched it, and he'd have trouble lifting a feather, but the range of motion seemed good.

I'm not crippled, he thought, with a rush of relief. Aloud he went on: "That *did* turn real nasty, ma'am. I'm surprised I lived."

"So am I, with the pneumonia. You'd been pushing beyond what your body could bear, but it wasn't your time," the older woman said; this time he was alert enough that he noticed a reserve in her tone. The younger looked at her and smiled.

"Mother stayed up with you for days," she said.

Judy shrugged. "It wasn't your time to make accounting to the Guardians," she repeated. "You'll be on light solids from now on, and your recovery ought to be very rapid. We'll start a physiotherapy program immediately."

When she saw he didn't know the word, she clarified: "Special exercises for the injured arm. There's scar tissue—you'll have to be careful to get full strength back."

"I'm most grateful, ma'am," he said. "To you and your folks. I hope I can do something in return."

Her gaze thawed a little. "Well, Mr. Vogeler, we *would* like you to answer some questions. And I think you're about strong enough to do that, soon, if not much else."

A yell came from somewhere not too far away. Ingolf started and paled; that was a woman crying out in pain. Judy Barstow shook her head. "Right on time," she said, and walked out.

Tamsin smiled at him before she followed, seeing the alarm on his face. "Childbirth," she said, and snorted. "It's Dechtire Smith. This is her third; she's strong as a plowhorse with hips like one too, but she always insists on the clinic and pretends she's dying."

"Well . . . it hurts," he said, relieved it was something so natural. "And it is dangerous."

Back home the men all went out and drank applejack when the midwife came, and pretended not to jump every time a shriek rang out. If it was bad enough for a real doctor, they drank more.

Tamsin nodded. "With two of my own, don't I *know* it hurts! But it doesn't hurt like *that*, when it goes well. We don't lose many mothers here, Mr. Vogeler—not one in a thousand. Believe me: that woman's not happy unless she's getting sympathy."

The brief flare of emotion had tired him, and the soup and bread were making him sleepy. He let his head fall back and slept once more.

*   *   *

Rudi Mackenzie bent and lifted the end of the Douglas fir onto the sledge, getting some of the sticky aromatic sap on his gloves as he heaved it up. Shouting and laughing, their breath puffing in the cold damp air amid the drifting snowflakes and the mealy scent of them, the others bent and heaved and the whole length was on it, and it was the work of a moment to lash it down.

He turned and bowed his head a last time to the stump while he rubbed the sap off the leather of his gauntlets; they'd made the usual apology and explanation when they cut it yesterday, which should satisfy Cernunnos. The tree was to represent His member, after all. Then he whistled.

A tall glossy-black horse brought her head up sharply not far away, where she'd been nosing the snow, more for something to do than from hope of finding anything edible; he could tell she was bored by the whole business. Despite the winter her midnight coat shone, and when she trotted over she seemed to float, barely tapping the earth with her hooves.

The reins leading to her light hackamore bridle were looped up over the saddlebow. Nobody had used a bit on Epona since they met; Rudi didn't need one, and it would be futile for anyone else to try. He'd had the horse since she was just under four and he was ten—that made her sixteen now, middle-aged in horse years, but even experienced wranglers usually put her at seven or eight at first sight.

"Well, you *asked* to come along," he said, scolding affectionately as he stroked her neck and she lipped at his hair. "You get all pissy about me taking someone else out, even your own get, and then I bring you and you sulk because it's boring."

She'd never liked seeing him working with other horses, not even her own daughters Macha Mongruad and Rhiannon. Rudi put a hand on her withers and vaulted into the saddle. He still remembered how proud he'd been the first time he could do that—she was just a hair under seventeen hands. Now it was as easy as climbing stairs . . . but he'd been able to ride her from the first, when nobody else could.

"We bring the Yule Tree!" he called. "On to the hall!"

That got him a cheer; everyone here was young, from his age down to six-year-olds running around pretending to help and pelting one another with snowballs; Mary and Ritva were doing that too, and giggling like the kids they'd been not too long ago. He smiled tolerantly—until one of theirs took him on the back of the head and knocked his bonnet off into a drift. They *weren't* kids anymore and they threw *hard*.

"Hey, watch that!" he called. "Not while I'm riding Epona!"

It wasn't that the big mare wasn't well trained. She'd spun under him in response to his shift of balance, moving as lightly as a deer. The problem was that she was trained for *war*, and fiercely protective of him besides, and didn't know the difference between a snowball and a rock meant to kill. He had to check-rein her then, and she snorted and shook her head and showed her teeth.

Epona was a genius of horsekind, but their intelligence was of a different type and order. You had to understand how they saw the world. He grinned at the thought; he was pretty sure that there were times when she thought *he* was a bumbling idiot who needed constant protection.

"Well, you were the one who was pining because I didn't take you out enough," he scolded her. "Be good!"

He kicked his right foot free of the stirrup, bent down and retrieved the bonnet. To calm her, he let Epona drop behind the rest of them; Odard and Matti were mounted too, and they all watched the shouting mob lead the two ponies pulling the sled through the snowy woods. A scramble and a push to help the team, and they were on a well-kept trail that ran east to Dun Juniper.

This forest had been Mackenzie land before the Mackenzies were a Clan, back before the Change; way back, since the family came out from east Tennessee in his mother's great-great-grandfather's time. Generations ago her great-uncle had started to tend and plant here—that was why there were so many oaks, and exotics like black walnuts, though nowadays every dun on this side of the valley spread them from the nuts and acorns. He halted under one walnut that reared a hundred feet above the trail and made a reverence to a small shrine there; it had a stone arch and two rosebushes trained to twine together.

"This is where they died," Mathilda said quietly. "Nearly twelve years ago now."

Rudi nodded; that had been in March of the last year of the War of the Eye, when Mathilda had been captive here. Her parents had sent a team of warriors to get her back; they had, and taken Rudi too, and killed the two Clan fighters guarding him, Aoife Barstow and Liath Dunling. He made an offering here every year on the anniversary of it, a handful of salt and wheat and a little of his own blood, to their spirits and the spirit of the tree; it had become a symbol to him that he'd be heading north soon, as part of the agreement that had ended the War.

She crossed herself and brought out her crucifix to kiss. "They fought very bravely, I remember that," she said gravely. "Holy Mary, Queen of Heaven, intercede for them, and for us all, now and at the hour of our deaths."

Odard repeated the gesture; they all sat silent for a moment in respect, then touched their horses into a canter and followed the sled.

It was already out of the trees, out onto the long lens-shaped stretch of benchland meadow that held Dun Juniper on the south-facing slope of the mountain. The snow was knee-deep, with more coming as the weather thickened. Mathilda tilted her head back and stuck out her tongue to catch the flakes on it. Laughing, Rudi did the same; even Odard joined in after a moment. They passed the tannery and bark mill and soap-boiling sheds, not in use in this season but still giving off a strong whiff of curing leather and boiled fat. The sled had gotten ahead of them, and they leg-signaled their horses to pick up the pace, until plumes of white flew up from their forefeet.

Dun Juniper lay at the middle of the oval, hard up against the flank of the mountain, halfway between the tannery at one end and the little waterfall and gristmill at the other. It had been a low plateau once, where his mother's kin had built a hunting lodge of great squared logs.

Rudi chuckled under his breath as he looked up at the walls looming through the snow; they were as high and strong as Sutterdown's, albeit the circuit of them was a lot less. Snow stuck in patches to the rough stucco, hiding the swirling designs of vine and leaf and flowers under the battlements.

And whenever he saw them, something deep within him said *home*, wherever he'd been.

"What's the joke, Rudi?" Odard asked.

"I was just remembering something my mother said. She showed up here right after the Change, and met her coven—she'd been in Corvallis; they were in Eugene. And she gave them this little speech, you know, to buck them up because they were all at sea and scared witless with it."

The other two nodded; they were all the children of rulers, in one way or another, and they'd grown up with the necessities of leadership. Rudi went on:

"And she said, 'It's a clan we'll have to be, as it was in the old days. . . .'"

Odard frowned. "What's funny about that? That's what happened, isn't it?"

"Yeah," he said, laughing outright now. "But she didn't actually *mean* it, not really. She thought it was, what are they after calling it, a *figure of speech*. She just meant they'd have to pull together to get through. It was the others who decided to *really* do that, and she says she pretty well just had to go along with it whenever they came up with something, like calling her Chief or Uncle Denni making the kilts when they found that load of tartan blankets. She says it shows how 'leading' means running fast enough to keep ahead of your people."

Mathilda joined in the laughter. "Well, my dad did something like that too," she said.

Rudi raised an eyebrow, intrigued. She didn't usually talk about her father much, naturally enough, since everyone outside Protectorate territory hated his memory. And a fair number within, too, for all that his tyranny had still saved their lives, or these days more often their parents' lives.

"Mom says he got a bunch of people he'd known in the Society together, that first day, Conrad Renfrew and the others . . ."

Odard and Rudi both nodded; a surprisingly large proportion of survivors had been members of the Society for Creative Anachronism and similar groups, and an even larger share of those had ended up in leadership positions. Enough so that in these latter days social climbers tended to invent Society parents if they didn't actually have them. Not just in the Protectorate, though that was where they'd been most influential, because of the Armingers.

For a while they'd been the only ones with weapons that worked, and who knew how to use them. In a world where you had to fight to take food and fight to keep it, a desperate man with hauberk and helm and shield, a sword and some faint beginning idea of what to do with it, had a *big* advantage over desperate suburbanites with kitchen knives and shovels. Mathilda went on:

". . . and after they'd talked about what was happening, and Dad had convinced them things weren't going to Change back and they had to do what he wanted or they'd all die, he said: 'What if a man were to take it upon himself to be king?' "

Odard grinned, catching the reference; or maybe he'd heard the story before. Even when Rudi was visiting in Association territory, people tended to avoid certain subjects—after all, his blood father, Mike Havel, and Norman Arminger had fought like bulldogs with a grip for ten years and then killed each other in a spectacular duel between the two armies they led, and his mother, Juniper, hadn't exactly been friendly with the Armingers either, to put it mildly.

He racked his brains; he'd read a lot of history, particularly of periods well back before the twentieth century—it was fun, and useful, and his teachers had encouraged him, starting with Juniper. Then the fact jiggled into place, along with a memory of his mother and himself curled up on a couch reading a heavy book with a leather cover.

Ah. That was what Oliver Cromwell said, when he was thinking of taking the throne of England, after he'd killed Charles the First. He never did, though. He just called himself the Lord Prot . . . well, Annwyn take it, was that where that bastard Arminger got the idea?

Matti went on: "And Count Conrad . . . well, he wasn't a count then, of course . . . said, 'Oh, hell, Norman, we'll just call you the Lord Protector. You can enter an insanity plea if the lights come back on, and we'll blame everything on you.'

"And Dad laughed and said: 'Lord Protector? I like it. We'll call ourselves the Portland Protective Association; it'll sound more familiar to the non-Society people I want to bring in. And if the lights come back on, Conrad, I promise to take the fall.' "

"Odd to think of important things starting by chance, like that," Odard said meditatively. "Though . . . when you're reading history, have you noticed how the older stuff seems more *real*, somehow? The people and the things they say and do, I mean. The closer you get to the Change, the more . . . weird . . . things seem. Except things like the Society; my mother's always on about that and how *her* father was king of some territory by right of combat. That sounds more like real life. It's all the stuff *around* it that doesn't. Opinion polls, and computers, and *Star Trek* . . ."

"The RenFaires, where my mother sang as a bard, they seem to have been pretty normal," Rudi agreed. "She'll be talking about them, and it's perfectly sensible, and then all of a sudden it's . . . the other stuff around it, like you said. Thinking about it is like trying to grab a live fish with your fingers; it's not impossible, exactly, but it's not worth the effort most of the time. And she sees it on my face, and calls me a Changeling."

They both gave chuckles of agreement as they followed the sledge through the four-towered gatehouse; they *were* Changelings, which was the slang term for people born after the world was remade.

The gates were wide open—it was the middle of the afternoon and peacetime—but Rudi made a reverence with steepled hands and thumbs on chin to the posts on either side; Lugh with his spear, Brigid with her sheaf and flame. There was a pleasant smell of woodsmoke, cooking, animals, infinitely familiar and welcoming.

Inside the walls didn't look as tall, since the bottom twelve feet were built into what had been the sides of the plateau, leaving the inner surface level. The ramparts were lined with small log houses, carved and painted with themes from myth or simple fancy, and in the central area were the buildings that served the dwellers here and the Clan at large: bathhouse, smithy, stables, workshops where every craft from glassblowing to hand-printing was practiced and taught, granary, infirmary, bad-weather Co-venstead, library and schools and more, divided by graveled lanes.

Just right, he thought affectionately. *Not too big like Sutterdown or, Mother-of-All help us, Corvallis; but big enough to be interesting, and the woods and fields right there outside.*

A crowd gathered around the sled with the big fir; most of the house-holds had their own Yule Tree, but this was one for the whole dun and all Mackenzies too. Rudi waved to them all and swung down from Epona's saddle; half a dozen youngsters sprang forward to take the bridle, and he picked one the mare had shown some liking—or at least tolerance—for. Another proudly bore off his sword belt and quiver and cased longbow.

The hall itself was the largest building, its shingled roof rearing over the rest like a dragon's scaly back, green in patches with moss beneath the thickening coat of snow. The foundation had been that hunting lodge, a big log box on knee-high fieldstone. Late in the first Change Year the early Mackenzies had doubled its size by the simple expedient of taking off the roof, adding more squared logs, and then putting the roof back, to give two tall stories and a big loft. A veranda and balcony ran around three sides, supported by pillars made from whole tree trunks.

Of course, there had been other modifications. . . . The pillars were carved in running knotwork and elongated stylized animals, then stained and painted with browns and golds and greens—anyone these days would recognize it as Mackenzie work; this was the original that other duns had copied. At either end the roof rafters crossed one another and rose to face inward in gilded spirals, sunwise and widdershins to balance the energies.

Where the horizontal beams of the balcony jutted out through the pillars they were carved in the shapes of the Clan's sept totems, the heads of Wolf and Coyote, Raven and Bear and Tiger; the grinning jaws held chains that supported big lanterns wrought of glass and brass and iron. The wicks within were already lit against winter's gloom, though it was only a little past noon, and they cast pools of warm yellow across painted wood and trampled snow. There was a reason these were called the Black Months.

The crowd was already freeing the tree from the sledge; they waited for Rudi, though, as he stepped forward to shoulder the heaviest load at the base.

"The Holly King grows old!" he shouted gaily. "Soon he will fall to the Oak King, and the Sun will be reborn!"

One of the twins was back at the other end—it had to be a woman there, of course, and an Initiate.

"The Crone is carrying Winter's child," she called. "But He will be born to marry the Maiden!"

A dozen shoulders took up the tree between them. Someone swung open the big double doors and they dashed up the stairs and into the hall itself. Inside was a great open space the length and breadth of the building, the walls carved and painted into a fantasy of leaf and flower and faces out of tales. A tub of water waited at the western end, with a screw-and-collar arrangement for holding the Yule Tree upright. He knelt with a grunt—the sapling was as thick as his thigh at the base, and this was going to be tricky. He guided the cut end into the circle with casual strength, then called, "Now!"

All the hands on the trunk and the forked poles laid ready for the moment were teenaged at least; it was a privilege to help with this. He put his shoulder to it, boughs scraping past his face, buried in softly aromatic green needles, and pushed, taking the strain carefully as he felt the weight come onto the muscles of his back and belly—that you were very strong didn't mean you couldn't put your back out; he'd seen it happen. Rudi had been around heavy weights and their handling all his life; he could sense when it began to tilt as the others pushed. . . .

"Easy there—*Imrim! Get behind it, man!*"

At last the tree was upright in the bath of water, a perfectly symmetrical shape of glossy dark green, the tip between two rafters and just six inches below the floorboards of the second story. Its scent filled the hall as the warmer air coaxed it out, bringing a breath of the spring woods. He knelt again and swiftly spun the screws until they bit into the thick dark furrowed bark and the wood below, then put on the board cover to keep overcurious kittens or puppies or toddlers from falling in or drinking the water. When he stood again, everyone who'd helped raise it stood in a circle around the tree and joined hands, throwing them up three times and whooping.

"Well, there it is," Rudi said to the crowd. "Jack-in-the-Green's little green Jack."

Groans and hoots, and people snatched up twigs and bits of bark that had fallen and pelted him with them. He retreated with his arms over his face, begging for mercy in a falsetto voice; then he sprang forward and grabbed two fourteen-year-olds and caught one under each arm, whirling them around with a back-cracking effort.

When the horseplay was finished he brushed down his jacket and plaid and went to hang them up, checking that his sword and dirk and bow had been placed properly. They had, of course; he touched the long orange-yellow stave of yew with its subtle double curve and black-walnut riser in the middle, there among the others. He remembered how he'd longed for a proper war bow of his own when he was a kid, practicing at the butts in the meadows below with the rest of his class—Mackenzie education gave the longbow a high priority.

Well, now he had it, from the hands of Aylward the Archer himself; his own height and a handspan more, a hundred and twenty pounds of draw, throwing a thirty-two-inch shaft at four to the ounce.

And it's just as much fun as I thought it would be!

He turned and saw his mother over by the hearth on the north wall, where the house altar rested over the great fieldstone fireplace and a low blaze of split wood burned down to embers. She waved to him: *come.*

Sir Nigel rose as he watched, and intercepted Sir Odard and Matti. "Come, and I shall thrash you at chess, young man," he said.

Rudi caught Mathilda's eye and gave a slight shake of the head, with an apologetic shrug added to it.

"I'll kibitz while Nigel beats Odard," she said, taking it with good enough grace; it wasn't as if she were a stranger to the concept of a state secret, or ever had been. "And then I shall thrash *you,* Sir Nigel. If you spot me your bishops."

That left only Juniper Mackenzie and Ingolf Vogeler in chairs by the hearth set into the northern wall of the hall. He was looking a lot better than he had; the shadow of the Hunter's wing wasn't on his brow anymore, but he was still painfully thin, the skin fallen in on the heavy bones.

She tucked up the soft blanket of beige wool that was around him and poured a little more of the hot mead that stayed warm in a nook in the wall of the fireplace. He thanked her with a shy smile that sat oddly on the battered warrior's face.

Mom's like that, Rudi thought proudly. *She's everyone's mother, if they have a good heart and need it.*

He'd complained about that once, when he was young, and she'd told him . . .

What was it she said? Yes: "Love isn't like money—the more you give away the more you get back, and the more you have to give."

And then she'd laughed and told him she loved him best of all, and he'd been all right again. He came over to the hearth and drew up a chair to sit, sinking into the leather cushions and enjoying the warmth of the flickering blaze.

"Glad to meet you when I'm in my right mind, more or less," Vogeler said, offering a hand. After the shake he looked thoughtfully at Rudi's long form. "Maybe we could spar a bit, when I'm back on my pins . . . I'd like to take the measure of a man who can take down two of the Prophet's cutters fighting in his underwear, and not get a scratch."

Rudi smiled broadly: "I'd like that, Ingolf. They say it'll be a while, though."

Sparring with the same people all the time could get boring—and dangerous. If you fell into a rut and stopped being surprised now and then you stopped learning.

The hall was returning to normal for a winter afternoon near Yule, which meant people sitting around talking or reading or telling stories, having a beer together or making plans and arguing . . . but nobody would disturb the Chief and her son at a conversation, and the buzz in the background actually made them more private.

There was a plate of sandwiches on the table beside Ingolf, some honey-cured ham with cheese, some roast venison; he'd eaten only one, and one of the dried-cherry scones.

Ingolf grinned as Rudi picked up a sandwich and raised an eyebrow. "Sure. I keep thinking I'm going to wolf down half a cow, and then I get full. You know how it is when you're getting over something."

He nodded, chewing and savoring the rich strong taste of the deer meat; he did know how it was when you were recovering from a fever or a wound. He'd had one about as bad, and on his gut, before he turned eleven.

After a moment Juniper spoke softly. "If you're well enough now, Ingolf Vogeler, it's your story I would have. Of your own will you're not to blame for what happened, but still one of my people is dead, and I must explain to an old friend why his daughter was killed in her own home. Also I am the Mackenzie, and the welfare of land and folk is something the Chief must account for at the last."

The easterner licked his lips slightly, took a drink of the mead, and spoke:

"I'm willing to tell you my story," he said, his eyes fixed on the distance. "Christ be my witness, I owe you folks my life and more. But it's . . . just so damned strange."

His mouth quirked. "Always told myself I was a practical type. But this has got weird stuff in it . . . would you believe a voice I heard in dreams sent me here?"

Juniper Mackenzie laughed, a clear peal. "Oh, Ingolf, you've come to the *one* place in all the world for *that* to be believed—though in truth, I might have thought you wandering in your wits if I hadn't had independent confirmation of some of it."

"And I haven't *had* the dream since I arrived. And by God, I'm thankful for that!"

Juniper nodded. "The Powers are at work here, but it isn't the first time they've touched my life, so . . . or Rudi's."

He gave a shy duck of the head. "Well, it's like this . . . the start's ordinary enough. After the war with the Sioux, I didn't want to end up a hired soldier, but there didn't seem to be much else I could do except get work as a farmhand. Not that I'm above any honest work; sheriffs from the Free Republic of Richland aren't so high and mighty that we never touch a pitchfork or a plow handle, not like some folk I could name but won't, like those arrogant bastards over to Marshall."

"Not welcome back home?" Rudi asked sympathetically. *That would be a terrible thing.*

"Not without more crawling than I could stomach," Ingolf said grimly. Then his tone became matter-of-fact.

"So some friends and I who'd fought together in the war, we got into the salvage business. Not steel and glass and stuff like everyone gets from the nearest ruins; that's low-value, and it's pretty tightly tied up most places too; you can't just go in and start mining. Not anywhere close enough to market that the cost of hauling wouldn't kill you."

"Yes, we have agreements on who can claim what here, as well," Juniper said encouragingly. "And there's more than enough steel and brass and aluminum and so forth, and will be for many an age. So as you say, it's cheap in most places."

Ingolf went on, his voice growing a bit more animated as he relived his great idea:

"What we went after was really valuable things—gold and silver, jewels, artwork that was famous before the Change, watches, machine tools that can be rerigged to run off water power, telescopes and binoculars . . . the sort of thing that's been worked out of places near to areas that still have people. Well, out east where I come from, that means going *farther* east, if you want to get somewhere unclaimed. East and south, down into the dead lands, past Chicago. I hear there are villages and farms up in parts of the Appalachians, but in the lowlands from the old Illinois line to the Atlantic it's . . . it's still real bad."

Rudi and his mother nodded. They'd heard the same from California, where a few explorers had gone lately, and similar things about Europe from Nigel and others. Nearly everywhere in thick-settled lands the streams of refugees from the great cities had overlapped one another; they'd eaten the land bare and then died. Except those who took to living off man's flesh, but that was a losing game in the long run, with the fate of the Kilkenny cats at the end of it. A few of the luckiest lived until the rabbits bred back.

Some of those little groups of grisly predators barely had speech or fire, since they'd started with feral children run wild during the chaos. They were primitive in a way no human savages had ever been before, without the great store of knowledge and skill real wilderness dwellers had. And they still ate men, when they could.

"So . . . we'd gotten a few good hauls, better as we went farther east, but the problem was that money . . . well, you can rent a room and buy your beer with cash, but if you want to make a life, you need to have a place where you're welcome to settle as something more than a laborer, and that's not so easy. Most places aren't too open to outsiders buying land, and without you're protected by law all you've got is what you can carry in your saddlebags while you fight off all comers, and a man has to sleep sometime."

True enough, Rudi thought.

The Mackenzies took in anyone honest, peaceable and willing to work, and they had little in the way of internal division of rank or wealth, but that was very much an exception.

"After a couple of years, all the people left in my bunch, they were those who didn't have a home they could go to and use what they'd got. Even young as we were, we were getting tired of knocking around, risking our lives and then blowing it all on a bender before some big shot could tax it off us. Then we got this offer from a bunch of sheriffs near Des Moines, and the new bossman too; he'd just succeeded his father and wanted to make a splash. . . ."

An aside: "Iowa's the biggest place going out east; the land's good, and they carried a *lot* of people through the dying time; there are more than two million there now."

Rudi whistled slightly, and Juniper nodded as well; that was as much as the whole Pacific Northwest, according to the best estimates they'd been able to get, and on only one-fifth the area. Ingolf continued:

"So you can go for days and days, and it's all tilled land and settlements, or at least pasture, and big towns now and then, cities even, hardly any real wilderness except right along the Mississippi and in the northwestern border counties. The Iowa farmers—ranchers, they say farther west; I don't know what you call them here—and the sheriffs, they're rich as rich."

Both the Mackenzies followed the tale easily enough; being familiar with what went on east of the Cascades they mentally translated *farmer/ rancher* and *sheriff* as *landed knights* and *barons.* Usually *deputy* or *cowboy* did duty for what most in the Willamette would call a *man-at-arms.* The descendants of starving townsmen were generally on the bottom of the social heap, sometimes bound to the soil, outright slaves in a few of the worst places.

"We don't have lords here," Rudi said pridefully. "But I know what you mean."

"We were lucky, too, with it," his mother whispered in his ear, and then pinched it in mild reproof.

Rudi jumped a little. Vogeler plodded on, his big wasted hands knotted together, his voice and mind in a different time and place. But trapped there, knowing what was to happen and unable to warn his earlier self, watching it unfold again:

"So they made a deal with us. I had a reputation for getting the goods, and they offered to let us settle, give us land and rank, if we'd go where nobody had gone before—all the way east to the sea, and the museums and art galleries and such. They still care for such stuff in Iowa, you see, more than most places. And the new bossman of Des Moines . . . they call him the governor when they're being formal . . . sent along this little rat of a guy to check it all. And that would be the price of our new homes. We could all be deputies at least. I don't much like the way they treat ordinary people there, but beggars can't be choosers."

Vogeler smiled grimly. "There was even talk of a sheriff's daughter for me, and *plenty* of talk about how I was a sheriff by blood . . . not that they really think any cheesehead's anything but a bear from the backwoods, that bunch. I thought they'd keep the deal, though, or at least most of it, so we signed up."

The hesitation left Ingolf's voice as he went on. "Well, it was a good deal, and like I said, we were all young. For a prize like that, we'd go to hellmouth and back, we thought. What I didn't know was who the little ratty guy, Joseph Kuttner his name was, was really working for. Neither did the bossman who paid his wages. So we crossed the Mississippi south of Clinton, all my bunch—we called ourselves Vogeler's Villains, same as my troop back in the Sioux War—"

CHAPTER FIVE

I ngolf cursed as sweat ran down into his eyes from the lining of his helmet—it was made from old kitchen sponges—and soaked the padding under his mail shirt. It was fiercely hot, with only a slight high haze, and wet as a soaked blanket with it, and the air buzzed with mosquitoes even a little past noon. If you went into the shade they ate you alive. At least he wore what they called a kettle helmet, with a wide sloping brim like a droopy canvas hat. He'd always preferred that to a close helm; the extra visibility and better hearing more than made up for any lesser protection, and it kept the sun off your face and neck. Plus in weather like this it let you breathe.

All he could smell right now was his own sweat and Boy's, and forest green from the scrubby sandy woods of oak and pine around, but his nose still tingled with trouble coming. Birds sang and insects buzzed; a swath of monarch butterflies swirled up from a patch of milkweed growing in cracks in the pavement. They passed another dead car, a heap of rust and shattered glass, amid a scorch mark that showed where it had burned.

There were bones in the ditches, under rampant weed and brush. Every time he rode Boy off into the endless woods they crumbled beneath the shod hooves; leached by twenty years of rains and frost, by acid soil and scavengers, but still so many to start with they were every-where, the skulls popping like eggshells.

The woods were also full of wet stagnant pits where basements had been; the houses had all been wooden frame, and they'd all burnt at one time or another. There must have been tens of thousands of them once all through this wasteland, and the thought made his skin crawl a little even now. All those little houses, in this place where no crops grew and you couldn't even find any decent water without digging and pumping, nothing but short twisty pines . . .

He found he hated this part of the lost lands even more than the dead cities. At least they were honestly alien; this never-a-city reverting to forest was neither one thing nor another. A sudden intense longing filled him, to see a herd of black-and-white cows grazing in green meadow, or smell bread baking, or to ride by a farmhouse in the snow and hear the rising-falling hum of a spinning wheel and a girl singing by it as she worked and smoke drifted low from the chimney. Anything that meant real life.

I thought I'd grown up free of the Change, not hagridden by it the way the old folks are, the way Dad was, so he'd drink too much and cry whenever he couldn't keep himself from thinking about it. I can't even remember it, not even the flash and the pain, nor the years right after when things were worst. I was too young. But here there's nothing but death and ghosts, and it's as if you can hear them all screaming and sobbing, hear it drifting on the wind. It'll be a thousand years before they stop.

He flung up his clenched right fist in its steer-hide glove and barked: "Halt!"

The whole train stopped in a slow clatter of hooves and squeal of brake levers, five big rubber-tired steel-frame wagons drawn by six horses each, and the two-score of guards and ostlers and salvage experts who made up Vogeler's Villains—not that every single one couldn't fight at need, including the four women. They all looked around; there was a wide meadow right ahead, and more of the scrub forest to their right and left, with sand showing through the sparse grass beneath. The meadow had the broken asphalt of the roadway looping around it in an oval and two roads leading south, so it had probably been a roundabout once. Nothing much grew there but some low green brush, and a couple of dead trees poking up through them.

Kaur stood in the stirrups and sniffed. "I think that's salt water," she said. "The maps say the ocean should be close, here, unless everything's silted up. Innsmouth's that way."

She pointed right south, the steel bangle on her wrist twisting. Her brother Singh nodded. Dark-skinned and hawk-faced in a way different from Injuns, they were both from a little village founded in the farming country west of Marshall by refugees from Minneapolis right after the Change, and both were three or four years younger than Ingolf's twenty-seven. They wore mail shirts like his; she had a plain bowl helmet and he covered his blue-black hair under a dark turban with a steel cap underneath, and the ends of his beard tucked up into the cloth on either side. They were Sikhs—he still wasn't sure exactly what that entailed even after six years together, since they didn't talk about it much. Apparently they were the only ones of their kind left in the world, as far as they knew.

The Lakota had burned out their people's settlement, and they'd found everyone dead when they came back from a hunting trip. He'd taken them into his troop during the Sioux war, and they'd been together ever since. During the war they'd fought with a cold ferocity that made even the wild raiders from the high plains afraid. What they'd done to prisoners to make them talk made him wince a little to recall . . . and he wasn't a squeamish man.

"Do a flit forward," he told them. "Mounted—quick and dirty. Don't take any chances, and get back before dark."

He *did* know they were both first-class scouts, the best in the Villains apart from him and Jose, and they could move quietly while wearing a mail shirt, which most folk couldn't. The band was shorthanded since Boston. Boston had been very bad. . . .

They nodded. Singh grinned in the thickness of his black beard; he was a big burly man, nearly as big as Ingolf, and the muscles bunched in his brown forearms as he picked the reins off his saddlebow. Sometimes when he'd had a drink or two he'd straighten horseshoes with his hands for a joke.

"We shall be like lions, Captain Ingolf," he said, and his sister nodded, a rare smile on her face.

"Like a lioness," she added.

They always say that, and they never say why it's funny, Ingolf thought, as they heeled their horses into a walk; Kaur dropped a little behind, covering her brother with an arrow on the string of her saddlebow.

I know what lions are. He had seen pictures in old books, and once a trader had brought a skin through, just before he left home. *They've got 'em down in Texas.*

One of his best men came from there, having wandered up the way people did every now and then and joined the bossman's army when Ingolf did; he'd told stories about them, how they'd bred up in the bush country until they were a major nuisance along the Rio Grande, the way tigers were farther north.

Sort of tiger-sized but colored like a cougar, and the males have a big black ruff around the neck, and they hunt together in packs like wolves. OK, a lion's big and fierce and sneaky, and so's Singh . . . well, his sister is medium-sized and fierce and sneaky. But why's it funny?

"All right, we'll camp here," he called loudly. Then he squinted at the sun; they still had eight hours to dark, this time of year. "Jump to it!"

Everyone knew what to do; some cleared the brush; others drove the wagons into a circle and linked them with chains and knockdown barriers of timber, shoved and fastened coils of razor wire under the vehicles, saw to the rest of the defenses, built fires, scavenged firewood, got the cooking gear ready. They had plenty of food, besides hoarded dried fruits and such to keep them from scurvy; this area swarmed with deer and duck, rabbit and bear, and some of the rivers were thick with fish, where the old-time poisons weren't still leaking from rusting storage tanks or lingering in the mud.

The natives were too thin on the ground nowadays to keep the game down, and they weren't really very good hunters, most of them. . . .

Not of animals, at least, he thought grimly as he swung down and handed over Boy's reins.

The stock were watered from buckets, and the wood teams also collected any green fodder around and piled it up for them to stretch the remnants of the parched corn. The Villains were cheerful enough, more so than he'd expected; there was even some laughing and horseplay, and after the main work was done someone got out a guitar.

I'm going to see every one of you gets a home out of this, if I can; so help me God and His mother.

He smiled to himself; homes for the ones who didn't just want to blow every penny on booze, whores and fancy duds, at least.

And me, I'm going to be rich, if I can, with a fort and land to the horizon. None of my kids are going to have to earn a living like this when I have 'em. And God knows I've earned it. . . . And as for you, my dear brother Edward, you can shit sideways, fold yourself in half and go blind back there in the old homestead. Maybe I'll come visit my nieces and nephews, with gifts fit for a bossman's heirs.

Kuttner came over, and Ingolf hid a grimace. Although the little man had turned out to be a lot tougher and less of a complainer than he'd expected back in Des Moines, and a hell of a lot better in a fight, that hadn't made him any more agreeable, just less disgusting. He was about thirty, a bit below average height—five-six or so—thin and wiry, with close-cropped brown hair and an unremarkable face that looked distorted, somehow, without being in any way abnormal if you considered it feature by feature.

"We should push on to Innsmouth, see if we can find a usable boat," Kuttner said, his voice always sounded as if he was in a hurry . . . which he generally was.

"Mr. Kuttner, you know I'm the best in this business, don't you?" he said, swatting at a mosquito.

It went *squit* and left a smear of blood on his cheek. He had bites under his armor, too.

"Yes, Mr. Vogeler, but—"

"Kuttner," he said, getting a little less polite, "did you ever wonder why the best man in this business is only twenty-seven years old?"

Kuttner stopped—which was a wonder, because he liked to talk better than listen—and looked at him out of his ordinary brown eyes. "No, Mr. Vogeler, I can't say that I have. Why?"

"Well, two reasons. First, it's a pretty new business, the way my Villains do it, because there hasn't been enough call for it till now. Second, those who take it up don't usually live very long, if they come anywhere near this far east. I *am* alive and I aim to get back to Iowa *still* alive, and collect what was promised. Are you sure we have to do this? The Bossman didn't mention Nantucket when we talked—we've got the stuff he wanted from Boston and that was the last on our list."

And I lost four good men doing it, he thought but didn't say.

That was a cost of doing business, and everyone in the Villains knew they took the most dangerous jobs. That didn't make watching an old friend die by inches of a punctured gut much better, or make it easier to make yourself give them an end to pain as the last gift.

"I have written instructions and the Bossman's authority," Kuttner said, running a hand over his close-cropped hair.

"Yeah—" Ingolf began.

The sound of drumming hoofbeats interrupted them. They could see a fair way down the roads to the south, littered with the rusting vine-grown heaps that had been cars and trucks. Kaur and Singh were coming along at a gallop, riding on the sandy median strip. The hard drumbeat of the hooves echoed through the woods, setting birds to avalanche-loud flight; it wasn't a sound anyone around here had heard for a long time.

Just when they'd broken free of the narrowest section something flashed in the sunlight, and Singh's horse stumbled, then went down by the stern with a short thick throwing spear in its back near the spine just behind the saddle. It began to shriek, enormous sounds that sounded like a woman except for the volume.

"Shit," Ingolf said, and looked around. "We're getting short of horses."

Jose had the section on guard, and he was already on it, leading his five riders towards the pair at a round trot. Kaur stopped, shooting over her brother's head into the woods; something screamed there. Singh crouched with his shield up and another javelin went *bang* off the surface, and a third hit the horse again. When Jose's men joined in the shooting he came erect and gave the wounded beast the mercy stroke, then started salvaging his gear; that meant that there weren't any more of the natives close enough to see.

"Everyone keep an eye out all 'round," he snapped.

A few started guiltily; everyone had picked up their weapons at the alarm, pikes and broadaxes, crossbows or bows, but a few had been staring at the action rather than their assigned sectors. Kuttner had his shete out and was looking around without more than a tightening of the lips.

Singh dropped to the ground from where one of the rescue squad had taken him up behind. "Ranjeet was a good horse," he complained to the air.

Then to Ingolf: "Captain, the woods are thick with them already. More coming from the direction of Innsmouth. I saw no bows . . . but we did not stay to be sure."

"About what I expected," Ingolf said, and looked at the circling woods, all beyond throwing range. "Good work. Cut a horse out of the remount herd."

Kuttner had the grace to look a little abashed. The captain of the Villains went on to him: "There were bound to be a bunch of them in Inns-mouth; they like to lair up in ruins when they can, and it's a good place for them—water, fishing, hunting here in the brush. This is the best spot to take them on. Without we give 'em a good hiding right away, we'll have little ambushes every second hour."

"They'll attack?" Kuttner said, peering at the woods.

Nothing was visible, though they both knew that red hating eyes were studying them. These were the ones who'd lived, or more likely their children by now.

"They usually do. But they'll come at night. Couple of hours past mid-night. That's how they remember doing it, or how their daddies told 'em to do it."

* * *

Kaur woke him by cautiously nudging his booted feet with her shete and stepping back as he uncoiled with steel in his hand. It was very dark, moonless, with the stars hard and white above; the walls of low forest around them were inky black, and only a faint red glow came from the campfires. The night had a dense green smell to it; the air was a little cooler, coming from the south. Lightning bugs blinked on and off, giving the illusion of little lamps as they drifted through the scrub.

"They come now," Kaur whispered, squatting and leaning on the sheathed weapon. "Many, Captain. They took the dead horse a little while ago, and now they come for us."

"*How* many?"

She shrugged; the brother and sister were good scouts, not magicians or witches. "Twice our numbers at least. Not more than ten times."

"Get everyone up—but quiet."

Her smile showed white in the darkness, and she ghosted away. He shrugged into his padded jacket, wriggling to get the mail shirt down and into place, and slid the carrying strap of his round shield over his head. He heard the howl of a coyote now and then, and the occasional *whit-whit-whit* of an owl; the preparations of his own folk were a little rus-tling and chinking only. He'd come a long way from that hulking clumsy nineteen-year-old who'd ridden off to make a name in the short glorious war against the Injuns.

God, I was useless. We all were. Everyone here now knows their jobs, though. Even the new ones hired for this trip.

The night was loud: wind in the trees, bullfrogs, cicadas, creak and rustle and groan, now and then the call of some foraging beast, once a distant squall of triumph as a catamount made a kill. Ingolf reached his commander's battle station, in front of one of the loopholed board barricades between two wagons. Jose the Tejano was there too, cradling a crossbow. He was a good few years older than Ingolf, old enough to have some strands of white in his black mustache, and he'd fought in most mixups between the Llano Estacado and the Red River of the North over the past ten years.

They looked out into the darkness, not straining their eyes, just waiting; he counted down internally, timing his breath to it and using that to calm himself. More mosquitoes bit, but he couldn't slap at them; the chance of the natives noticing it and learning their prey was onto their attack . . . was small but not zero. One thing he'd learned long ago was that mistakes could kill you, even little ones.

Of course, just being in the wrong place at the wrong time could kill you, even if you were an expert and careful as hell. A sudden high-pitched shriek of surprised pain came from out in the darkness.

"*Now!*" he shouted.

A deep *tunnng* sounded from the center of the encampment, where a man pulled the lanyard on a small heavy machine of springs and levers. It threw the dart-shaped projectile upward nearly a thousand feet; there was a sizzling popping sound, and the magnesium flare burned with explosive brightness—as close to an explosion as you could get in the Changed world, that was. He didn't look up; the spot of fire would kill his night vision, and hopefully a lot of the attackers who weren't expecting it *would* look, by reflex. From overhead it lit the clearing with a pitiless blue-white radiance, the huge shadows jerking and twisting; the flare swung and twisted beneath the parachute as it drifted down.

The *crink-crink-crink* of the winch's gearing sounded as the crew wound the thrower again, ready to launch another flare before the first hit the ground. The Bossman of Des Moines really had laid out for the very best on this trip, including choice items from his own armory. For some reason Kuttner seemed to find the sound disagreeable.

Out in the clearing the light showed a carpet of dark ragged furtive

crawling movement, studded with gleams from eyes and teeth and ancient knives. His mouth went dry; there were a lot more of them than
he'd thought there would be, at least a hundred and maybe twice that,
eeling towards the circle of wagons on their bellies. A half dozen bands
must have gotten together for this, a rare degree of cooperation among
the wild men, who invariably hated one another with the malignant
loathing born of a generation of stalking and eating the unwary, often
starting the process of eating before death.

But then, an intrusion by outsiders was rare too. Apart from the meat
of men and horses, their well-made gear and weapons would be a prize
beyond price. None of them could let their rivals gain such strength.

A massed squealing arose, an endless *AitAitAitAitAitAitAitAit*—

Some part of him realized that it was a word, or had been once: *Eat*.

The natives rose and rushed forward in a wave, like rats exploding out
of a neglected grain bin when you opened the lid and shone a lantern
inside. Seconds later about half of them started hopping and screaming,
where they'd run into the mesh matting his people had spread around
right after they camped. Lying flat and artfully camouflaged with soot
and sand and pine duff, the nets were studded with upright razor-edged
three-inch spikes.

Some of the enemy fell onto the points and slashed themselves open as
they tried to roll away. Others just kept coming, hitting the bare patches
by luck or in a frenzy great enough to ignore the pain.

A couple of the squad leaders shouted, *Fire!* Ingolf didn't bother, since
everyone knew what to do and he personally had always disliked someone bawling at him in situations like that. He just drew to the ear and
shot into the mass of them and reached for another arrow; there were
boxes of them on the inside of the prefab barricade. The snap of bowstrings and the *tung!* of crossbows sounded, and shouts and curses of the
salvagers, and the unearthly throbbing squeal of the wild men. Even as he
drew and loosed, he realized . . .

"They aren't stopping for shit! *Ready for it, you Villains!*" he roared.

A whistling, and he ducked as a shower of little throwing spears came
down out of the night, driving into the sandy ground with a dry crunch,
or into wood with hard cracks; the ones that hit the triple-ply canvas of
the wagon tilts made a drumhead sound and hung there like porcupine
quills. One went into the barricade next to his eyes, and he could see that

the head was a ground-down table knife. He used the moment to slide the shield from his back and run his left arm through the loops, and then the luckiest or fastest of the natives were at the barricade. This was the south-facing edge of the wagon-fort, and they were thickest here.

"*Richland!*" he shouted as he surged up.

He wore his shete over his back when he was on foot, the hilt jutting up by his left shoulder. He swept it out and cut with the same motion. A snarling face with a shock of greasy blond hair and a human finger bone thrust through the septum of its nose fell back in a splash of red. An ancient shovel crashed down on his shield, *bang*, and a kitchen knife probed at his armor. He jerked the shield downward and broke both the savage's arms; then he thrust across the thrashing body with his shete, the blade skidding on the wood of the shovel handle and taking off the fingers of the wielder. . . .

A long snarling scrimmage around the edge of the wagons, steel glittering in the light of the second flare, gasping breaths, banging and rattling and shrieks. The horses in their paddock snorted and reared against the ropes; the half dozen spearmen of the reserve came pelting up in a line where some of the savages had gotten onto the top of a wagon's cover, and thrust them back with their long weapons. A few more minutes, and the attackers realized what the odds were of storming what amounted to a fortress held by men with real weapons and good armor, trained in fighting as a team.

Then they ran; Ingolf stuck his shete point-down in the sand and snatched up his bow again to shoot at their running backs, and so did everyone else except the wounded.

Kill enough and the rest would hide safely far away.

Silence fell as they waited to be sure the enemy would *keep* running, deep silence except for the pop of another parachute flare going off, panting breath, and the moaning of wounded savages. Then the night sounds slowly began to return, which meant that there weren't any humans running through the woods.

Men went around outside the wagon circle with spears and crossbows and lanterns, making sure of any enemy still moving; their two medics switched weapons for kit and went around inside, bandaging and cleaning—nobody seemed to be dead, or to have a crippling injury, but a couple had nasty bites that would fester if not swabbed out carefully.

That included himself; he hadn't noticed it at the time, and swore mildly at the sharp hard sting when the doctor irrigated the little wound on his neck with disinfectant.

A few wild men had been caught in the razor wire under the wagons and had to be finished there. Ingolf sprang up to the bed of a wagon and looked out carefully.

"They won't try again tonight, or anytime soon," he said.

"You think, *Capitán?*" Jose said. "They were pretty fierce, this bunch."

"We probably killed off half the swinging dicks in three or four bands—and all the stronger ones. They'll be fighting each other for weeks, settling who eats who."

"*Sí.* Good thing we were ready for them, though."

The commander of the Villains nodded; if they'd gotten right up to the wagons where they could use their numbers, everybody in the Villains would have died. Quickly, if they were lucky.

"Hey, maybe you'd better look at this, though," Jose went on.

Ingolf turned and waved to the thrower crew so they would stand down; they didn't have so many flares that they could keep lobbing them indefinitely. Then he vaulted over the barricade and followed his second-in-command a short way into the dark.

A wild man lay there; there was a bolt through his thigh, his feet had been slashed to ribbons by crossing the spikes, and he was trying to crawl away around them. As they approached he turned, glaring. He had a finger bone through his nose too, and one through each earlobe; on his body was an ancient threadbare pair of jeans, loose on his skinny shanks and patched with rabbit skin. A cloak of the same had been about his shoulders, and from the smell roughly piss-tanned. There was a big gold necklace around his neck, lying on the bare chest and glittering with diamonds. It was all pretty fancy, by local standards.

What really caught Vogeler's eye was what Jose had noticed, the weapon near the man's hand.

"Probably their *jefe*, their bossman," Jose said. "That's funny that he has a shete, isn't it, *Capitán?*"

"Damned odd," Ingolf agreed, his eyes narrowing. "It's not a machete—that's new work."

The modern weapon was longer and thicker at the back of the blade than the pre-Change tool which had inspired it.

"Want to try to get the story out of him?"

The wild man snarled at them and barked, an *ough-ough-ough* sound, snapping with little lunges of his brown-yellow teeth, his hands scrabbling for something to throw.

"No, I don't think this one's a great talker."

"*Sí*, he doesn't look like it, does he?"

Jose shrugged and brought the crossbow to his shoulder and aimed carefully. *Tunngg*, a flash through the dark, and right beneath it a meaty whack. The scrawny body jerked and went slack; Jose bent, set the spanning hook on the string, and cranked the crossbow taut again.

"You've got the watch until dawn," Ingolf said to his second-in-command, kicking the mysterious shete farther away from the body before picking it up.

He didn't want to go near the dead man; the lice and fleas jumped ship when a man died, and these probably carried disease. Safer to leave the burial detail for a day or so. Which reminded him . . .

"If they try to drag the bodies away, let them."

"*Capitán?*"

"Don't want them stinking the place up." *Any worse than it is now,* he thought.

Smell was inevitable when you cut men's bodies open. At least the sandy soil would sop up the liquids; it would be safer to bury any remaining tomorrow.

"This is the most defensible campsite we're going to find around here, I think, so you'll be stuck in this location for a while."

He took the captured shete back under the lamps—not much point in trying to sleep more tonight—and as he cleansed his hands and arms with sand and then water, he studied the weapon.

It was a fairly typical example of what horsemen used everywhere he knew of, from the Big Muddy to the Rockies and south to the Rio Grande; a yard-long piece of slightly curved steel, three fingers broad at the widest spot near the tip, sharpened all along one edge and four inches down the other from the point for a backhander. The hilt had a simple cross-guard and a full-length tang, with fillets of wood on the grip and a wrapping of braided rawhide that was coming loose in one or two spots; the pommel was a plain brass oval.

This one was better made than most, forged by a real smith and not simply ground and filed out of old-time stock. He tapped it against a wagon's frame, and the almost bell-like sound was right, and so was the elastic way it sprang back when he bent it against a tree stump by sticking the point in and leaning on it.

Still sharp, he thought, feeling cautiously with his thumb. *Shame the way it's been let rust. Looks like it hasn't been cleaned or oiled in a month . . . maybe a bit less, with the air here.*

He rotated his wrist, whipping the steel through a blurring figure eight; the air hissed behind it. It was lighter than he preferred, but it felt alive in his hand.

Over at the fire he got out his cleaning kit and went to work. When he'd finished and held it out at arm's length towards the flames his brows went up. There was a rash of rust pits, no way around that the way it had been neglected, but the surface of the metal rippled in the firelight under the thin coating of linseed oil he'd applied, full of wavy lines—not just forged, but *layer*-forged from a mixture of spring and mild steel, and then hardened on the edge.

There was a very slight roughness in the steel along the working part, the point and about a foot back from there; that was blood etching, the way the salt and acid of blood attacked the softer layers even if you cleaned it immediately.

This beauty would set you back fifty, sixty dollars in Des Moines. More in Richland or Marshall, since the Iowan capital attracted the best craftsmen. That was the price of a good ordinary horse, or two months' wages for a laborer, but it was a working tool that had been used hard, not a dress weapon—no fancies like inlay.

Wait, I lie, he thought.

Symbols had been graven in the surface in the same spot on both sides, not far from the hilt: a stylized rayed sun, and within it three letters—*C* and *U* and *T*.

"Well, that's what it's for," he said. Then he called out: "Hey, Kaur, Singh!"

The scouts came over; Singh was still rubbing a cloth on the serrated head of the mace he used for close-and-personal work. It smelled if you left the results in the grooves. There were spatters on his turban, as well.

"Ranjeet is well avenged, Captain," he said, his dark eyes sparkling.

Ingolf felt a little uneasy about these two on occasion. Revenge was all very well, but there were times when he thought the pair of them were a bit monomaniacal on the subject.

"Take a look at this," Ingolf said. "One of the wild men had it."

They both looked surprised; they hadn't seen anything more complex than tying a knife onto a stick since they got east of the Illinois Valley.

"It's modern work," Singh said, turning it over in his big hands. "Well-done, too."

He had been a blacksmith's apprentice before his village was wiped out, and still dabbled usefully in it. Now he flicked a fingernail against the edge of the weapon to test the sound, and tilted it so that the firelight would pick out surface features.

"See the wavy line along the cutting edge, just a finger's width in? I have heard of that. It is done by coating all the blade except the edge with clay, then packing it in red-hot charcoal, letting it cool, and then retempering. It makes the cutting edge very hard, glass hard, without turning the whole blade brittle, but it requires great skill. The heat treatment has been well-done, too!"

He was waxing enthusiastic. His sister leaned forward, a frown on her dark comely face.

"What is that doing here, Captain?" she said, toying with the long single braid of her hair. "These wild men, they can't even take apart a pair of old garden shears to make knives. Make shetes?"

She made a complex dismissive sound that involved gargling and spitting.

"Yeah, that's the question," Ingolf said. "So they must have stolen it off the body of someone in from the Midwest like us. I don't think I know of more than three or four other expeditions that've gotten east of the Ohio."

"There could be more that we don't know of, more so if they were small and done quietly," Singh said. "If they died here, who would hear anything?"

Ingolf grunted skeptically. "News travels slowly, but it does get around," he said. "And it would take a big outfit, well found, to get this far."

He took the shete back, reversed the blade and held it out to Kaur. "This is a little light for my arm, but it should be about right for you."

Her eyes lit as she took the blade and ran through a series of cuts and thrusts, feet moving like a dancer's as she whirled and lunged. "Yes! Thank you, Captain. This is a very fine weapon, better than mine or my spare."

"And see if anyone else knows what those marks on the blade are," he said.

Kuttner was standing by his bedroll. Ingolf got out his pipe and fixings and lit it with an ember held in a green twig as he sat and leaned back against his saddle. He didn't smoke much. If nothing else, tobacco was too hard to find outside the Republic of Richland, or too bad if you did—good leaf and fine cheeses and apple brandy were his home country's main exports. But sometimes it was an aid to thought.

And hopefully it might discourage the mosquitoes, or at least Kuttner, who he'd noticed hated the smell. He dragged the smoke across his tongue and blew a ring into the darkness, watching it catch faint light from the lanterns and coals of the fire and enjoying the mellow scent.

"Why did you give the shete to the woman?" Kuttner asked at last.

Noticed he doesn't like Kaur. Doesn't like Singh either, but he really doesn't like Kaur. Doesn't seem to like women in general much, at least none of the ones with us, but I don't think he's queer, either.

"It's the right weight and length for her. You've seen her fight," Ingolf said reasonably, then described the etchings. "You ever seen anything like those marks?"

Firelight was good for playing poker; the shadows cast on a man's face made it harder to lie. He could see the slight hesitation in Kuttner's response, and the way his eyes flicked aside for a moment.

"Not really. I think I've heard that someone uses those symbols in the far West, but no details—there isn't much trade that way."

Ingolf nodded; it was true enough. Iowa had plenty of cattle and wheat from its own fields, and the metals trade mostly went up and down the Mississippi and its right-bank tributaries. But there was something. . . .

He's not telling all he knows, that's for sure.

* * *

A dozen of them rode into Innsmouth the next morning, as soon as the sun was high enough—too many shadows were convenient for ambushers. They came out of the forest, and into what had been the town proper; their hoofbeats echoed off the walls that flanked the broken pavement.

This part didn't have many tall buildings; most of them had burned out at one time or another, their soot-charred windows like eyes in a skull. Bare black frames occupied half a street where the vacant spots weren't covered in second growth of saplings and sumac and brambles. Then they were back among brick structures that still stood.

It looked like the final collapse here hadn't come at once the way it had in Boston; there had been an effort to get the streets clear by pushing the vehicles off, and peeling, faded paint on a big warehouse-looking building read, EMERGENCY FOOD DISTRIBUTION CENTER.

That one had been inhabited more recently; you could tell by the stink, stronger than the silt-salt of the nearby sea, and the flies. And the crude wooden rack outside with the rows of skulls was a giveaway.

Dead giveaway, he thought mordantly. *But it feels dead now, uninhabited.*

"Check it out," he said.

They waited, bows ready, eyes traveling to the roofs on either side; the horses shifted nervously under them. Singh and Kaur swung to earth with their shetes in their hands; when they came back out they both looked disgusted, but relaxed and with the steel sheathed.

"Nothing, Captain," the man called. "They were here, but they cleared out last night. I think you were right—they fought among themselves a little when they got back from rushing us."

"Nothing?"

"Nothing living, and nothing I wish to remember having seen," Singh said, and spit.

Considering some of the things he'd seen Singh do himself in the war, he decided he really didn't want to look inside—no point in putting things like that in your head unless you had to. Instead they cantered down to the water's edge. There they found what they wanted; an old-time warehouse for boats, where they were stacked up several layers high in metal racks. He'd seen that before in the ruined cities on the Lakes, and the guidebooks listed several here.

The ground floor was smashed remnants where small animals scurried amid the tendrils of shade-loving vines, hiding as the humans dismounted and looked the place over; storm surges had come up the town's narrow central harbor several times in the past decades. Beams of sunlight lanced down from holes in the rippled plastic of the roofing, catching on a chain, turning the bulks of cabin cruisers and catamarans into shadowy vastness. Birds flew in and out, tending to their nests.

Ingolf sighed and did some climbing—not easy in armor, but he certainly wasn't going to take it off. His limbs felt heavy after little sleep and a bad fight last night, but he was used to working while he was exhausted; it was a requirement in both the trades he'd followed since he left home. A lot of the boats were made of the old-time material called fiberglass. He was familiar with it; some bowmakers used it instead of horn on the belly of a saddlebow, though it was getting rare back in civilized country. It had the advantage of not rotting if kept out of the sun, and at last he found a good sailboat with a folding aluminum mast.

"This one'll do," he called down.

More birds flew up at the echoes. Everyone in the Villains was used to working with pre-Change machinery, and more than one of this group had dealt with boats before, on the Lakes. It was still long hours of nightmare work to get the rusted slideway working, with only the spells of watch duty to break the hot monotony. He had barked knuckles and a sweat bath worse than the usual summer-in-armor by the time the boat was in the wheeled cradle on the ground. Scavenging had found them enough Dacron and cord to rig the simple lug sail.

As the others were stowing the supplies, Jose drew him aside and spoke softly, with a glance at the Bossman's agent.

"*Capitán*, this *cabroncito* wants to go to that Nantucket place really bad, let *him* go. So he's close to the Bossman, close enough his farts don't make no sound anymore, but that don't make him no friend of *ours*."

Ingolf smiled at the other man's worry. "And which friend of ours would I pick to send with him, to do something I'm afraid of, Jose?"

The Tejano blew out his lips in a gesture of frustration. "OK, I know what you mean. I still don't like it."

"*I* don't like it. Doesn't mean it doesn't have to be done."

Then Jose grinned, a quick white flash. "So now I complain how you take Kaur and Singh both. I'd feel better here with them to spot for us if the wild men sniff around. They're the best sneakers we got."

"That's why I'm taking them! And you know they don't work apart. It's the smallest number that'll do the job—me, the Sikhs, Kuttner."

Unspoken went: *And the least loss if we don't come back.* Losing three more wouldn't fatally weaken the Villains for the trek back to the living lands. He clapped his second-in-command on the shoulder and nodded back towards the wagon camp.

"Just keep it together for ten days. If we're not back by then, then break camp and *head west* on the eleventh day. That's an order. We've already got all the stuff the sheriffs and the bossman wanted, apart from this, and enough gold to start a mint. We'll catch you up, but you *move*. You hear me, trooper?"

"*Sí*. Doesn't mean I have to like it either."

* * *

The harbor mouth hadn't silted up quite enough to catch the sailboat's keel, possibly because it was protected by the half-sunken hulk of a great ship whose bow reared out of the water like a dull-red hill. There was a little lurch of contact as the four of them labored at the sweeps they'd found, and then they were over the bar and out into Nantucket Sound.

Ingolf found himself relaxing as the green-brown shoreline faded. That wasn't very logical—drowning killed you just as dead as a sharpened shovel in the brain, and if they were shipwrecked anywhere around here it was right back into the stewpot. The fresh breeze and clean salt air and bright sunlight must have something to do with it, and the fact that he was finally out of his armor; it was bound up with a couple of cork life vests, like all their gear. They had enough smoked venison and biscuit to last them for a few days, fishing line and hooks, map and compass, and their weapons.

Birds went by overhead, gulls and some sort of pigeons moving in a big flock. Not far away a whale breached; he couldn't tell what kind, except that it blew its spout forward in twin jets.

The wind was from the northwest, just off the starboard quarter. He looked at the map again, at his compass, and then up at the sun. Spray came in over the rail and flew backward, stinging his eyes with the salt, and he squinted into the brightness over the blue water and its white-topped waves.

"Should be there just before sunset, unless it moved," Ingolf said, lolling back with the tiller under his arm.

Neither Kaur nor Singh spoke, which was fairly typical. They were ready at the lines, with the care of people who liked to do things right but weren't entirely sure they could; their experience in boats was more limited than his, and he was no expert, just competent enough to set a straight course in not-too-bad weather. Kuttner didn't speak either, which *wasn't* like him. He usually had some order or observation or complaint. Now he was tensely silent.

Ingolf shrugged. *I like him better this way, except that he looks like he's about to snap like a lift beam under too much weight. I suppose it was too much to hope he'd get seasick and call the whole thing off.*

Instead he concentrated on his sailing. As they passed out of sight of land, the Sikhs' silence grew a little tense too. After an hour or so Ingolf spoke:

"Hell, you two, we don't even have to tack for a while. I've been out on Michigan in rougher weather than this."

And nearly died, he didn't add.

For all his cheerfulness—you had to show willing and look confident if you were the leader, which necessity made it easier—he also let out a *whuff!* of relief when a low line of beach showed on the southern horizon. The sun was only a handspan over the horizon to their right, and it was starting to cast a glitter path on the water, tinging it with red. As they came closer Ingolf began to frown.

"Singh!" he said. "Take the tiller!"

When the other man had, he moved cautiously to the bow and stood with one hand on the stay line that ran from there to the mast, peering ahead. Then he unshipped his binoculars, careful to settle the loop around his neck—they were big military-grade field glasses, an heirloom from his father, irreplaceable if dropped over the side—and took another look.

A long shore, sandy beach backed by fifty-foot bluffs, interrupted here and there with lower parts. And . . .

"What's wrong?" Kuttner said.

"The books said Nantucket was covered with scrub and thicket, with a few trees here and there, and lots of those houses like back on the Cape," he said.

"Well?"

"It isn't. That's forest there, dense forest. Oak, I think. Maybe hickory, and some pine, but lots of oak."

"That could have grown up since."

The three Villains looked at him; surely nobody could be *that* ignorant?

"Not in twenty-two years it couldn't," Ingolf said. "And it's sandy there, and there's the salt wind. That's *old* forest. Not very tall, yeah, but it's old. Take a look."

He handed over the binoculars reluctantly and kept a hand ready to grab; as far as he knew, Kuttner had never been afloat on anything but the Mississippi before this trip.

The smaller man's lips went tight. "We must land," he said, but it was as if he had to force himself to say it.

"Yeah," Ingolf said, equally unhappily. "It's getting too close to dark to head back."

"I do not know," Kaur said. Ingolf looked at her in surprise, and she went on: "It is as if something tells me, *Go away.*"

She shivered. "Perhaps this place is cursed."

Her brother nodded. Ingolf was surprised; usually the two of them had the steadiest nerves of anyone in the company—sometimes he suspected they really didn't care much if they lived or died.

"We don't have a choice. Let's go for it."

An opening in the straight line of the coast showed. It wasn't where the maps said it should be, but it did break the surf-bound ramparts.

"And see that?" he said, pointing to a faint trickle of smoke rising there. "That means men. We'd better be cautious."

The three Villains kept the boat's head into the wind as they all put on their fighting gear; the choppy up-and-down motion made it awkward, but they managed. Ingolf and the others wolfed down rabbit cooked that morning and some biscuit, grimacing at the sawdust taste of the thrice-baked bread. It hadn't been very warm out on the water and it was cooling now, enough that the padding and armor didn't make you sweat much. Kuttner wore his usual odd cuirass of overlapping plates of leather boiled in wax, with metal buckles and trim, its color a russet brown contrast to the oiled gray of the others' mail shirts; his helmet was round-topped, with a spike in the center of its dome and hinged cheek guards.

Ingolf settled his shete over his shoulder, made sure that his bow was protected in its waterproof oiled canvas case by his feet—moisture could play hell with the laminations of a horn-and-sinew recurve—and then turned the boat into the sheltered waters.

Those were shallow; the keel gave a nasty *tick* that made the rigging groan and everyone lurch as they crossed in from the sea.

"What was that, Captain?" Singh said, pointing west.

"I didn't see anything," Ingolf answered, concentrating on avoiding the green patches as he wended his way towards the shore.

"I saw a flash of light to the west, farther up this coast. Like sun on glass, I thought."

Kaur nodded. Ingolf sighed: "There weren't supposed to be any tall glass buildings here, either. We'll see."

Ingolf had been right; the land around the low spot was mostly forest where it wasn't reed-rustling salt marsh. The trees weren't very tall, forty or fifty feet at most, but the trunks were thick and gnarled, with a dense understory of bushes. He recognized white and black oaks, chestnut, beech, maple, pine and hickory; the broadleaf trees predominated, lush in their summer foliage, and there were a lot of dead elms. The smell reached him, strong even compared to the sea salt and the marshes, earthy and wild, familiar from the wooded hills of home and yet a little strange.

Compared to their surroundings, the habitations looked small. Six boats were drawn up, wooden twenty-footers; he got the binoculars out and looked. They were open undecked craft made of planks that looked hand-sawn, with oarlocks and unstepped masts and furled gaff sails. Behind them was a little hamlet of six long rectangular houses, built low with a mud-and-stick chimney coming out of the shingle roofs and earth heaped up against the sides. The chimneys were idle, and the smoke came from a central open hearth in a cleared space.

He switched the view; there were fish-drying racks with the catch on them, and more fires—very low smoldering ones, giving off a dense haze that clung to the ground.

That must be to smoke 'em, he thought.

Ten or twelve acres around the hamlet were planted, amid haggled-off stumps that showed how the land had been cleared. Lush growth hid the soil; there were cornstalks wound with beans, pumpkin vines, tomatoes, the tops of potatoes, turnips and more. A buzzing midden a thousand yards away looked to be mostly oyster-shell; when the wind backed and shifted they got a powerful whiff from it. Otherwise the community seemed pretty tidy; there was even a paddock fenced with split rails, though no stock in it he could see.

"I don't think this bunch are wild men," he said. "Not the usual kind at least. How many do you think, Singh?"

"Forty. Sixty if they pack close in those houses," Singh said. "Perhaps twenty fighting men at most, counting boys."

His sister gave him a look, and he cleared his throat and went on: "And perhaps some strong women. That would be as many as could row those boats, as well. You are right, Captain. That is not a wild-man den. Those are people."

Ingolf nodded. "Doesn't mean they're *friendly* people, necessarily."

He focused on the edge of the woods. "Looks to me like they cleared out when they saw us coming in, but they're watching from there."

Decision firmed. "We'll go in, but cautious. Get one of the anchors and some line."

Two hundred yards from shore they dropped it; it splashed in and sank away to the bottom twenty feet below, and he could see the puff of sand as it struck through the clear water. Then they jerked the heavy rope to see that the flukes had set, and paid out line as they sculled the sailboat closer to shore. He halted them when the bow just touched bottom; that way they could snatch themselves out fast if they had to, pulling up the line. They dropped another anchor and secured it with a slipknot; he took a deep breath.

"Let's go."

The water was cold on his skin as he jumped in and waded ashore, filling his boots. The long shadows of twilight went ahead of them. The others followed, holding their bows above their heads to keep the wet off; then the Sikhs went on first while Kuttner and he covered them as they looked in each of the long huts in turn.

When they came back Singh handed him a leather pouch. The deerskin was well tanned, butter-supple, and worked with a design of porcupine quills and shell beads, with bits of plastic and old glass added.

"That's good tanning," he said, sniffing at it; the rich mellow scent of leather was strong, along with smoke and some herb it had held once. "Brain and bark, I think."

Singh nodded. "There are three or four families in each of the houses,

Captain, from the bedrolls. The tools are mostly from before the Change, but look at this."

It was a hoe, with a skillfully shaped handle; the head was a large shell, probably adequate in this light sandy soil.

"Right." Another deep breath. "Let's talk to them."

He walked beyond the buildings. They all held up open hands, yelling about their peaceableness and waving *come on*. Eventually people did, moving out of the thick brush along the forest edge with a skill that made him blink. A dozen men in hide breechclouts led, aged from early teens to their forties; their hair was shaved on either side of the head and gathered up into a standing roach, with a pigtail behind, and they held light javelins settled in the groove of a yard-long throwing stick ending in a hook. They had steel knives, too, and hatchets.

Behind them came an older man in similar dress, and a woman in a buckskin tunic that reached to her knees; as they got closer he saw that her braided hair was gray-streaked yellow, and she was the man's age or nearly, looking a bit older because she'd lost most of her teeth. He was Injun, though of no tribe Ingolf knew, with ruddy light brown skin and flattish features, stocky and looking very strong for his size, with thick scarred forearms.

Hmmm, he thought, looking at the younger folk again. A couple looked like white men, a couple like Injuns, and the rest mixed. *Nothing odd there; I've seen enough blue-eyed Sioux out west, and redheaded Anishinabe up north.* People had shifted around a lot, right after the Change, and settled where they could.

The woman looked at him steadily. When she spoke, it was as if the English language came haltingly to her, the sound a little rusty; and there was a trace of an accent he didn't recognize, one that turned *are* to *aaah*.

"You are . . . not . . ."

The man beside her was probably her husband; he spoke himself, in a complex-sounding language full of quick-rising, slow-falling sounds, then made a crook-fingered grabbing gesture with his right hand.

"The Eaters of Men," she said, probably translating; it sounded that way, not quite English phrasing.

The other locals lowered their weapons, a few smiling at the strangers.

"No, we're not, ma'am. We're from the Midwest—Wisconsin, me. We're . . . explorers."

Suddenly tears were running down her face. "Oh, it's been so long!"

* * *

" . . . came out here from Innsmouth three weeks after the Day," said the woman who'd been Juanita Johnson once, and now thought of herself as Sun Hair. "The Emergency Committee had cut the ration to just one little bowl a day at the Distribution Center and there was fighting every day with the refugees. . . ."

The Day? She must mean the Change, Ingolf thought, nodding.

"My father and mother, my uncle John and aunt Sally and Mr. Granger and Lindy, the Smiths, and us kids . . . I was fifteen. Things were already very bad, and the rumors . . ."

She licked her lips again, then took Ingolf's bowl and reached out to spoon more fish stew into it with a wooden ladle; the cauldron was made from the bottom half of an aluminum trash barrel. It was good stew, full of chunks of white cod meat and scallops and vegetables. The firelight shone on the faces—the warriors closest, and the two-score of women and children behind. He caught glimpses of a naked toddler huddled up against her mother, of another younger one at the breast. They murmured among themselves; mostly the odd-sounding language, but in it were English words he caught or half caught.

It was cooler now that the sun was down, not chilly but close enough to it that the fire's warmth felt grateful on his skin. A couple of the older people had cloaks or blankets around their shoulders, made of glossy pelts.

"Later we realized they must be true. A few times in the years after that, boats came here . . . hunting . . . and we had to run or fight. Dad and Uncle John loaded everything we could find, the tools and seed and the three goats from Uncle John's place we'd hidden from the Committee, and we headed out. I don't know where Dad was really hoping for—he talked about going north to Maine. But there was a storm, and we were cast ashore here; we managed to get most of our stuff out but the boat was wrecked."

She frowned. "I haven't thought about it for a long time . . . I *knew* about Nantucket. I'd been there. This isn't Nantucket. It looks a little like it, but the trees . . . and the people. They're the . . . we're the . . ."

Another word in that language; she smiled and thumped her forehead with the heel of her hand.

"The People. Or the Sea-Land People. They're Indians, and they'd never heard of white men. Or metal, or growing corn, or . . . or anything. They said nobody had—they used to visit the mainland before the Day, only they say it was all forest too, and relatives of theirs lived there, not cities and things. Then there was a dome of fire, colored fire, and when it went away they were *here*. When my family got here they were sick; someone had already come here and left . . . I think it was chicken pox. Most of the People died of it. There'd been about a hundred, but only two dozen lived."

All the watchers shuddered at the words *chicken pox*; some of them made signs that were probably for protection against evil magic.

"But they're good people . . . and they had food; they knew how to fish and hunt. We stayed, and we helped with the sick, and learned to talk to them, and showed them things, and they showed us . . . My dad died six years later, drowned while he was out fishing. Mom got sick with something a year after that, I don't know what, it was awful; she had this pain in her stomach. . . . Uncle John built boats for a hobby, so he knew how. . . ."

Ingolf finished the food and set the plastic bowl aside as Sun Hair rambled through her tale of years, of children born and folk dying, of learning and forgetting.

I don't think she's really wandered in her wits, he thought. *Just a little strange, like a lot who had a hard time in those years. Hers wasn't as hard as some. But Christ, this is weird!*

He knew the history of America before the Change, at least in outline; he *was* a sheriff's son, after all, an educated man who could both read and write fluently and cipher well. He'd read through an entire book on it, the *Time-Life* one, and another bound together from several carefully preserved *National Geographics* with wonderful pictures. This island was near where the first English had settled, four hundred years ago. And the Injuns they met had been farmers, albeit without iron or cattle or horses. How long since Nantucket had been covered in oak trees, peopled by folk who'd never seen corn?

His mind quailed at the gap of years. *Of course, it must be possible. It's* here, *isn't it? And if God made the Change, why not this?*

Kaur and Singh were looking bewildered. Kuttner looked like he was three sheets to the wind, and had been smoking something strong along with it. His eyes glittered, a look like lust. He leaned forward and cut in: "And Nantucket town? There?" he said, pointing east.

Sun Hair began to cry; her husband put an arm around her. "That's where my boy Frank went!" she sobbed. "And he never came back! He never came back to me!"

* * *

"I don't like doing this to them," Ingolf said, looking back at the Sea-Land People.

This was as close as they came to the great fishhook harbor where the maps said Nantucket town should stand. So far all they'd seen was forest and game trails, weaving to avoid patches of marsh and a few open old-field meadows. They were lamenting, weeping and throwing their hands rhythmically into the air at this act of suicide by their guests.

Morning sunlight speared through gaps in the forest canopy, thinner here right near the sea, and seemed to surround the locals with a nimbus of light as they wept and swayed.

Good people, he thought.

They'd had plentiful reason to fear and suspect outsiders from the mainland, but they'd taken the travelers in without hesitation once they saw they weren't wild men. One girl in particular had been *very* friendly later that night . . . though he suspected part of it was that they had a real limited selection of mates here if they wanted to avoid inbreeding. Singh was looking sort of sleek, too.

They moved forward; the trail was overgrown, and Singh and Kaur unlimbered their shetes and cut at ferns and blueberry bushes. Then they were in open country, on a neatly trimmed stretch of green, though that might be the angora goats the Sea-Land People kept, descendants of the original nanny and her two kids.

Light flashed, through his eyes, through his upraised hands, through his mind as he shouted in protest. The moment of pain was endless, and over instantly. And—

* * *

Sheriff Ingolf Vogeler sat in his chair of judgment, looking down at the bound thief. It was a formal room, with a shelf of books, and black-bordered pictures of his father and brother Edward on the wall behind. . . .

* * *

" *Christl!*" he wheezed.

For an instant, two complete lives warred for possession of his mind, and he realized he didn't even *like* the pompous self-righteous bastard he might have been.

* * *

Troop-lieutenant Ingolf Vogeler looked down at the Sioux arrow that sprouted in his chest; he toppled slowly forward in the flame-shot night, dropping his shete as the choking salt invaded his lungs, dead on the day of his nineteenth birthday. . . .

* * *

Ingolf Vogeler looked at the slowly rotating hologram model of the molecule and *knew* he wasn't going to get the parasmallpox to do what he wanted. . . .

"Save, store and restart from one-C," he growled, reaching for the can of Mango cola.

* * *

Somewhere his body took another step forward. Images of the land ahead of him strobed through his eyes—or perhaps not through his eyes. A quiet cobbled street lined with brick buildings. Ruins. The same cobbled street, with people in weird clothes or nothing, and vehicles that floated on turning silvery balls that seemed *liquid* somehow.

Planes of crystal light turning through spaces that hurt his mind like razors slicing at his flesh, too *big*, too *big*. Something stretched, gave way, like a guitar string stretched around the universe, shivering with a note that vibrated from fire to darkness and back to fire.

And Ingolf Vogeler was stumbling forward. He walked; there were stones beneath his feet, but someone else was walking just a second to the side of him, like standing between two mirrors and watching yourself recede into infinite distance. The building ahead of him was square, with

five windows across the upper story, four and a door flanked by white pillars below, comely in an antique fashion like some of the older buildings
back home, what an old man had told him once was called the Federal
style. A flag hung from a pole over the white-painted door, the old US
flag of Stars and Stripes.

The door opened. His hands and feet moved at normal speed, but
somehow it took an endless effort of will to keep them in motion, a
harder struggle than freeing a bogged horse once, when he stood in the
muck and strained until the muscles of his stomach started to tear loose.
Blurred afterimages floated behind every movement.

A hallway, with strange magnificent pictures—one of a blond woman
in a skirt made of strings. And a voice, a voice that spoke within him, a roar
of white noise that he struggled to understand. He felt like a tiny spout,
with a torrent vaster than a waterfall trying to force its way through. He
could not, and he must.

You are not the one. You must find him. Travel from sunrise to the sunset, and seek the
Son of the Bear Who Rules. Tell the Sword of the Lady what awaits him.

A door swung open, slowly. The light behind it was terrible, and more
than anything in all the world he wanted to turn away, turn aside, but he
knew it would shine wherever he turned his head. Blood dribbled from
his bitten lips, and the sting was sweetness.

The sword hung there. He craved it, and dropped to his knees, beating his fists on the floor, wailing the anguish of denial.

CHAPTER SIX

"You poor man," Juniper said, leaning forward and putting her hand on Ingolf's.

The easterner looked wasted again as he stopped. Rudi frowned; he wanted to know about the sword.

First and foremost if it's real, he thought. *That was a wild tale!*

A glance at his mother's face brought him back to a host's obligations. She frowned at Ingolf's silence, then leaned forward and tapped him on either cheek.

"Uh!"

His eyes were wild and blank for a moment. Then he licked dry lips and took the cup of hot borage tea she pressed on him, drinking with a trembling hand and spilling a little.

"Sorry," he said huskily. "Haven't . . . I tried to keep from thinking about that." He swallowed again. "So, I'm crazy, right?"

"This sword," Juniper said. She met his eyes and held them with her own. "It was a longsword, double-edged, with a guard like a crescent moon, and a pommel of moon-opal held in antlers. Is that it?"

Rudi's breath caught. She had shared that vision with him, but as far as he knew with no other. A great relaxation came to Ingolf's face, as if some tension were unwound at last.

"Christ, I'm *not* crazy, then?"

"No, my poor Ingolf, you're not. It's far worse than that."

Just then Aunt Judy walked into the hall. She gave an angry hiss as she saw Ingolf's face, came up and took his pulse. Then she examined his eyes; he moved his face obediently to her prodding, passive as a child.

"Juney, are you *trying* to kill my patient? I said he could talk, not be wrung out like a dishrag!"

"I'm sorry, Judy," Juniper said meekly. "We can stop now."

"We certainly can! I want this man in bed, *now*. I'll get some green oat milk in wine to calm him."

"I want—" Ingolf began.

"You want a good night's sleep, so you can tell us the rest tomorrow," Juniper said. "We've a guest room ready for you here in the hall. And Judy's word is final on matters of health!"

Unprompted, Rudi came forward and helped the other man rise, then took an arm around his shoulder. When they'd put Ingolf to bed he stopped in the corridor outside the guest room and looked at his mother.

"Who's the sword for?" he asked bluntly.

Juniper looked at him, and he was shocked to see that the leaf-green eyes were full of tears.

"Oh, my son," she whispered. "You know as well as I. What did they call Mike, your blood father?"

The Bear Lord.

"And what did the Powers speak through me, when I held you over the altar in the *nemed*?"

He didn't need to speak that, either. That was when she'd named him *Artos*, in the Craft. And . . . to himself, he whispered what she'd said:

> *Sad winter's child, in this leafless shaw—*
> *Yet be Son, and Lover, and Hornèd Lord!*
> *Guardian of my sacred Wood, and Law—*
> *His people's strength—and the Lady's Sword!*

"I don't want to go," he said softly. "I thought . . . not yet." His eyes went out past the walls of his home. "I'm not a boy anymore, Mother."

They both knew what he meant; that he was old enough to know how easily and quickly a man could die. Ingolf's tale had rammed that home anew. He went on: "And I don't want to leave you and Father and Maude and Fiorbhinn," he said. "Or the Clan, and home. Someday, yes, but . . . not yet."

Love and sorrow warred in Juniper's eyes. "I don't want you to go either, my darling. I just don't think you've much choice."

Rudi's temper flared for a moment: "I thought we were the Lord and Lady's children, not their slaves!"

Her palm reached up to cup his cheek. She was a full nine inches shorter than he, but he felt like a child again at the gesture. Then she tweaked his ear sharply and he jumped.

"Yes, we are Their children," she said. "So are cockroaches . . . and crocodiles . . . and crocuses. We are *not* the sum whole of the scheme of things! So don't be thinking that They'll necessarily favor *you*, any more than I'd put you before your sisters."

"Sorry, Mom," he said after a moment. A grin. "I've been hanging around with Christians too much, sure and I have. Nice people, a lot of them, but they've got a strange way of looking at things."

"Oh, my dearest one," she said.

Her voice choked a little. Suddenly he noticed how many gray threads there were in the mane that had always been so fiery fox-red.

When did that happen? he asked himself, and put an arm around her shoulders. She turned into it and rested her forehead on his chest.

Her quiet voice went slowly on: "And They can be as harsh as sleet and iron, as the wolf in winter and Death itself. They have given you so many of Their gifts for a reason. And a man who refuses a duty They lay on him is . . . not punished . . . but . . . forsaken. And he will never know love or honor or happiness again."

He shivered at the look in those infinitely familiar green eyes; they were looking *beyond*.

Then they squeezed shut, and tears leaked out, sparkling in the lamplight; she grabbed him by the plaid.

"But how I wish you didn't have to go to that dreadful place! I am so frightened for you, and it will only get worse!"

"There, and I was just grousing," he said, holding her close and remembering her rocking his troubles away. "I'll come back with a shining sword and fine tale, since the Powers would have it so. It's just that I would have them be a bit more open about the reasons for it all!"

* * *

Rudi Mackenzie dreamed. The air was sweet and mildly warm, smelling of earth and growing things; some crop that grew in leafy blue-green clumps stretched to the edge of sight in neat rows separated by dark, damp turned earth. A well-made road ran through it, neatly cambered with crushed rock, and a milepost stood nearby. It was granite, hard and smooth, and the rayed sun on it was cut deeply, but time had still worn it down until the shape was visible only because of the slanting rays of the real sun setting in the west.

A crack and a wretched gobbling sound came from behind him. He turned, or at least his disembodied viewpoint did. A score of . . . creatures . . . were working their way down the rows of the crop.

They look like men, he thought absently.

A little; they stood on two legs, and their hands held tools, digging sticks of polished wood set with blades of smooth stone. But their legs were too short and the arms that hung from their broad flat shoulders too long, and the heads sloped backward above their eyes. Those eyes were big and round, on either side of a blob of nose and set above big chinless thin-lipped mouths; it made them look like children, somehow, and the more horrible for that. The naked bodies were brown, sparsely covered in hair.

A nondescript-looking man with a loose headcloth covering half his face rode a horse behind them, a long coiled whip in his hand. He swung it again, seemingly to relieve his boredom; the creatures were working steadily and well, jabbing the sticks downward in unison every time they took a step forward. Another worker jerked and moaned as the lash laid a line across his shoulders, then turned his too-big eyes down and drove the stone-headed tool into the earth again.

No. They're not men, but their ancestors were, Rudi's bodiless presence thought.

Then he woke. Shudders ran through him, and he could feel sweat running off him to soak the coarse brown linen of the sheets. That turned chilly quickly in the damp cold air of winter. The girl who was sharing his bed had awoken too; she snapped a lighter on the bedside table and touched it to the candle in its holder.

"What a dream." He gasped, clutching at the blanket as if it would help him keep the shattered, fragmented images clear. "My oath, what a dream!"

"It must have been, Rudi!" Niamh said.

Her blue eyes were wide as she tossed back tousled straw-blond hair. Like half the people in Dun Juniper she was an apprentice from somewhere else, in her case studying under Judy Barstow. They'd been friends and not-very-serious occasional lovers for years; she didn't want anyone long-term here, since she planned to go back home to Dun Laurel when she was consecrated as a healer.

"You clouted me a bit, thrashing around the now, and I couldn't wake you."

"Sorry, Niamh," he said contritely, shaking head and shoulders and letting the dream go. "Maybe it was just a sending from the fae."

Who weren't all kindly, he knew, particularly those from the wildwood. Looking around grounded him; he'd slept in this room ever since he stopped using a pallet in his mother's. It had a cluttered look and a lot of souvenirs; there was his baseball bat and glove—he'd been first baseman for the Dun Juniper Ravens Little League team as a kid—and the images of the Lord and Lady over the hearth he'd carved when he wasn't much older. A shelf was stuffed with his books and ones he had out from the dun's library. A stand in the corner held his armor and weapons.

The blanket was of his mother's weaving, done while he was a captive of the Association in the War of the Eye, a bit worn now but still beautiful with its subtle pattern of undyed wool in shades of white and brown and gray. He smoothed it and lay back.

"What was it, then?" she said, yawning and laying her head on his shoulder. "A sending? Or just a dream?"

"It's never *just* a dream," he said. "But . . . you know how it is."

She nodded. There were dreams, and then again there were dreams, and deciding which meant what was as important as it was difficult.

"On the whole, I think it was the Powers telling me to get my shoulder to the wheel and my arse in gear." He sighed.

"Oh," she said. Then: "Something to do with that cowan Ingolf?"

His mouth quirked in the candlelit dimness; cowan was a term for those who didn't follow the Old Religion . . . and not an altogether polite one, either.

"So much for secrecy. Yes, but don't ask me anything more about it . . . yeeep!"

"Anatomy. I'm just studying anatomy."

* * *

CASTLE TODENANGST, WILLAMETTE VALLEY NEAR NEWBERG, OREGON
JANUARY 14, CY22/2021 A.D.

"Yes, I gave them hospitality in Gervais," the dowager baroness of that holding said, glaring at the three faces across the broad malachite table from her. "Why shouldn't I?"

She was a gaunt woman with gray streaks in her blond hair; Sandra thought the green silk of her long cotte-hardi dress went badly with her rather sallow complexion.

The Lady Regent of the Portland Protective Association answered calmly: "Why? Because it would have made me look very bad if it came out that a noblewoman of the Protectorate had done that, particularly if this man they attacked had been killed . . . and our own children were there. Questions raised in the Lords. Questions raised in Corvallis at the next Meeting. Embarrassment, fines laid on the whole Association . . . I do *not* like being embarrassed, Mary. *Do* you understand?"

Sandra was an unexceptional woman in her fifties, petite and round-faced. Her stare could still make others flinch; it did now.

"I understand, my lady regent."

"Good. Then don't let it happen again. You have my leave to go. *In proper form, Mary,*" she said.

The baroness halted, made a sardonically precise curtsy that bowed her head just a hair more than manners required, and stalked out.

Sandra steepled her small elegant fingers and cocked her head a little, looking at the door through which Mary Liu had just gone in high dudgeon. It was massive, of light-colored oak over a solid steel core, and Liu hadn't been able to slam it, which must have annoyed her no end.

"Do you know the problem with the Dowager Baroness Gervais?" the Lady Regent asked.

Conrad Renfrew, Count of Odell, took a walnut out of the bowl on the table between them and cracked it between finger and thumb, tossed the nut meat into his mouth and thought for a moment while he chewed.

"Is the problem that she's an evil, murderous, spiteful bitch who's conspiring with these assassins from the cow country?" he replied meditatively.

He was a thickset man in his fifties who'd always been built like a fire-plug and had put on a little solid flesh lately. He wore casual-formal dress, a wide-sleeved shirt of snowy linen beneath a brown T-tunic cinched with a studded sword belt, and loose breeches tucked into half boots; a heraldic shield on the tunic's chest held his arms—sable, a snow-topped mountain argent and vert. His face was hideous with old white keloid scars, his eyes blue under grizzled brows, and his head as bare as an egg with less need of the razor he'd used in his youth.

"No, that's not the problem," Sandra said, toying with one of the trails of her silk wimple.

"She's a *stupid*, evil, murderous, spiteful woman who can't even speak a simple English sentence without *translating* it into High Formal Bitch?"

"No, she's bright enough. What she lacks is self-knowledge. I, for example, am fully *aware* of the fact that I'm an evil, murderous, spiteful bitch. And that I like it that way. Mary Liu just thinks she's hard-done-by and never given her due and has to stand up for her rights in a hostile, unfeeling world. And her habit of self-delusion leads her to do things that are quite unwise. Attempting to deceive me about helping this Prophet fellow, for example. If I said, 'Mary, darling, as one evil bitch to another—don't . . .' Why, she'd be *quite* insulted."

All three of the nobles sitting about the table in the presence chamber chuckled. It was in the Silver Tower, sheathed outside with pearly granite originally stripped from banks in Portland and Vancouver when Castle Todenangst was built by the Lord Protector's architects and labor gangs in the second and third Change Years.

That color scheme continued within: white marble floors, light silk hangings, elegantly spindly furniture of pale natural woods or antiques salvaged from mansions and museums in the dead cities, only the rugs providing a blaze of hot color. A workshop in Newberg had spent two decades rediscovering the secrets of Isfahan and Tabriz carpets, but with modern themes: local wildflowers, hawks among trees and tigers creep-ing through reed beds beside the Willamette.

The air smelled slightly of jasmine and sandalwood; the closed windows kept the noise of the great fortress-palace and the cold bright January day at bay, leaving only the slight hissing of the gaslights and an occasional gurgle from the recessed hot-water radiators behind their screens carved with scenes from *Le Morte d'Arthur*.

Conrad of Odell cracked another nut, dropping the shells into a Venetian-glass bowl.

"Stop showing off, Conrad," the third person said. "So you can still crack walnuts with your fingers. So what?"

She put one on a ceramic coaster and tapped it open with the plain brass pommel of her dagger; the two halves of the shell fell neatly apart. Then she continued: "Big fat hairy . . . hairless . . . deal. You're Lord Chancellor now, and I'm the new Grand Constable. Breaking things is my job, and the method doesn't matter as long as the job gets done."

Tiphaine d'Ath—Baroness d'Ath in her own right, very unusually for a woman in the territories of the Portland Protective Association—was the youngest present by fifteen years, which put her in her mid-thirties.

In contrast to Lady Sandra's headdress and long-skirted cotte-hardi of pale silk and dazzling white linen, she wore male garb; in her case, black silk and velvet, with arms of sable, a delta or over a V argent in the heraldic shield on her chest. Her face was calm, as it usually was: strong-boned, with pale gray eyes and hair so fair it would take a long while for the first gray strands to show, worn in what another age would have called a pageboy bob. She was tall for a woman, just under five-ten, built with compact long-limbed grace. Some people called the Regent *the Spider*. They called her henchwoman *Lady Death*, in a pun on her title.

Nobody laughed. It wasn't that sort of joke.

"*I'm* not spiteful, in any case. Murderous, evil and a bitch, yes; *spiteful*, no," Tiphaine added, taking a sip at her glass of wine after eating the nut.

"Some would say a duel a month for six months shows a certain amount of spite," Renfrew said, smiling; she'd been his protégé too, if not for so long as she had been Sandra's. "Particularly since you cut them to ribbons and they died by inches, screaming. Quite a performance; you couldn't have done better with a dungeon and its entire staff. Fulk De Wasco looked like he was naked and nailed to the floor even while he still had his sword."

"No, that was policy, not just fun. If Lady Sandra wanted me as Grand Constable, since I'm a woman I had to kill some of the more inveterate assholes, and in a way that would intimidate the others. A sword through the throat doesn't scare them enough; they're mostly too stupid to be cowards. Doing a little preliminary carving and trimming around the edges does give them pause for reflection at the closed-casket funeral, for some reason."

"Everyone knew you were good with a blade," Renfrew said. "Even Norman realized that, and he wasn't what you'd call the equal-opportunity type."

"He was smart enough to believe his eyes, when he didn't let his obsessions get in the way. With some people you need to use visual aids to make a point. I'm still a freak of nature, but I'm a freak they don't dare to diss."

A long-haired Persian cat jumped up on the table. Tiphaine dumped it unceremoniously down; Sandra smiled slightly.

She wouldn't have dared to do that once, she thought, tucking a lock of her graying brown hair back under her headdress; the silver-and-platinum band around it chinked softly.

Aloud: "Isn't it interesting that this Prophet fellow was prepared to send assassins all the way to Mackenzie country? And isn't it even more interesting that they knew this Vogeler was heading there? What do we know about these people? Refresh my memory; I've had more pressing business lately."

"It's a father-son team running a cult," Tiphaine said, speaking without consulting the notes in the folders before her. "Our sources aren't certain if the son is natural, or adoptive and the natural son of the woman who ran the cult before the Change."

"The Church Universal and Triumphant, yes?"

"Yes, my lady. Generally known as *the Cutters,* or at least their musclemen are, or the Corwinites, from their headquarters. It's in the country just north of the old Yellowstone National Park. They were there before the Change, and already had a couple of rungs missing from their ladders if you ask me, but the Prophet moved in and took them over with a group of followers in late 'ninety-eight and added a lot of new stuff."

"He's not native there?"

"Rumor has it he was in California on the day of the Change itself.

He'd been blowing up scientists in the eighties and nineties—had a major hate-on for technology—and he was in jail in Sacramento. He escaped in the confusion, felt that God had personally answered his requests with the Change, and headed for Montana. That he got there *does* say something about his survival skills."

They all nodded thoughtfully; California had been a charnel house as bad as anywhere on the globe, that day when the lights went out . . . and the water stopped coming through the pipes that kept nearly two-score million alive in a natural desert. Not one in a thousand had lived through it, the ones who'd run early and fast; reports said there were places where the desiccated corpses still lay three deep on the edges of the Mohave, despite a generation of sun and wind and crows and coyotes.

Dead as LA, went the proverb.

Tiphaine went on: "The new management of the CUT started small just after the Change, but they've been expanding recently, both by straightforward conquest and by conversion; they cover most of what was Montana by now, and chunks elsewhere. If they take over you convert or die, so it snowballs. I've looked into the theology. They're . . ."

Her tone remained flatly unemotional as she paused for a moment to search for the appropriate phrase and then resumed: ". . . mad as Tom O'Bedlam. Living on a different planet. Fucking bughouse nuts."

"Yes, I've perused it a bit, too," Sandra said. "Even stranger than the late unlamented Pope Leo here. Sort of a mishmash of Christianity and Buddhism and every lunatic and charlatan from Madame Blavatsky on, with an explanation of why God sent the Change, too—floods having been tried before, as it were. And they're getting uncomfortably close, if they win this war with New Deseret. I wish we had access to this easterner Vogeler who was involved. The Mackenzies didn't exactly brief Mathilda on it."

Conrad's brows went up; when the scars on his face moved, he looked more like a gargoyle than ever. "The CUT are a bit far away to worry about, surely?"

"That's the time to worry. Knowledge *is* power. And now that we've absorbed the Palouse—"

"The western half of it," Tiphaine said, with pedantic accuracy.

"—there's only Boise and Deseret between us and them."

Conrad shrugged massive shoulders. "You're the sovereign. They're basically a bunch of sheep shaggers, though. And they think anything with gears in it is sacrilegious, don't they?"

"Yes, but you should read more widely in history, dear Conrad. There are any number of cults which've caused no end of trouble, though their first followers were few and poor. Especially when they preach salvation at the sword's edge. In the event of trouble, how are we placed?"

She knew most of the answer, but it never hurt to go over the facts again. Conrad's blue eyes took on a slightly abstracted look. He'd been an accountant by trade before the Change, as well as a fellow member of the Society for Creative Anachronism and a close friend of Norman and Sandra Arminger.

"The treasury's got a full year's revenue on hand in cash, our paper is trading at par and we can borrow at excellent rates if we have to— the customs and excise taxes are blossoming nicely with the way trade's picked up. It would be even better if it weren't for the Haida raiders and plain-and-simple pirate scum all over the Pacific basin."

"The pirates we'll have to leave to the naval powers like Tasmania, but for the Haida we need a Warden of the Coast. But who to appoint Marchwarden? Piotr has the most lands in that direction, but . . ."

"But I wouldn't appoint him to supervise an orgy at the Slut and Brew," Conrad said.

Tiphaine nodded. "There's Juhel Strangeways, Lord de Netarts. He's competent, and even fairly honest. And he already has County Tillamook in ward, for Lady Anne. It'll be—"

"Five years until she reaches her majority," the regent said.

"By then, he could have the place organized. He already dealt with that Haida raid, October before last."

"A matter in which our Rudi had a hand," Sandra said thoughtfully, stroking the cat in her lap. "He attracts trouble as sparks fly upward, that boy."

"Coincidence?" Conrad rumbled.

"I'm far too paranoid to believe in coincidence, Count Odell."

The other two smiled. "Neither do I," the man said, and Tiphaine nodded. "De Netarts, for Marchwarden of the West, then?"

Sandra nodded, and he went on: "The basic mesne tithes are coming in without too much trouble as well; it's easier now that we don't have to split them with the Church."

Sandra smiled like a cat. That had been one of the many reasons she'd unobtrusively arranged for Pope Leo to shuffle off his mortal coil, and for Portland's Church to be reunited with Rome—or rather with the Umbrian hill-town of Badia, which was where the Swiss Guard had escorted the remnant of the Vatican when Rome went under.

Poor Norman, he did so want a pope of his own in true medieval style, and Bishop Rule was just the sort of madman to suit the role, once he'd decided that God considered everything since about June 15, 1297 a mistake. Of course, the Change was some evidence for that . . . on the whole, though, Pope Log is preferable to Pope Stork.

Despite the occasional tussle with Benedict and his successor Pius XIII over things like the nomination of bishops, and despite how useful a tame inquisition had been. One sane pope six months away was far easier to deal with than an all-too-active lunatic in Portland, and it had made reconciliation of a sort possible with Mount Angel and the other so-called Free Catholic bishoprics. Mount Angel's mutant order of warrior Benedictines was becoming uncomfortably influential, through its budding university and with its daughter settlements helping the more badly battered areas get on their feet again.

Stalin had meant mockery when he asked how many divisions the pope had, but in the end his bewildered successors had found it didn't matter; and men-at-arms and castles could come into the same category. At seventh and last men were ruled from within their heads by ideas as much as by clubs from without, and a careful ruler kept it in mind. The Church of Rome had outlasted any number of systems that looked stronger than iron at the time, and had ridden out many storms that claimed to be the wave of the future; she was wise with years, and infinitely patient, and bided her time.

Best to take advantage of that, for herself and her daughter and her daughter's children to come, rather than trying to build dams against it.

Conrad nodded, as if reading her mind. "We're making a mint off the salt-works on the coast and the Columbia tolls, too. Basic population has more than recovered from all those laborers who left after the Protector's war."

They both scowled slightly; of all the conditions imposed after the Portland Protective Association's qualified sort-of defeat in what everyone else called the War of the Eye, the one allowing peons to leave without paying their unpayable debts had hurt hardest. Everyone had a lot more land than farmers to till it, even now. People were wealth in the most fundamental sense, strong hands and backs to work and fight.

"Between natural increase and immigration from the more chaotic areas like Pendleton, which unfortunately goes to the other realms as well as to us, and the fifty thousand left in the Palouse when we annexed it—"

Sandra smiled her cat smile, and Tiphaine d'Ath nodded, and Renfrew grinned. It had even been voluntary.

At least, it was voluntary on the part of the collection of sheriffs and strong-arm types who took over there after the Change, she thought. *And their sons.*

They'd been unable to compose their own feuds—not least because of the Association's subtle pot-stirring—and had been left in the end with a choice between the neofeudalism of the PPA and the iron-fisted centralized autocracy of the United States of Boise under General-President Thurston. Now the Free Cities of the Yakima League were surrounded by Protectorate territory on three sides, too, and could be squeezed, as long as she was subtle and indirect about it.

Conrad went on as she mused: "—we're up to about four hundred thousand people all told. Portland-the-city's nearly as big as Corvallis now."

Sandra shifted her gaze to Tiphaine; the military was her responsibility. She'd been Conrad's deputy there for years, before getting the top command last year when the Count of Odell decided to concentrate on his chancellor hat.

"The sons of the knights we lost in the war are grown now, or mostly," the Grand Constable said.

Which was fortunate. It took *years* to train a mounted lancer; the best had to be virtually born at it.

"What with that and new creations, when we call out the *ban* and the select militia, we can field twenty thousand men and keep them in the field as long as we need. A thousand knights, four thousand men-at-arms, a couple of thousand good light cavalry—horse archers, mainly—and the rest infantry. Half crossbowmen, who finally all have modern rapid-fire models, and the rest spearmen. I think we should raise some pike units like the Bearkillers and Corvallans, but that would take a lot of re-training time."

Tiphaine and Conrad started an argument about the relative merits of eighteen-foot pikes versus spear-and-shield; Sandra ignored it while she thought. She'd never pretended to be a soldier of any sort, any more than she was an engineer. You found people who knew what they were doing and left them to do it . . . provided you also found ones you could trust.

"—admit the phalanx has an advantage on open ground but pikemen are too specialized for my taste. Spearmen are more flexible, and—" Conrad said.

Sandra cleared her throat. "The big picture, please. Proceed, Tiphaine. And if we're pressed?"

"In an emergency? Forty thousand if we call the *arrière-ban* for a defensive war, though of course those won't all be as well trained and it would be awkward during the harvest. The castles in our core territories are all in good shape, the armories and emergency food stores are full, we've got reserves of trained destriers to replace horses lost in the field, the river fleet on the Columbia is fully ready, and we've finally got the field artillery up to spec as well as the siege train."

"Problems?"

"The Palouse. We haven't had time to get it castellated properly yet, so it's vulnerable in a way the rest of our territory isn't. The strongholds there are mostly earthwork-and-timber, motte-and-bailey at best. The local lords can't afford to rebuild right away. Also the roads there are lousy—the fools haven't even been filling in the potholes or keeping bridges from washing out, and the railroads are a wreck. But if we try to make them repair twenty-two years of neglect overnight, they'd be bankrupt. Except that they'd revolt first, of course."

"I presume we have the necessary plans ready to fix the situation?"

"Of course, my liege; we started on that before the annexation. It's simply a matter of money . . . a very great deal of money."

"How much?"

Tiphaine named a figure, and Sandra winced slightly. Then she held up a finger.

"Conrad. Do you think you can get the Lords to approve a special subsidy for infrastructure improvements in the Palouse, along the new eastern border at least?"

The stocky man winced in turn. The Association's landholders didn't like paying even the standard assessments, and an extra one would cost him political capital—which was to say soft-soaping, bribing and threatening.

"Yes, if you think it's worth the trouble. And it *will* cause trouble," he warned.

"Twist the necessary arms—I have some files you'll find useful. It'll keep the new lordships in the east sweet if we loan them the money and supply engineers and materials. I *could* pay it out of the Privy Purse, but I prefer to keep that for unforeseen emergencies."

Renfrew gathered up his papers. "I'd best get on to it; young Lord Chaka will see sense, I think. His mother will help. Stavarov will cause problems but I can talk him 'round if I offer some of his people land. . . ." He raised an eyebrow at her.

"By all means, but bargain hard. I want to keep as much of the vacant areas of the Palouse in the Throne's demesne as I can. Granting land is a lot easier than getting it back, unless there's a convenient case of escheat for treason."

He nodded and made a formal bow, kissing her extended hand and grinning like something carved on a waterspout. "Farewell for the nonce, Sandra, you evil bitch."

"That's 'my sovereign liege-lady and regent of the Association' evil bitch to you, Conrad."

Laughing, he bowed again and turned to go. Sandra pulled at a tasseled cord; the door opened smoothly and showed the corridor outside, with the guards standing to attention; their mail gleamed with a gray oiled sheen as they brought their spears to the salute.

When the door closed again, Sandra stood, gently stirring a cat out of her lap. "Come," she said to Tiphaine.

The warrior-woman helped her into a long robe of white ermine, and they walked out onto a balcony, closing the sliding glass doors behind them. The day was bright and sunny for January in the Willamette, with only a few drifts of high cloud; you could just see Mount Hood's white cone to the east, over the battlements. Above it a glider swooped, its long slim wings dark against the aching blue of the sky.

The two women's breath smoked as they looked down into a flagged hexagonal courtyard twenty feet below. It was overlooked by two stories of barracks and storerooms on all sides as well as the Silver Tower. Todenangst was full of things like that, unexpected crannies and vantage points. She'd put most of them into the plans herself; Norman had been much more . . . straightforward . . . and not nearly as fond of Peake's work as she.

"They say this castle had a man's bones in it for every ton of concrete poured," she said, with a nostalgic smile for the grand adventure of those early years.

Sometimes I think we got away with it only because nobody could believe how crazy we were.

Tiphaine nodded; she'd been newly come to the household then, and barely fourteen. "I remember a bit of it; they used to throw the bodies into the mix, sometimes. You kept telling the Lord Protector it could wait until we had the farms fully up and running again, and he said it *could* wait, but he just didn't want to, he wanted his castle and he wanted it now."

"Poor Norman, that was his great fault. He was in too much of a hurry to realize his dreams; it killed him in the end, as much as Havel did. If only he'd known how to wait, he'd be alive today . . . and we'd have it all. I miss him."

The courtyard below was one where her private guard exercised. Rudi and Mathilda were there now, in Protectorate-style armor, based on early medieval models; she was resting for a moment, watching him take on three knights of the household. Odard called the start with a flourish of his white-painted wand:

"Kumite!"

The knights spread out; Rudi waited for a moment, smiling faintly. Then he leapt, so quickly that it wasn't even a blur, more as if he stretched out impossibly for a second. A flat crack sounded as he slammed into the closest of them, one big kite-shaped shield slapping into another, Rudi's tucked close into his left shoulder in perfect form. The knight was knocked flying with both feet off the ground, to land flat on his back with seventy pounds of armor and gear to drive the wind out of him. His sword pinwheeled through the air to land with a dull clang.

Rudi whirled before knight or blade landed, caught a sword on his own shield and cut backhanded into the side of the second's helmet with a crashing *bonnnggg*, and met the third blade-to-blade before he could strike himself. The knight was good—the household took only the best, and trained rigorously—but he seemed to be moving like a slo-mo scene in the movies in the old days, while Rudi wasn't.

Or he moves like that tiger we had at the baiting, the one they matched against the bison bull. So much power, and so fast . . .

After a flurry impossible for an untrained eye to follow, the Portlander stopped and looked down at the rounded point of the blunt practice sword just inside the split skirt of his mail hauberk and prodding at the leather of his breeches. In a real fight it would have hamstrung him and opened the femoral artery.

He swore admiringly and stepped back, letting the point of his own blade drop to the earth and his shield dangle from the guige, the diagonal strap around his neck. He and the young Mackenzie high-fived each other as the other two clambered groaning to their feet, grinning ruefully.

"He's very good indeed, isn't he?" Sandra asked.

"Yes, my lady," Tiphaine replied, without taking her cold gray eyes from the scene below. "When my team took him back in the War, he was ten—and he cut a grown man badly with his knife and would have killed another if he hadn't had a mail-lined jacket on. Now . . . You know what the pagans say of him?"

Sandra nodded, smiling. "That his secret name is *Artos*, and that he's the chosen Sword of the Lady? Yes? There was the prophecy at his birth, and that thing with the raven right after the war, at his mother's wedding. That was a wonderful touch, if Juniper stage-managed it."

Tiphaine shuddered slightly at the memory. She had been there, although not in the front rank, and she tried not to remember it . . . because when she did the all-sufficient cynicism her mentor had taught her was shaken. The rumors hadn't lost in the telling over the years, either. Instead she hung on to her clinical detachment as she went on:

"Well, he's so far up the bell curve that I'm tempted to believe it myself, sometimes. It's not *natural*—and I helped train him these past twelve years, on his visits."

"I do believe in his legend," Sandra said, then chuckled quietly at Tiphaine's raised brow. "Oh, not the pagan gods; they're as much a myth as Jehovah or the Risen Christ, whatever dear Juniper thinks. Myths are lies; but I believe in the *power* of myths the way I believe in rocks . . . rulers have had the various pantheons carrying water for them since the first con man met the first sucker, and priestcraft was born. That was long enough ago that they were probably both walking on their knuckles."

Mathilda took up her shield and walked out to face Rudi. The mail hauberk she wore rippled in smooth gray-white, a treasure that had taken a team of experts more than a year to make from double coils of titanium wire.

"And my daughter?" Sandra asked.

Tiphaine pursed her lips; her duties had included the warlike part of the Princess's education since the girl turned nine. She also knew that Sandra Arminger hated inaccurate information with a passion.

"It's a disadvantage being a woman, of course, even if it's not as much of one as our macho idiots think. The Princess is . . . very good, enough to hold her own on most battlefields. About as good as Odard, say. That means she's better than him in natural talent, since he has an extra twenty-odd pounds of muscle on his upper body. And she really works at it. But she's not in the same class as Rudi. Not in mine, either, frankly. She's fast, far faster than average, and very strong for her weight . . . but Rudi's faster than that."

Sir Odard was standing ready again with the referee's white baton. He waited until they faced off, then brought it down sharply and shouted, "Kumite!"

Tiphaine hesitated for a moment, then went on: "He's faster than me—and I've lost only a hair off my best speed so far."

Tiphaine was a little past thirty-five, and she'd been an up-and-coming junior gymnast before the Change, only out of the running for future Olympics because she was too tall. Sandra had rescued her and seen the possibilities. . . .

"And he's strong even for his size; he can lift and toss twice his own body weight, even in a full hauberk. I've got a lot more experience, which makes up for it . . . so far."

"Interesting," Sandra said, narrowing her eyes. "Of course, Mathilda will be ruling, not fighting with her own hands. She only has to be good enough to win respect among, as you so accurately put it, our macho idiots. Iron on their shirts, iron between the ears."

Tiphaine chuckled slightly, which was the equivalent of a belly laugh for her.

"And the joke is?" Sandra Arminger said; normally the remark would have won only a slight narrowing of the eyes in amusement.

"Here we are in the Land of the Iron-Shirted Machos, and the people making the decisions at the top are nearly all women. You, my lady, me . . . Mary Liu, the Dowager Baronesses of Dayton and Molalla. And Juniper Mackenzie and Signe Havel, down south."

Sandra's own laughter was warm and genuine. "Well, not so surprising, Lady d'Ath, Grand Constable of the Association. So many of the first generation of the male upper nobility got themselves killed, one way or another."

"That happens in this business," Tiphaine replied, tapping at the long hilt of her own blade. "You have to be smart *and* lucky to die old—which our distinguished chancellor looks to be doing. I probably won't," she added clinically. "Too many people hate me and more will before it's over. You should start grooming possible replacements."

Mathilda and Rudi were circling, the big round-topped kite-shaped shields up under their eyes, longswords held over their heads hilt-forward. Mathilda attacked first, boring in with a fixed snarl visible even from above and through the bars of the practice helmet.

"Haro, Portland! Holy Mary for Portland!"

"Morrigú! Morrigú! Blackwing!"

Blades clashed, banged on shields, rattled on mail, thrust and cut and parry in arcs that glittered silvery-cold in the winter sunlight, striking at head, hip, thigh, neck without pattern or warning. The supple young bodies moved with a beautiful minimalism despite the weight of the metal confining them.

"Mathilda seems very determined," her mother said.

The heir to Portland moved aside from a shield-up rush by letting one bent knee relax and swing her out of the way, cutting at the back of Rudi's leg with a viciously economical swipe. He caught the blow aimed at his hamstring on the long tail of the shield, whirled. . . .

"Oh, she is. She's got the anger, the fire in the belly; most of the best fighters do. She hates being taken lightly or coming in second in anything, which I can sympathize with, and it drives her hard. It's like fuel, once you learn to ride it rather than be ridden."

"Rudi, on the other hand, always struck me as a very sunny-spirited boy," Mathilda's mother observed.

Tiphaine's long fingers tapped at the vines carved into the marble of the balustrade. "True . . . and he kills without fear, or anger, or hate, with regret even, simply because it's necessary. That's rare, and it's rarer still among the really first-rate. God help the enemy that finally frightens him or makes him mad."

When they went back into the chambers, Tiphaine sank to one knee and formally kissed Sandra's hand.

"My lady liege," she said. "I'd better start getting things ready, if you scent a war."

"My dear, as one evil bitch to another . . . it's beginning to smell very much like that."

Alone, Sandra sat again and toyed with the cat that leapt into her lap, teasing it with the ends of her wimple. She had always found that an aid to thought.

*   *   *

"Hello? Mother?" Mathilda said, as the guards thumped the door shut behind her.

"Ah!"

The slight figure in the chair started, and the cat gave a silent *meow* and jumped down. Mathilda turned and called, "Agnes! The lights, please."

A silent maid-cum-secretary in double tunic and tabard came out and turned up the gaslights and returned to wait against the wall at the far end of the chamber, hands folded.

"I was deep in thought, love," her mother said. "Is it dinnertime already?"

The early January sun had set; Oregon was farther north than you might think from the climate, and the winter days were short. Soon the yellow flame made the mantels glow bright, and Mathilda sank down on the rug near Sandra's feet, taking off her hat; it was the usual round flat type with a roll of cloth around the edge and a broad silk tail at one side.

"Not quite. I thought I'd sit with you awhile, if that's OK and you're not too busy. I always enjoy sparring with Rudi; it makes me better even though he wins. But I don't like it as much as *he* does."

"Likes to fight, does he?" Sandra said thoughtfully.

"Oh, yeah. He says there are only two reasons to fight."

"Which are?"

"Joy and death."

Her mother's brows went up. "Joy in death?"

"No, no . . . For joy, to stretch yourself with a friend; or death, to kill as quickly as you can. Nothing in between." She frowned. "I can see what he means, but it isn't that way for me, not most of the time. I mean, I *like* practicing with arms, but you put a sword in Rudi's hand and he's . . . transported."

"And waxes poetic about it. He's a young man of some depth, our Rudi . . . but if it's going on for dinnertime, you should change to a cotte-hardi for the meal," Sandra said gently. "We'll have important company. You have to wear skirts occasionally, you know, or . . . ah . . . people will talk."

"Or people will think I'm Lady Tiphaine's girlfriend?" Mathilda said dryly. "Or vice versa, accent on the *vice.*"

Sandra gurgled laughter. Her face was still smooth in her fifties, and the wimple was kind to it, but that made the laughter lines stand out around her brown eyes. Mathilda joined in the chuckle; in fact, Tiphaine's lover was and had been for twelve years a miller's daughter from Barony d'Ath by the name of Delia. Who was in theory a lady-in-waiting to the baroness and who'd been ennobled by an equally theoretical marriage to a knight who had no more interest in women than the current Grand Constable had in men. Her children had been the result of intervention by a pre-Change turkey baster. The two women were quite ridiculously devoted to each other and completely monogamous.

The cream of the jest was, of course, that Lady Delia de Stafford was delicately beautiful in an entirely feminine way and a complete clothes-horse and *never* wore anything less than the height of fashion—female fashion. Since she was cheerfully ready to lie truth out of Creation about it (being a secret witch, as well, and therefore not in awe of Christian sacraments), her naively sincere confessor was among the few at court who didn't at least unofficially know or guess. Tiphaine's own chaplain had been carefully chosen for complaisance, guaranteed by the files Sandra had on him.

I suppose that's sinful, what they do, Mathilda thought.

She certainly liked boys herself; she'd enjoyed kissing a couple, Odard and Rudi among them. But she was also fairly proud of the fact that she was still a virgin, and intended firmly to remain so until her wedding night. And she fully confessed everything she could think of in meticulous detail, tried her best to repent, and dutifully did every penance set. Sometimes the thought of her mother's files made her a little queasy; even more so the thought of reading and using them herself, even on priests. Better than chopping off heads or burning people at the stake, but . . .

A ruler has to kill sometimes, for the good of the realm and the people. Blackmail, that makes you feel . . . dirty. Mom has to live like the spider they call her, at the center of a web of paper and secrets.

"Rumors aren't a joke, though. They can hurt; they can kill," Sandra said. "As a ruler, you can protect someone like Tiphaine . . . which helps ensure they're loyal . . . but if people believed rumors like that about *you*, it could threaten your position. Which means threatening your life. Don't ever doubt that."

Mathilda nodded. *And it's a sin even if it doesn't hurt anyone else. But it's not as bad as a lot of things some people do, like bullying peasants or waging blood-feuds over some piece of nothing. We have to kill to live sometimes, but it's not something you should ever do lightly. Besides, I like Delia. It's lucky I don't have to confess other people's sins. Father Donnelly is sort of strict . . . I wonder why Mom picked him for me, and not someone she could control?*

That reminded her of her worries. "Mother . . . I've been thinking."

"Something I heartily recommend," Sandra said, her eyes shrewd as always.

It was a bit daunting, sometimes, to realize that she was *always* thinking, and always had been. Even more daunting to think of living like that, never saying or doing anything without having a dozen possible consequences dart through your mind.

"Mother . . . when I'm Protector . . ." She'd come of age for that in five years; you had to be older than the heir to a lesser title. "Will I *really* be Protector?"

"Ah," Sandra said; she sounded satisfied somehow. "I was wondering when you'd ask that."

"Well, *will* I be? Like Father?"

Sandra smiled again. "There will never be another Norman Arminger," she said. "What you mean is—will you really hold the power, as I do?"

Mathilda nodded, and her mother went on: "That depends entirely on you, my dear. It won't be easy. Half the nobles will want to marry you, or have their sons marry you, and rule through you; and you *must* marry, and fairly soon—a ruler's first responsibility is to have an heir, to keep the peace after you're gone. It would really be best if you married and had a child *before* you come to the throne; a ruler should have an *adult* heir, and at least one spare, and it's better if *they* have an heir in turn before coming to the throne. Your father and I would have had more children, if we could have."

Unspoken was what would have happened if one of those had been a son. Mathilda went on: "But if I married anyone here, or their heir, wouldn't that turn the others against me? As long as I'm single, I can sort of keep them guessing and trying to court my favor. The way Elizabeth did."

Sandra silently clapped her hands. "Bravo! But you don't want to die childless the way she did, do you, my dear?"

"Well . . . no. I want kids, someday. But not whole litters, like Victoria; just four, that would be perfect—two boys and two girls. A small family's better, I think . . . what's funny?"

"Nothing, my dear. Just reflecting on how perspectives change."

"Like you said, I can't *not* have *any*. I mean, we don't have a lot of relatives; nobody like James Stuart was to Elizabeth the First. It's my kid or they fight over the throne till the last one standing takes it. And they might rip the Protectorate apart doing it." She made a moue. "James wasn't any great prize, but he was better than a civil war."

"Smart Stuarts were few and far between," Sandra agreed. "Charles the Second, maybe, though he was lazy."

"And . . . there's Rudi. He wouldn't be, you know, *here* a lot; he'd never want to live here all year 'round. And the Mackenzies are *definitely* going to hail him Chief after his mother, now that the Assembly's made him her tanist. And the fighting men here all respect him. A lot. If it didn't turn everyone against me, those who *were* against me would really think three times about revolt—I could call on the Mackenzies for help. And I like him muchly, and God knows, he's cute as hell."

Sandra nodded. "You know his mother and I have talked about that. But it would be chancy. He's a witch; he'd never take the Faith even in form, and the Church isn't as much under our control as it was in your father's day. Plus there'd be the question of what religion your children followed—no witch could ever rule here, and no Christian in Dun Juniper. A lot of our believers and priests would be angry enough at a pagan consort. That could mean trouble; assassination attempts, say."

"If I died without an heir, who *would* succeed? The Grand Constable?"

Sandra looked at her and smiled again, this time slow and fond. "That's my girl! No, Tiphaine couldn't lead a big enough faction. It would be Conrad, probably. Though only after a fight. He doesn't actually want to be Lord Protector, but he'd take it rather than let some of the others in."

"And the Stavarovs and the Joneses and the others know that, and that helps keep me alive," Mathilda said.

"Bravo! And he *does* have an heir already—three—and very able lads they are, too, with very good matches already lined up. But your father built all this for *you*, my dear. You have a duty to his blood."

Mathilda nodded slowly. Her mother went on: "And some of the rest of the lords will try to rule through you whether you're single or not, and some will be ready to bring the whole Association down in wreck as they jockey for power, if they're not restrained . . . or occasionally, killed. I'll advise you as long as I'm around, of course, but the decisions will be *yours*. You'll have Conrad and Tiphaine and a few others you can trust, but ultimately it's your wits that the realm will depend upon."

"I think . . . I think the common people will support me. And the town guilds. If I offered charters . . ."

Sandra nodded; Mathilda could see she was pleased.

"Yes, for what that's worth, they *would* support you; they know what a cabal headed by someone like Count Piotr Stavarov would be like, and they want a strong protector to keep the barons in line. But remember, this isn't the Clan Mackenzie or Corvallis or even the Bearkillers. What counts here in the end is the great tenants-in-chief, and their vassals and men-at-arms and their strong walls, and if you do anything that unites all of them or nearly all of them against you, they'll destroy you. Your father knew that—it's a balancing act. They have to be afraid of you, but not *too* afraid, or for the wrong reasons. You'll be stronger than any one or two or three of them, but not all of them. They've tolerated me because I leave them alone beyond enforcing their dues and keeping them from killing one another too often. And because we got hurt badly in the war and the uprisings, which left a lot of widows ruling for underage sons—you won't have that advantage."

"A lot of them would like to make the peasants serfs again," Mathilda said with sudden bitterness. "The older ones, they give me the chills, sometimes. I know . . . I know that Dad did a lot of hard things, but he had to."

Or did he? a small voice within her wondered.

She lashed back at it:

He did *save all sorts of people! Portland is the only big city we know about that didn't have everyone die! And the whole country around here has more people than almost anywhere else that was near a town before the Change. If it weren't for Dad there wouldn't be anything human left between Seattle and here and Eugene except bones boiled for stew.*

"But the Change is a long time ago. We don't have to be like that anymore. I want to be a *good* ruler," she said, the words tripping over one another. "I want my people to love me."

She managed to throttle back the next part: *I don't want to rule like Dad . . . or even like you, Mom.*

Sandra looked at her, and there was no fathoming her expression, except that there was love in it.

"Those are two things that don't always go together, my darling," she said.

CHAPTER SEVEN

Abbot-Bishop Dmwoski rose from his knees before the image, feeling them creak and pop as he signed himself and turned back to his desk and sank into the swivel chair. He was a broad-shouldered man who had been thick-muscled most of his life, but going a little gaunt now as white and gray replaced the blue-black of tonsured hair and short-cropped beard. Pale blue eyes showed beneath his shaggy brows, in a square pug-nosed face graver than the smile lines said was natural. He put his palms on the silky polished wood of his desk and sighed.

It was not the one of plain pre-Change metal he'd used for so many years; on this last Christmas he'd come in to find that the brothers had replaced it with one they'd been working on in secret for years. *This* one was mostly burl-grained walnut, and the panels on the sides and front were carved with biblical scenes, and the top shone with the intricate patterns of the dark grain.

He sighed again. He hadn't had the heart to demand that they replace his old desk and turn this one over to the town mayor down in town, as had been his first impulse.

I still miss that old monstrosity, he thought. *I have seen so much change in my life—the Change most of all—that I find myself craving stability more and more. Perhaps not the worst of yearnings in a monk, but I must be cautious that it does not cloud my judgment as head of the Order. Even God knew mortality and change when He became flesh in this fallen world, and we must remain supple before time's gales.*

The top of the desk was painfully neat with its piles of paper, inkwell, seal, pens and typewriter for very private correspondence; he had been a soldier before he found his vocation, and then again after the Change when Mount Angel became the core of survival in this corner of the Willamette, and he was a precise and methodical man by nature and training. The office walls held a crucifix, a Madonna and Child done in a spare style that looked—and was—both Eastern and very old, and abundant bookcases, stocked with works on everything from agriculture and medicine to theology, tactics and engineering.

There were few personal items. A framed photograph of a middle-aged woman with a square face, tired and lined and resembling the abbot's own more with every year. Also framed was the Rule of the Order of the Shield that Pope Benedict had returned with his approval when contact was reestablished, together with an addendum in his own hand: *Well-done, thou good and faithful servant.*

He opened several files and arranged them before him, pulled the plug out of the speaking tube and called: "Send in Father Ignatius, please, brother."

The young soldier-monk came in, bowed and kissed the bishop's extended ring, then stood at the Order's equivalent of parade rest—feet at shoulder width apart, head slightly bowed above braced shoulders, hands clamped together beneath the concealing sleeves of the robe. Behind an immobile face, Dmwoski smiled at the earnest discipline of the young man. It reminded him of himself, once—though there were aspects of the younger generation he would *never* understand, short of heaven.

We are separated by the death of a world and the birth of another. Perhaps never since Noah and his grandchildren has there been such a division.

"Your reports on the Vogeler affair have been excellent, my son," he said. "Be seated."

Ignatius perched uneasily on the edge of the chair. "Thank you, Father," he said.

"You have familiarized yourself with this?" the bishop went on, tapping another folder.

The younger cleric drew a deep breath. "Yes. Extraordinary! Nantucket *is* the center of some disturbance of space and time, possibly the epicenter of the Change itself."

"That is apparently so. The Holy See's information and the . . . evidence . . . that the British visitors brought make it plain."

"I wish they had stayed longer, Father."

Dmwoski shrugged. "They had told all they knew. What is *also* plain—not least from your work, my son—is that the Mackenzies have other information from this Vogeler with respect to Nantucket. Information that they have not shared with us."

Ignatius frowned, though his hands rested motionless on his thighs, one sandaled foot flat on the ground and the other bent back slightly beneath him. Dmwoski's lips quirked slightly—the young man was in the First Position for Swift Drawing, quite unconsciously ready to leap, whirl and strike. Mount Angel's martial training bit deep. There were times when the Order of the Shield reminded him a little of tales about Shaolin monks from the old days.

"Father, I think that . . . they would do so only in a religious context. The Mackenzie herself does not keep secrets for the pleasure of it, and the Clan, frankly, usually leaks like a sieve. I would ordinarily say that while capable of many wonderful things, they cannot keep their mouths shut for any reason whatsoever. But in this case . . ."

Dmwoski nodded. "Yes. In their view of the world, the Change must necessarily be of supernatural agency."

Ignatius looked up, startled into showing his surprise: "You do not think so, Father?"

Dmwoski allowed himself a smile. "All things are accomplished according to the will of God, but He usually acts through mortals and through the natural world. Miracles would not be miracles if they happened every day, would they? Their purpose is to show us a possibility."

The abbot's face grew somber: "And while even evil is made to serve His purposes in the end, those purposes are beyond our comprehension. If it serves His purpose to deliver the world to a catastrophe such as the Change, He may well have done it by allowing . . . oh, the aliens that the Corvallans postulate . . . or wicked or heedless men misusing or misunderstanding the laws of nature. Or it may have been God allowing the Adversary to exert his power."

"Or, with respect, Father, it might have been a veritable miracle, as when He stayed the sun above Joshua."

Dmwoski nodded. "All things are possible to Him, brother. If that *was* the cause of the Change, then of course no probe of its source can do further harm. If, however, mortal hands and minds were the agency . . . who knows what might result? Even to the destruction of the world."

"Pray God and the saints that may not happen!" Ignatius said, eyes wide in shock.

"Pray indeed; but God imposes on us a duty to *act* in this world. I would be much more comfortable if one of our own were involved in any expedition to Nantucket. The more so as the followers of the false Prophet seem to have an interest in this—and perhaps know things which we do not."

Ignatius looked down in thought. "You mean to give me this task, Father? I will of course obey, but would not an older and wiser man . . ."

He is frightened, Dmwoski thought. *But not for himself; he fears failure only. Good! God deliver us from recklessness and arrogance masquerading as courage!*

"Such a journey will require a young man in his full strength," Dmwoski said. "Also you have already successfully completed several difficult missions, both military and diplomatic; your teachers give you excellent reports."

"Thank you, Father. But how exactly am I to gain access to any mission the Mackenzies launch? I am reasonably well liked there, for a Christian cleric and an outsider, but I *am* a Christian cleric and an outsider and the Clan are . . . clannish. I presume that is your intention, rather than the Order sending an expedition of its own?"

Dmwoski nodded. "Needs are infinite, resources always limited, my son," he said. "With the threat of the CUT, the Order will need all its strength. One man—one man of unusual abilities—we can spare. More we cannot."

His blue eyes grew shrewd. "And if the Mackenzies send their tanist—"

"They will, Father. Given the legends which surround his birth and early life, it would appear inescapable to them. And he is a . . . a most formidable man. As a warrior I have not met his match, save possibly the Grand Constable d'Ath; and he has equal intelligence. And much more charm as well."

Dmwoski nodded. "Just so."

He supposed there must be some people who liked her, but even putting her private life to one side, personally he'd met *snakes* who had more charm than Tiphaine d'Ath. He knew the cardinal-archbishop had contemplated excommunication, and had refrained only when a tacit agreement was reached that she would abstain from the sacraments most of the time.

Aloud he continued: "But consider also the relationships which Rudi Mackenzie . . . *Artos* Mackenzie . . . has acquired in that storied and adventurous young life of his."

"Ah," Ignatius said, and bowed his head in respect. "The princess. She and Rudi Mackenzie—"

"Have been raised together and took the oath of *anamchara*. Which requires the sharing of secrets. If Rudi is to investigate these matters for his mother, he will tell her. She will not allow him not to."

"What do you think she will do, Father?" Ignatius said. "I have little knowledge of her beyond matters of public record and a few meetings."

"She will, I think, find some way to accompany him."

"With respect . . . I cannot see her mother allowing that!"

"Neither can I," Dmwoski said dryly.

The unspoken *and teach your grandmother to suck eggs* made the young man flush, but the Abbot smiled to lessen the sting and went on: "Nevertheless, she will try. She may or may not succeed. We cannot in good conscience abet her possible defiance of the regent; it would be politically suicidal as well. But we *can* . . ."

". . . help her if she succeeds in it," Ignatius said.

"Just so. She is a most loyal daughter of Holy Mother Church, in an independent and occasionally self-willed manner," Dmwoski said.

"Well, she *is* a princess, born to rule, not an apprentice dairymaid," Ignatius said.

Dmwoski nodded. Wryly, to himself: *And to you, my son, a 'princess born to rule' is the most natural thing in the world, whereas I must every now and then remind myself that such things do again walk the world . . . the Changed world . . . even if gryphons and unicorns do not.*

Aloud he went on: "Considering her parentage, we have been blessed indeed that she earnestly seeks the good. Hence she is likely to *accept* our help, if events take the turn that I expect."

"But her contacts are primarily with her confessor, and the hierarchy in the Association dioceses, are they not, Father? I assume we are keeping this hypothesis secret from them?"

"Yes. It is necessary. Working through the regular hierarchy in the Association territories is an unacceptable security risk in this matter. They are too intimately involved with the Protectorate's secular governance. Frankly, I would be afraid of the Lady Regent's learning too much if we consulted in that direction. Nor do they have any man of your particular abilities."

"And the princess does not share the prejudice so many Association nobles have against our Order," Ignatius said, nodding thoughtfully.

"Precisely, brother. If anything, she favors us—from appreciation of our work, and also from reasons of policy as a counterbalance to the Dominicans. Many of whom regret the ending of the schism and the disbanding of Antipope Leo's inquisition."

Ignatius had lost his doubts; his mind was working quickly behind an impassive face. Dmwoski nodded.

"We must consult others of our brothers, speak at length, and pray for guidance. But I think, my son, that your first step on this journey will be towards Portland."

∗   ∗   ∗

FLYING M BARONIAL HUNTING PRESERVE, COAST RANGE FOOTHILLS
PORTLAND PROTECTIVE ASSOCIATION, OREGON
JANUARY 30, CY22/2021 A.D.

This is a bit different from our last hunting party, back last Samhain, Rudi thought.

He inhaled deeply. All he could smell was the damp snow, and the deep sweet pungency of conifer forest. The sun was a little west of noon and well south, which made him squint as he watched the edge of the woods ahead, where the snowy natural meadow narrowed down to a point between two steep hills.

The twins weren't with them; they didn't like visiting Association territory, for which he couldn't blame them, and they'd gone off to stay with *Hiril* Astrid at Stardell Hall. Mathilda was the only woman in the half dozen actual hunters, though there were a few young ladies-in-waiting and a middle-aged chaperone back at the lodge. Everyone else was a young male Associate, a nobleman; then there were the beaters ahead of them on the other side of this stretch of forest.

Rudi held up his right hand. The others came to a halt, spread out across the field where sun-cured grass stuck through the snow in beige-upon-white. Especially after Mathilda hissed at them about hunt discipline.

The Flying M was in a valley that wound up from the Willamette near Yamhill into the Coast Range ahead and to the west. They'd come farther where the tall forest of Douglas fir and hemlocks closed in with a tangle of steep forested ridges, rippling around them in tall dark green ranks. The branches were heavy with the white of the recent snowfall and the Alaskan air mass was still over the valley, keeping the air well below freezing.

The wind was cold in his face, and the sound of the hounds was a musical belling at least a half a mile farther on—though sound was tricky among woods and hills, particularly after snow. A hundred yards behind them the horses were starting to snort and plunge in the hands of the grooms. Epona bugled her challenge to the scent of predator drifting in from the west.

"He's coming," he said, softly but clearly.

Grins of excitement to match his own ran up the line, breath coming heavier and puffing white in the chill air. The villagers in the first manor east of here said the tiger was a big male, and it had taken several sheep and a cow; they were terrified that it would be a child next.

That *might* be simply fear talking. The old man-eaters who'd escaped or been released right after the Change had died out by now, though the memory of them remained vivid. As humans grew scarce and better armed, stalking natural prey like deer and elk and feral cattle and swine in the burgeoning wilderness became a wiser strategy for their descendants. Those who learned, lived.

Still, nobody wanted to take chances. To a tiger a human looked temptingly edible, just about the size of a deer, and winter was their hungry season too. You had to teach them to avoid men and their homes. . . .

There was a deep stillness, the snow-hush drinking sound, with their own breath as loud as the quiet creaking of boughs under their white burden. He was in Portlander outdoor dress, quilted jacket and stout wool breeches and fur-lined leather boots, his feet only a little cold, but he'd kept his own yew longbow rather than the crossbow they favored.

The shaft on the string had a hunting broadhead, a razor-edged triangle whose ultimate origin had been a stainless-steel spoon. Mathilda was armed Clan-style too—she'd grown up using longbows part of the year—and the rest carried hunting crossbows with spring-steel prods, the wicked four-bladed heads of the bolts glittering when the intermittent sun broke through the clouds. Everyone had a hunting spear too, with a broad razor-edged head and a crosspiece below that, standing upright with the buttspikes driven into the ground.

Crack-crack-crackle...

He caught that, and Odard, and Mathilda, then the others. That was the sound of frozen snow-laden brush breaking under heavy paws as the great cat moved quickly; Rudi's consciousness focused down to a diamond point, everything growing crisp and clear and slow. Then a call, as the king predator realized there were men in front of it as well as behind.

A moaning *mhgh... mhgh... mhgh*, building to what wasn't quite a roar, then a deep guttural snarling sound of anger and fear: *ouuurrrh... ouuurrrh*...

Mathilda spoke: "He's going to break cover! Rudi and I have first shot!"

The tiger eeled through the brush at the edge of the clearing with a delicacy astonishing in an animal that weighed as much as a pony, and stood looking at them from two hundred yards away.

"Big 'un," Lord Chaka Jones said exultantly, his chocolate-brown face alight with pleasure. "Damned big. Siberian, and pure or nearly."

He was right; it was a six-year-old male in its prime, with its shaggy winter coat a pale yellow-white between the black stripes.

"Ten feet without the tail," Rudi agreed. "Six hundred pounds, easy, maybe seven hundred."

Seeing them it snarled, a sharp racking sound, baring teeth like ivory dirks, ears laid back and golden eyes blazing, tail held stiff and low, twitching slightly at the end. A white puff of breath obscured its head for an instant. It half turned as if to go back in the woods, but the sound and scent of the hounds brought it around again. The great head went back and forth, looking at the six humans, and then it began to pace forward in a half crouch, belly almost touching the snow.

"Remember, these things can jump thirty paces in a single bound," Odard Liu said.

"Yes, teacher," one of the others grumbled.

At first the tiger moved step by step, placing each foot carefully, just like a housecat stalking a ball of yarn. Then it began a rocking trot . . . and suddenly it was coming at a flat-out gallop, a series of amazing bounds with a puff of snow shooting from under its rear feet every time it took off and then again when it landed, seeming to float in long gravity-defying arcs.

"You first, Matti," Rudi called.

He bent his bow nonetheless, the yew limbs flexing back into a shallow curve as he drew Mackenzie-style past the angle of his jaw, eyes locked on the white patch on the big cat's chest.

Snap.

The sound of the string hitting Mathilda's bracer was sharp and crisp. The arrow blurred out in a smooth shallow arc, and it met the tiger's latest leap at its peak. The elastic grace turned to a squalling tumble; the tiger landed whirling, trying to bite the thing that had hurt it, and he could see the peacock feather fletching of her shaft against its rear flank. That would kill it . . . but not quickly.

Then it screamed and charged, belly to the ground now, broad paws churning a mist of snow that glittered in the sunlight.

Snap. Snap. Snap.

He shot twice, Matti once, in the next six seconds. All three arrows struck; her last buried itself to the fletching right in the V at the base of the beast's throat. And still it came on with a roaring coughing growl, blood smearing the snow now as it tensed for the last leap.

Then it collapsed, the fierce grace turning to tumbling limpness, flopping not five feet from Mathilda's boots.

"Streak, 'ware streak!" Odard shouted frantically, trying to get into position to take a shot without chancing hitting a human.

Rudi pivoted automatically. He saw blurred yellow-and-black, a second tiger just taking off for the final killing bound, its huge paws spread with the claws ready to grip and the mouth gaping for the bite to the neck. He shot once and threw himself forward under the leap, snatching his spear as he went by. That meant landing in an ungainly heap, and the ashwood shaft cracked him painfully on the knee. Rudi forced himself into a shoulder spring, coming to his feet and whirling at the same time.

The tiger landed where he'd been, then turned in a whirling spray of snow and blood and slaver, screaming its challenge. It came up on its hind feet; his arrow had struck it low in the belly, but the wound wasn't crippling or a quick kill. Now it hunched and drove for him. Massive paws slapped forward with the claws out like giant fishhooks in a left-right-left-right that melded into a single slamming blur of movement, each blow strong enough to crack bone or disembowel.

He screamed a snarl back at it, giving ground but jabbing fiercely at its face, short quick stabs to keep it distracted and make it rear and expose the vulnerable underside. One blow landed on the broad spearhead, numbing his hands but splitting the paw against the razor edge as well. The cat screamed again, recoiling from the pain.

"Haro!"

Mathilda drove her spear into the beast's side with a meaty thump, the blade sinking between two ribs until the crossbar stopped it. A second later, Chaka's hit it a little farther back, with all the burly black nobleman's two hundred pounds lunging behind it.

Rudi poised for a stroke of his own, but the blaze in the animal's sun-colored eyes went out. It moaned, dropped to the snow and bit savagely at the whiteness with red pouring out between its fangs, then went limp.

Rudi paused, panting and grinning. The three who'd made the kill spent a minute thumping one another on the back and asking if anyone had been hurt.

"Not a scratch," Rudi boasted.

"No?" Chaka said, wiping sweat off his face. "Then how come you're bleeding?"

"I am?" Rudi said, then felt the sting.

A probing finger found a tiny patch of skin gone from the outermost tip of his nose, flicked off by a claw. Just a little closer and his whole face would have gone the same way . . .

He shrugged off a complex shudder and cleaned his spear by jabbing it repeatedly into the snow and the wet earth beneath it, then wiping it down. The air was full of the smell of blood and the rank tomcat musk of the tigers, and their own sweat. His longbow's string had snapped, probably cut by the spearhead, but it was fine otherwise and he slid it back into the carrying loops beside his quiver; there were arrows to retrieve as well.

Then he stooped, leaning on the spear, and touched a finger to the blood, mingling it with his own on thumb and forefinger and touching it to his forehead.

"Go in peace to the Summerlands and hunt beneath the forever trees, brave warriors," he said quietly. "We honor the fight you made; speak well of us to the Guardians, and be reborn through the Cauldron of She who is Mother to us all."

Then to the woods: "Lord Cernunnos, Horned Master of the Beasts, witness that we kill from need and not from wantonness, to protect our farms and our folk; knowing that for us also the hour of the Hunter comes at last. And to Your black-wing host, Lady Morrigú, I dedicate the harvest of this field."

A few of the Protectorate nobles crossed themselves or touched their crucifixes in alarm as he invoked the Powers—though this time not, he noted, Mathilda or Odard. Rudi suspected some of them were giving thanks that Matti hadn't been hurt for reasons other than love of their princess; he wouldn't have liked to have to account for an injury to the Lady Regent himself. Then everyone was smiling and exclaiming over the size of the tigers and the rareness of finding a *streak*—a group—of young males together. Usually one would drive all others out of his territory, even his siblings.

"They might as well be our nobles," Matti said dryly.

Everyone laughed at that. Chaka unstoppered a chased silver flask and they all took a sip of the brandy as the foresters and varlets came up to skin the kills. Odard took out a tape measure and sized them both.

"Nine feet six inches and nine feet eleven inches, nose-tip to base of the spine," he said, and stood back to let the servants do their work.

"Not a record, but close," Chaka added. "That's a day not wasted!"

One of the foresters grinned up at Rudi as they turned the animals on their backs to begin the flaying; he was an older man in his thirties, a little gray in the close-cropped yellow hair.

"I've never seen a man move so fast, my lord," he said. "That was a good piece of work, keeping the tabby in play with the spear. You saved yourself a bad mauling there, maybe your life, and perhaps saved a couple of others as well."

Rudi nodded thanks and handed him the flask; he'd never liked being called *lord* or having people wait on him hand and foot—Juniper

Mackenzie had always done her share of the chores, and seen that he was raised the same way. The forester looked surprised, then took a quick swallow and handed it back, with a gasp of thanks; it was good brandy. Rudi drank again and returned the flask to Chaka, then puffed out a cloud of white breath.

"I was just barely fast *enough*," he said.

"That tiger had reflexes like a cat!" Odard said.

Rudi groaned. "Too close for comfort!"

"Let's get back to the lodge," Mathilda said. "It looks like more snow, to me."

Rudi cocked an eye skyward. It had been cold all day; now the temperature was falling again, and the wind was from the north. The tall firs swayed with it, sending showers of fine white crystals from the last day's fall down, and whipping up a ground mist. Snow rarely lay more than a few days in the valley flats, but this was a little higher; it might stick as long as a week here, in a cold winter. He swung into the saddle with the others and they headed back along their own trail; everyone started an old hunting song with a fierce bouncy tune, "The Eye of the Tiger."

"A good hunt," Chaka said again when they'd finished. "Nothing like it on a winter's day."

Rudi nodded agreement. "It is one way to liven up the Black Months, and it needs doing. Though it's more fun still if you stalk them alone or with one or two others. The best way is to use a blind over a water hole or a game trail."

Mathilda smiled quietly; a couple of the others probably thought he was putting it on.

"Oh, come on." One of Odard's friends, a knight named Drogo de Gaston. "I know you Mackenzies are supposed to be hardy and all that, but that's going a bit far, isn't it?"

Rudi grinned. "Well, we don't have as many tigers down in our part of the valley," he said. "Also all our crofters have longbows, and know how to use them."

That brought more good-natured chaffing, for all that some of these young men had lost fathers under the Mackenzie arrowstorm in the War of the Eye.

Soon the hills swung back, and they were at the lodge. The Flying M had been a place for country pleasures long before the Change, and it was built in rustic style of notched logs. Smoke whipped almost horizontally from fieldstone chimneys as they pulled up before the veranda of a long low main building; there were some detached cabins for the staff, plus stables and paddocks, and an airstrip with a ramp-and-catapult arrangement that was used to launch gliders in the summertime. Rudi found it homelike, and flying was one of life's great pleasures, right up there with sex—his blood father had been a pilot by trade, and had been aloft on the day the engines stopped.

Dinner was roast venison they'd killed two days earlier, and a lot of fun—though he suspected it would have been a good deal rowdier if Matti weren't present, and the making of assignations with the servant girls was reasonably discreet under her eye. Rudi refrained entirely.

Though why she minds when she doesn't want to sleep with me herself, I don't understand, he thought. *Strange folk, Christians.*

When the cake had been demolished, they had the luxury of real coffee. That was still rare and very expensive, since it had to be shipped in from Hawaii or South America, through seas that were often stormy and which held more pirates every year—his mother refused to serve it, except at feasts where everyone could have some. He was cautious about it, because he wanted to be able to sleep tonight. The same trade had brought in the oranges and dates and figs that went around with the sweet dessert wine. The liqueur was from the valley's own vineyards but also an import to the Protectorate, from Mount Angel and done *Trockenbeerenauslese*-style.

When he and Mathilda were alone by the fire she sipped from the golden-colored stuff in her glass and looked at him levelly before she said, "All right, Rudi, spill it."

He shrugged. " 'All my secrets I will share,' " he quoted, from the *anamchara* oath they'd sworn as children. "But these aren't all *my* secrets. They're the *Clan's* secrets. And you're the one who has to tell your mother *no* when she asks . . . which isn't something I'd want to have to do."

She winced slightly, then sighed. "I've done it before and I'll do it this time. Now spill it."

"OK, you remember that guy from the east, Ingolf Vogeler?"

"Yeah," she said dryly. "Seeing as we all nearly got killed saving him. You and he and Juniper were spending an awful lot of time talking."

"It was a story worth hearing," he said, and told it.

"*What?*" she said when he was finished, sitting up and putting her empty glass down, impatiently waving away one of the servants who came up to refill it. When they were alone: "Are you bullshitting me again, Rudi?" Her eyes narrowed. "Because if you are, this is no time for one of your jokes—"

"No, no, I swear it by Brigid and Ogma, may they curse me with stutters all my life if I lie, and that's how we had it from him."

Mathilda's mouth dropped open slightly. "And you all *believed* it? *Juniper* believed it?"

"We had reason," he said, going a little grim; and he noted that she thought he was more likely to be credulous than his mother.

Well, fair enough . . . Juniper had once told him there was nobody more skeptical of charlatans than those who'd been genuinely touched by the Divine. *And I've seen a few try to fool her over the years.* Anyone stupid enough to try came away sorry and sore; nobody tried twice.

"I'm not all that happy about it, you know, Matti. Things are . . . awkward. Mother went to the *nemed.*"

"The sacred wood? Why, what happened?" Mathilda said, startled and alarmed.

She had never been there except as a spectator for public rites like Juniper's wedding to Sir Nigel at the end of the War of the Eye; even that was pushing the limits of what her faith permitted. She knew what Rudi was talking about, though: a circle-casting and questions asked of the Powers. That was dangerous at the best of times, and when Juniper Mackenzie called, *They* were all too likely to answer.

I love the Lord and Lady, but They can be dangerous, he thought, remembering her white-faced exhaustion afterwards.

And They show us the Aspect that is in our hearts. Whether the pot hits the kettle or the kettle hits the pot . . . I think that's why They move so indirectly in this world. They are . . . too real . . . for it to be safe for us to meet Them face-to-face on this side of the Veil. So we see Them in dream and vision and prophecy, and through Their world itself instead. Even for people like Mom, meeting Them directly isn't something that can be done too often.

He looked up at her. "What is that bit in your Christian Bible? About asking for bread, and getting a stone? They told her something about me—have been saying it since I was just born. And it frightens her. Frightens her for me, and also for all of us."

Matti bit her lip, then shook her head as if clearing it. After an instant she burst out: "How can you think They're good, if They do things like that?"

Rudi found himself chuckling ruefully. "You can't tell everything to a two-year-old, can you?" Then he quoted, with malice aforethought: " 'Father, if it be possible, let this cup pass from me,' eh?"

Mathilda winced and smiled at the same time, started to say something, then decided not to—they'd learned a long time ago that religious arguments were pointless. Particularly when, as she said, arguing doctrine with a witch was like trying to cut fog with an ax. Then she shook her head, as if trying to bring it back to the world of men.

"Well, what happened after he saw this so-called Sword of the Lady? Wait a minute—aren't *you* supposed to be the Sword of the Lady?"

"Yeah. It's a Mystery."

Mathilda sighed; there was no answer to *that*. "What happened next?"

Rudi paused for a long moment, staring into the low blue-and-crimson flames that danced over the coals in the hearth. He shivered a little, remembering the haunted look in Vogeler's eyes whenever he forced himself to think of what had happened on the island.

"Then he came out of that place on Nantucket. . . ."

CHAPTER EIGHT

Ingolf Vogeler could hear screaming. After a moment he realized that his own voice was one of the chorus. He staggered backward, and turned his back. His face was slack; before him burned the sword, and the Voice, the Voice . . .

Travel from sunrise to the sunset, and seek the Son of the Bear Who Rules. The Sword of the Lady waits for him.

He quieted himself, his throat raw. Singh was trembling and gray; his sister's face was wet with tears, the first time Ingolf had ever seen her weep, even when they'd taken a barbed arrow out of her back with nothing for the pain but a slug of whiskey and a leather strap to clench between her teeth. Kuttner lay on the ground, his wide unseeing eyes staring up into the sky, making little mewing sounds where froth and blood mingled on his lips and bubbles blew to his short panting breaths.

And a fourth, a teenager in the dress of the Sea-Land people. He was visibly the chief's son, but light-skinned and his features sharper than his father's, his eyes hazel-green.

Ingolf tried to speak, but it was as if his mouth had forgotten the trick of it. He started to stumble forward, then stopped and grabbed at each of his companions in turn, shoving them towards the forest. Kuttner was the hardest; at first he tried to wiggle on his belly, then crawl forward on all fours like a beast, and in the end Ingolf had to stagger along with one of the smaller man's arms held across his shoulder.

The burden grew less as they walked into the shadow of the gnarled forest, keeping their backs to . . .

Ingolf felt himself shudder again. *I couldn't describe it to save my life. When I try to think about it I hear the Voice again.* And the presence of a hundred unlived lives jostled in his head. *Who is Ingolf, then?*

That pressure faded with every step; the world itself grew more solid around them, and the memories that weren't died away into a jumble of alien images. They were on a narrow trail through oakwood and smooth-barked beeches, panting and shuddering and looking at one another.

"Mother," Kaur mumbled. "Father. Kalil. Goolab—"

"*Chub'rao!*" Singh mumbled; it was the language he'd heard the two using between themselves occasionally, mingled with English. "Be silent! That was lies, lies, they are dead, they are dead these six years! *Daghabazi!* Treachery!"

The young man in the Sea-Land costume was looking around with growing excitement, but it was tinged with fear. He spoke unexpectedly in halting English:

"Time . . . time is summer?"

Ingolf nodded.

"I go . . . Place of Dreams . . . get man-dream . . . snow on ground. *Winter.*"

Ingolf grunted, scarcely taking it in. They went farther, and Kuttner could walk on his own, in a shambling sort of way. Ingolf thought of asking what he'd seen, then looked into his eyes and decided not to. His own brain was starting to work again, and he wondered why the tribe weren't still standing there watching. Had there been something that they could see way back there? He found the place they'd stood . . . and the tracks were old and faded.

It's rained since then, he thought.

He looked at the faint dimpled impressions of bare feet and moccasins among the leaves and litter, and the marks of his own folk's boot heels, and his mind began to whirl again. A beetle walked down into the mark, crumbling a little more sand into it. The outline was soft, not crisp and sharp and recent. Then he looked up at the leaves; they weren't as full and lush as they'd been; in fact, they were starting to look tattered. Sweat prickled him under his armor.

"Let's get going," he said roughly.

They strode down the forest trail. He inhaled deeply to savor the musty scent of leaf mold, the weight of his shete and quiver on his back, anything *real*. A squirrel ran up the rough bark of a pine and chattered at him. A deer had gone across the trail not too long ago, mark of the cloven hooves still sharp and distinct.

Finally they came across one of the people from the village, a girl about the age of the young man who'd unexpectedly turned up. She was clothed in a deerskin wrap around her waist, with long reddish hair falling past her shoulders, and carried a reed basket full of wild blueberries. She stopped as she saw them, gave a small shriek, dropped the basket and fled with a twinkle of heels, screaming rhythmically as she sprinted. By the time they'd reached the little inlet and the garden fields around the houses, everyone was lined up. They looked frightened. . . .

Ah, Ingolf thought, flogging his brain into action. *They're afraid we're back from the dead.*

"We're not ghosts!" he called—despite a momentary uncertainty; what if they *were*?

The young man with them suddenly cried out and dashed forward. Sun Hair pushed past her husband and caught him fiercely to her.

"Frank! Frank!"

The tense silence broke in joyful shouts.

* * *

"You should stay," Sun Hair said a day later.

"Can't do that, ma'am," Ingolf said, shaking her hand.

They were at the water's edge, and the tide was in; it was barely dawn, and the water farther out looked like purple streaked with cream as the sun broke over the eastern horizon. Kuttner had recovered enough to be looking visibly impatient. Even the gulls' sharp *skreek-skreek-skreek* overhead seemed to be urging him on—though he knew that was probably his own fear. Singh and Kaur were already on board and hauling up the anchor, which was a hint too.

Her husband was there to see them off, along with most of his folk, and his son Frank. The older man spoke to his wife, but his eyes were on Ingolf. She translated the sonorous words:

"My man says you have brought back his son who he thought was dead for half a year. You have good luck with your spirit that turns aside evil magic, and you are a strong man who can hunt and fight and make strong sons and daughters. If you stay, we'll give you our daughter for a first wife, and build you a house and a boat for fishing and whale catching, and help you clear planting land. The . . . the . . . family—"

She waved around at all the people present; the word she was looking for was probably *tribe* or *clan*.

"—will be glad to welcome you. Your friends too."

Touched, Ingolf held out his hand to the older man; they shook, a firm hard grip.

"Tell him I'm honored," he said, which he found was true. "But I have my own people, who are depending on me. I am promised to them."

The chief of the Sea-Land tribe nodded; then he held up one hand with the palm out in a gesture of farewell. Ingolf returned it, then waded out into the chill water and vaulted over the side of the sailboat.

And it's over two weeks since I landed here, though I only lived two days of that. And young Frank was there six months, and he thought it was only an eyeblink too. I'm getting as far away from here as I can!

He shuddered as the Voice murmured at the back of his mind. It had been loud in his dreams last night. Would he ever be free of it?

"Let's see how getting really far away works," he muttered to himself. The others didn't notice, lost in their own thoughts. "It wants me to go west, anyway. That sounds *fine* right now."

Even half a continent empty of everything but ruins and vicious savages didn't sound too bad compared to staying close to *that* place.

* * *

"It's a whiles after the date I told Jose to clear out," he said as they neared Innsmouth. *A full week, in fact,* he thought with a slight shudder.

"Then why are we heading back *there?*" Kuttner asked.

He squinted across the bright water; the wind had been strong and favorable, and it was midafternoon. Nothing moved but birds, and leaf and branch waving in the stiff onshore breeze. Farther out all you could see was green; now they were close enough to see the buildings staring at them with empty eye sockets, and smell the faintest tinge of rot and ancient smoke under the greenness of the returning forest.

I will not be back east, even if I lose everything I made on this trip, Ingolf knew suddenly. *I'll hoe spuds for a living and sleep in a barn for the rest of my life before I come east again. This country is poisoned.*

"Why?" Kuttner said again, more sharply.

"Because I told Jose to go, but I'm not sure he did; he could have stayed a bit, thinking he could talk me around if I showed up. If he did go, he'll have left a message. It's not going to be easy, getting out of here alive on foot. Not easy to catch a mounted caravan on foot, either, but we'll be a lot less likely to go into the stewpot if we can."

With fifty men and a train of wagons, you could just bull your way through. Four alone would have to spend a lot of time dodging and hiding. Even on horseback, they'd have trouble catching up. On foot . . . that would be hard. Everyone was perking up; Singh and Kaur nodded soberly.

Of course, Ingolf thought, *if we can get out of here alive, it'll be a lot easier with those two along.*

They stopped outside the harbor bar to suit up. The tension was almost welcome as they docked and sprang ashore, weapons ready, but the silence remained. Hot sun baked smells out of earth and sea—some familiar, some oddly alien, sharp metallic pungencies and oily half sweetness. They waited tensely, but nothing moved.

"Wait a minute," he said, and jumped back into the boat.

There was a satisfaction in chopping through the bottom, even though the springy material resisted his tomahawk, and then he nearly lost it when it did punch through a weakened patch at last and the splintered fibers gripped it. Water came bubbling through as he wrenched it free; then he slid the handle back into the loop at his back and drew his shete to slash the rigging and the furled sail to ribbons. When that was finished he bent the mast against the joint by hauling on a rope fastened to its top. That took a moment of straining effort, but he was rewarded with a grating rip of metal, and the aluminum pole tipped over.

"Why are you wasting time?" Kuttner said, when he jumped back to the dock; the sailboat was already listing.

"Because someone might have been watching and getting ideas," Ingolf said, as he sheathed the yard of steel in the scabbard across his back and took up his bow again. "I don't want any of the wild men going sailing for their meat; that would be poor thanks for the folks who helped us. They're less likely to try it if they don't have an intact boat. Now let's get going."

There *was* a message, left in a hide bag fastened to a tree with a dagger. That was a message in itself—none of the wild men had come back, for they would certainly have taken both. He reached inside and unfolded the papers.

One was a letter on thick cream-colored modern paper; some of the fibers in its coarse surface scritched on his calluses. The other was a piece of crumbling pre-Change glossy, with a tourist map of Innsmouth on it. The note was short and to the point:

Capitán, stuff at the X. Killed more wild men second attack seventeenth August; lost Smith, Alterman and Montoya. We left twenty-sixth; see you in Des Moines if not before. Go with God.

X turned out to be a warehouse, a blank windowless building of rusty pressed metal. On the ground in front of it was a circle of fresh scorch marks, where a dozen of the magnesium flares had been set off. He looked more closely, and saw the trip wires of a deadfall setup; there was a wild man, too, dead with a crossbow bolt through the chest. From the looks of the swollen, blackened body and the oily-sweet stink and the maggots, the man had been there for at least three or four days, in weather like this. Kuttner had his shete out and was glaring around.

"Relax . . . relax a bit," Ingolf said.

The Iowan indicated the body. Ingolf nodded. "And nobody came back to eat it," he pointed out. "Jose set this up. Let's see what he left us."

They approached the doors warily, which proved to be wise: Singh pointed out another trip wire, grinning as he stood aside and triggered it with a long stick. A *tunng* sounded from within the warehouse, and a bolt flashed through the air, landing with a *cruch* sound in the body of a rusted FedEx delivery van across the road.

"That Jose, he is a clever man!" the big Sikh said, looking more natural than Ingolf had seen him since they landed on Nantucket.

"And inside is what'll save our lives."

He'd been pretty sure of what *was* inside, from the barnyard smell: their horses, plus a remount each and a couple for bearing packsaddles. There was just enough water left in the buckets and containers set up to last them another day, and the food was about gone. The animals were frantic-glad to see them; Boy came and nuzzled him carefully, making extra-sure it was really him, and incidentally checking him over for anything edible. He gave the horse some dried apples he carried, pushing off the others and trying to decide whether he was angry or grateful.

Some of both, he decided. *Sure, they would have died of thirst soon or the wild men would have eaten 'em, and I really* like *Boy. On t'other hand, in the end people matter more than critters. He didn't weaken the Villains much by leaving these, and he probably saved our lives. And Jose isn't sentimental about animals.*

That was true even by the standards of a farm boy, or a horse-soldier who'd seen the trail of equine carcasses a hard-pressed pursuit left. Their tack was there too, plus some extra supplies—jerky and dried berries, spare arrows, presized horseshoes so their mounts could be cold-shod, tools, and basic camping gear. *And* a substantial share of the melted-down gold and selected jewelry, neatly lashed into bundles of convenient size—convenient for a packhorse, and convenient to grab and run if you had to leave the beast behind.

Ingolf swore admiringly and shook his head; Jose did think ahead. But then, the Tejano had been a wandering paid soldier for a long time, nearly as long as the profession had existed post-Change. He'd told a lot of stories, including some where the hired soldiers robbed the ones who hired them. And others where the employers were suddenly struck with the thought—after the fighting was over—that dead men didn't draw pay.

Jose's loyal to his friends, he thought. *That's for damned sure.*

"Let's get going," he said, lifting his saddle and blanket off a crate stenciled to proclaim that it was full of TV remote controls, whatever those were, from South Korea, wherever the hell that was. "I want to be a long way from here by dark."

* * *

CENTRAL ILLINOIS
OCTOBER 30, CY21/2019 A.D.

The prairie's just so goddamned huge, Ingolf thought.

That was the biggest thing about it: the sheer *size*, and around here it was nearly flat, with a roll you had to concentrate to see over an hour or so of jogging along at walk-trot-canter-trot-walk. In a generation the grasses had conquered anew the empire that the settlers' steel plows had ripped away, and the wildfires had burned out most of the remnants of house and barn and fence.

Tall grass rippled in endless green-bronze surging waves under the mild dry breeze, to a horizon infinitely distant in every direction. The sound of it was an endless *sssssSSSSSSsssss*, growing and then fading again as each wave went by, over and over, like ocean foam on a sandy beach. Even the noonday sun seemed to hang unchanging for a while overhead.

The scent it baked out of the grass was like lying in a haymow, but wilder and with a spicy tang to it. And there was the first hint of winter to come; it was just cool enough to be comfortable in a mail shirt with a padded gambeson beneath, but the crisp air held a hint that told you a blizzard could hit anytime from now on and leave you hip-deep in snow.

The land wasn't much like the forested hills and tilled river valleys of Ingolf's home, but the weather gave him a pang of nostalgia for the long cool days of Indian summer along the Kickapoo. Homelike too were the geese and ducks that made ragged Vs in the afternoon sky above, their honking a lonely chorus to accompany the beat of hooves and creak of saddle leather.

He'd spent a lot of time in country like this, in Iowa and Nebraska and southern Minnesota. The only trees were clumps marking old windbreaks around farmsteads, and many of those were dead and burnt. A few maple and burr-oak saplings had taken root in breaks in the asphalt—it protected them from the fires and competition from the grasses. This wasn't his kind of country, but it was a kind he'd ridden often enough, and that was almost a homecoming.

"Don't get overconfident," he said, sensing the growing cheer of his companions. "We're not home until we cross the Mississippi—or catch up to Jose and the guys."

Singh grunted. "If we ever do, after the way we've had to go back and forth," he said.

Which was fair enough. The last delay had been when they tried to take a shortcut and got stranded in thousands of square miles of renascent wetland the maps didn't show, before finding the trail again—you couldn't just barrel down the old interstates, not these days. This road was a guess at Jose's probable choices. Too many bridges and overpasses were out. He couldn't even rely on his second-in-command taking exactly the same route back as they'd used coming out, since the local wild men would be on the lookout for that.

He could have gone farther south, to cross the Illinois where it runs north and south instead of east and west, Ingolf fretted.

This had been a secondary road in the old days, two-lane blacktop, and it lay on natural high ground, running northward to cross the Illinois River and connect with old US 80, which would give a good run west to cross the Mississippi at Muscatine. The grass alongside the cracked remnants of pavement was mostly big bluestem, seven or eight feet tall in this season, where it hadn't been flattened by the weather; you had to stand in the stirrups to see over it. The heads branched out into three lobed "turkey feet" over long reddish blue stems thick as a man's little finger.

Now and then they passed the tilted, rust-tattered remains of a silo or barn; a drumlike booming came from one where the breeze buckled a stretch of sheet metal like a saw flexing between two hands, echoing with lonely persistence over the empty land.

It's just as dangerous here as the East Coast, even if it isn't as spooky, he reminded himself. *More so, perhaps.*

The hordes from the Chicago metroplex had met those from Peoria and even East St. Louis here, and the die-off had been bad; many had been so ignorant of country life that they'd perished fighting for scraps in the shadow of grain elevators and silos still mostly full.

The children of the survivors were perhaps a bit less like two-legged rats than the ones farther east; for one thing they'd been joined over the years by desperate outlaws and broken men drifting in from Iowa and north Missouri over the Mississippi. A few had taken to trading across the river in hides and furs, and most of them didn't eat human flesh anymore. That didn't mean they wouldn't rob and kill—and they had horses and bows and shetes to do it with, many of them.

A stirring in the long grass brought his bow up, but it was only a mob of feral cattle. There was no point in shooting, since they had the better part of a yearling elk across one of the packhorses. The herd crossed the old roadway eastward in a bawling, surging mass as they became aware of the humans, their heads up in fear. Several hundred went by; animals had crossed the river too, and bred back swiftly in these rich empty lands.

They'd seen plenty of deer and elk and beaver as well, and sign of catamounts and wolves, bears and tigers, even a few buffalo. These cow-beasts were lean and rangy and long of horn, but their smell was nostalgic. His father had been a great cattle breeder, and had made Readstown famous throughout the Kickapoo Valley for his Angus and Holstein studs bred up from stock . . . acquired . . . right after the Change.

Kaur came trotting back across the fields from the northwest, riding bent over so that she was invisible until she was in earshot except as a ripple in the grass. She shouted their cry—"The Villains!"—to alert them and reined in, throwing him a casual salute as she came within speaking distance. The brother and sister were ragged and filthy; everyone in the little group was, after two months of flight and occasional fight winning their way west. She and Singh still managed to look as if they were about to be inspected, somehow.

"I saw their campsite, Captain," she said.

"Good! Whereabouts are they headed?"

"The bridge is still up at Spring Valley," she said, pointing back with her bow hand. "Just go one road over; it's US 89 on the map, straight north on that. But once you're up out of the river flats and the old town-site on the north bank the land is black for a couple of miles—that was as far as I went—prairie fire. Still smoking. Jose left the 'proceeding as normal' sign at the bridge."

"*Thought* there'd been a fire," Ingolf said—they'd seen the smoke passing from east to west ahead of them earlier that day. "Well, we'll get through the burn fast as we can."

Not having any grain for feed cut how hard and long you could push horses, even switching off with your other mount several times a day; particularly if you wanted them to have any reserve for an emergency, when losing a horse meant losing your life. They stopped to let them graze for an hour or so. He ate some of the elk they'd cooked that morning with notable lack of enthusiasm.

"What I'd give for fresh bread and French fries and catsup," he said.

"Or some vegetables," Singh agreed. "Or an apple."

He looked around at the ground where they squatted, then dug at it with his bowie for a moment, pulling up a clump of bluestem. He had to lean back to do it, with all the strength of his body behind it before the main stem cracked audibly. Some of the roots were as thick as a pencil, and the ground that clung to it was a fine dark gray whose clods would be coal black when they were wet.

"This is good land," the Sikh said. "It seems a pity it isn't farmed."

Ingolf nodded; the thought had occurred to him and Jose. "Yeah," he said. "But you'd need at least a thousand people to make a settlement here in the wild lands—and a fort, windmills, all sorts of stuff besides stock and tools and enough to keep you for a year or two until you had a big enough crop in. Not safe otherwise."

Kaur snorted and picked a piece of gristle out from between her teeth. "I will not farm again," she said quietly.

Ingolf tossed a gnawed rib aside and wiped the back of one big hand across his mouth before taking a swig from his canteen. "Let's get to it."

There was the usual short delay as a horse decided it wanted to stop for the night right here, but they were all hobbled and easy to catch. The short route to the bridge lay off the slightly raised roadbed; as they turned into the grass visibility shrank to less than the length of a lance, but that worked both ways—they were no longer visible themselves. Pushing through the tall coarse growth slowed the horses, and you had to watch out for pits and traps; old basements and foundations, pieces of farm machinery that had lain out for better than twenty years, and tangles of elderly barbed wire. Posts burned but the wire endured until rust broke it, unless someone harvested it to make chain mail or a new fence.

The iron-shod hooves crushed a path, and trampled nodding yellow-petaled black-eyed Susans like giant daisies, clusters of purple-blue iron-weed with flocks of silver-spotted skippers hovering about them, and blue gentian. Quail burst out from under their hooves occasionally; Kaur nailed one to the ground with an arrow before it could flog itself into the air, bent in the saddle and scooped it up, then dropped back to the packhorse that held their meat.

"Bit of a change." Ingolf nodded.

They came up onto another road. He grunted in satisfaction at the sight of saplings crushed down where they'd taken root in broken spaces in the pavement; that and a neat circular space trampled flat in the long grass meant that Jose and the others had come through here with the wagons. He looked at the campfires and over at Kaur.

"Last night?"

"Last night." She nodded with satisfaction.

"By God, if we're lucky we may actually catch them by first dark!"

The river ran through a depression in the flat land with scalloped sides, an irregular ribbon of woods through the grasslands, bare-branched gray except where faded yellow and dark red tatters told of autumn's blaze and burn. The road bridge was a metal truss on concrete piers; a fresh gash in the railing on the western side showed where someone, almost certainly the Villains, had pushed an ancient truck over the side. It stood like a new island downstream, the water rippling around it, shedding the rust of a generation to join the Mississippi.

Ingolf sniffed. The scent of burning was strong now, and there was still a little gritty ash drifting in, making him blink watering eyes. They all wet down their bandannas from their canteens and tied them across their mouths before they left the ruins of the little city of Spring Valley.

Out on the flatlands north of town the grassland was burned down to stubble, leaving an empty plain of blackness. Smoke drifted over it from patches still smoldering; nothing stood above ground level save the charred stumps of trees and an occasional snag of wall. The desolate appearance was deceptive; in a single season this would be lush prairie again, growing all the stronger for the layer of ash. The tall grasses kept much of their bulk down belowground, and however hot the flame it didn't kill out the roots. The seeds of some of the other plants *needed* fire to germinate. Every season's fire gnawed away a little more of the works of men, though.

He coughed into the damp cloth. "I hope our folks got out in time," he said, worry in his voice.

They all nodded, familiar with the dangers of a prairie fire. In old dry grass like this the wall of flame could be twenty or thirty feet high, traveling faster than a galloping horse and ready to scorch out the lungs of anything it caught. He stood in the stirrups where the road turned west and peered under a sheltering hand, squinting against the midafternoon sun.

"Doesn't look like the fire's still going," he said. "Not enough smoke."

Singh nodded. "The wind's shifted," he pointed out. It was in their faces now, carrying gusts of smoke and ash. "It's usually westerly around here anyway. That would push the fire back onto the burned ground."

Ingolf jerked his head in anxious agreement. "Think the wild men could have set it?" Kaur said, jogging along a little ahead.

"Could be. Could be they did it to drive game—it's time for their big fall hunts."

Or they could have done it to cover an attack, Ingolf thought. *Or even if they didn't, they'd take the chance to kill and rob anyone caught in it.*

By unspoken common consent they legged their horses up into a canter on the shoulder of the road. Out in the burned-over fields small explosions of crows and buzzards took off from the blackened corpses of animals caught in the fire. After a half mile Ingolf swore and got out his binoculars for an instant.

"That's the wagons, all right. *Hup!*"

They rocked up into a hard gallop. The five big vehicles were strung out on the road in marching order. One was burning, the stores-wagon, with little bitter gouts of flame when the flames hit something like linseed oil or the varnish on a spare bow. The four with the loot weren't; someone had taken the trouble to lash down the spare tilts over the everyday ones and lace everything tight, which gave sparks few places to light on vehicles mostly made of pre-Change metal. For the rest, from the signs they'd just taken all the horses and bolted when it became clear the fire was going to hit, which was sensible.

He and Kaur and Singh threw their lassoes over bits of the burning wagon, snubbed the lariats to the horns of their saddles and backed the animals, pulling it lurching and smoking a safe distance from the others. The horses snorted and protested, but they were too well disciplined to really balk. Then they turned west again, riding hard.

"Shit," Ingolf swore; it was far too serious for *uff da*.

The first body was an ostler named Sauer they'd hired east of Kalona; he'd quarreled with his farmer and been turned out of his cottage and job, but he'd always pulled his weight on the trip. Sauer had burned, and died of it. The rest of the bodies were hidden by a heaving carpet of buzzards and crows and ravens, but they were just *off* the scorched zone, where streaky fingers of black stretched into the bronze-brown of untouched prairie. The bluestem was trampled flat for several hundred square yards. Carrion birds took wing in a black cloud as the riders came up, revealing the arrow stubs.

"Hit them as they came out of the smoke," Singh said grimly, pointing to where a ragged line lay, along with several dead horses.

Ingolf nodded, his throat too tight to speak. A straggling trail of bodies showed where the pursuit had gone.

"These took one with them each," he said with angry pride, reading the signs on the ground.

A circle of bodies marked where Jose and about a dozen had made a last stand. The suddenness of it winded him, like someone starting a fight with an unexpected punch in the gut; half an hour ago he'd been looking forward to seeing the man again, and now there he lay on his back with the stubs of two arrows through his mail shirt and most of his face gone from the birds. There was blood on the broken shete that lay near his hand; he'd gotten that much at least.

Six years I knew you, he thought. *Battle and hunt and camp and barroom. We saved each other's lives more times than I can count. You taught me better than half of what I know. Go with God, brother.*

He dismounted and knelt for a second with head bowed over clasped hands, asking that there be mercy for the soul of Jose Menendez, one-time sergeant in the Lomas Altas Emergency Guard, of late troop leader in Vogeler's Villains. Then he covered the ravaged face with a broken shield.

And for you, Greg, Tommy, Dave, Will, he thought, fury building. *You all deserved better than this.*

Singh was gray-faced and shaking. "The wild men will suffer for this; their tents will burn and their women will weep," he said thickly. "We will avenge them, we will—"

"Wait!" Kaur said. "Would the wild men leave their armor? Harness on the horses?"

Ingolf took a deep breath and then another, scrubbing a hand across his face, the rough leather of his glove scratching and pulling at the hairs of his cropped beard.

"Think, you cheese-head hayseed, goddamnit," he whispered savagely to himself.

His eyes darted about. "Yeah, and the arrowheads, and everything else . . . cloth, tools, shoes . . . they'd have stripped the bodies bare and dug out all the broken arrows. And scalped them. And butchered the dead horses for their meat and hides. All that this bunch took was the live horses and the shetes and knives and bows."

"You are right," Singh said.

He pulled a broken lance shaft out of a horse's torso with a grunt, then stabbed it into the ground to clean it off. The three of them stood around it and looked, with Kuttner still mounted and keeping an eye out.

Ingolf grunted again. The lance head was about eight inches long, fastened to the mountain-ash shaft with a skillfully forged tubular socket heat-shrunk onto the wood. It wasn't quite the style of any he was familiar with, but it was far too well made for a wild-man troop, even this far west. And . . .

He took it from the Sikh and held it so the westering sun caught the surface and showed irregularities, especially where dried blood stuck. A rayed sun was etched into the steel.

"Kaur!" he said. "Your shete!"

She drew and held it out beside the broken lance; the design on the sun figure was identical.

"Something stinks here," Ingolf said grimly.

A sound from Kuttner interrupted him, and then Kaur's cry of alarm an instant later. Ingolf vaulted into the saddle and got out his binoculars. The sun was winking on more lance heads, and beneath them the distant dots of riders. He rough-counted. . . .

"At least thirty," he said. His head twisted around. The ground here was flat as a tabletop and devoid of cover, no place to make a stand. "We'll head south for the river—there's broken country there."

"Wait!" Kuttner said. "Give me two more horses and I'll lead a drag."

The three Villains looked at him, surprised. Leading a drag was a standard trick of plains-country warfare, to raise a plume of dust and deceive watchers. Volunteering for it here was also suicide. . . .

"Better me than all of us. You can escape and tell the bossman in Des Moines what happened to his expedition."

Nodding in grudging respect for the man's loyalty, Ingolf started to help. It took only a few seconds to rig some gear on the end of a rope; Kuttner took the leading reins of the two packhorses and spurred his mount straight east. He didn't even bother to take his remount. Ingolf

felt a slight pang—one of those horses was carrying the bundled pro-
ceeds that Jose had left for them back in Innsmouth—but living through
this and finding out who was responsible for the massacre was more
important.

The three of them paused only to sling spare quivers to their saddlebows and then turned south at a gallop, each leading a single remount.
Grass whipped at his thighs and the horse's face; Boy ran with his head
lifted, and the sound was a constant *shhhsshsh* beneath the drumbeat of
hooves. Distantly behind them a bugle blew; the enemy, whoever they
were, had spotted them. Now everything depended on how fresh the
killers' horses were and how their luck went.

They went flat-out for two miles, just outside the line of burned
ground, then reined in to a canter; the horses were beginning to blow,
fruits of two thousand miles of hard work. Luckily they'd all been reshod
recently, so they'd be less likely to go lame unexpectedly. They all looked
over their shoulders as well. Kuttner's dust plume was clear, where his
drag scratched the ashy soil of the burn. And behind him . . .

"A bunch of them split off after Kuttner," Kaur said. "At least a dozen
are still after us, though, Captain."

"A dozen's better odds than thirty." Ingolf grunted thoughtfully.

It puzzled him; the stunt Kuttner had pulled was the sort of thing you
did for comrades-in-arms or close friends, and the man had never even
tried to be that, despite their going all the way to the Atlantic and back
together. He'd always been a disagreeable bossy son of a bitch; they'd
come to grudgingly respect him, but no more.

They turned onto the burnt ground—trying for the river would be
impossible otherwise, but it made their dust plume a lot worse. As they
switched horses Singh and Ingolf exchanged glances; they both rode a
lot heavier in the saddle than Kaur, by at least thirty or forty pounds. Her
horses were less tired to start with and would last longer in a stern chase.
Useless to try to get her to bug out, though.

Ingolf's next glance was over at the sun. *Three hours to dark,* he thought.
Just low enough to get in our eyes, not enough to do us any good.

A few instants after that the extra plume of gray ash told him their
pursuers had crossed onto the burned ground too. Canter-trot-canter-
walk . . . the dust grew closer; the enemy were pushing their horses hard,
or they had lots of fresh remounts, or both. Probably both.

"*Uff da*," Ingolf swore.

That they couldn't hope to win an arrow duel was so obvious none of them had to say anything about it. There *weren't* any good options when you were outnumbered by five to one, but riding over an open plain and shooting was about the worst possible choice. If you had any choices.

"Which we don't," Ingolf muttered to himself.

"They think they can pin us against the river before we can cross," Kaur said clinically.

It turned out they were right; the riders were in close sight before the fingers of lower land stretching down to the Illinois River came in reach, no more than three or four hundred yards behind. Ingolf peered over his shoulder again; there were fifteen of them and all had helmets on, and of the same variety—low rounded domes with a central spike and cheek flaps. He made a hissing sound between his teeth. Even most full-time paid soldiers didn't usually wear uniform equipment. That was the sort of thing you saw only on a Bossman's guards.

And not the Bossman of Des Moines. His folk's gear is different, shaped more like the old army helmet.

He couldn't see for sure what they were wearing for armor, but he could be certain it wasn't the bright-polished chain mail favored by the household troops of Iowa's ruler.

They carried lances, little upright threads tipped with an eyeblink of metal. The bottom four feet or so of each was probably resting in a scabbard—a tube of boiled leather slung at the right rear of the saddle, which kept it out of the way when you were doing something else. Right now the something else was drawing their bows. . . .

"*Incoming!*" Kaur shouted and ducked, hunching in the saddle so that the shield slung across her back covered the largest possible share of her body.

A dozen arrows fell in a hissing sleet, mostly five or ten yards short but uncomfortably well aimed and bunched. A single exception slammed into the back of a remount with a hard wet *thmack* sound, and the animal collapsed behind them, its hind legs limp, screaming like an off-key bugle as it struggled and jerked and the shaft in its spine waggled.

As one, they all signaled their horses up to a gallop and turned in the saddle to shoot back, rising in the stirrups and clamping their thighs hard against the leather in the moment they loosed. The surviving pair of remounts galloped ahead as their reins were dropped, herd instinct keeping them from doing the sensible thing and scattering. Ingolf exhaled as he drew, the thick muscles of his right arm bunching against the sinew and Osage-orange wood and horn of the recurve. Thousands of hours of practice starting when he was seven guided the angle to which he raised the bow before letting the string roll off the fingers.

Snap of bowstring against the scarred steel surface of his bracer, and the recoil slammed him back against the high cantle of his saddle. *Snap-snap*, and the brother and sister fired as well.

The arrows slapped out, seeming to slow as they arched towards the distant dot-sized figures of the pursuers. More came back, and those seemed to go *faster* as they approached. Two went by with unpleasant *vvvvvptttt* sounds before burying themselves in the ash-black ground, *shunk-shunk*.

This wasn't the first time he'd done something like this. It was just as unpleasant as he remembered, and would have been worse if he hadn't been so caught up in surviving moment to moment. That sound of arrows going by was the sort you remembered years later, leaving you depressed and sweating just when you were about to kiss a girl or bite into an apple.

Assuming I ever get to do either again, he thought, hearing Boy's valiant laboring beneath him as he shot and shot again.

Then the lip of the ravine leading down to the river was close. Another flight of arrows came in just as they urged their mounts over the edge. The animals went down it fast, sometimes squatting on their haunches, then hit the old path at the base running until they were around a corner two hundred yards eastward, with tall oak and maple all around and thick brush between the trees, the steep bank close to the water's edge.

Kaur's gasp of pain was bitten off. Ingolf didn't look over until they'd stopped. When he did his stomach lurched. Not that the wound was mortal in itself; the chain mail and the padded canvas underneath had absorbed most of the force of the arrow, leaving only a few inches of it sticking into her hip. Red was leaking out through the mail already, and running down her leg, though not the arterial pumping that spelled a swift end. With nursing and care she could recover. But with the arrowhead lodged in bone, it would be impossible for her to ride fast, or to run and fight.

Right now, that meant death. He saw her accept it, biting her lip until the blood flowed; then her brother did as well.

"We will see *pitaji* again," she said. "I knew when we saw their faces again in the place of magic that we were fated. *Karman.*"

Singh nodded, then turned his face to Ingolf: "This is as good a place as any. We'll hold them as long as we can. Ride hard, my friend."

They leaned over to clasp hands for an instant. "It has been an honor, Captain. Avenge our blood."

Ingolf nodded, not wasting time on saying what they both knew. Singh swung down and handed him the reins of his horse.

His teeth were bared as he turned and got Boy back to a gallop, and clods of earth flew up from the hammering hooves. No point in holding back now; he had to try to break contact before the enemy caught up with him, and he ignored the low branches and brush that flogged at his face or rang off his helmet as he ducked and wove. The Illinois River was to his right, flowing from east to west here as he rode upstream, a long bowshot across—call it three hundred yards. It flowed quietly, with only a little gurgling chuckle at the edge. His own harsh breathing sounded louder in his ears.

A yell came from behind him, faint and far now. Then another, a man screaming in astonished pain, and then a clash of steel on steel. That followed him for perhaps a hundred of Boy's long strides; then it stopped, and he knew the two Sikhs were dead. He glanced behind as he went down a long straight stretch, and caught the first glitter of steel.

"Shit!" he snarled, and reached over his shoulder for an arrow. "They must have sent men around Singh."

The pursuers dropped back as he shot again, dropped out of sight, though that wouldn't last for more than seconds. The path twisted around and split. He made an instant decision and turned right, throwing aside the leading reins of Singh's horse and slapping it on the rump with his bow as it went by. Then he took the right-hand branch, down to the edge of the water.

It was nearly under the piers of the Spring Valley bridge; Boy gave a single are-you-sure-boss snort and jumped into the water, striking out strongly for the opposite shore. Ingolf let himself slip out of the saddle, holding his bow above the surface with one hand and clinging to the saddle horn with the other. Water sloshed into his clothing with a cold shock, and he could feel the dragging weight as the padding under his mail shirt soaked it up. You could swim in war gear . . . but not for long.

He was three-quarters of the way across and in the shadow of the bridge when the first of the enemy went pelting past the spot he'd left, galloping flat-out. That meant the men in the lead were either very brave or completely reckless; there were any number of nasty tricks you could play on a narrow trail.

One . . . two . . . three . . .

The total had gone up to nine before one of them reined in, bringing his horse up on its hind legs. That took skill; so did avoiding a tangled collision by the two behind him, who split around the rearing horse. The too-alert one pointed to the ground, then across the river. Yelling, the three horsemen spurred down to the water's edge, and into it.

"Shit!"

That had been a long shot, and it hadn't panned out. But three-to-one was a lot better odds than twelve-to-one. As Boy came out of the water he thought quickly while hooves went clattering on rock and making wet sucking sounds in the muck. The horse shook himself, spattering more water around; Ingolf got into the saddle and headed east again, on the south side of the river this time, urging the most out of his mount. The trees grew thicker as they blurred past; this path had been graveled once, but it had seen only the hooves of deer and elk, mustangs and feral cattle for the past generation.

One hour to sunset now, he thought. *Only an hour.*

Rock grew higher south of the river, layers of banded sandstone that caught the dying sun bloodred. They made sound echo, and sometimes treacherously die off or seem more distant than it was. The more so as he bore south and high walls closed around him on both sides, dark where the rock blocked the sun. Hooves clattered on stones and thudded on sand, where the ancient floods had carved this passage.

There.

The right spot, where a bulge of rock narrowed the passage through the canyon. His bow went into the saddle scabbard, and he brought his shield around from his back and slid his left forearm into the loops.

He reined in and slid from Boy's saddle while the animal was still moving; it carried on around a curve in the canyon wall, slowing down and looking back. The man plastered himself flat against the rock; in the same motion he drew his shete, holding it high with the point back, suddenly conscious of his own panting breath, and how paper-dry his mouth was, while the rest of him streamed water. The pursuers' gallop hammered at his ears, bouncing off the stony walls around him, making it hard to judge just where they were.

He could hear their barking, yelping cry, too: "Cut! Cut! *Cut!*"

"I'll give you a cut, you son of a bitch," he snarled to himself.

A lance point flashed as it came around the corner, giving him a fractional second's warning and showing where the man's arm must be—poised to thrust it into his back as he fled.

"Richland!" he bellowed.

As he shouted Ingolf pivoted with tiger precision and swung, whipping the long cutting blade forward with every ounce of strength his shoulders and back could muster. Combined with the speed of the galloping horse the sharp metal cut through a mail-shod gauntlet, through flesh and bone and flesh and then through the tough shaft of the lance itself. The mounted warrior rode on for a dozen paces, screaming in shock and staring at the stump where his hand had been, the blood spurting out with fire-hose speed, then toppled and lay flopping and twitching.

The one following him slugged his mount back on its haunches with desperate brutality, dropping his lance and going for his shete. Ingolf ignored it, dropping his own weapon and darting in to grab one booted foot and heave with all his strength. The rider flew out of his saddle and into the rock wall of the canyon as if springs had pulled him. The helmeted head went *bonnnngggg* on the rock and the neck snapped beneath it. That horse went past too, riderless, buffeting Ingolf back with a force that brought a grunt as he was slammed into the canyon wall.

The third rider had an arrow on his bowstring. He drew and shot, in the same instant that Ingolf's hand whipped up across the small of his back and forward in a throw. Tomahawk and arrow crossed each other in flight. The arrow banged painfully off Ingolf's mail-clad shoulder, and the head of the tomahawk sank with a meaty smack and crunch into the rider's jaw. He toppled backward over his horse's crupper, trying to scream and succeeding only in gobbling. Gauntlets beat at the ground in futile agony as Ingolf pounced. The back of the wounded man's neck was protected by an aventail of steel splints fixed to rings on the helmet brim, but they bent and snapped as Ingolf drove his boot heel down again and again.

Silence fell, except for the sound of the wind hooting through the rock, and the horses stamping and moving restlessly. Ingolf limped back to his shete—where had that small cut on his left thigh just below the mail shirt come from?—and sheathed it. That gave him a chance to examine his opponents for the first time. They were young men, younger than he was, of middling height but with the broad shoulders of bowmen and dressed alike in coarse blue woolen pants and tunics and high horseman's boots. They'd all been armed with dagger, shete, bow and lance, and all wore the same equipment, not just the helmets; back-and-breasts of overlapping leather plates, chaps of the same protecting their legs, mail sleeves. In fact . . .

That's like the gear Kuttner *was wearing!*

Things went *click* behind Ingolf's eyes. He'd been furious before. Now the rage went coldly murderous. For certainty's sake he examined one of the shetes; it was a twin to the one he'd taken from the wild-man chief near Innsmouth, though not quite as good.

"Time to get out," he muttered to himself.

Boy had stopped a hundred yards down the canyon, and the other horses were milling around, unable to get past him. He didn't bother to investigate the gear; time enough for that later. Instead he simply looped the stirrups of each up over the saddle horn and improvised a leading rein. Taking them in hand he looked up at the sky; it was turning dark blue in the east, nearly nightfall.

There was just enough sunlight to gild the arrowheads, when he came out of the eastern mouth of the canyon and found a semicircle of the enemy waiting for him, their stiff horn-and-sinew recurve bows drawn to the ear.

Kuttner sat his horse behind them, grinning. . . .

* * *

FLYING M BARONIAL HUNTING PRESERVE, NEAR YAMHILL
PORTLAND PROTECTIVE ASSOCIATION, OREGON
JANUARY 30, CY22/2021 A.D.

The fire had died down to coals while he told Ingolf's story. When Matti spoke her voice was as quiet as the blue-and-yellow flickering over the embers.

"That would be hard, to lose your best friends all on the same day, and then be betrayed like that."

"Yes," Rudi said somberly. Then he smiled. "But you know what Mom said to him?"

"What?"

"She told him what his friends' names meant—the Sikhs. He hadn't known. . . . She said—"

His gaze went beyond the wall, recalling that night in Dun Juniper.

* * *

"*Lion*," the Mackenzie chieftain said softly. "*And Lioness.*"

Ingolf looked up, startled out of memory. "Ma'am?"

"That's what Singh means: *Lion*. And Kaur means *lioness*. Your friends died faithful to their ancestors, Ingolf."

* * *

"We'll have to get by the . . . Cutters? The Cutters, yes . . . when we go east," Mathilda said thoughtfully.

She picked up the poker and stirred the embers; they crackled and let a few dull red sparks drift upwards. The hall was silent now; they were alone, though there were servants within calling distance.

Rudi sat up. "Wait a minute!" he said sharply. "What's this *we*?"

Mathilda looked at him, her brown eyes hurt. He'd seen it done better . . . and they'd spent a *lot* of time together since they were children.

"We're *anamchara*."

"Yes, we are," Rudi said.

They'd been children when they went through that rite, back during the War of the Eye, when she was held prisoner by his people and before he'd been taken captive by hers; they'd done it to make sure that they weren't caught up in the quarrels of their parents. That didn't make it any less real, or less binding.

"But that doesn't mean you can run off with me, soul sister," he said. "You're heir to the Protectorate, for sweet Brigid's sake!"

"And you're heir to the Mackenzie," Mathilda shot back.

Her back had gone stiff, and she wasn't trying the puppy eyes on him anymore. Rudi ran a hand through his red-gold mane.

"I am not! It's not hereditary!"

She made a rubbing gesture between thumb and forefinger. "That's the world's smallest violin playing for you 'cause you'll be tossed out to starve or go beg in the gutters of Corvallis, Rudi. The assembly made you tanist, didn't they?"

He flushed, which was unfortunately obvious with his complexion; not quite as milk white as his mother's but pale enough to show the blood mounting to his cheeks, particularly in winter. There wasn't much doubt who the Clan would hail as Chief . . . but he didn't want to think about his mother taking the voyage to the Summerlands, not yet. That might be a long time, anyway; she was only in her fifties, strong and healthy.

"Look, Matti, I'd love to have you along. There's nobody in the world I'd rather have my back. But you *can't* go. Your mother would never let you do something that crazy."

She pounced. "If it's that crazy, why is *your* mother letting *you* do it?"

"I'm of age," he said, and instantly regretted it as her lips narrowed.

Oops. Matti doesn't come of age until she's twenty-six. That had been part of the agreement at the end of the War.

"And besides, you heard about the dream Ingolf had. I'm *supposed* to be doing this. Mom doesn't like it, of a surety she doesn't, but she knows I have to."

"Pagan superstition," Mathilda spit.

"Hey!" Rudi replied, dismayed. *I did get her angry, and no mistake!*

Then she took a deep breath and relaxed. The problem was that she relaxed the way a lynx did, waiting on a branch for something edible to pass by. And he recognized that expression; it was too much like her mother's. She was *thinking*.

"Well, who *is* going with you?" she said reasonably.

"Ingolf, of course," Rudi said. *Anamchara did* have to share their secrets. "And one more—I think Edain, Sam Aylward's son. He showed very well in that dustup with the Haida last year."

Mathilda nodded; they both knew the young man well. "And?" the young woman went on ruthlessly.

"And two Rangers."

Mathilda's eyes narrowed dangerously again. "Any *particular* Dúne-dain?" she said.

"Well . . . my sisters." At her look: "Well, *half* sisters."

She nodded quietly, got up and left. Rudi stayed and sat staring into the fire. Then his eyes turned towards the staircase where his best friend had gone. They'd known each other half their lives. . . .

"That was *much* too easy," he muttered to himself.

CHAPTER NINE

"*E-ndan Ingolf warn?*" Astrid Larsson said, when Ritva finished the tale that Ingolf Vogeler had told.

Mary and Ritva Havel halted on a footbridge. For privacy they and the commanders of the Dúnedain walked the Path of Silver Waters, past waterfalls frozen into arching shapes of glittering white, fantasies that shone with an almost metallic luster beneath the pale brightness of the winter sun. Likely they would melt in the next few days. Mithrilwood—what had once been Silver Falls State Park, and a good deal around it—was higher than the Willamette valley floor, and colder, but not as winter-frigid as the great mountain forests that ran eastward from here until they met the glaciers of the High Cascades.

"Then the man Ingolf surrendered?"

The language they were speaking was Sindarin, the tongue most often used in a Dúnedain steading. There was a slight tinge of distaste in her voice.

"*Alae,* duh! *naneth-muinthelen Astrid,*" Ritva said, in the same language.

Her version used more loan words than Astrid's book-learned variety; she had come to it as a living tongue.

"*Well,* duh, *Aunt Astrid.*"

Light flickered bright through the boughs of the firs and hemlocks, and the bare branches of oak and maple; it was still three hours to sunset, though there were clouds gathering in the north and she thought it smelled like more snow tonight.

She went on: "*E-ndan i guina.*" Which meant: *The man lives.*

"His friends asked him to avenge their blood," Astrid pointed out.

There was a persistent rumor that she *was* an elf, or at least half-Elven. Ritva had to admit that as far as looks went it might have been true; her mother's younger sister was tall and willowy-graceful, with white-blond hair that fell almost to her waist and features that had an eerie cast, eyes too large and rimmed and streaked with silver through their blue, chin a little too pointed. Which was the way elves were supposed to look, pretty well. Only the slight lines beside those disturbing eyes belied it; she was thirty-six this year.

"*Apa rasad pilinidi terëaldamo mengiel?*" Mary Havel scoffed. "Sort of hard to avenge anyone after he'd gotten a dozen arrows through his brisket. As it is, he escaped eventually—we didn't get the details on that—and he still has a chance to get vengeance someday, maybe."

"You have a prosaic soul, Mary," Astrid said regretfully; she used the same tone she would have to diagnose a skin disease.

The Lady of the Dúnedain could tell Mary and her sister Ritva apart easily. How, nobody knew; their own mother had more difficulty. Her consort Alleyne was with them, and her *anamchara* Eilir and *her* man John Hordle, but the six of them were alone apart from that.

The thing that worries me most is this story about the sword, Eilir Mackenzie said in Sign.

Eilir was the same age as the Lady of the Dúnedain, the same five-foot-nine height, and had the same graceful sword-blade build; her features were a little blunter, her hair dense raven black and her eyes green. She had been deaf since birth, as well.

John Hordle snorted, and spoke in a basso rumble: "Well, if there's a bloody magic sword involved, at least the sodding thing isn't stuck in a *stone!*"

Astrid scowled at him for a second; the big Englishman could make even the Elven-tongue sound as if it were being spoken in a country pub over a pint. Or possibly at the top of a beanstalk, since she barely came to his shoulder, and he was broad enough that he looked almost squat.

Beside him Alleyne Loring walked like an Apollo, six feet of long-limbed blond handsomeness, with the first gray threads appearing in his mustache in his fortieth year.

Astrid nodded at her soul sister, speaking with hands as well as voice, as had become second nature since they met in the first Change Year.

"It's the sword that bothers me, too. Obviously, it's important; obviously, this Prophet doesn't want us to get it. Or at least that's the way it looks to me. From what Ingolf said, he made at least two attempts to probe Nantucket—one that failed completely, and then by stealth with Ingolf's band, through the spy they had at the court of the bossman of Iowa."

Alleyne spoke thoughtfully: "Or the Prophet could have planted it all as a story to get Rudi out of the valley and where he could get at him. Plenty of people know that . . . ah . . ."

"Prophecy," Ritva said helpfully.

"Yes, that prophecy about Rudi."

Astrid smiled at him. "No, I don't think so," she said. "If they just wanted to kill him, there are a lot less complicated ways."

Which they seem to have tried at Sutterdown, Eilir pointed out.

"No . . . no," Astrid said. "Rudi got involved with that only by chance—if chance you call it. They were after *Ingolf.* Which means they didn't *want* us to hear the story; and it couldn't have been collusion to give credence to his story; he very nearly *did* die before he told us."

"They were trying to kill him, all right," Ritva said, recalling the night in the Sheaf and Sickle's upper corridor; her nostrils widened slightly, smelling again the iron-copper rankness of blood and fear-sweat.

Her sister Mary nodded: "That slash on his shoulder and arm must have let out half the blood in his body. From the look of it, the Cutter was aiming at his neck."

She described it again, and they all nodded; everyone here was a warrior, and intimately familiar with the ways edged metal had with human flesh.

"We're both going," Mary added flatly, preempting her aunt as she drew breath to speak.

"Going where?" Alleyne said, arching one brow.

"On the *quest,* Uncle," Ritva said, feeling a great happiness bubbling up under her breastbone. "The *quest* for the *sword,* with Rudi . . . with *Artos.* I mean, isn't it obvious?"

Out of the corner of her eye she saw Aunt Astrid opening her mouth. They moved to forestall her.

"You *can't* go! You're *Hiril Dúnedain*, the Lady of the Rangers, and there may be war here—you can't go off into the wilderness," Mary said.

"You're like Elrond or Théoden," Ritva added, using the clinching arguments. "You have a people and a place to ward. We're just *ohtar*."

The word meant *warrior-squire*, one rank down from *Roquen*, knight-commander.

"But there should be Dúnedain involved," Ritva added.

She did *not* go on to say that it was the best they could do in the absence of real hobbits, dwarves or elves, though the thought made her smile and exchange a glance with Mary. They loved the stories of the elder days—the two of them wouldn't be here if the tale didn't speak to their hearts—but Aunt Astrid took them with an appalling literal-mindedness sometimes. So did a lot of other people in the Dúnedain Rangers, for that matter.

But this is the Fifth Age of Middle Earth, or possibly the Sixth; the Third was who knows how long ago, and things have changed.

Alleyne caught her eye, and one of his moved in the slightest hint of a wink.

"I think that would be wise, my lady," he said gravely to his spouse. "After all, Thranduil sent his son Legolas on the quest of the Ring, and Glóin sent Gimli likewise—they didn't go themselves."

Eilir and Hordle nodded vigorously. Astrid sighed deeply, and Mary hid her relief. Wild horses hitched up with triple-reduction gearing couldn't shift Aunt Astrid once she got her mind set on something; she was the only person the twins knew who could outstubborn them, though their mother, Signe, came close.

Eilir went on, signing emphatically: *I'm not leaving Beregond and Iorlas. They're too young. And I'm your* anamchara, *not your nanny; you're most certainly not dumping your three on me and going off on an adventure!*

"I suppose so. Though Thranduil was thousands of years old and I'm thirty-six. Oh, well, it's the Doom of Men."

"I suspect we're all going to get our fill of adventure much closer to home," Alleyne said grimly. Then he shook off his mood. "But we'll have some time to get ready . . . and time to live in."

Astrid sighed again. "Yes, yes, Mary and Ritva have leave go on the . . ." She hesitated, then brightened. "The Quest of the Sunrise Lands."

"*Ring!*" Mary said.

"*Cool!*" Ritva echoed.

You have to admit that Aunt Astrid has a way with words. She always comes up with a neat phrase.

Voices were singing as they turned and walked along the path beneath the cliff towards Stardell Hall, a party of hunters in from the woods with their dogs trotting at their heels, bows in their hands and a brace of elk over their packhorses. But it might have been anyone here; a good singing voice wasn't exactly an essential qualification for membership in the Dúnedain Rangers, but it helped. This tune had a happy sound with a fast-tripping chorus:

> *Sing ho to the Greenwood!*
> *Now let us go—*
> *Sing hey and ho!*
> *And there shall we find both buck and doe*
> *Sing hey and ho!*
> *The hart, the hind, and the little pretty roe*
> *Sing hey and ho!*

Stardell had been old when the Change came, originally built by the CCC as the headquarters for the park. There was some cleared land nearby for turnout pasture and gardens, snow-covered now. But this steading got more from hunting, and more still in payment for the services of the Rangers. The core of it was tall forest with the high-pitched shingle roofs of the log buildings scattered beneath; homes and workshops, stables, barns and a granary built of rough stone, a Covenstead and a small chapel for the Catholic minority.

Ritva looked up. Several of the larger trees bore flets, round platforms cunningly camouflaged high above the ground, some with walls and roofs above; there were more of those farther up in the mountains, and cave redoubts as well. The flet on the big Douglas fir was where she and her sister stayed when they were in the steading; it had bunk beds and a very pleasant little cast-iron stove.

There were people in plenty bustling about on the ground, near two hundred at this time of year. This was the largest of the Ranger stations, and their main work was as seasonal as farming: guarding caravans and running down bandits and evildoers, with a sideline in destroying man-eaters, carrying messages and small valuable parcels, rescuing the afflicted and defending the helpless. Evildoers liked camping out in the cold no more than respectable folk, bandits were no more able to cross snowed-in passes than merchants, and this was the time of year when messages could wait.

There were shouts of greeting as the *Hiril Dúnedain* and her kinfolk came back from their long stroll. A pair of tow-haired girls of not quite three came out of the hall, stumping along in their snowsuits with the mittens dangling on strings. At the sight of Ritva and Mary they sent up a shout:

"Gwanûn! Gwanûn!"

"Yes, we *are* twins," Mary said, and took Fimalen up on her hip; Ritva took Hinluin.

"And so are you, little Yellow Hair," Ritva said.

"And you too, little Blue Eyes," Mary said.

They're so cute, they almost *make you want some of your own,* Ritva thought. *Someday. Not yet! And it was a bit thoughtless of Astrid to give them interchangeable names like that.*

The Larsson family ran to blonds, as did the Lorings. The Larssons also tended to produce twins, both fraternals and identicals, but Astrid's eldest—her son Diorn—was a singleton. He was also black-haired and gray-eyed and preternaturally serious for a ten-year-old.

"Mae govannen, gwenyr," he said gravely, putting hand to chest and bowing: *Well met, my kinswomen.*

They replied with equal formality; Ritva remembered her struggles with the complex vocalic umlauts in the Elvish plural form and envied his being brought up with it from birth. Then everyone trooped into the hall, after shaking out their cloaks. Stardell looked a little like the hall in Dun Juniper, but there was no second floor, only a gallery around what had been the roofline before they raised it. And the carving on the pillars and vaulting rafters above was more restrained, the colors mostly greens and pastel blues and silver-grays, and the old gold shade of oak leaves in the fall.

The style was what her mother, Signe, had once told her was more Art Nouveau and less Book of Kells than that the Mackenzies favored, eerily elongated dancing maidens and their lords, sinuous trees with blossoms of iridescent glass, and little gripping trolls grinning with bone teeth, peering from corners and holding up the stone finials of the hearth.

The sisters went over by the fire; there was a pleasant smell of pine boughs and hemlock amid the grateful warmth, and a scatter of children's toys on the floor—a hobbyhorse, a little elk on wheels, a stuffed tiger on a rug made from the hide of a real one. The black gold-embossed leather covers of the Histories stood above the hearth on the mantelpiece, flanking images of the Lord and Lady as Manwë and Varda. A Corvallan was waiting there, a small rather dumpy man in the four-pocket jacket and pants that people from the city-state favored when they were traveling.

Ritva hadn't seen him here before, and he was looking around with the *I'm seeing it but it can't be real* expression outsiders often got in Stardell, lost amid the pleasant liquid trilling of Sindarin conversation.

"*Mae govannen,*" Astrid said curtly, and then dropped into English: "Well met, if you prefer the common tongue."

"Lady Astrid, Lord Alleyne," he said, bowing courteously. "I'm here about that little problem you were concerned with."

Alleyne grinned to himself. Ritva caught the expression and suppressed an urge to giggle, and heard Mary snort as she did the same. It wasn't a good idea to diss Aunt Astrid at the best of times; right now she was feeling sore as a tiger with a nail in its paw because there was finally a *real* quest, for a sword of power . . . and she couldn't go.

I'd feel mangly bitter about that myself, in her position, Ritva thought. Mary gave her a little nod. *Squared. This is going to be fun . . . to watch.*

"It isn't a *little* problem," Astrid said, glaring at him with a cold fury that made him wilt visibly. "By the treaty which ended the War of the Eye, all the realms of the Meeting pay a subsidy to the Dúnedain Rangers for the work we do. By the same treaty, the People and Faculty Senate of Corvallis, as hosts of the Meeting, are responsible for collecting it and forwarding it to us. Quarterly."

"There have been problems—not everyone pays on time, and I'm sure you realize that means we have to take out short-term paper—"

"And I'm sure *that is your problem and not mine!*" Astrid roared, an astonishing husky sound.

Everyone in the hall stopped and looked; Fimalen and Hinluin hid their faces in Mary's and Ritva's necks, and Diorn stared with bristling suspicion at the man who'd angered his mother.

Astrid went on: "*Spay snur khug!* What do you think I am, some huckstering dog of a merchant like you, a banker, a debt collector? *I* have my people to feed and my warriors to arm! *You* have a debt of honor for the blood we shed in the wilds to keep you fat!"

The Corvallan looked around, licking his lips. The eyes on him were not particularly friendly, and in unconscious reflex he searched for someone who wasn't glaring. Eilir tapped her ear with two fingers and shook her head at him with a look of pity that he found disquieting. John Hordle was smiling . . . but he was also leaning an elbow on the pommel of the four-foot sword he usually carried slung across his back, with his right hand on the long quillions of the guard. When their gaze met, his thumb jerked out to point to Alleyne Loring.

The envoy made a mute appeal to Alleyne, and the Englishman shrugged slightly and silently mouthed, *Pay up!*

The Corvallan sighed and reached a hand inside his jacket. When it came out he held a rectangle of black leather; he opened it and pulled the fountain pen out of its loops.

"Will you take a check drawn on the Faculty Senate's account with First National of Corvallis, Lady Astrid?"

"By all means," Astrid said, all graciousness again. "Make it payable to Dúnedain Enterprises, Limited, if you prefer the common tongue. In *Edhellen,* that would be *Gwaith-i-Dúnedain, Herth.*"

* * *

CORWIN, VALLEY OF PARADISE, MONTANA
FEBRUARY 1, CY22/2021 A.D.

The Church Universal and Triumphant had come to the high green pastures of Paradise Valley a decade before the Change. Their leaders had told them that the end of the world would come soon, in nuclear fire. The elaborate maze of underground shelters and stockpiled weapons hadn't been very useful when the end came instead with a soundless flash of light, but the massive stores of foodstuffs and tools and clothing most emphatically *bad*. Still, they had been deep in quarrels with the local ranchers when the Prophet arrived with a few followers, fleeing the great dying of California. The Church had taken him in, and its leader proclaimed that his vision was from the Ascended Masters. . . .

Sethaz felt himself sweat as he backed out of the Presence. It was getting worse, the darkness and the smell and the long ranting harangues. Thank the One that it had been fairly comprehensible this time. It was almost as bad as his mother had been, once the Alzheimer's had progressed. The pillow had been a mercy. Perhaps . . .

No! he thought. *Not yet.*

The path outside was lined with his personal Cutters, Guardians of the House of the Ascended, the Sword of the Prophet; they went to one knee in the snow as the Son of the Prophet appeared, the sheathed tips of their shetes resting in the snow ahead of them, their heads bent over the hilts. The red-brown of their lacquered leather armor showed brilliantly against the pale carpet of winter, with the golden-rayed sun on their breasts; if they'd been on a mission instead of guarding the House of the Prophet, they'd have worn white cloth over it.

The cold lay on his face as he looked up to the Absaroka Mountains to the east, so intense that it made the air seem liquid. Snow peaks cradled the Valley of Paradise on both flanks, floating high and holy where the air thinned between the world of Man and the Beyond. Between him and the mountains loomed the unfinished bulk of the Temple of the Dictations, swarming with workmen even in winter. Smoke drifted high against heaven, smelling of hot brick and scorched metal.

There was a long silence as he stood and watched the morning light tinge the jagged white horizon with a hint of pink, letting the clean wind blow the nausea out of him. He wasn't an imposing sight in himself, a man just short of thirty, a little on the tall side of medium, his cropped hair brown and his eyes an everyday hazel, slender and strong with a swordsman's thick wrists and an archer's broad shoulders. Yet the aura about him was enough to keep others at a deferential distance.

At last Councilor of the Way Charom came over, boldest of a knot of ecclesiastical bureaucrats. They had grown over the domains of the Church Universal and Triumphant like mold over bread these last ten years, but there was no way to do without them.

"What is the word of the Prophetic Channeler, your holiness?" he said.

"Wheel may turn wheel, and that wheel may turn a wheel or a shaft, but no more, lest the anger of the Ascended Masters be again turned on us, and mankind's pride be broken in the dust again."

The stout shaven-headed man in his wool and furs bowed over linked hands, but he couldn't hide a flicker of relief. Sethaz inclined his own head, very slightly, but a mark of acknowledgment all the same. It would have been *very* awkward if the gearing necessary to run windmills to pump water had been declared Abomination. The Guardian of the Way was what a secular state might have called an interior minister, and it would have been his responsibility to enforce the edict.

There was enough trouble making sure that all the women covered their hair.

"May I ask how the Prophet is?" he asked, greatly daring.

Sethaz thought, then decided to allow it. "His earthly, human shell of this embodiment grows weak," he said, which everyone knew. "One day soon he will rejoin the Unseen Hierarchy and cast aside the envelope he wears. It is a burden and a torment to him, though one he bears willingly for us."

Charom nodded again and spoke with unctuous relish: "It is good that you will be here, his chosen Son and successor, trained through many Embodiments to receive the Dictations."

You mean it's good that you got in with the winning side early, Sethaz thought, and flicked a hand in dismissal. The minister withdrew.

Alone he paced between the compounds, with only the six triads of Cutters that accompanied him everywhere. Little remained of pre-Change Corwin; most of that had burned in the fighting when the Church took full control of the valley. Now it was a complex of new buildings, most built in two-story blocks of gray stone and shingle roofs set around courtyards, a few of the older ones of timber; covered walkways connected them above the streets. In the summertime the gardens were very beautiful, but now they lay dormant, banked under earth and straw and mounded snow that glittered with ice crystals.

The snow was colored brown with dirt where sleds carried loads through the tree-lined streets; grain in sacks, salvaged metal bound for the smithies or weapons and tools out of them, firewood, charcoal, frozen sides of beef and mutton, a thousand other things that came in as tribute from the regions that acknowledged the Dictations.

People swarmed as well, women in headscarves and long skirts and overcoats, men in pants and jackets and fur caps, officials of the Church in their heavy robes, expressionless slaves in thick rags carrying burdens or pulling sleds. All paused reverently when a priest climbed a podium set beside the street and read a brief passage from the Dictations. He caught a snatch of it.

" '. . . Vigil of the Violet Flame, but the soulless minions of the Nephilim prevailed over the men of Camelot, and . . .' "

"Amen! Amen! Amen!" the chorus thundered out when he'd finished, and then the folk turned back to their business.

Sethaz went in under an arch marked with the sun disk; he liked to do unannounced inspections. If you relied too much on written reports or scheduled visits there was always the danger you'd end up in a puzzle palace of deceptions stage-managed by underlings. The guards there—trainees were strictly segregated—slapped left fist inside right hand and bowed low. This building was one of the Prophetic Guard's; the courtyard was roofed over, rising in a laminated timber barrel vault with many skylights, with the cells of the students looking down from all around and open classrooms, offices and libraries and refectories below. The layout made it easier for a single observer in the courtyard to keep track of everything that occurred, as well: it was called the panopticon, and the Dictations attributed the method to the Ascended Master Plato.

Several dozen of the youngest students knelt in one end of the court, resting from physical training and chanting:

> The beloved Maha Chohan gave me a grant
> Of many good and fine life streams
> Like a golden chain, girdling the Earth,
> Is the Unseen Hierarchy of the Ascended Lords.
> Without the Unseen Hierarchy,
> The Earth would long ago
> Have passed into oblivion. . . .

A senior student prowled behind them with a rod of split ash, waiting for an error or hesitation. The faces of the novices were glazed with the effort of the endless repetitions; only so could the Truth be ground into the soul, with sleeplessness and hunger. Not an eye of the juniors flickered away from the Preceptor who led the chant. The rattle and thud of weapons practice came from the center of the courtyard; for a moment Sethaz and his personal guards watched.

The trainees were young, their faces smooth and hairless, scalps shaved, a mixture of levies from the newly conquered regions and the sons of ambitious families closer to the core territories. The Sword of the Prophet were like the priesthood, a pathway to office and power. The older classes were sparring, stripped to the waist, using wooden swords or staffs or hand-to-hand. There was a constant clatter of wood on wood, an occasional thump and grunt as a blow went home. Sweat ran down their shaven scalps and muscular torsos, giving the air a musky pungency under the scents of wood and soap and stone; the instructors here were in the armor of Guardians, often nearing middle age, always scarred. Some lacked a hand or foot or were otherwise crippled.

The students bore scars as well, of the scourge and hot iron, from punishment or self-inflicted efforts to reach the trance state where you became one with the Masters. Pictures of those Ascended Lords graced the walls, above the mirrors and stretching bars; Christ and Zoroaster, Muhammad and Gautama Buddha, Blavatsky and Mundy, his own mother and the current Prophet.

Sethaz watched the practice in silence for a few minutes. Then he snapped his fingers and the senior instructor came over. He had the chin beard and close-cropped hair of a warrior elder, streaked with the first gray hairs. He'd been a fighting man even before the Change, and joined the Church not long after.

"How do they progress, Commander Sean?" the Prophet's son asked.

"Son of the Prophet, they're doing fairly well," the man said. "But we haven't the training cadre to expand the program as quickly as I'd like."

Sethaz cocked an eye at the oldest class, the eighteen-year-olds. He was less than thirty himself, but he felt like one carved from the granite of the hills compared to them.

"They look to be shaping well."

Sean nodded. "Yes, Dispenser of the Word, and they can help with the basics for the new intakes. But their knowledge is still theoretical. They need combat experience before they're fit to be instructors themselves."

Sethaz nodded. "Let's see how they do at second-level trials."

Then he stripped off his heavy winter coat, and the sweater and silk shirt beneath it. One of the students let that distract him, and went down under his opponent's staff. The instructor added a few hearty kicks before he rose.

"Those three," Sethaz said.

Staff scurried to bring practice armor, much like the combat variety except that it was more battered and worn, and blunted blades—a step up from the lath-and-wood of everyday drill. After the suit had been strapped on he reached out his arms, and shield and shete were there. The rest of the students grouped themselves in files of three and went to one knee, watching silently and controlling their breathing with drilled ease.

Sean was grinning as he turned to the similarly outfitted students. "The Son of the Prophet does you a great honor. Push hard on the word of command . . . *fight!*"

The students didn't waste any time on preliminaries; the center man of the triad lunged with blade outstretched.

"Cut! *Cut!*"

Not bad, Sethaz thought, as he swayed aside and clubbed the trainee on the back of his helmet with the edge of the shield, a short chopping stroke. In the same instant he caught the second's stroke at the side of his leg on his own shete and kicked him in the belly, hard. The armor spread it; the steel-toed riding boot would have killed a man without the plates and padding, and even with he doubled up with an *ooof*.

That left the third. He came on gamely, shete flashing. It cracked hard on Sethaz's shield, then rang on the steel of his blade. After a moment he found the rhythm of it, and left an opening. The student's shete lunged and then it was caught between his right arm and his flank, clamped hard by the inside of his arm. The trainee foolishly tried to wrestle it clear rather than abandoning it and going for a dagger, and took a head butt in the face. Sethaz pulled the blow; that was another one that could kill. It jarred him a little, even with the steel of the helmet and the padding between him and the impact. The youngster's nose broke with a crunching sound and he lurched back to the matting, lying dazed with blood pouring down over his mouth.

Sethaz kept the grin off his face, standing and making the air whine as he whipped the blunt practice shete through figure eights.

"What have you learned from this?" Sean barked at the kneeling spectators.

One of them raised a hand. At a curt nod, the youth said, "Sir, that a fighter should not think only of his shete, just because he has a shete in his hand. Everything is a weapon to the warrior's mind."

"Correct," Sethaz said. "And always use conditions and circumstances, which are unique to each fight. Remember that."

He let the servants strip off the armor, went through into the bathhouse, showered and took the cold plunge. Then he sighed and changed into a robe.

Back to business, he thought, crossing over a street in the enclosed walkway and into the building that housed his private offices and quarters and his Women's House.

The sanctum he used for most of his despised but could-not-be-avoided paperwork held only a mandala, desk and office furniture, but the broad windows looked out across a vista of river and cottonwoods and snowy pastures, up to the green of ponderosa-pine forest and the glaciers above. A murmur and click of abacus beads came from the offices on the ground floor, but he felt private here—except for a triad of the guards, of course, and his secretary, Geraldine. It had been a refuge when he was younger, still uncertain and feeling his way as the Prophet withdrew into his visions and the generals and priest-bureaucrats jostled for power.

More servants brought him fresh bread and a bowl of lamb stew with onions and potatoes as he read through the most important dispatches. Things were going well down in the Powder River country; the last of the powerful ranchers there were asking for terms, ready to accept the Dictations. And the Sioux had finally yielded all the Hi-Line, retreating eastward into their strongholds in the Dakotas and agreeing to allow missionaries from the Church to preach in their camps.

Let's hope that works, he thought. *They make poor slaves but they'd be very valuable subjects.*

He clapped hands to have the tray taken out, and sat sipping borage tea. Which left another matter, one less easily solved with a few regiments or preachers.

"Bring him in," he said.

The secretary genuflected and went to the door, and a near-naked figure was thrust through to stumble to a halt and stand blinking. Kuttner was in his thin drawers, teeth still chattering from the cold of the unheated basement cell. His hands were bound before him, and the guards had thrust a pole between his elbows and his back, and were steering him by it. They pushed him down on his knees; Kuttner bent to touch his forehead to the tiles of the floor. There was a crusted slow-healing scar on his left cheek, ending in an empty socket.

"I beg for mercy, Son of the Prophet!" he wailed. "I have failed the Prophet and the Church Universal and Triumphant. Mercy!"

Then he sensibly fell silent. There was no excuse for failure; it showed a lack of proper openness to the Dictations.

"I am disappointed in you, Kuttner," Sethaz said, offering none of the usual titles or formulae of politeness. "We had great hopes . . . and the Prophet himself has said that the matter of Nantucket is important."

If that's not just his madness speaking, Sethaz thought, then pushed the deadly siren song of doubt away. *I must have faith.*

Kuttner licked his lips. He was a capable spy, and they'd spent years infiltrating him into the household of the young bossman of Iowa before he inherited from his father; his file indicated that he was cynical, but fundamentally loyal, ambitious, and highly intelligent. Brains were in far shorter supply than zeal. Now there was something in his single remaining eye that made Sethaz a little uneasy.

"Son of the Prophet, the Prophet's words were truer than my weak and doubting spirit could have imagined. There *is* something dangerous on the island. Something . . . I don't understand, something beyond the world of men. Our previous expedition disappeared without trace, until I found that shete with our mark. *My* attempt penetrated the mystery."

"Yes," Sethaz said, looking down at the report on his desk.

How much of it can I believe? he mused. *Kuttner used to be a reliable man.*

"And we'd have known more of it if you hadn't let this man Vogeler escape. To be precise, *he* penetrated the mystery; you were lost in visions."

Kuttner licked his lips again. "I was sure that he had made submission to the Church and was ready to learn the Dictations," he said.

"And you thought you had established a secure control link."

"I was not wrong, Son of the Prophet. I . . . just didn't have time to use it. I was careless."

"And lost an eye because of it," Sethaz said.

Though that is fortunate for you, he thought. *If you had not been so badly wounded, we might have suspected collusion.*

Kuttner went on in desperate haste: "But Son of the Prophet, he *did* tell me of *his* vision before I revealed myself. He had no reason not to, and no reason to lie while he still thought I served the bossman of Des Moines. The vision of the sword, and the dreams that told him to take the news to the far west and seek this Sword of the Lady."

Sethaz came to a decision, and motioned. One of the guards drew his shete and flicked twice at the cords in the same blur of motion. Kuttner remained motionless while the knife-sharp weapon went *tick* against the wood of the pole. The staff clattered on the floor of the sanctum; another flicker of steel between his bound hands, and Kuttner grunted as he rubbed his wrists and felt the pain of circulation returning.

"However, the men I sent to the west didn't do too well with Vogeler either," Sethaz said. "A most obdurate apostate and traitor. In fact, the observation team saw him carried out of this Sutterdown place towards the lair of the Witch Queen herself . . . and that is precisely who we wanted to keep Vogeler's story *from*. You are pardoned, provisionally, and restored to your rank of High Seeker of the God-flame. You have until snowmelt to come up with a plan. Consult the archives and interview agents as you wish."

Kuttner rose to his feet, met Sethaz's eyes, gave a single bow of precisely the right depth, turned on his heel and left.

Sethaz smiled to himself and opened a drawer, taking out a box and resting it on his table. In it was a clock; not just a pre-Change model, but made new of steel and brass, its exposed interior a mass of gearing. If the pagan witchcraft of the far West wasn't enough to bring the attention of the Church Universal and Triumphant, such blasphemous meddling with forbidden things would be.

He glanced at the agenda on his Rolodex. "All right, Geraldine. Generals Walker and Graham next."

The war against New Deseret was necessarily on hold for most of the winter, but that didn't mean there weren't steps that had to be taken before the spring grass grew enough to support horse soldiers.

* * *

BARONY GERVAIS, PORTLAND PROTECTIVE ASSOCIATION
WILLAMETTE VALLEY, OREGON
FEBRUARY 18, CY22/2021 A.D.

"Welcome home, my lord baron!"

Odard Liu caught the apple the shopkeeper tossed. It was still fairly crisp, and he bit into it as he rode through the gloomy drizzle of a February afternoon, waving thanks with his free hand as he enjoyed the rush of sweet juice.

The rain fell in a mist of steady silver-gray, flattening the smoke from the chimneys and dappling the puddles in the asphalt streets. Hooves—his palfrey, the chargers of the two men-at-arms and the rouceys of the half-dozen mounted crossbowmen who followed him—landed on it with an endless hollow wet *clop-clop-clop-clop*; he could catch glimpses of the streaked concrete of the castle's towers over the shingle roofs. The column of horsemen swerved now and then to avoid an open oxcart full of split firewood, or covered ones hauling bales and boxes and sacks. A priest signed the air as he went by in his one-horse, twin-wheeled carriage with its collapsible hood, and they all bowed their heads in respect.

Gervais wasn't very large, more of a big village than a town or city, and not much survived of the pre-Change settlement save the southwest-northeast grid of the layout and the roadside trees. Lamplight spilled out onto the street, amid a pleasant tap and tinkle and clang of folk at work, with the whirring moan of spinning wheels and the rattling thump of looms beneath it. A wave of doffed hats, respectful bows and curtsies and greetings followed him, often with umbrellas above.

Odard liked being popular here. It wasn't very difficult; he didn't chase any girl who really didn't want to be caught, collected no more than his legal due and was ready to remit a bit when times were hard, made sure the baronial court was honest, and kept his vassal knights from fighting out their quarrels over the tenants' crops and homes. Most of that had been his mother's policy before him and he intended to continue it now that he was of age.

He sighed heavily. Unfortunately, his mother didn't seem to realize that he *was* of age, or that he wasn't always going to fall in with her idea of what the Baron of Gervais should do. He hoped Mathilda didn't have the same problem with the Regent when *she* turned twenty-six.

I'm not looking forward to this homecoming.

A wet moat separated the castle from the town, but the drawbridge was down and the portcullis up. Spearmen and crossbowmen snapped to attention to either side of the gate and on ramparts and towers above, and a trumpet sounded.

Castle Gervais was built to one of the standard plans the Association had used back in the early days. A curtain wall with towers had a gatehouse facing the town and another on the eastern wall. Within was the Outer Ward, an open paved space on all four sides. Within that was the keep, a square block with tall round towers at all four corners, and two big U-shaped ones for the inner gatehouse, all built to overlook the outer works.

He rode through the inner gatehouse with more ceremony, and dismounted in the Inner Ward, ringed around with smithy, stables and the great hall and lord's apartments. Odard returned the salute of the watch and nodded to his escort. From the bustle and the lights a welcoming feast was in preparation; nobody was in the stocks in the center today, he noted.

"Gavin, Armand, go get dry, get something hot to drink and then report to the seneschal. I'll be here some days, possibly weeks."

The men-at-arms had hooded cloaks of the same unfulled wool that Odard wore, but theirs were over helmet and hauberk, a gleam of oiled gray under the wet cloth. The pennants on their tall lances drooped likewise, the wet canvas clinging to the ashwood. Sergeant Gavin grinned at him, the smile white in his brown face; he was in his late thirties, old for his trade, and as a young man had served Odard's father, the first baron.

"Yes, my lord. Good to be home, eh?"

"Better than being out in the rain."

The steward greeted him in the vestibule of the hall with a mug of priceless hot cocoa, along with the rest of the senior staff.

"Ah, Romarec, you're a lifesaver," he said.

He sipped at the hot sweetness as a servant took his cloak and another offered him a heated towel to dry his face. There was a slug of good brandy in the cup, too.

"Your lady mother waits to greet you in the solar after you've refreshed yourself, my lord," Romarec said.

Well, that's Mom, Odard thought wryly, nodding to several of the others and giving his old nanny a hug before heading for his private quarters.

His valet had come ahead by train from Todenangst with the baggage. Odard's own rooms were in the southeast tower of the keep, four stacked one above the other. All of them were brightly lit, with fires crackling on their hearths, and had been for long enough to take the curse off the winter's day—not easy, in a structure made of thick mass concrete and in this climate, even when all the walls were paneled and hung with tapestry.

Alex Vinton was a small foxy-faced man with red hair and freckles, about six years older than Odard, wearing a soberly rich tunic of russet-dyed linen, shoes with turned-up toes, and a gold-link belt. He did *not* wear the usual servant's tabard over it, and wore only a discreet livery badge clasped to the brim of his hat. He'd proved extremely useful in a number of ways.

"Hi, Alex," Odard said, lowering himself into the steaming lavender-scented water of the bath. "Christ, that feels good. . . . Been busy?"

"Yes, my lord," he said, folding the clothes Odard had discarded. "I've been back two days now and there's quite a bit of gossip."

"Oh, God and His merciful saints"—Odard steepled his hands in mock prayer and rolled his eyes upward—"*tell* me she didn't have those assassins here at the castle!"

"No, no, my lord," the valet said. "The hunting lodge over at Fairfax."

"Ten miles away and in a swamp, that's *something,*" Odard said meditatively, scrubbing at his fingernails with a small brush; he was a fastidious man and bathed every day when he could. "When did she meet them?"

"She didn't, my lord. She had her younger brother Sir Guelf do it."

"That's also something. Not much, but something."

Alex held the towel for him as he stepped out on the mat, then helped him dress with foppish care in the latest fashion, just below the court-appearance standard—dark trousers cut closer than had been the custom in his father's time, tooled-leather shoes with little golden bells on the upturned toes and ceremonial gold spurs on the heels, a knee-length tunic of heavy indigo-dyed silk with silver embroidery on the square-cut neck and elbow-length sleeves whose flared points extended halfway to his knees, and a white silk shirt beneath it. He added a ring or two and examined himself in the full-length mirror, smiling at what he saw.

"Not bad," he said, taking a belt of leather covered in worked-silver plates and buckling it around his waist.

It had a purse and a ten-inch poignard; the hilt had patterned silver and gold wire inlaid in the black stag-horn grips, and a pommel in the shape of a silver cat's head. You didn't usually wear a sword inside in time of peace, but a gentleman didn't go unarmed outside his own chambers, either. Alex added the round hat with the roll around its brim and flicked the long silk tail from the side to lie over Odard's right shoulder. The badge at the fore was the *mon* arms of the House of Liu in a turquoise that set off his eyes.

"You're the pattern of chivalry, my lord," the valet said unctuously, then spoiled the effect with a grin.

"All right, I admit it, I like looking well," Odard said.

"Tell the comptroller when he has to pay the bills, my lord," Alex said, grinning still wider.

There was something to that. Barony Gervais was rich in anything grown or made within its boundaries or available in local trade, but the silk came from Burma or New Singapore or Hinduraj, and it cost—regular trade with the portions of Asia not irretrievably wrecked by the Change was just getting started again. The price of fashion was one reason he was just as happy to get away from court for a while.

"See if there are any details you could find," he said to the valet. "Talk to Guelf's men; maybe you can smoke out something."

Odard whistled a tune he liked as he walked through the corridors towards the solar, looking his usual cheerful self. Hearing it, someone within earshot began to sing the words—a woman's voice:

> *I forbid you maidens all*
> *That wear gold in your hair*
> *To come or go by Carter Hall*
> *For young Tam Lin is there—*

Inside, he was on edge; a little like the time just before a fight when you wondered which bush hid a man with a crossbow bolt ready to punch through your armor, or a hunt for a tiger or boar. Usually politics was something he enjoyed, even the junior jostling for position that heirs did, and he'd been getting more and more involved in the real thing as he approached the magic age of twenty-one. Having to play the game with your own mother was another kettle altogether.

It wouldn't do to let it all show. Instead he raised his own voice for a moment:

> *None come or go by Carter Hall*
> *But they leave him a pledge—*
> *Either your rings or green mantle*
> *Or else your maidenhead . . .*

And then laughed as he took the spiral staircase.

The castle solar was in the south-facing upper turret of the southwestern tower, the one nearest the hall; that height let it have real glazed windows all around the circumference of the big round room rather than arrow-slits, though today more light came from lanterns of brass and mirrored glass. It glowed on the tapestries, the pale tile of the floor, on polished metal and bright rugs, on a big rood cross of black walnut inlaid with semiprecious stones.

The Dowager Baroness Liu was sitting there with her women—mostly sisters or daughters of knights who held land in fief from the barony—and his younger sister Yseult. Everyone stopped what they were doing and rose as he stood in the doorway, except his mother; as he turned to her the ladies-in-waiting curtsied, a wave of colored flowers in their cotte-hardis and headdresses.

"Ladies," he said, taking hat in hand and bowing in return with a sweeping gesture. "I'm enchanted to see you all again. Would you excuse my mother and me? We've a good deal to discuss, and I'll see you all in the hall at dinner."

He smiled charmingly as he said it. Some of the younger and prettier women smiled back invitingly, but he wasn't going to make a fool of himself in *that* direction, beyond a little light flirtation. They were all of a rank that could expect marriage, and he was the heir to the barony and a notable catch. Almost all of them also had male relatives equipped to resent misbehavior with edged metal; people of their generation were a lot stricter about such matters than their parents had been. Odard fancied himself with a sword, but he also disliked real fighting without a very good reason.

Yseult squealed and ran towards him and then—being just turned fourteen—slowed her pace and curtsied gravely. He reached out and tweaked her nose, which made her squeak again and got their mother frowning.

"Greetings, my lord brother," she said, kissing his extended hand, and then both his cheeks.

"My lady Yseult," he said, bowing in turn. "You're looking good, sis."

She was; she'd gotten their mother's blond hair, worn loose to her shoulders under a simple headdress in maiden's fashion, but more of their father's face, high cheekbones, blue eyes sharply slanted and nose a graceful tip-tilted snub, complexion like pale honey. He suspected that in a few years she'd be making the young gentlemen of the district do some real suffering to win the right to carry her handkerchief to a tourney.

"My lady mother," he went on, with a deeper bow.

She nodded and stuck her needle in the half-finished tapestry in its frame by the hearth. The women were working on yet another something with warriors and dragons and a very large wolf, probably from the cover of some trashy book his mother had liked when she was young—it seemed that every woman who'd been in the Society before the Change had *that* weakness, even Lady Sandra, and the others had all caught it, like some chastely ideational form of the clap.

Dried sachets scented the air, along with the fruity smell of the alcohol lanterns and faint cedarwood from the hearth. A page in livery sat on a stool not far away, strumming a lute—his younger brother, Huon. He frowned at that. The kid should be doing page service in someone else's household, to bind the families and get the best training as page and then squire, but his mother had been dragging her feet about it.

So . . . *No time like the present to establish publicly who's boss now.*

"Hello, Huon," he said, as the boy stopped playing and came forward to pour a cup of the mulled wine from the flagon heating on the tiled stove. "Lord Chaka says he could use a page, and then a squire, over in Barony Molalla."

The boy's dark eyes lit with eagerness. Odard went on: "Talk to me about it after dinner."

Several servant women in their double tunics and tabards stood motionless on call, eyes cast down and hands folded before them. One glided forward to refill a teacup from a pot that rested over a little spirit lamp; they all turned and tripped out of the room when he made a gesture.

When everyone was out of earshot, he kissed his mother's hand and then her offered cheek, kicked a padded leather settle over close and sat. His mother's eyes were as blue as his own, and colder—nobody had ever said Mary Liu operated on charm—but he favored his father in his lithe build. His features were a compromise, which left his nose straight but short, unlike her slightly hawkish beak.

"Were you *trying* to wreck the family fortunes?" he demanded, preempting her complaint about Huon. "You and my precious hothead of an uncle?"

He could see her considering denying everything. Instead she stuck her needle in the fabric and shrugged.

"It was an opportunity to get some revenge for your father, and my older brother," she said flatly. "With . . . plausible deniability."

"Plausible to *the Spider*?" Odard asked incredulously. "You expected to keep it *secret* from *the Lady Regent*?"

She frowned, lines appearing between her plucked fair eyebrows and touching her wimple.

"That was a risk," she admitted.

"Risk to my own precious personal hide, Mother—I ended up in the middle of that cluster . . . heap in Sutterdown."

For a moment genuine distress showed in her eyes: "I didn't mean for *that* to happen, darling!"

"Mother, that doesn't mean those lunatics weren't trying to *kill* me."

"It . . . went wrong. You shouldn't have been there. That was unfortunate."

"That was *stupidity*!" he replied. "And what exactly do you think Lady Sandra would have done to our family if they'd killed the *Princess*? Besides which, do you *know* how many years of effort I've put into cultivating Mathilda?"

"Years spent hanging around with that Mackenzie brat as if you were his boon companion!" she spit suddenly.

"There are worse companions to have," Odard said, and held up his hand. "Don't explode, Mother. I'm as aware of the debt I owe my family as you are. Unlike you, I'm also aware that a man can walk farther than he can run."

"I made a policy decision."

"And one that ended putting *me* in a fight to the death with the men *you* let use *my* land as a base!" he repeated.

That made her look embarrassed; but her face also closed in like a fist, and he knew that it took something drastic to shift her when she started looking like that.

I suppose I'll have to be frank, Odard thought. *Deplorable. Give me honeyed equivocation anytime.*

"Mother, I came of age several months ago," he pointed out with gentle implacability, holding her eyes. "I *am* the baron. If you wish, you can select one of the demesne manors as a dower house, and establish your own household there."

And sit and rot with the servants and some gossiping old biddies, he thought grimly.

"Or you could have apartments at court."

And have Lady Sandra keeping a very close eye on you twenty-four-seven.

Shocked, she followed the thought. "I . . . Darling, I just want to be of help to you!"

He smiled. *She* is *my mother, after all. With all that that implies.*

"I know, Mom. You do a great job of keeping the comptroller and the bailiffs in line and the mesne tithes coming in, which frankly makes my life a lot easier."

His face went stern. *"But you will* not *interfere in matters of high policy again without consulting me. Mine is the final word. Do . . . you . . . understand?"*

Their eyes locked. After a moment hers turned aside, and she nodded.

"But . . . contacts with the new power in the East could be valuable . . ." she said. "I have assurances from them—passwords and signs—"

"Perhaps. But *I* will be the judge of that from now on," he said. "And not so incidentally, there's something very strange going on here. That man Ingolf the Cutters are so hot to ventilate *saw* something out there in the barbarian lands. Rudi and his mother are very interested. Mathilda's interested. Which means *I* am interested . . . and I want any information you get. Understood? And I *will* use it as the Princess requires. From now on, a double block and tackle and a team of oxen couldn't get me away from her."

She nodded again.

"Excellent. Let's go down, then."

He rose and extended an arm. She followed and laid her fingers on it, and together they paced down towards the hall.

And someday, one way or another, I will be Lord Protector.

CHAPTER TEN

Everyone who could in Dun Juniper was out on one excuse or another, after the long confinement of the Black Months; the bright chill air booming down from the mountains smelled of fir sap, sweet grass, apple blossom, the faint cool scent of hawthorn flowers from the hedges.

"We should start the quest *soon*," Ritva said.

She was panting slightly after the sword-and-targe bout with her sister Mary. Ingolf and Rudi watched with professional appreciation for their quicksilver lightness of movement. The easterner also looked as if he appreciated their looks.

Hmmm, Ritva thought, looking at him. *He is shaping up nicely. Possibly . . .*

Mary took up the conversation seamlessly, leaving Ingolf looking a little nonplussed. It took a while to get used to their conversational style.

"The high passes will be open in a few weeks. Or there's the Columbia gorge; it's year-round."

They were all armored for practice; a blunt blade could still kill you. Rudi was in a Clan-style brigandine; the twins wore what the Dúnedain used for light armor on scouting trips, a mail shirt a lot like Ingolf's but riveted to a covering of soft dark green leather to make it quieter and less conspicuous.

A crowd of excited six-year-olds went by, shepherded by a teacher in an arsaid—an ankle-length version of a wrapped kilt and plaid—showing them plants and telling them the names and uses. Usually they'd have ignored Rudi, or waved; he'd grown up here, after all, Chief's son or no, and Dun Juniper wasn't all that populous. Now a number of them looked at him with awe, and some pointed and murmured.

"Now, by the Dagda's club, how do you start off on a secret quest when everyone knows your face and who and what you are and how that ancient prophecy about you seems to be coming to life?" Rudi said, mouth quirking.

"Hell with me if I know," Ingolf Vogeler said. Then he brightened: "But at least I haven't had any more of those damned dreams."

The pasture below the dun's gates and past the hillside orchards was thick grass starred with yellow dandelion and blue camas-flower; it stretched away on either hand beneath a bright blue sky, and the scent alone was enough to make a man feel as if he were sixteen and had just gotten his first kiss. It must be better for someone recovering from wounds and illness that took him close to death.

"Sure, and the regard of the Powers can be uncomfortable," Rudi said.

He began a pattern of cuts and thrusts, moving slowly at first and then speeding up, feeling muscles warm and stretch. The longsword moved easily in his hand.

"I doubt you'll have any more trouble with them, provided we go and see about this sword," he said.

"I thought *you* were the sword," Ingolf said dryly.

Rudi cocked an eyebrow at him and grinned. The eastern wanderer was a nice enough sort for a Christian, but he was obviously a bit disturbed to be fulfilling a prophecy made by the pagan gods.

"Well, it's never simple when *They* are involved," he said cheerfully. "Both, neither, all at once. You can't bind Them with words . . . not even true ones."

"I suppose if I got the Villains in and out, I can get you there and back," Ingolf said. His face went bleak. "And I won't have a dirty little traitor along this time, either."

Rudi blinked, not letting his eyes narrow. "I'll be careful to listen to your advice," he said—carefully. "You having the local knowledge and the experience and such."

Ingolf was examining a practice shete he'd had made up—the long point-heavy slashing swords were what he'd trained with all his life, and it would be more trouble than it was worth to switch styles.

"Just a minute there," Ingolf said, the flat rasp of his native accent strong. "I'm shepherding you to the East Coast, right?"

Rudi shook his head, meeting the other man's eyes. *Best keep things straight from the beginning.*

"Indeed and you're not," he said quietly. "It's my quest, Ingolf. I'd rather it wasn't, but the Powers have marked me for this task all my life, and it's myself must lead. Not that I won't listen to you, for I can see you'll be a right-hand man to me, none better." A smile. "I'm young, but not a young fool, sure."

"*I'm* the best salvage boss in the business," Ingolf said, obviously not relishing the prospect of being right-hand man to someone half a decade younger and still only shaving every second day.

"I don't doubt it," Rudi acknowledged.

"Hell, I'm the only one who's ever gotten to Nantucket and back . . . and I don't think many have gotten out of Corwin alive, either, *or* crossed the continent. No offense, Rudi, but you haven't done any of it. Hell, you've never left home."

"You've done more than a little in the way of traveling," Rudi acknowledged. *Though I've been most places in the valley, and round about it from the ocean to Bend.*

His voice was friendly but with a trace of iron in it as he went on: "But it doesn't alter the fact that this is *my* journey. I'd like your help with it, Ingolf . . . but if you can't accept that, then I'll go without you, and thank you for the message you brought."

The other man's heavy brows drew together. He grunted without speaking. They'd left unspoken the matter of whether the Powers would leave his rest alone if he dropped out of the matter. Ingolf thought for a moment, then brought the shete up in a salute.

Mary Havel was refereeing; she waited while they settled their helms. When Rudi flicked the visor of his sallet closed she chopped her hand down.

"Kumite!"

Fight!

His blade flicked into motion towards Rudi's neck—

Crack.

The shete smacked into the young Mackenzie's buckler. He knocked it away and thrust in riposte. Ingolf jerked his body back from the waist without moving his feet; it wasn't a counter Rudi was familiar with, but it worked, leaving him extended and off balance for an instant with the tip of his sword just touching the other man's mail shirt before his shield knocked it up.

The easterner used the motion to bring his shete round and down in a diagonal slash that would have beheaded an ox, or taken off a man's head and his shield arm at the shoulder too. His shield stayed well up all the while, not thrown to one side and leaving an opening. Rudi swayed out of the way as far as he could, and brought both buckler and blade up to meet the blow.

Crack-clung!

The force of it drove him down on one knee and numbed his left hand so that he almost dropped his buckler.

Cenn Cruaich, this one is strong! he thought, eyes going a little wider.

Ingolf cut three times before Rudi could get back on his feet. The Mackenzie parried with his sword—not directly, which would have driven it down on his own head, but by slanting the metal to shed the blows, *ting-ting-ting*, a threefold shivering crash faster than heartbeats. The big easterner hit like a blacksmith with a forging hammer, but he didn't let the force of his own blows throw him off balance either, which was always likely to be a problem with a point-heavy weapon like the shete.

Rudi feinted a thrust at his opponent's knee to break the rhythm of the attack and then bounced erect. Ingolf stepped backward and shook his head.

"That's enough for me today," he said. "Too much and you lose more than you gain. I'm still a little short-winded."

"You pushed me hard there," Rudi said, grinning. "Not bad, for an old man just up from a sickbed."

"Same back at you, youngster," Ingolf said in turn.

He smiled himself; he was doing that a little more often now.

"All right," he went on soberly. "I'm the guest here. I'll just have to not all right," he said. "I'm *old*, boy, and there's no cure for it. Some bones I had broken on me when I was about your age caught up with me for a bit there."

Edain was worried still. He was young enough for his gut to think that his father and mother went on like the rocks and trees while he changed. Some of his first memories were of sitting like this, watching his father at his bowyers' craft. Often while his mother made the loom thump at the other end of the big room, amid the smell of glue and varnish, sawdust and linseed oil and wax, with his elder half sister helping her and the youngsters in the cradle or crawling about with Grip and Garm, his father's hounds.

But I'm old enough to know *different. Even trees don't live forever,* he thought with a chill. *Grip and Garm are dead.*

And his younger brother, Dick, was fifteen and insufferable now, and his youngest sister, Fand, was twelve and worse.

Even rocks don't go on forever.

And his father *was* old; in his sixties. His hair was still thick and curly, but the brown had turned mostly gray or white, and the flesh had fallen in a bit on his strong square-jawed face. He still got about well enough and did most of a man's work, but he'd retired as first armsman some years ago now.

"So, spit it out," the elder Aylward went on, leaning back with his elbow on the table with its clamps and vise.

"Ah . . ."

Edain shuffled his brogues on the well-swept concrete of the floor. But for the age he looked much like his father, only a finger above average height but broad-chested and stocky-strong, with muscled arms and the thick wrists of a plowman or archer—both of which he was. His eyes were the same gray as the older man's; his hair was a little lighter, with a touch of yellow in the earth-brown, and he wore it shorter than most male Mackenzies of his generation, though longer than the short-back-and-sides his father had always kept to.

"Ah, it's a trip, Dad, one that Rudi was talking about," he said, feeling sweat breaking out on his forehead. "Talking about us doing it together."

He was too old now for a swat on the backside, but he'd learned early never to lie to his father. No matter what scrape he got into, honesty

hope you can listen as well as you fight, which is pretty damned good. But you're not going to cut your way across the continent, no matter how good you are with a blade."

Off to their right in the next field archers were practicing, ninety-nine of them and a bow captain, most of the dun's First Levy standing in the staggered three-deep harrow formation.

"Nock shaft!"

Right hands went back over the shoulders to the quivers, twitched out one of the arrows, set it to the string with the smooth economical motion of an action as familiar as walking.

"Draw!"

The varnished yellow-orange staves of the yew bows glistened in the bright spring sunlight as they rose and bent, drawing past the angle of the jaw.

"Let the gray geese fly—wholly together—*loose!*"

The strings of the longbows slapped the bracers all at once, like one great snap. The long arrows slashed upward with a multiple *shsshshshsh* sound like a distant whickering and came almost to a halt at the top of the trajectory. The pile-shaped heads glinted as they plunged downward towards the target, a line of shields propped near the hedge at the southern edge of the field, two hundred paces distant. The hammerfall of the arrows was still as sharp as heavy hail on a tile roof; they drove deep into the wood, and they would have punched through most armor. Three seconds later the second volley hit, and two more were in the air before they struck, and more followed in a steady nock-draw-loose rhythm.

"You're not going to be taking them with you, either," Ingolf said, nodding at the archers. "Much as I wish we could."

Mary and Ritva sighed with heavy patience. "If you two are through with playing little-boy games, what does Lady Juniper say about it?" one of them asked. "About the *quest*, not who can pee farthest."

"She's not happy about it, but there doesn't seem to be much choice," Rudi said. "If I didn't know her better, I'd say she was procrastinating. She *has* given me the go-ahead. The details are up to me; Mom's good that way."

"No, there isn't any choice, Sword-of-the-Lady-Artos," the other twin said with malice aforethought.

They unpacked the picnic basket. Rudi unstoppered a jug of fresh milk, and took a long draft of the cool rich creaminess; it always tasted a bit better after the grass really got going again. Ingolf bit into a sandwich of sharp cheese and smoked pork loin and slivers of pickle while Mary and Ritva opened the crock of potato salad. None of them took off their gear, except the helmets; you had to keep yourself used to the weight and constriction.

"One thing that's bothering me," Ingolf said hesitantly. Then he went on: "Look, that . . . Voice . . . told me to go *find* the Sword of the Lady. But it *showed* me a sword. That's sort of . . ."

"Contradictory," Mary or Ritva said helpfully. "Is Rudi the Sword of the Lady, or is the *sword* the sword?"

Rudi nodded. "That had occurred to me. Well, it's an oracle—they're *usually* gnarly and hard to figure out. But it doesn't change what we have to do, the which is get to Nantucket, sure."

"Get *you* to Nantucket, like a bolt at a target," Ingolf said. Somberly: "I've already been there, and I wish to God I didn't have to go again. Even without the weirdness, it's not exactly a merry outing like sugaring-off in the spring."

"Let's break it down," Rudi said. "We need to make the preparations; then we need to go, and preferably we need to do it quietly so this Prophet doesn't get wind of it."

"How many people?" Mary or Ritva said. "Nine is traditional."

Rudi looked at them, unable to decide for an instant if they were putting him on. It was a very Rangerish thing to say, but . . . he decided they were; the bland butter-wouldn't-melt was the giveaway.

"As few as possible," he said in a quelling tone. "We have to sneak there and back—we *couldn't* take enough to cut our way through, not if we turned out all the troops of the Meeting."

"Right enough," Ingolf said, sounding a little reassured. "But not *too* small. Most of the country we'll be crossing isn't what you'd call easy. We'll want enough to discourage bandits and look out for one another. Nine sounds good—in fact, I'd be happier with a dozen or so."

"We've got one asset already," Rudi said thoughtfully. He pointed at the twins. "You two."

"That's true, but you're not usually so perceptive, Rudi."

He snorted and went on: "You're Dúnedain *ohtar*. Rangers go all sorts of places and deal with all sorts of people; I mean, yeah, you're my sisters

and your dad was Bear Lord, but by now people are used to you showing up wherever without a lot of fuss. And the Prophet's men won't be looking for you specifically yet."

"And you're gir . . . women," Ingolf said. At their inquiring look: "The Cutters don't hold with women doing much besides keeping house and raising kids, or working the churn and loom," he said.

"*Canuidhollin*," Mary or Ritva replied crisply. Which meant roughly: *What complete idiots.*

"Yeah, but they'll be less likely to notice you."

"Notice us do *what*?"

"Here's my plan . . ." Rudi went on.

* * *

DUN FAIRFAX, WILLAMETTE VALLEY, OREGON
APRIL 16, CY23/2021 A.D.

Edain Aylward Mackenzie stopped and took a deep breath at the entrance to his home. This part of it had been a *two-car garage* in the old days; someone had told him what that meant once, but he'd forgotten. He was nineteen . . . well, nearly nineteen. All his life it had been the place where his father made bows and fletched arrows, and his mother wove at the big loom, when they weren't out about the chores of house and farm.

Umm, Dad . . . he began mentally, rehearsing what he'd say, then wrung the flat Scots bonnet in his hands. *Oh, Wild Hunt take it, I could never fool him!*

If he stood here eventually someone would ask him what he was doing; the Aylward house was only one of twenty inside the log palisade that enclosed Dun Fairfax. He took a deep breath, said, "Stay, Garbh!" to the shaggy half-mastiff bitch at his heel, then opened the door and plunged in, blinking as he went from light to shadow.

There he stopped in alarm; his father was seated at his workbench, bent over with a hand pressed to his side.

"Are you all right, then, Dad?" he blurted sharply, his own burden forgotten.

His father grinned back at his seriousness and straightened. "No, I'm hope you can listen as well as you fight, which is pretty damned good. But you're not going to cut your way across the continent, no matter how good you are with a blade."

Off to their right in the next field archers were practicing, ninety-nine of them and a bow captain, most of the dun's First Levy standing in the staggered three-deep harrow formation.

"Nock shaft!"

Right hands went back over the shoulders to the quivers, twitched out one of the arrows, set it to the string with the smooth economical motion of an action as familiar as walking.

"Draw!"

The varnished yellow-orange staves of the yew bows glistened in the bright spring sunlight as they rose and bent, drawing past the angle of the jaw.

"Let the gray geese fly—wholly together—*loose!*"

The strings of the longbows slapped the bracers all at once, like one great snap. The long arrows slashed upward with a multiple *shsshshshsh* sound like a distant whickering and came almost to a halt at the top of the trajectory. The pile-shaped heads glinted as they plunged downward towards the target, a line of shields propped near the hedge at the southern edge of the field, two hundred paces distant. The hammerfall of the arrows was still as sharp as heavy hail on a tile roof; they drove deep into the wood, and they would have punched through most armor. Three seconds later the second volley hit, and two more were in the air before they struck, and more followed in a steady nock-draw-loose rhythm.

"You're not going to be taking them with you, either," Ingolf said, nodding at the archers. "Much as I wish we could."

Mary and Ritva sighed with heavy patience. "If you two are through with playing little-boy games, what does Lady Juniper say about it?" one of them asked. "About the *quest*, not who can pee farthest."

"She's not happy about it, but there doesn't seem to be much choice," Rudi said. "If I didn't know her better, I'd say she was procrastinating. She *has* given me the go-ahead. The details are up to me; Mom's good that way."

"No, there isn't any choice, Sword-of-the-Lady-Artos," the other twin said with malice aforethought.

They unpacked the picnic basket. Rudi unstoppered a jug of fresh milk, and took a long draft of the cool rich creaminess; it always tasted a bit better after the grass really got going again. Ingolf bit into a sandwich of sharp cheese and smoked pork loin and slivers of pickle while Mary and Ritva opened the crock of potato salad. None of them took off their gear, except the helmets; you had to keep yourself used to the weight and constriction.

"One thing that's bothering me," Ingolf said hesitantly. Then he went on: "Look, that . . . Voice . . . told me to go *find* the Sword of the Lady. But it *showed* me a sword. That's sort of . . ."

"Contradictory," Mary or Ritva said helpfully. "Is Rudi the Sword of the Lady, or is the *sword* the sword?"

Rudi nodded. "That had occurred to me. Well, it's an oracle—they're *usually* gnarly and hard to figure out. But it doesn't change what we have to do, the which is get to Nantucket, sure."

"Get *you* to Nantucket, like a bolt at a target," Ingolf said. Somberly: "I've already been there, and I wish to God I didn't have to go again. Even without the weirdness, it's not exactly a merry outing like sugaring-off in the spring."

"Let's break it down," Rudi said. "We need to make the preparations; then we need to go, and preferably we need to do it quietly so this Prophet doesn't get wind of it."

"How many people?" Mary or Ritva said. "Nine is traditional."

Rudi looked at them, unable to decide for an instant if they were putting him on. It was a very Rangerish thing to say, but . . . he decided they were; the bland butter-wouldn't-melt was the giveaway.

"As few as possible," he said in a quelling tone. "We have to sneak there and back—we *couldn't* take enough to cut our way through, not if we turned out all the troops of the Meeting."

"Right enough," Ingolf said, sounding a little reassured. "But not *too* small. Most of the country we'll be crossing isn't what you'd call easy. We'll want enough to discourage bandits and look out for one another. Nine sounds good—in fact, I'd be happier with a dozen or so."

"We've got one asset already," Rudi said thoughtfully. He pointed at the twins. "You two."

"That's true, but you're not usually so perceptive, Rudi."

He snorted and went on: "You're Dúnedain *ohtar*. Rangers go all sorts of places and deal with all sorts of people; I mean, yeah, you're my sisters and your dad was Bear Lord, but by now people are used to you showing up wherever without a lot of fuss. And the Prophet's men won't be looking for you specifically yet."

"And you're gir . . . women," Ingolf said. At their inquiring look: "The Cutters don't hold with women doing much besides keeping house and raising kids, or working the churn and loom," he said.

"*Canuidhollin*," Mary or Ritva replied crisply. Which meant roughly: *What complete idiots.*

"Yeah, but they'll be less likely to notice you."

"Notice us do *what?*"

"Here's my plan . . ." Rudi went on.

* * *

Edain Aylward Mackenzie stopped and took a deep breath at the entrance to his home. This part of it had been a *two-car garage* in the old days; someone had told him what that meant once, but he'd forgotten. He was nineteen . . . well, nearly nineteen. All his life it had been the place where his father made bows and fletched arrows, and his mother wove at the big loom, when they weren't out about the chores of house and farm.

Umm, Dad . . . he began mentally, rehearsing what he'd say, then wrung the flat Scots bonnet in his hands. *Oh, Wild Hunt take it, I could never fool him!*

If he stood here eventually someone would ask him what he was doing; the Aylward house was only one of twenty inside the log palisade that enclosed Dun Fairfax. He took a deep breath, said, "Stay, Garbh!" to the shaggy half-mastiff bitch at his heel, then opened the door and plunged in, blinking as he went from light to shadow.

There he stopped in alarm; his father was seated at his workbench, bent over with a hand pressed to his side.

"Are you all right, then, Dad?" he blurted sharply, his own burden forgotten.

His father grinned back at his seriousness and straightened. "No, I'm not all right," he said. "I'm *old*, boy, and there's no cure for it. Some bones I had broken on me when I was about your age caught up with me for a bit there."

Edain was worried still. He was young enough for his gut to think that his father and mother went on like the rocks and trees while he changed. Some of his first memories were of sitting like this, watching his father at his bowyers' craft. Often while his mother made the loom thump at the other end of the big room, amid the smell of glue and varnish, sawdust and linseed oil and wax, with his elder half sister helping her and the youngsters in the cradle or crawling about with Grip and Garm, his father's hounds.

But I'm old enough to know *different. Even trees don't live forever,* he thought with a chill. *Grip and Garm are dead.*

And his younger brother, Dick, was fifteen and insufferable now, and his youngest sister, Fand, was twelve and worse.

Even rocks *don't go on forever.*

And his father *was* old; in his sixties. His hair was still thick and curly, but the brown had turned mostly gray or white, and the flesh had fallen in a bit on his strong square-jawed face. He still got about well enough and did most of a man's work, but he'd retired as first armsman some years ago now.

"So, spit it out," the elder Aylward went on, leaning back with his elbow on the table with its clamps and vise.

"Ah . . ."

Edain shuffled his brogues on the well-swept concrete of the floor. But for the age he looked much like his father, only a finger above average height but broad-chested and stocky-strong, with muscled arms and the thick wrists of a plowman or archer—both of which he was. His eyes were the same gray as the older man's; his hair was a little lighter, with a touch of yellow in the earth-brown, and he wore it shorter than most male Mackenzies of his generation, though longer than the short-back-and-sides his father had always kept to.

"Ah, it's a trip, Dad, one that Rudi was talking about," he said, feeling sweat breaking out on his forehead. "Talking about us doing it together."

He was too old now for a swat on the backside, but he'd learned early never to lie to his father. No matter what scrape he got into, honesty was the best policy with Samuel Aylward, late of the Special Air Service Regiment.

"A hunting trip?" his father prodded. "Or a jaunt for the sake of the thing, like that trip to Tillamook?"

The beads of sweat grew and he suppressed an impulse to wipe them away.

"Quite a bit of a trip, a long 'un," he said. "Weeks or more. We'd be going off right away."

Horned Lord and Mother-of-All, do you have to ask so many bloody questions? he thought desperately. And then: *Oh, bugger, I let it slip.*

Normally he spoke with nearly the same accent as any other Mackenzie his age, except that it was a bit stronger since he lived close to Dun Juniper. That musical lilt and its rolled R sounds were natural to him, though he'd heard that it had started right after the Change when people tried to imitate Lady Juniper's manner of speech. His father always found it irritating or amusing, depending on his mood.

When he was in the irritated phase, Sam Aylward called it life imprisonment among the stage Irish, whatever that meant.

But when he was under a strain more of his father's own voice came out in his, and Sam Aylward had been born in England—on a farm near Tilford in Hampshire, to be precise—and the soft burr clung to his tongue despite more than twenty years here in the Willamette.

Edain could see his father relent; he laughed then, and the younger man flushed.

"It's all right," Sam Aylward said. "Just that you're about as good at keeping something off your face as I was at your age. Still, you're a better than good shot and useful otherwise for a long trip."

"You *know?*" Edain blurted.

His father grinned like a wolf. "I may not be the first armsman anymore, but Lady Juniper *does* still ask me for advice, I'll have you know. I was your age when I took the Queen's Shilling, pretty much, and ended up on a transport to the Falklands not long after. Your mother knows too, by the way."

That was no surprise. His mother was high priestess of the oldest coven in Dun Fairfax, and she heard everything from this world and the Otherworld both.

"You want to go?" Sam Aylward asked.

He looked at his father in astonishment. "Well, of course I do, Dad!" he said.

"Ah, I should remember what nineteen's like," Aylward senior said. At Edain's affronted look: "You'll understand in a while."

"It's the farm I was worried about, with the spring work and all," the younger man said awkwardly. "I mean . . ."

"Lambing and shearing's over," Aylward said. "And besides, we've got Tamar, and her man's about the place now, and young Dickie is getting to be a real help, and your little sister with your mother. We'll manage."

Edain blew out his lips in relief. A huge excitement grew beneath his breastbone; it dimmed only a little when his mother came through the door from the main house with his siblings, including his elder half sister, Tamar—she'd been born a little before the Change that killed her father—and her handfasted man, Eochu, and their firstborn in her arms.

Baby Forgall just gurgled quietly, but everyone else *looked* at him. His mother with worry; she had the upper section of her arsaid over her head like a hood, which meant she'd just been at some rite before the house altar. Dick was looking at him with naked envy. Young Fand was nearly as distressed as their mother, her fair redhead's face flushed.

Then her expression changed and she spoke: "I guess we can't tell Eithne, sure?" and giggled, back to her usual hateful twelve-year-old self.

That made him feel better about it. For one thing, Eithne would be spitting mad that he was going and she wasn't when it all came out, so he wouldn't be sorry she *didn't* hear of it. And things had never been quite the same with them since that trip north last year. He felt even better when his father snapped in a tone harder than his usual: "No, and if you want your brother back alive, you'll keep your mouth bloody well *shut,* girl!"

She looked properly abashed. Then Sam Aylward went on to his eldest son: "Rudi has the gear you'll need for the first part ready. But you'll need a spare war bow."

There were dozens racked on the walls, finished or in the making. Edain's eyes went wide when he saw the one his father took down. It wasn't new—he'd gotten a new one as a gift at his birthday this spring, just after Ostara—but it was beautiful, from the darkly shining riser of black-walnut root to the carved horn tips at either end. The staves were yew, the whole weapon six feet long with a subtle double curve, out a little from the riser and then back again, what the old books called reflex-deflex.

His father was known as Aylward the Archer throughout the Willamette, and his marksmanship was only half the reason.

"That's your war bow, Dad!"

"Too heavy for me, these days. I get a twinge in me shoulder at full draw with it. A hundred and fifteen pounds with a thirty-inch arrow . . . Give it a try."

Edain flushed again at doing it with everyone watching. The actions were automatic: he strung it Mackenzie-style, with the lower tip braced against his left foot and his right thigh over the riser. Then he brought it up and drew, pushing out his left arm and pulling with the muscles of his torso and gut as much as the right arm. A little to his surprise it bent easily, and he held the draw without any betraying quiver.

"You'll do," his father said when he'd eased off from the draw, then pulled him into a quick rough hug. "You'll do me proud, boy."

His mother was crying a little; she was a decade and more younger than his father, but he suddenly realized with a shock that her yellow-brown hair had gone mostly gray too. When had that happened?

He knelt before her. She made the invoking sign over his head—a pentagram, starting with the top point—and spoke with a catch in her voice:

> *Through darkened wood and shadowed path*
> *Hunter of the Forest, by your side*
> *Lady of the Stars, fold you in Her wings:*
> *So mote it be!*

The whole family joined in on the final line of the spell-prayer. It made him feel stronger; then his mother handed him a sack.

"Just a few extra things. There are some simples in the white box; they're all labeled in case you take a chill. Try"—her face worked—"try to come back safe!"

He was glad to finally get out and on his way; good-byes were all well and good, but he had to *go*. He strode down the graveled lane between the houses and sheds, the Covenstead and the big communal barn, and out through the gate, with Garbh padding at his heels. It was midmorning, and most of the folk were out in the fields; he passed a few younger children playing or watching still younger siblings, and the odd adult whose work kept them in the dun even now. Outside the gate he paused to leave a few crumbs by the grave of the Fairfaxes, the old couple who'd owned the farm around which the dun had grown, and then turned east.

He kept to the road, passing people busy in the garden plots with their eternal battle against slugs and couch grass and creeping shoots, their hoes flashing as they sang a working song:

> *Remember what old granny said*
> *These beetles are pretty—but better off dead;*
> *They can be compost—and we can be fed!*

Eithne gave him a look and went back to work; he winced a little. Her mother gave him a look that was even worse and called out, "Care to try a spell at the hoe, if you can spare the time from a walk in the woods?"

He shrugged and kept walking. "No, no, these mysteries of the Earth Mother are too sacred for my eyes!" he called with mock solemnity.

That got him a chorus of good-natured hoots and jeers, particularly from the men and boys working there, and he waved back as he went by. Nobody was too upset; they knew he wasn't one of Dun Fairfax's few shirkers. This was a solidly prosperous settlement and proud of it— prosperous by standards no older than Edain, which meant that everyone in it had plenty of food all year 'round, at least two spare sets of clothing and a clean bed of their own. But it stayed that way because everyone in it worked very hard indeed.

The fields narrowed as he went east towards the head of the valley. A quick skip from rock to rock at a ford put him over the river that flowed down from Dun Juniper's hillside bench. Then he was into the green gloom of tall forest, land that had been Mackenzie-owned in the old days, Lady Juniper's land; that meant a century of careful tending since it was last logged. Red alder grew tall along the stream, ten times his height, with its bark mottled white and the new leaves green and tender. Fir and hemlock and red cedar stood taller still and candle-straight on the drier ground; beneath the forest floor bore a carpet of low-growing red-stemmed kinnikinnick, starred with pink flowers in this season.

Birds were many; away in the middle distance he heard the mating-season *boom-boom* of a blue grouse, and closer to hand a pair of hummingbirds hovered above a patch of iris. It was all nearly as familiar as his family's house, or the fields. He still smiled to see it. . . .

But I'm leaving, he thought. *I'm going far and far away, and I may never be back again!*

He stopped for a moment to look back for a last glimpse through the trees and down at the valley's dappled spring quilt of plowland and pasture and young wheat. That was enough to sober him for a few minutes; with every pace away he could feel how his heartstrings were deep in that good brown earth. And it made him look at each tree and turn of the creek in a new light as it went past; but he was cheerful enough again in a few minutes. He was young, and strong, and the Chief's tanist had chosen *him* as his companion on the great journey.

When he came near the old overgrown logging trail above Dun Juniper he was grinning again. He decided to approach on the quiet—and was congratulating himself on how well he was managing, though only deer and elk and the odd hunter had kept fern and brush from totally closing the way. It was Garbh's low growl that alerted him; he wheeled with a sudden start of alarm.

"Not bad, kid," a voice said from behind him.

He knew from the flat harsh accent that it was the foreigner Ingolf. Very slowly he turned, cheeks blushing with embarrassment, biting down on anger.

He outsneaked me! he thought indignantly. *And on ground I've hunted over all my life!*

Rudi stood grinning, leaning on a quarterstaff. Three big A-frame packs rested at his feet, and another of the walking sticks.

"Ready, Edain?" he said, tossing it.

Edain caught the length of ashwood and looked up through the trees to the high white peaks eastward. Mackenzie Pass would still be cold this time of year. . . .

"Ready, Chief!" he said, rearranging his quiver and shrugging one of the packs onto his back with a grunt of effort.

Usually Rudi didn't like being called that; and technically he wouldn't be, not until his mother died or stepped down, and even then only if the Clan hailed him—though that was pretty well a foregone conclusion now that they'd made him tanist. This time he shrugged it off with a grin.

"Then let's get going!"

"After you, Chief," Ingolf said with a smile.

Rudi *did* scowl at him; then they set their faces eastward and walked into the forests and towards the peaks that walled the world.

CHAPTER ELEVEN

"It really is worth coming here for the blossom time," Mathilda Arminger said wistfully, taking a deep breath of the cool morning air. "Too bad we have to leave right away."

This had always been fruit country, and still was; neat orchards mantled the rolling floor of the valley on every side, apple and cherry and pear, a froth of cream and pink and white, the scent as intoxicating as cool wine. Petals fell in drifts from the trees on either side of the road to catch in her hat and hair and the russet-brown suede leather of her jerkin, and there was a deep murmur of bees amid the blossoms.

The great white cone of Mount Hood hung in the sky to the south, looming over the valley that ran north to the Columbia Gorge. The cream of its summit was tinged with a little pink from the rising sun. It looked a bit odd to see the snowpeak there, even though this was far from her first visit to the chancellor's home fief—in Portland and the Willamette you saw the mountain from the west.

The ferroconcrete bulk of Castle Odell on Lenz Butte behind them was two years younger than Mathilda, but the bright white-stucco mass might have loomed there for generations, with banners flying from the high turrets and terraced gardens falling from the outer edge of the moat to the valley floor. Odell Town huddled at its base as if for protection, its churches and dwellings and workshops mostly red-tiled and built since the Change; a half-finished cathedral in the fashionable Cypriot Gothic style was already the tallest building in it.

Steep forested hills rose green and blue with distance on either side, and Middle Mountain a few miles south separated the lower valley from the upper. A few fleecy clouds floated overhead, and the air was busy with birds journeying north. The road their horses trod came out through the town's western gate and followed the old Union Pacific. Trains of ox-drawn cars went by northward on the steel rails, mostly with barrels of fruit brandies and cordials, apple vinegar and honey mead; south the return cargoes were grain and wool from the count's vassals in Grass and Tygh valleys.

As the road and rail turned west and then south they passed manors and villages and even a few isolated farms—the latter very rare in Association territory, and a sign of long peace. Peasants cutting hay in a riverside meadow paused to wave their straw hats; a friar on foot told his beads as he walked and raised a hand in blessing as they passed; once a raggedy-gaudy troubadour with a lute slung over his back doffed his cap and bowed as they rode by. A little later a half dozen mounted crossbowmen on road patrol saluted smartly.

And now we have to figure out how to get rid of Lady Catherine, she thought as she returned the gesture with a wave of her riding crop.

As princess she was exempt from most of the usual rules, but Catherine was young—daughter of one of the Countess of Odell's ladies-in-waiting—and took her duties as chaperone seriously, sitting primly on her palfrey in her modest divided skirt and leggings. Her lips were compressed; it had taken a direct order to stop her hauling along a round dozen mounted attendants and guards. Mathilda's own mouth quirked.

Chaperone, indeed! As if I couldn't kick up my heels anytime I wanted! And Odard would be happy to cooperate—he isn't a pest about it, but you can tell. There's no real guard against impurity but determination.

The hills closed in on either side as the way turned south and closed with the Hood River, brawling and leaping white over rocks with spring's snowmelt. A roadside shrine caught her eye, a miniature carved wooden shed above a saint's image. It was a naked man with one hand on his chest and the other holding a cross.

Saint Dismas, she thought, *the thief who'd been crucified at the side of* Jesus. *The one who repented, that is. Patron saint of criminals who've gone respectable.*

Conrad Renfrew wasn't openly old-fashioned, but he had an odd sense of humor she'd noticed sometimes in those who'd been adults before the Change. It was just like him to find a special devotion to that particular member of the calendar.

"Let's stop and ask the saint's help," Mathilda said.

That was always a safe thing to suggest, and in this case she really wanted it as well. They reined in and dismounted; Odard gallantly gave her a hand down, which was sort of superfluous—Catherine was the one who might actually need it. As he did he whispered, "I'll fix her saddle to slip off when she remounts. She couldn't ride a rocking horse bareback and she won't notice until it's too late. Then we can just gallop away and she'll have to walk back to the castle."

Mathilda nodded unhappily; the count wasn't at home, but his lady and his eldest son *were,* and they'd smell a rat as soon as Catherine got back to town, and couriers would start galloping in every direction and heliograph messages would fly to the outposts all around. It would be touch and go whether she and Odard could make it south to the border before a *conroi* of lancers caught up to "escort" her home . . . and there would be hell to pay from her mother.

The three young nobles tied their horses to the hitching rail, dropped a few copper coins in the box and lit the small tapers provided, planting them before the image. Then they knelt on the dense green turf, signing themselves, kissing their crucifixes and taking up their rosaries. Mathilda continued with silent intensity as they all bowed their heads in prayer:

Saint Dismas, patron of the repentant, I am not sure that what I plan to do is right, and I am torn between my duties. I know I should obey my mother, but God has called me to guard the folk. I can see no other way than this to best fulfill my oaths and help my friend in this task, and so do what is best for both our peoples. If I do wrong, misled by my rebellious heart, help me to repent. May God bless this quest and my companions on this road. Saint Dismas, teach me the words to say to Our Lord to gain pardon and the grace of perseverance; and you who are so close to Him now in heaven, as you were during His last moments on earth, pray to Him for me that I shall never again desert Him, but that at the close of my life I may hear from Him the words He addressed to you: "This day thou shalt be with Me in Paradise."

As Mathilda stood and brushed off her knees she heard a quick beat of hooves from the northward. She looked up in alarm, a hand going to her sword hilt, but it was a single rider leading a pair of packhorses.

As he came closer she could see that it was a monk with his dark robe kirted up over practical-looking deerskin pants and stout riding boots; a telltale chink and shift hinted at a short mail shirt beneath the coarse dark robe. A longsword and dagger hung from his belt, beside a steel crucifix and a rosary of maple-wood beads, and a bowcase and quiver rode at his saddlebow. One of the led horses had a four-foot shield strapped to its packsaddle.

The canvas cover was still on that, but she suspected she knew what it would show: a raven over a cross. And his face was vaguely familiar. . . .

"Knight-brother of the Order of the Shield of Saint Benedict," Odard said quietly, agreeing with her unspoken thought. "Not the worst possible news. He won't be reporting to the Regent, or Cardinal-Archbishop Maxwell. But they're an independent-minded bunch."

Mathilda nodded. The Benedictine monastery at Mount Angel had come through the Change on its own and had been a rallying point for resistance to the Portland Protective Association and its then-schismatic Church. Mount Angel and the Protectorate both sent delegates to the Meeting at Corvallis these days, but there was still a lingering suspicion. And she knew that her mother resented the influence of the Order's missions and daughter houses in the interior and the far south.

"Wait a minute," she said as the man drew closer. "I recognize him. That's Father Ignatius—he's a priest as well as a brother—he was in Sutterdown when the Cutters attacked. He's been at court in Portland lately, too, some sort of diplomatic mission from Abbot-Bishop Dmwoski."

The hood of his robe was thrown back to show bowl-cut black hair and a tonsure. The face beneath was weathered like leather and had a scar along the right side of the square jaw, but it was only a few years older than hers, the eyes dark and watchful and slightly tilted, shaped a little like Odard's. He was of medium height, only a bit taller than she, but broad-shouldered. The hands on the reins were shapely but large, with thick corded wrists.

The warrior-cleric drew rein and signed the air. "Bless you, my children," he said. *"Dominus vobiscum."*

"And with your spirit, Father," they replied. The priest went on to the young chaperone: "Lady Catherine, it was thought that I would make a more suitable escort for Her Highness, since she plans to push on to the upper valley to see the scenery there, and may stay overnight at Castle Akers in Parkdale. The chatelaine there can see to her needs."

Duty warred with sudden hope on the young noblewoman's round plump face. Mathilda gave her a smile and a nod, and she burst out happily: "Thank you, Your Highness, reverend Father!"

Mathilda fought down both relief and suspicion until the other young woman had heeled her placid gelding into a trot back towards the civilized comforts of the castle solar. Then she turned narrow-eyed inquiry to Ignatius.

"Who exactly did you mean when you said 'it was thought' you'd make a better escort, Father?"

The priest's brown eyes were calm. "I suggested it to the countess, my child," he said. "Without, I'm afraid, drawing attention to the fact that I did not say I would be *returning* from there. It allayed her worries about you, and you won't be missed until tomorrow evening at the earliest. . . . You *are* planning to escape over the border and join Rudi Mackenzie on his journey to the east, aren't you?"

"Why, Father, why would you suspect any such thing?" she asked in turn, controlling a gasp of dismay.

Answer a question with a question when you don't want to answer, she thought, and then went on: "That would be a reckless thing to do!"

"Daughter, don't lie to me. For starters, you're rather bad at it."

He began to tick off points on his fingers. "*Primus,* you were with Rudi Mackenzie when the assassins attacked. *Secundus,* you were privy to his tale of the mysterious events on Nantucket—"

Her eyes went wide in shock. "How do you know about *that?*" she said.

He smiled grimly, showing teeth that were white but a little uneven.

"Holy Mother Church has many sources of information—and from well beyond this corner of the world. *Tertius,* you and Rudi Mackenzie and his half sisters and Baron Odard here have all dropped out of sight . . . heading east. The inference is obvious. I might add that as soon as your mother hears of your disappearance, she will know what you have done."

"I left a letter for her with someone I trusted," Mathilda said sullenly.

"Clever clerics give me heartburn." Odard chuckled. "They tend to push in where they're not wanted. Shall I rid you of this troublesome priest, Princess?"

He laid his hand on the hilt of his sword and raised a brow at her.

"Oh, stop posturing, Odard," Mathilda said impatiently. "I know you'll bash whomever I tell you to bash, but that's ridiculous here."

At least, I hope he's posturing. Priest murder is sacrilege! she thought. Aloud she went on: "And in case you hadn't noticed, he's got a sword too."

"I did," Odard said, with the same lazy smile. "A man who wears a sword should expect to have to use it, tonsure and robe or no."

"I am willing to use it," Ignatius said. "Against the enemies of peace, and of the Faith, whom we've been given dispensation to fight by the Holy Father. Do you wish to join one of those two categories, my lord Odard?"

"A knight-brother knows how to *use* the sword too," Mathilda pointed out. "Let's hear what he has to say."

The priest turned his gaze to her. "Daughter, are you determined on this course? For as you said, it *is* reckless."

"You're not my confessor, Father!" she snapped.

Unexpectedly, Ignatius smiled. "For which, thanks be to God!"

Mathilda found herself chuckling for an instant, and abandoned the attempt to hold on to her anger.

"Then what are you questioning me for?" she asked. "Father," she added after a moment.

"My child, being who and what you are, your actions affect more than yourself. This is your responsibility; God gives us each a cross to carry, as heavy as we can bear—neither more nor less. *My* responsibility is to the head of my Order . . . and *he* has ordered me to investigate the matter of Ingolf Vogeler, and the assassins who pursued him here. The Order of the Shield has been watching the growth of this dangerous cult in Montana for some time now. What we know does not please us; and we must know more."

Mathilda arched her brows. "You don't intend to try to stop me?" she said bluntly.

Ignatius shrugged. "The Regent is not my ruler; Abbot-Bishop Dmwoski is. Furthermore you will be Lady Protector in only a few more years, and it is my judgment that your displeasure then if I, ah, fink you out would do more to endanger the interests of the Order than angering your mother now. Besides which, if we hurry we can probably cross the border well before anyone finds out what's going on. When . . . if . . . we return, things will be very different."

Mathilda stood for a moment, and then threw up her hands with a laugh. "Let's go, then. It'll be a comfort to have the sacraments available on the way. Not including extreme unction, I hope!"

When Ignatius grinned, you suddenly remembered he was a young man himself. He slapped his sword hilt and replied, "Perhaps I can help us *avoid* that one."

Odard bowed slightly. "As the princess commands," he said. Then after a long considering look at the priest: "And perhaps it's just a good idea anyway, too."

They swung back into the saddle and headed south at a ground-covering pace, walk-trot-canter-trot-walk; she and Odard had chosen their horses carefully. Not the big destriers that cost more than a knight's armor—those would be waiting for them in Bend, if all went well—but good-sized long-legged palfreys. The cleric's horses were fine stock as well, and not carrying too much weight; he was whipcord and sinew rather than bulk. Mount Angel had rich lands, including stud farms with a growing reputation.

The narrow passage along the river opened up into broad fields and orchards again southward; the skin between Mathilda's shoulder blades crawled as they passed the last castle of the Upper Valley, where the rail-road stopped and just before the valley floor rippled up into the ridges around the base of Mount Hood. The tall square tower of the keep flew a banner with a saw-edge circle, sable on argent. Those were the arms of the Akers family, barons but not tenants-in-chief, vassals of the Counts of Odell rather than the throne. She expected the garrison to be as alert as any of her mother's own household forces, but they evidently didn't consider a monk and two gentlefolk heading *out* of the valley any of their business.

"Phew!" Mathilda said as the last field gave way to forest.

It was cooler under the shade of the great Douglas and grand firs, and the ground was rising; they were more than a thousand feet higher than the Columbia gorge now. The faint smells of woodsmoke and habitation were gone, noticeable only by their absence. The tiny white and pink flowers of shade-loving sourgrass bloomed under the tall trees, and snowy-colored trillium; ferns were sprouting through the damp litter of leaf and needle, and a patch of yellow violet trembled gold beside a stream. After the first few miles they saw few traces of human hands except the road itself. Birds were noisy with their spring mating rituals, and once a small herd of elk crossed in front of them and went crashing eastward in alarm.

The area of the old Mount Hood wilderness and much besides was Lord Protector's personal reserve, land under forest law where nobody could hunt or cut timber without special leave. Odard and the priest looked over at her as she snorted laughter.

"It's just that technically speaking, this is *my* land we're on. Yet I'm sneaking through it like a poacher afraid of a whipping from the verderers!"

The two men chuckled. Odard lifted his head. "And speaking of poachers, I think I smell venison cooking. Good man, Alex. And a dab hand with a crossbow."

Mathilda tested the air; there was woodsmoke and grilling meat, sure enough. A minute later the narrow road turned and revealed a small stretch of meadow, an ancient campground. Twenty-odd years and heavy rains had left nothing of picnic tables save green mounds, but the stone hearth was still usable. Odard's manservant Alex was there, with five hob-bled horses, their packsaddles . . . and yes, pieces of venison on skew-ers over glowing coals, giving off a smell that made her mouth water. The neatly butchered carcass of a yearling doe hung in sections from a branch; Alex had wrapped the chunks he was cooking in bacon from the supplies, since the meat would be lean this time of year.

It had been a long time since their breakfast at Castle Odell, and it would have looked suspicious to pack along supplies for what was sup-posed to be a short trip to look at the flowers.

"Your Highness," Alex said, bowing, not even a twitch to show he was surprised at seeing three riders instead of two. "My lord Odard. And most reverend father in God. No sign of the foresters who ought to be patrol-ling. Even if the Princess was graciously pleased to give me a signed war-rant, they should have *checked,* the idle bastards. It's not as if I'm hiding."

Odard grinned; he'd told her Alex could manage getting their gear ready and meeting them with it, and evidently he'd been right.

"No problem getting past the road patrols?" he said to his servant.

Alex shrugged. "I'm just another commoner, my lord. Nobody notices us—and there's no tax on goods *leaving* Association territory. It's not like the old days, when they were on the lookout for runaway peons."

Ouch, Mathilda thought. *Well, those were hard times; hard measures were necessary.* The thought was well-worn and increasingly unsatisfying.

She dismounted; they took a moment to unsaddle and hobble their horses, and pour out oats from the packsaddles. Those contained a little food, but mostly the essentials of their gear, things you couldn't buy in a town market. Principally their armor, since a really first-class suit had to be fitted like fine clothing. Her battle harness included a set of titanium mesh-mail, the priceless work of half a dozen specialists laboring for years, stronger than even the best steel and only a third the weight, besides being rustproof.

Sneaking it out of the palace had been a major pain. She'd felt a quiet glow of accomplishment when she managed it without—she very much hoped without—anyone important noticing. Right now the venison kebabs *felt* more important. Alex had fresh bread with them, and butter and soft cheese and pickled vegetables. . . .

* * *

Two days later Mathilda's horse drank, and then raised its dripping muzzle from a pool. The spring that made it flowed from a split in the dark basalt lava, and they'd paused to fill their canteens and let their mounts drink. Hers nosed towards a tall purple stalk of larkspur; she put her hand on its muzzle and pushed against the hairy weight to distract it—the plant was pretty, but its other name was poison delphinium.

"How *did* you beasts survive before we people came along to look after you?" she asked it with rhetorical indignation and fed it some dried apple.

Then the animal lost interest in water and feed both. Its ears cocked forward and it raised its head, snorting and staring westward. A crow launched itself from the boughs of a willow that stood a little downstream trailing its branches in the water, calling *gruk-gruk-gruk* as its wings flogged the cool air. A pair of pintail ducks swam away, then decided to follow it, skittering down the little creek with their feet splashing at the surface as they made their takeoff.

"Heads up, Your Highness, Father," Odard said quietly. "*Told* you we were on Warm Springs land by now. The Three Tribes are touchy about their borders, too. There was a lot of raiding around here in the old days."

"Yeah," Mathilda said, tightening the girth. "Someone spotted us yesterday, I think. They probably hightailed it for help."

She swung back into the saddle, and stopped her hand on its way to the bow cased at her knee with an effort of will; they weren't here to fight. Her warning hiss made Alex stop his hand reaching towards the light crossbow he kept hanging at his, and the four of them rode up out of the hollow onto a long open swelling. The grassland was green with spring and starred with white flowers and sage that gave a strong clean scent when hooves crushed it, and scattered with dwarf juniper. Mount Hood loomed directly west, which meant they *were* on reservation land.

The rumble of hooves grew louder, and a dozen horsemen came out of the rise half a mile southward. They headed straight for the travelers at a gallop, and then split and surrounded them amid high yelps and *ki-yi!* yips and thundering hooves; that was good tactics, and it would give them a psychological advantage. All of them had bows, quivers over their backs, shetes at their waists and lariats hanging from their saddlebows. They had round painted shields as well, and one or two carried light spears; their hair was in braids, and most wore feathers in it. More feathers and beads and shellwork picked out their gear and horse harness and the leather vests they wore over colorful shirts or bare skin.

"Let's hope they're honest," Odard murmured as the noise and dust enveloped them.

Mathilda nodded, and her mouth went a little dry; their horses and gear were worth a good deal. The strangers' leader reined his own beautiful white-spotted Appaloosa in; he had a band of white paint across his upper face and black circles around his eyes and a tanned wolf head on his steel cap, with the muzzle shading his face like the bill of a hat and a fall of hide covering his neck.

He looked as if he were about thirty, with raven-black braids hanging past his shoulders and halfway down the steerhide vest sewn with stainless-steel washers he wore as display and armor. He also had the nearly beardless ruddy-brown skin, high cheekbones and narrow black eyes of a full-blood Indian; his followers were all younger, and they ranged from looks much like his to tow hair and blue eyes. People had moved around a lot right after the Change, even out here where the die-off hadn't been so bad, and then mostly copied the customs of whoever took them in. Or the customs those people put together out of half memories and legends in a world gone mad. . . .

"So," he said, after looking them over. "You folks are from the Protectorate, right? And maybe the priest, too?"

Mathilda felt herself flush at the tone. He could tell where she and Odard and the servant came from by their dress—boots, baggy pants, and belted T-tunics worn over full-sleeved linen shirts. She and Odard had left off the golden spurs of knighthood and avoided the distinctive roll-edged round hats with dangling side tails that nobles wore, using broad-brimmed Stetsons instead. She flushed again as she realized that the man had seen her reaction.

The other Indians talked among themselves in a language she recognized—Chinook Jargon—but couldn't speak. She didn't think they were making compliments, though; and they were probably using the tongue to psych out the intruders, since she knew they spoke English at home most of the time. Her temper boiled over.

"The charter of the Meeting at Corvallis says people from all member states can travel freely through the territories of the others on peaceful and lawful business," she snapped. "Last time I looked, the Confederated Tribes of Warm Springs were members of the Meeting."

The men circling them bristled at that. "I'm in charge of this section of the council's border guards," their leader said sharply. "Foreigners have to give an account of themselves. You could be bandits or rustlers—we've lost some stock lately."

The priest raised a soothing hand.

"I'm Father Ignatius, from Mount Angel," he said. "We're peaceful travelers heading for Bend."

The narrow dark eyes of the Indian leader flicked from her to the priest, to Odard's politely watchful smile and to Alex's blankness.

I shouldn't have said anything, Mathilda told herself. *I'm noticeable enough, in men's clothes.*

That wasn't actually forbidden in the Association's territories anymore, but it was fairly rare.

"If you're heading for Bend, you're doing it way off the main road," the Indian said. "Except on the highway nobody travels our land without our leave."

"Yes, we are off the road," Ignatius replied in a friendly tone. "But just passing through nonetheless, and taking nothing but a little water and grass."

The other man thought for an instant and then gave a slight nod; his followers relaxed.

"Name's Winnemucca," he said, extending a hand.

The priest shook; there was a jostling and shifting of horses as the others of their party did. The Indian's eyes widened a little as he felt the sword calluses on Mathilda's hand, and the strength of it. His own was like a rawhide glove over living metal.

"Thank you for giving me your name," Father Ignatius said.

Winnemucca laughed, and some of the others grinned in more friendly wise.

"We've got a scholar with a sense of humor here," he said. Then to Mathilda's obvious incomprehension: "That's what *Winnemucca* means, in Paiute. *He Who Gives.*"

He leaned his hands on the horn of his saddle. "Maybe you'd like an escort south to CORA territory?"

Mathilda tried to hide her wince. Just what they needed; something to draw more attention!

I'm lucky photographs are so rare and expensive now, she thought despairingly. *But it looks like I can't keep myself hidden for a single day. If only we could get farther from home . . .*

"But maybe not, eh?" He Who Gives said. After a moment's pause: "You can be on your way then. If you're not looking for company, head a little west as you go south—we haven't moved our herds up that far yet."

He gave a high shrill call and wheeled his horse, shaking his bow overhead. The others followed him like a torrent, until only the sound of their hooves was left, a faint fading rumble in the earth.

"Phew," Mathilda said, wiping her forehead.

"Your Highness, I thought for a moment there he'd made us," Odard said. "Or would have if the good father hadn't intervened."

"I think maybe he did," Mathilda said. "But maybe he'll keep his mouth shut, too. Let's get going. It's another day's ride to Bend."

* * *

NEAR BEND
CAPITAL OF THE CENTRAL OREGON RANCHERS ASSOCIATION
APRIL 19, CY23/2021 A.D.

"Well, that's a relief," Ritva Havel said.

She looked at the dusty white road ahead of them as they ambled along behind the horses they were driving, and at the irrigated fields of wheat and potatoes and pasture to either side, divided by rows of poplars, drowsing under the afternoon sun. Puddles and lines of water glinted between the young green of the spring crops.

Her sister nodded. The Santiam Pass had been *cold*. They hadn't been caught in a bad snowstorm—you had to be really unlucky for that, towards the end of April, even over six thousand feet. But the ground beside the road had been wet and it had gone down to freezing every night they were up in the high country, often with sleet accompaniment. They were young and in hard condition and they had the equipment they needed, but that didn't make it fun the way it would be in July, or even the way a winter hunting trip on skis could be.

Bend was three thousand feet lower than the summit of the pass, and it was sunny and mildly warm and Lord-and-Lady-bless-us *dry* this bright noonday, and the smells were of river water and turned earth and woodsmoke as well as everlasting pine sap as they came towards the city. The white fangs of the mountains—she could see Three-fingered Jack and the Sisters and Mount Jefferson—were merely pretty from here. Up there at this time of year you soon started thinking they hated the tribe of men, like Caradhras in the histories of the War of the Ring. At least there weren't any orcs, or bandits either in this season.

"And I wish you wouldn't snore when we have to share the same little tent," Ritva went on to her sister.

"I do *not* snore!" Mary said indignantly. "Besides, our flet back at Mithrilwood isn't much bigger."

"Yes, you do snore, and at home there's a wall between our beds at least," Ritva said, and continued with ruthless logic: "Besides, *I* snore. And therefore *you* snore."

"How do you know you snore? *I* was never rude enough to tell *you*," Mary said.

A boyfriend had informed Ritva that she snored like a water-powered ripsaw and slept with her mouth open—something not easy to express in Elvish, *and* it was among the reasons she'd dropped him—but she wasn't going to say *that* right now.

"How do I know you've been eating beans?" she said snidely instead, and they both laughed.

Epona chose that moment to start a purposeful move towards a cartful of baled alfalfa hay on the road before them. They both moved their mounts to cut her off, and the big black mare stood staring at them with one hind foot slightly raised, swishing her tail, ears just a bit back. For a horse, Epona was extremely intelligent, disturbingly so; you could see the thoughts moving in her great dark eyes as she looked at you.

"Remember what Uncle Will said about her when she's doing that?" Ritva said.

"Yeah." Mary chuckled, and dropped into Texan-accented English for a moment. " 'Girls, she ain't lookin' at us that way 'cause she loves us.' "

The other horses fell back into an obedient clump when Epona decided she wasn't going to make trouble, even her daughters Macha Mongruad and Rhiannon. Contrary to what a lot of people thought, it was the lead mare that ran a horse herd . . . and there was absolutely no doubt about who was boss mare when Epona was around. The problem was that when she was away from Rudi she got less and less interested in what people wanted.

They had their own mounts and a spare each, dappled gray five-year-olds with a big dash of Arab blood; and besides Epona and her get there were six others, all big warmbloods and battle-trained—what Portlanders called destriers, bred and taught to carry armored lancers in battle.

Destriers weren't much seen this side of the mountains. Folk out here favored quarter horse and other ranch breeds, mostly: agile and tough and suited alike to working range cattle or to the quicksilver eastern style of mounted combat. Destriers of the quality they were bringing cost more than a knight's armor and weren't common *anywhere*, the Association's territories included. They'd let the coats get rough and shaggy, and the light packsaddles were an additional disguise, but there was only so much you could do to hide their quality from people who knew horses.

Epona wasn't carrying anything, of course. She never did, except to bear Rudi.

It was good to get the fortune-on-hooves they were driving to the paddock of the livery stable the Dúnedain used here, a bit outside the walls of Bend, over towards the forested slopes of Pilot Butte. The proprietor was busy when they came up, giving a worm-killing herbal drench to a blindfolded horse, a messy but essential task you had to do every couple of months at least, involving funnels and rubber hoses; they'd treated theirs before the trip started. A couple of his employees ran to open the log-frame gate. Part of the turnout had fine grass, watered from the Falls North canal, and a larger section a little higher bore gray-green sagebrush on good firm dry soil. There was a strong smell of manure from the heap beside the stables, and a smell of scorched metal and *ting-ting-ting* from the farrier's shop.

The owner himself came over when he'd finished the task, looking muddy and swearing under his breath. Horses didn't like having their mouths held open and things pushed down their throats; despite steel-toed boots he limped a bit where this one had stepped on his foot accidentally-on-purpose.

"*Mae govannen,*" he said, which sounded odd in a ranch-country twang.

Then he dropped back into English, since that exhausted his Sindarin: "Pleased to see you ladies again."

"Good to see you again too, Mr. Denks," Ritva said, mentally pushing the lever that switched her thoughts to English likewise. "You don't look too busy."

"Still the quiet time of year," Denks said as she leaned over to shake his hand; he hitched at his suspenders and then ran a hand over his glistening bald scalp. "We get some traffic down from the Columbia in winter, and from out east, but you're early to come over Highway 20."

Then, cocking an eye at the horses and making a *tsk* sound: "Look rid hard and put away wet, these 'uns."

Epona was doing a circuit of the five-acre field, tail and head high, followed by her progeny. The others headed straight for the water and feed. There wasn't much grazing in the high country this time of year, and anyway horses like these couldn't get by on grass alone.

"Nice-lookin' critters if you like 'em big," Denks went on.

"Well, we'll be here long enough for you to feed them up a bit," Mary said; they'd slung bags of milled oats over each horse's back to get them over the mountains. "And have them reshod. We'll be needing some more stock—nothing fancy, enough to pull a Conestoga; harness-broke mules would do. And we'll be having a good deal of stuff dropped off here."

The man nodded without asking questions, which was welcome but not unexpected; he'd done business with the Rangers for years. They stored most of their gear with him in a hayloft as well, taking only their swords, some money and documents, and a change of clothes into the city proper.

That involved a half-hour walk through the outskirts—places where suburban tracts had lain, burned over or torn down for their materials. Now they housed everything from truck gardens to warehouses full of raw hides to the tanyards that turned them into leather with a stink of lye and acrid bark juice to plain weeds and sagebrush and greasewood and stubs of wreckage. The city walls were the usual type, concrete and rubble around a core of salvaged-steel girders; they were thick and strong, but the inhabitants hadn't bothered to smooth the outside as much as some places did, leaving it rough and gray-brown with edges of rock sticking out.

Which was a good metaphor for Bend in general. The clotted knot of would-be entrants on the road outside the eastern gate wasn't very big, but it wasn't moving much either, besides yelling and waving their arms and making their horses rear and snort. Being on foot the twins could push forward until they saw the reason; a Rancher and his cowboy-retainers arguing with the gate guard. Ritva smiled to herself as he grumbled and eventually paid over the entrance tax the city charged.

The CORA—the Central Oregon Ranchers' Association—was as much of a government as this area had; its assembly met here in Bend, and its lariat-and-branding-iron flag flew over the gatehouse. But though the city of Bend had shrunk drastically, there were still fifteen thousand souls living within the circuit of the walls in a bend of the Deschutes River. Its town council was scrappily independent of the big herding spreads, and so were the small farmers of the irrigated areas north and south of town.

Just to add spice to life in these parts, the ranchers all quarreled with one another regularly too, partly from things like strayed unbranded mavericks ending in the wrong roundup and partly from sheer bullheaded cussedness. They got the essentials like defense and keeping up the dams and canals done, somehow, but you always wondered how when you saw their usual barroom-brawl notion of governance.

"Not much like Corvallis," Mary observed.

"*They're* organized down to their bootlaces," Ritva agreed. "I'm glad Bend doesn't do that peace-bonding nonsense on your sword."

Inside the streets were more crowded, as was inevitable in a walled town; empty spaces had been built up, and some of the single-story buildings raised a story or two. More people were on horseback than in a town west of the mountains, but by way of compensation there were good if thronged brick or board sidewalks, and squads of dung scoopers.

They walked past cobblers' and harness makers' shops—Bend was famous for its leather goods—and bookstores, furniture makers, stores selling pre-Change and modern cutlery and pottery, clothiers and tailors with a hum of pedal-driven sewing machines, a print shop, cookhouses and taverns, and an entertainer strumming his guitar and singing with a bowl in front of him. They didn't drop any change in it; he used the whining nasal style of singing popular around here, and neither of them liked it.

"Mah horse is gone bad lame, mah dog done died, my woman don't love me no more and I ain't got no money for *beeeeeeerrr*," Mary crooned, in the same fashion.

Ritva laughed. It sounded a lot funnier when you said it in the Noble Tongue.

"You've created a new style, sis," she said. "Country and Elvish."

For a moment Mary's face turned sad. "The reason I don't like that type of song is it reminds me of Dad," she said. "*He* liked it—or something a lot like it, I think."

"Yeah," Ritva said, putting an arm around her sister's shoulders for an instant. "I miss him too."

They'd been two years short of ten when he rode away to war and never came back, only his body in a box, and their mother was different after that. These days their recollections of him felt *faded* somehow, as if they were memories of the memories rather than the thing itself. But she could remember the effortless strength as he scooped both of them up, one under each arm, and twirled them around until they were all breathless and laughing. . . .

Then they passed a school where children sat on the steps eating from their lunch boxes.

"*Meren aes*," Mary said.

Ritva could feel she was making herself cheerful; she nodded agreement as she realized she was hungry too. Time dulled grief, which was a kindness of the Lord and Lady to humankind. The smells of grilling and roasting and frying from the cookshops and taverns and street vendors were making her mouth water.

"*E yaxë olgaren nubast gwasolch,*" Mary went on.

"Yeah, I could use a hamburger and fries," Ritva replied.

The phrase translated strictly as *cut-up cow beneath bread with edible roots,* but usage had made the modern meaning plain.

"I like that spicy ketchup they make here."

Macy's Traveler's Rest was familiar too; it had been a motel before the Change, though now the courtyard parking spaces held a timber bunkhouse for those without the rather stiff charge required to rent a room for themselves. The same people owned the grill/bar next door, and beyond that was a public bathhouse with a good reputation and plenty of hot water; between them an alleyway had been turned into a bowling alley–cum–shooting gallery. Voices and an occasional shout and hard thunk came from there as they walked down from their room—the Traveler's Rest was safe enough to leave ordinary gear unattended.

A hopeful voice called out, "You girls new in town?"

The words were unexceptional, but the tone wasn't and neither was the low whistle; from his worn leather clothes, the man was from the outback, probably in town for a spree, and it was only too apparent he and his friends hadn't visited the bathhouse yet. He wasn't much older than they were. Ritva sighed internally; that wouldn't have happened back west over the mountains, but the Rangers weren't quite as familiar here. They both turned so the loungers could see the trees-stars-crown on the front of their jerkins and take in the left hands resting casually on the long hilts of their swords. Another of the men started whispering in the ear of the one who'd spoken, but the speaker pushed him aside.

"Anyone can sew stuff on their shirt," he said, then turned what was probably intended to be an ingratiating smile on them.

It would work better without that black tooth, she thought.

The hangers-on had been whiling away time throwing tomahawks at the target down at the other end of the closed-in alley; it was a balk of seasoned oak, and they were throwing hard at a chalked-out human outline on it. You *had* to throw hard to make a hatchet stick in an oak target fifty feet away, as well as getting the rotation just right—several had hit without the blade striking and bounced back halfway to the thrower's bar. One or two of them had wooden mugs of beer; and throwing edged iron around while you were drinking was *truly* stupid.

"Toss me one of those," Ritva said with a smile.

"Hey, these are dangerous; the edges are sharp," one of the others said.

He tossed one anyway, slow and underhand. Ritva caught it and flipped it to Mary, who threw it back.

"A couple more."

The men looked at one another; a couple of them grinned. They started throwing more of the hatchets, some of them harder and faster, but without hostile intent. The twins intercepted them and began flipping them back and forth to each other, a pair, then four, then six, then eight. Then they turned so that they were both facing towards the target and walked up to the throwing line; the onlookers scattered as the whirling figure eight of sharp iron approached.

"*Hathyl hado!*" Ritva cried, and suited action to the words: *Throw the axes!*

Thunk! and the first tomahawk sank into the chest of the target, its handle quivering. Then they had to snatch the hatchets out of the juggle with one hand and throw with the other; that took concentration, but they'd been practicing tricks together a long time. *Thunk—thunk—thunk . . .*

"Thanks for the entertainment, boys," Mary said to the spectators politely, and they walked on towards the bar and grill, leaving an echoing silence behind them as the men contemplated the neat grouping in throat, midriff and crotch.

"*Rym vin thûannem,*" Ritva said, feeling slightly guilty at her own enjoyment.

"Well, yes, we *were* blowing our own horns," her sister acknowledged. "But remember what Aunt Astrid said about spreading legends. That's a help to all the Dúnedain who ever come through here in times to come."

Ritva snorted. "Just a conjuring trick, anyway. Tomahawks are more trouble than they're worth."

A couple of the customers scurried back from the windows to take their seats again as the twins pushed through the swinging doors of the bar and grill and into the dim interior, their feet scrutching in the sawdust on the plank floor. A plain middle-aged waitress in a yellow dress and white apron came over. They returned her smile as they pulled out chairs at a vacant table and hung their sword belts over the backs.

"Hi, ladies," she said—they'd been promoted from *girls* the last time they visited. "Welcome back to town—what'll it be?"

"Two bacon-cheddar burgers, Sarah," Ritva said, and then sighed in exasperation as she realized she'd stopped thinking—and speaking—in English again, and her Sindarin had gotten an amused raised eyebrow.

She repeated it in the common tongue and added, "Mayonnaise, onions . . . got any tomatoes?"

"Dried or pickled?"

"Pickled. Two mugs of root beer."

The twins passed the time waiting for their food by playing mumblety-peg, resting their daggers' hilts on the backs of their hands and trying to set them point-down in the floor by flicking them off—they weren't the first by a long shot, to judge by the state of the boards. The hamburgers' smoky richness was a welcome change from venison jerky; hard work outside in cold weather made you crave fats. And they were only ten cents each for patrons of Macy's.

As they left, Mary looked down at the list she'd taken out of a pocket in her black Ranger's jerkin. Bend was a good place to pick up supplies for a trip; routes from north and east and west and south funneled trade and travel here, and sellers came where the buyers congregated. So did the best makers and artisans this side of the Cascades.

"One steel-axle twenty-foot Conestoga wagon with extra covers for the tilt, spare wheels and hubs and tire rims," she began.

"*Náyak!*" Ritva said, wincing slightly and thinking of the price: "*Painful!*"

"It's not our money, sis. Hmmm . . . shovels, picks, axes, hauling chains, grease bucket and keg of good-quality axle grease, heavy jack, caltrops, lariats, hemp twine and rope, canvas, extra shoes and boots, sweaters, hats, knit socks, underwear, needles and thread, soap, blankets, oilskins and tarpaulins, three tents, saddler's tools and leather, horseshoe blanks for cold-shoeing, small hollow anvil, farrier's tools, nails, lanterns, alcohol for lanterns, flints and wicks for lighters, water barrels and a keg of water purification powder, medicine chest, *horse* medicine chest . . ."

"Did you ever wonder how the Fellowship made do with only one pack pony?" Ritva said, looking over her shoulder.

That ordinary-looking man *might* have been following them. On the other hand, he went into a shop as she watched, so probably not.

"They probably didn't change their underwear or use soap," Mary said.

Aunt Astrid would have been appalled. They both had the thought at the same time, and giggled.

Then: "And there's the food."

Buying first-quality in bulk would be expensive this time of year, before the crops started coming in.

"We shouldn't load too much," Ritva said.

They both knew you ended up foraging or buying locally eventually on a long trip; that was why modern trade routes tended to detour around deserts, unlike the pre-Change interstates. But . . .

"I think Rudi's going to be taking us through out-of-the-way places where foraging takes real time. With a twenty-footer we can afford a little weight, and Denks will help us with stowing the loads. Let's see . . . barreled salt pork, smoked hams, bacon, jerky, hardtack in sealed boxes, dried beans, dried peas, dried fruit, shelled nuts, cornmeal, whole-meal wheat flour, yeast in sealed packets, milled oats with molasses for fodder, sea salt . . ."

"Did you notice who got stuck with the *chores* on this glorious quest?" Ritva added as they came out of a feed store several hours later, squinting up at the afternoon sun over the Cascades. "Admittedly we're the ones who can do it without attracting much attention, but . . . They'll have us fetching the tea, next."

"Well, if we're spending other people's money, let's blow some on *plastic containers*"—in English perforce; nobody had come up with a Sindarin equivalent—"for the bulk foodstuffs—less chance of weevils, if we're careful. Those old trash barrels are getting ragged, but the fifty-gallon kind are still good."

"Expensive, but they're worth it." Ritva nodded, then looked down at the list again. "Just the weapons, and we're done."

The proprietor of A. E. Isherman's Fine Arms and Armor knew them of old and greeted them beaming under the swinging sign—THE RIGHT TO BUY WEAPONS IS THE RIGHT TO BE FREE—not far from the old Town Hall. He was a short dark strong-featured man of about forty with shoulders like a blacksmith, two fingers missing from his left hand and a remarkable set of scars that ran from the angle of his jaw under the rolled top of his sweater. They looked very much like someone had tried to tear out his throat with their teeth once, and come quite close to succeeding.

"If it isn't my favorite elf-maidens," he said with a grin and a bow that showed the little knit skullcap on the back of his head. "On your own this time, eh? Still *ohtar* or have you been promoted to *Roquen* yet?"

Ritva smiled slightly and caught the *let's play* vibe from her sister. Ish was one of the ones who couldn't tell them apart when they were putting it on.

"*Ohtar.* But we're not elves," she said loftily.

"It's the Fifth Age," Mary continued. "The Age of Mortal Men. And Mortal Women. The Fourth Age ended with the Change."

"There haven't been any elves around for a long, long time," Ritva continued.

"Not since the *early* Fourth Age, probably."

"The elves all departed into the Uttermost West long ago; *everyone* knows that."

"Which is *even farther west* than Oregon."

"We just *talk* Elvish."

"Isn't it interesting, though: the kids at Stardell Hall are probably the first people in Middle Earth to speak it from the cradle for . . . well, nobody knows how long ago the Third Age was, really."

His head went back and forth like someone watching a tennis ball, and then he shook his head and made a broad welcoming gesture.

"Only the best for the Rangers, mortals or not. Come on in."

They both made a respectful gesture to the little silver scroll beside the door as they entered. The big siding-clad frame building had been a fishing outfitter's store in the old days; despite the new skylights and a couple of good modern lanterns it was rather dim inside, and the new potbellied stove probably didn't keep it very warm in winter either.

There was an enticing smell to the weapon shop of Isherman, though: the sharp acrid scents of oiled steel and brass, the richer mellowness of leather and seasoned cedarwood, boxes of horn and sinew and wicker baskets full of gray goose flight feathers. Spears and polearms gleamed in horizontal racks or rested with their butts in wire cages like sheaves of demonic pruning hooks; bundles of arrows bristled from barrels, and arrowheads rested gleaming in little kegs. Armor stood on old store mannequins, looking like ghostly headless warriors in the gloom, and helmets hung like bunches of huge grapes from the ceiling.

Isherman didn't manufacture most of it, but he had contacts with plenty of the best craftsfolk east of the mountains, and some west of them—Ritva recognized a set of Sam Aylward's bows.

"We'll be taking quite a bit," Mary said, looking at her list again, and began mentioning quantities.

"Going on a long trip, Ms. Havel and Ms. Havel?" Isherman asked when she'd finished. "The Rangers getting a big caravan together? Planning to start your own war?"

"Ish, what's the polite way to say 'if I wanted you to know, I'd tell you'?"

He stroked his black chin beard with the remaining digits on the mutilated hand and looked at the two young women.

"There *is* no polite way to say that, Ms. Havel . . . though it's usually men saying it to ladies."

"Shall I think of a *more impolite* way to say it?" Ritva inquired with a bright, cheerful smile.

Isherman shrugged and smiled himself as he waved a hand at two chairs in front of a table he used as a desk. It held ledgers, piles of paper, and several inkwells and sets of trimmed quills.

"Isaac!" he called to one of the teenaged sons who worked with him. "Some clover tea and honey and biscuits for our guests!"

"Aha, serious haggling is in store," Mary said, and rubbed her hands. "*Gell!*"

Ritva left her to it; her sister had more natural talent in that direction, though neither of them was really in Isherman's league. She drank some of the sharp-sweet tea and nibbled at a shortbread biscuit rich with pinyon nuts while the samples were brought out and gravely considered.

Everyone on the expedition had their own personal armor and sword, custom-made and better than Isherman's best, but you always needed spare arrows and makings, and bits and pieces to maintain your war harness in trim and repair damage, down to little bottles of fine linseed oil for keeping the straps supple. A few good bows were also advisable; bows were fragile. And while a first-rate sword could be passed down several generations with proper care, even the best shield was lucky to survive one hour of strong arms and heavy blows; they ended up buying a couple for each member of the party, adjusted to their height and heft, both ordinary round ones and the big kite-shaped Norman style Association nobles used.

"And twenty lances. Knight's lances, ashwood," Mary said.

The long poles were another thing that was unlikely to make it through more than one fight. So . . .

"And another twenty spare shafts," Ritva amplified.

Isherman's eyebrows went up, and he looked as if the urge to ask questions were about to make steam come out of his ears. Instead he shrugged and showed them what he had in stock. The weapons were ten feet of gently tapering wood, with a head like a narrow two-edged dagger a foot long heat-shrunk onto the end and a weighted butt cap to make it balance two-thirds of the way back from the point. These were the very latest type, with a hand guard like a small shallow steel bowl fastened just ahead of the grip.

"Good spring steel for the lance heads, and properly retempered, not just ground down," he said.

"Ish, you never try to short anyone on quality," Mary said severely. "Prices the Gods couldn't afford, yes; quality problems, no. And *don't* tell me how it pains you to part with the lances. Out here, they're not real popular."

"I'll go down another twenty dollars, but no more." The man shrugged with a wry smile. "Inferior gear would get my customers killed, not to mention my reputation. So, is it a deal?"

"Deal."

Both the sisters shook with him to seal it; he added an *omayan* and they invoked the Lord and Lady and the spirits of the Uttermost West. The proprietor looked happy—sort of—as Ritva took out her checkbook; it would be insulting for him to look *too* happy, since that would mean he'd diddled them to an excessive degree. She dipped the quill pen in the inkpot on top of his desk and made one out to Isherman's Fine Arms and Armor, drawn on the Dúnedain Rangers' account at the First National, and carefully noted the amount in the registration book at the back.

Uncle Alleyne pitched a fit if you weren't careful about accounts.

We might have gotten another five, ten percent off if we'd split up the purchases and gone all over town, Ritva thought. *But that wouldn't be worth the time and trouble since we're in a hurry—and Ish is more reliable on quality than anyone else here.*

"And you're not going to tell me a word about what this is all in aid of, are you?" he said as he waved the check in the air to dry the oak-gall-lampblack ink and slid it through a slot into his strongbox, then made out an invoice.

Ritva cleared her throat and looked at her sister; Mary had stepped over to the door even as one of the apprentices opened it in curiosity. There was a small open park across from the shop; locally it was called Free Speech Corner, and by convention everyone from wandering religious enthusiasts and local politicians to general wingnuts with a new theory about who, Who or what had caused the Change could address whoever would listen there. There were even a couple of conveniently shaped rocks, so that you didn't have to bring a bucket, barrel or chair to stand on.

"What's that?" Ritva called; all she could see from here was people's backs, many of them standing on wagons.

"Some new preacher who's been tearing up the scenery lately. The ranchers don't like 'im, which means some here in town *do.*"

They caught a few phrases through the rumble of the crowd: "Ascended Master Jesus Christ . . . wrath of God on us again, like the Change . . . arrogance of the rich, whom God will surely humble as He exalts His poor . . . soulless minions . . ."

"Hey, who you calling a soulless minion?" a cowboy standing on one of the wagons shouted. "You bossless son of a Rover whore!"

Someone in the crowd below grabbed him by the ankle and dragged him down; he yelled twice, once in outrage and once in pain as he thumped against the hard ground. Two of his friends jumped down and started kicking and punching the man who'd grabbed their friend. Someone jumped on the back of one of the cowboys and began punching *him.* . . .

"Uh-oh," Mary said.

"Uh-oh," Ritva agreed.

Then a knife glinted and they heard the distinctive *wheep* of a sword coming out of a sheath. Normally they would have to help the locals restore order—Rangers were supposed to do that. This time they couldn't.

"*Ere!*" Mary said. "Rudi will *kill* us if we get ourselves killed right now."

"*Ere,*" Ritva agreed. *Shit* seemed appropriate.

"There's one of the pagans!" a scrawny man in well-worn clothes screeched, pointing at the tree-and-stars on her jerkin, visible in the doorway. He threw a rock at her.

Crash. The two-pound cobblestone went through an irreplaceable pre-Change window and knocked over a stand of arrows. A number of people in the crowd-turning-into-a-riot started their way.

Ritva and her sister looked at each other and picked up two of the round shields, slipped on their helmets, and each grabbed a yard-long ax handle from a bin.

"Isaac! Reuben!" Isherman called.

His two sons were seventeen and eighteen; otherwise they looked almost as much alike as Mary and Ritva, and much like their father, down to the skullcaps. The young men scooped up helmets and shields and clubs. Half a dozen other shopkeepers from up and down the street were coming out as well, carrying everything from sledgehammers to black-snake whips.

In Bend, most respectable citizens were sworn in as deputy peace officers in advance. You could riot here pretty freely, as long as you accepted that the local taxpayers were just as free to bash your head in for it.

Bang!

Another rock cracked off the two-foot circle of bullhide-covered plywood on her arm as she hopped down into the street off the board sidewalk. She took a dozen paces and made a long lunge of the sort she'd have used with her sword and poked the man in the belly with the end of the stick, hard. He went *uffff!* and folded over. Unlike someone stabbed in the gut with a longsword, he'd be getting up again; Mary rapped him behind the ear with carefully calculated force as they went by to make sure his resurrection didn't happen too soon or too comfortably.

"Adventure," Ritva said, as they moved in well-drilled unison and tried to watch all directions at once.

I really wouldn't like to get stabbed in the back here, or have my brains knocked out with a brick.

"*Ere,*" her sister said, nodding.

* * *

THE HIGH CASCADES, CENTRAL OREGON
APRIL 20, CY23/2021 A.D.

"We're not moving fast enough," Ingolf said, hitching his thumbs into the straps of his pack.

His teeth wanted to chatter. It was an effort of will not to be depressed—the sensations of being wet and cold were similar enough that it was easy to let the one slip into the other. And another effort not to snap at Rudi's indecent cheerfulness.

White flakes were falling out of the sky, drifting down silently between the tall dark green firs and hemlocks, muffling sound, making even the smells of sap and wet earth seem faded. The flakes that landed on him were big and fluffy and a little wet, the sort you got at the beginning and end of winter back home as well. So far they were sticking on the branches but not much on the ground, and the rocky dirt of the game path was turning to rocks mixed with cold mud. But the temperature was falling with the sun, somewhere up above the gray ceiling that was coming closer and closer.

The breath of the three men steamed in the cold air, and Garbh was walking along with her head down and a white scruff starting to build up on her black-and-gray fur.

The clouds already hid the mountaintops, and now the thin air was wet at the same time. Luckily the pathway ran along the slope here rather than up and down the forty-degree mountainside. You could trust a couple of generations of deer to find the easiest way through.

"At least you two know how to handle cold weather in these mountains," Ingolf said. "Cold winters I'm at home with, but I was born a lowlander and I nearly got killed coming over the Cascades last year."

Something in the way Rudi's shoulders set ahead of him made him go on a little sharply: "You *are* experienced at handling winter weather here, right? It's only a couple of days' walk from where you *live*."

Rudi stopped; behind Ingolf, Edain did as well. "No, I'm not," Rudi said shortly, turning to face him. "Nobody comes up this *high* except in summer, usually. Not even bandits."

"No point," Edain said helpfully. "The big game all migrates down to the foothills or the valley in wintertime. And these are wet mountains, here on the western side, as wet as wet can be."

Rudi chimed in: "They get a *lot* of snow, twenty, thirty feet in a winter, sometimes more. And it can happen right up until June."

"Yeah, I can see that," Ingolf said dryly. "If we *really* didn't want anyone to notice us, this was the way to come, by God."

He looked up the boulder-strewn slope where the old granulated drifts were still waist-deep, the surface rapidly disappearing under the new fall. Off to the right a fair-sized river was rushing unseen in a deep cleft, hard enough with the first of the spring flood that sometimes it shook the rock under his feet. The temperature was dropping faster now, and the snow fell more thickly. But not in straight lines out of the sky; the tips of the tall pointed trees were beginning to move a little, and the snow slanted as it picked up speed.

A low moaning began as the wind strengthened, at first the sort of teasing almost-sound that you couldn't swear to, then louder and louder.

"Look, we *have* both lain out in the woods often enough in wintertime," Rudi said.

Ingolf nodded, but that was *not* the same thing. Down on the floor of the Willamette snow lasted a week at the outside, usually a lot less. He'd been told that some winters didn't have any at all. There was nothing like the months of hurt-your-face freezing weather he was used to back home in the Kickapoo country on either side of Christmas. Or the blizzards that he'd experienced out on the high plains in the Dakotas, which could kill a man trying to get from the campfire to a tent fifteen feet away. Up here, six or seven thousand feet higher than the valley floor, it probably got *just* that bad—or possibly even worse. Judging from what he'd gone through last year in the Santiam Pass, which was lower and warmer than this area . . . it *was* worse.

The trouble was that every particular stretch of the world had its own way of killing you, and the countermeasures were usually highly specific too. What worked in the Kickapoo country wouldn't always work in the north woods, and neither set of skills would map right onto the shortgrass plains of the Dakotas. He guessed that went double for mountains . . . which, to date, he'd mostly traveled in the summertime.

"OK, it looks like our luck has run out," he said, jerking a thumb upward.

Rudi and Edain looked up, took deep breaths to taste the weather, looked at the snow, blinking as flakes drove into their faces.

"You could be saying that," Rudi said with a wry smile, and the other Mackenzie added:

"Just a wee bit."

Rudi went on: "I'd say we're in for a really bad one—last of the season, perhaps, but bad. By tomorrow morning it could be twelve feet deep. Good day to stay home drinking mulled cider and roasting nuts by the fire and telling stories."

Ingolf joined in the laugh. They *were* experienced woods runners and hunters, after all. Just not in as many environments as he'd seen. Rudi wrapped his knit scarf around his face, leaving only the eyes uncovered.

"And cold enough to freeze off your wedding tackle," Ingolf said. At Edain's grin: "I'm not joking, kid. I've seen it happen."

The young man looked stricken and visibly refrained from a reassuring clutch at himself. Rudi thumped him on the back.

"And are you glad you switched to trousers the now, eh?" he said.

Edain shuddered and nodded. They were all in thick wool pants over long johns and fleece-lined boots of oiled leather, with bulky sheepskin coats worn hair-side-in and knitted caps and good gloves; that and the heavy packs made them look like fat white snowmen in the growing blizzard. They had their cased bows and quivers over their backs as well, and the two clansmen wore their plaids and carried six-foot quarterstaves of ashwood with iron butt caps. The warm clothes weren't perfect protection against freezing to death, particularly if they got wet. And they would, if they kept walking too long, or they'd simply get buried, if the snow could come as deep as the other two said.

"OK, let's keep an eye peeled for someplace to fort up," Ingolf said; louder now, to override the soughing of the storm. "You guys have been up here in *summertime*, right?"

"That we have," Rudi said, and Edain nodded vigorously. "In the general area, as it were."

An hour later Ingolf was starting to get really worried. The wind was slashing at them like a Sioux raiding party off the high plains, coming from any direction or none without any warning; and it carried enough snow to feel as if someone were socking you with a snowball every half second or so. He could barely see ten yards, and that only when a gust cleared the way, and the snow was up past his knees. That meant even with the pants bloused out and tucked into the boots snow was working its way inside, then melting and running down into his socks; the burning in his calves and thighs was bad enough to distract him from the feet.

Ingolf thought Rudi was looking a little worried too—it was hard to tell when all you could see of a man was snow-covered eyebrows, what with the cap above and the scarf wrapped around his face below. And of course Rudi wouldn't *show* it. The best way to keep fear under control was simply to refuse to acknowledge it; not to others, and not to yourself if you could help it.

He scraped the wet clinging stuff off his face with one glove and peered ahead. "I think that overhang ahead is our best bet," he said, pointing. "Unless you know about a real cave around here?"

"No, I don't," Rudi said. He hesitated, then nodded. "Better than nothing."

The snow was starting to sting when it hit exposed skin, ice crystals hard and sharp in the colder air. They fought through a gust like a punch in the stomach and into the shelter of the overhang, where the rock of the mountainside showed bare and leaned a little over the trail. It wasn't a cave by any means, but it did slope in six feet back from the trail proper, with a floor that was nearly horizontal. From the way dirt and needles had mounded up there it didn't flood. Ingolf looked around as best he could.

"We need some saplings!" he shouted into the others' faces. "These firs are too big!"

Edain was lost in a stolid misery, ready to keep going until he dropped but more likely to do that and die than think; Garbh nuzzled at him, whining. The elder Mackenzie shook Edain until some semblance of humanity returned to the gray eyes.

Then Rudi shouted back to Ingolf: "I think there's an old burn just down from here!"

They all threw their packs down in the back of the overhang, where the snow was thinnest, laid their swords over them, then took off the coils of rope tied to the outside of the horsehide haversacks. Those had metal clips swagged onto their ends, and snapped together.

"Work as if your life depended on it," Ingolf said. "Because it fucking *does!*"

Rudi turned out to have some old-time metal tent pegs in his pack. Ingolf beat two of them into a crack in the rock with the back of his tomahawk.

"You've got to be ready to haul up!" Rudi yelled at Edain. "Are you ready, clansman?"

Edain whacked himself on both cheeks with the palm of his glove. "That I am, Chief!" he shouted back through the white noise of the wind.

The rope went through the notches in the steel pegs; Edain took a hitch across his back and wrapped it around his left arm, paying out with his right. That way he could walk backward against the weight when he was hauling in. The two older men went down the rope swiftly, using it more to steady themselves than to bear their weight, through a screen of snow-heavy bush and into a patch of tall thin Douglas fir saplings, wrist-thick and fifteen feet long. He couldn't tell how big it was, not with the snow swirling thick about them, but it was more than enough.

"Perfect!" Ingolf said. "Get 'em!"

They both had hatchets—his own was his tomahawk. He cut a sapling off at knee height with two strokes, forehand and backhand, and pushed it over; it caught on half a dozen uncut ones as it started to slither downslope. The next time the round handle turned against the slippery surface of his glove; he wrenched himself aside, and it was the flat that bounced against his boot rather than the cutting edge . . . enough to hurt, but he broke a cold sweat at the thought of what a wound would mean here and now.

By the time they'd sent four bundles of saplings up to Edain, Ingolf was afraid that everything would blow away anyway. He and Rudi climbed back up to the trail to find that the younger Mackenzie had already started stacking the saplings in a half-moon, their butts braced with rock and the tops trimmed and jammed against the stone, each woven to the next with their branches. The other two men pitched in; by the time the little shelter was complete snow had already covered its sloping sides six inches deep.

When they crawled inside and pulled the small door of branches to behind them the—relative—quiet was more stunning than the noise outside had been. They all lay panting in the dense dark while their ears recovered enough to hear the muted wail outside. Cold got Ingolf moving again; it was actually better in here, and improving as the body heat of three men and a dog warmed the still air, but not what you'd call comfortable . . . and between sweat and melted snow, he *was* wet at the skin.

Snick.

The flame of his lighter showed the rock of the overhang and the semicircle of trail the sapling shelter covered. When he began scraping a circle clear and piling tinder—of which they had plenty, since the ground was covered with fir branches—Rudi and Edain looked at him in alarm.

"You can't light a fire here, Ingolf," Rudi said. "We'll smother—the snow's making this as airtight as a kitchen bread box. Our body heat will keep us from freezing."

Ingolf grinned as he stripped off his gloves. It felt good to be able to smile without ice crackling from his face.

"Watch and learn, children," he said.

He'd brought in a fair amount of bark, as well as deadwood; the bark was from some fortunate mountain larch trees, thick and furrowed and fairly fire-resistant. He tied sections into a rough hollow square tube, reinforced it with sticks, and thrust the completed article up along a crack in the rock at the edge, through the sloped saplings and the snow on top of them. More of it made a smoke hood beneath the improvised chimney, and then he got a small fire going on the floor. Flickering reddish light opened out the little chamber they'd made, seeming to push back the noise of the storm a bit. The men stripped off their outer garments and hung them from the saplings, making added insulation and an opportunity for them to dry as well.

"Well, we're not the first here," Edain said grimly, as he spread the boughs across one corner of the overhang.

What had seemed like another brown rock was in fact a skull. The bone was clean and dry, long since picked bare by insects and decay; the gold in the teeth gleamed in the firelight.

Ingolf nodded. Edain reburied the remains, and Rudi made a sign over it and murmured a few words he didn't catch. None of them were much put out; you still found the like pretty well everywhere except places where people had lived since the Change to clean things up. A *lot* of people had died that year, and skulls lasted.

The fire cast a grateful warmth. The little shelter would have been habitable without it, given the depth of snow piling up outside to insulate it. But it certainly helped to have their own temporary hearth.

"This is a good trick," Rudi said, grinning at Ingolf. "Home away from home."

"Well, I wouldn't go quite as far as to call it *homelike*, if you take my meaning, Chief," Edain said. "I'll remember the way of it though, if I'm ever caught out like this again."

"I learned it from an old Anishinabe named Pete—Pierre, actually—Pierre Walks Quiet. He worked for my father," Ingolf said. "Wandered in from the north woods a couple of years after the Change and ended up bossing the Readstown forests for us—timber runner, looking after the game, stuff like that. He helped teach me woodcraft when he took me and my brothers on hunting trips . . . and scared the bejesus out of us with stories about the Windigo. We get a *lot* of snow, and we get it every damned year."

Rudi stretched and yawned. The sun was probably barely down outside, but they were all ready for rest.

"I'm part Anishinabe myself," he said. "One-eighth. My father's mother's mother was Ojibwa. My blood father came from your part of the world—farther north and east a bit, if I remember the old maps."

Ingolf nodded. You wouldn't have thought it from the way the young man looked, except maybe the high set of his cheekbones and the slightly tilted eyes.

"And I'm a member in good standing of the tribe called *hungry*," Edain said.

He mixed meal from a bag in his pack with melted snow and set the dough on a thin metal plate over the fire that he greased with a pat of butter. It rose and browned, filling the shelter with a mouthwatering smell that was not quite like baking bread but close enough; Ingolf felt his hunger return as warmth and the scent reminded him of just how much effort his body had put out today. The meal was premixed with baking soda and a little salt, a Mackenzie trick he admired; it gave you something a lot better than the usual travelers' ash cake.

The rest of their supper was the last of the pork chops and trail food; after today they'd be down to leathery, salty smoked sausage for meat to go with the hard cheese and dried fruit. Oatmeal and some of the fruit went into a pot of water, to cook overnight in the ashes and be ready for breakfast.

"When you're hungry enough, this all tastes good," Rudi said.

"When you're hungry enough, your bootlaces taste good," Ingolf said tolerantly. "Hope we don't come to that on this trip."

Though we probably will, sooner or later, he thought, and went on aloud: "Now for another trick."

He'd collected the saplings he needed along with the firewood, and he had plenty of leather thongs in his pack; a few minutes' work gave him two teardrop-shaped snowshoes, a little crude but usable. The Mackenzies watched carefully as the shavings peeled away from the wood beneath his knife and he tied the ends together and knotted the webwork across. The only tricky part was the square opening in the middle and the loop to catch the toe of a boot.

"I've heard of those, but I've never actually used them," Rudi said, turning one over in his hands. "Skis yes, sometimes, snowshoes no. Not much call for them down in the valley."

"There's nothing like them for deep snow in the woods," Ingolf said. "Especially when you don't know the ground; you've got better control than you do on skis, even if it's slower. Your turn."

He watched closely, but the two younger men were both good with tools and used to handling wood and leather, and produced passable if not elegant results. Then they played paper-stone-scissors to see who'd take which night watch. Nothing was likely to hit them from the outside in weather like this unless it was a particularly mean bear, but someone had to keep the fire carefully, given the combination of open flame and the tinderbox materials of their shelter.

Then the two Mackenzies made their evening prayers; it made Ingolf feel a little self-conscious about the way he'd gotten lax over the years, so he said a rosary. It would have made old Father Matthew smile, anyway.

"Wish we were over the mountains already, though," Edain said, wrapping himself in his sleeping bag and stretching out on the crackling, sweetscented boughs. A smile: "Mom told me not to get my feet wet, you see."

Garbh curled up against his stomach; now that it wasn't so cold in here it smelled powerfully of wet dog, the wet leather of their boots and gear and the tallow that greased it, and the more pleasant scents of fir sap and the sputtering coals and the slowly cooking oatmeal. Even the muted howling of the wind was comforting, with a full belly and a soft place to sleep.

"Wish we didn't have to leave at all," Rudi added. "Curse the Prophet and whatever it was you saw on Nantucket both, Ingolf. Nothing personal."

"Not much point in cursing it, any more than the weather," Ingolf said, twisting to find a comfortable position. "Mind you, times like this I wish I was settled down somewhere with a nice warm girl and a good farm, myself."

"No, it doesn't help . . . but cursing it makes me feel a *little* better," Rudi said, flashing him a grin.

"I'd settle for the nice warm girl right now, meself," Edain said. "Not that you two aren't good companions for the trail, but you're a mite hairy and smelly for perfection."

"Bite your tongue," Rudi said. "You might be camping out with my half sisters."

"No offense, Chief, but . . ." Edain said, and shuddered theatrically.

"You two done much traveling together?" Ingolf asked. *In other words, "Why did you pick this kid?"*

"Just a wee bit, you might say," Rudi said. "And he was with me up at Tillamook last year, when the Haida hit us."

"So was Garbh," Edain said, and thumped the dog's ribs.

"Yeah, but she wasn't so useful," Rudi said. "Tell the man about it, Edain—we're all going to be together a *long* time, and we need to know one another."

"Chief—"

Modesty, Ingolf decided, listening to the protest in the tone. *Who'd a thunk it?*

"Wait a minute," he said. "Wasn't that the fight where Saba's husband got killed?"

"Sure and it was," Rudi said. "He was on a trading trip; the Brannigans and their kin are all good at that. Myself and Edain and a few friends had been traveling up north, seeing the sights, you might say, and went along with Raen and his wagons for the last bit when they headed to Tillamook. I know the baron there, and could introduce them. Then . . . ."

Edain stayed silent. Rudi snorted. "You tell him or I will, boyo!"

"Everything was fine until we got to the coast," Edain said at last, starting slowly, as if dragging things out of the well of memory that wanted to stay submerged. "This was . . . by the Wise Lord, more than a year ago now. Fall of the year before last. We were riding along and singing—"

* * *

COUNTY TILLAMOOK, PORTLAND PROTECTIVE ASSOCIATION
COASTAL OREGON
OCTOBER 1, CY21/2019 A.D.

It was upon a Lammas night
When corn rigs are bonny
Beneath the Moon's unclouded light
I lay awhile with Molly. . . .

The song died away, muffled in the clinging mist, and they rode on in silence; though usually you couldn't get four young Mackenzie clansfolk to shut up, riding abroad for adventure and strange sights. The air was too thick, and the way it drank sound made the song forlorn.

I feel like a ghost, Edain Aylward Mackenzie thought, peering through the fog.

Then he shivered a little at the thought, spitting leftward to avert the omen and signing the Horns. Thick morning mist off the sea puffed and billowed about them, and moisture dripped from the boughs of the roadside trees. Drifts wandered over the graveled way; the fetlocks of the horses stirred it like a man's breath in smoke. Slow wet wind soughed through the Coast Range firs behind him, louder than the sounds of the little caravan's hooves and wheels; the Association baron and Rudi Mackenzie rode directly ahead.

"These clansfolk have come all the way from Sutterdown to see about your cheeses and smoked salmon," Rudi said, jerking a thumb over his shoulder towards the wagons. "Not to mention that attar of roses stuff you wrote about. If trade's not below your notice, Juhel."

"Men with wheatfields and vineyards in their demesne and Portland on their doorstep can afford to get picky about *dérogeance*," the young baron growled. "What I've got is trees, grass, cows, potatoes and fish. God has given this land and these people into my charge—and now that I'm Anne's guardian, the whole of goddamned County Tillamook's on my plate till she's come of age, not just Barony Netarts. It's up to me to see to it the people prosper. I'm sick of courtiers making jokes about Tillamookers in wooden shoes."

Edain listened and snorted quietly to himself. He'd seen enough in this visit to know that any Association aristo would *say* that sort of thing, and a lot of them were right bastards all the same. Evidently Rudi thought this one meant it, though—he'd gotten to know the man while he was up north in Protectorate territory on his yearly visits.

That was why Juniper Mackenzie's son and tanist had agreed to speak for the wagon train's owners. Edain and his three friends had come along for the fun of the thing, this being after Mabon and slack time on their parents' crofts. There were casks of Brannigan's Special and carved horn cups from Bend and raw turquoise and such packed in the wagons, and blankets and cloaks woven on Mackenzie looms—his own mother's and sister's among them.

He let the conversation blur into the background noise of hooves and wheels on gravel and looked around instead; he'd come along on this trip with Rudi to see new things.

That I have! he thought.

The ruins of Salem, the steel gates of Larsdalen, great empty-eyed skyscrapers in Portland staring like lost spirits of the past at the present-day pomp of tournament and court, the majesty of the Columbia gorge and hang gliders dancing through it like autumn leaves, Astoria and its tall ships and crews from as far away as Chile and Hawaii, Tasmania and New Singapore and Hinduraj . . .

And the sea, the Mother's sea. And whales! And sea lions!

His eyes went left, towards the ocean about a mile away. The great gray vastness of the Pacific was out of sight now—fog still clung in drifts and banks over the flat green fields of the Tillamook plain.

It gave them glimpses as if curtains were drawn aside for an instant and then dropped back. They rode past drainage ditches and levees and rows of poplars with leaves gone brown-gold and the skeletal shape of a windmill that pumped water to dry out the soggy land. Cows with red and yellow and brown coats grazed between rose hedges, mostly on the rich grass of the common pastures; now and then there were fields that looked like reaped oats, and potatoes; others bore ranks of rosebushes, an odd-looking thing to be grown like a crop, and he wished he could see them in summer's glory.

He could *smell* the sea, though, the wild deep salt of it, and the rich silty scent of the vast salt marshes on the seaward edge of the plain. They were full of wildfowl at this time of year too, and the gobbling and honking and thrashing of their wings came clear.

A village passed, stirring to the morning's work and giving off a mouthwatering scent of cooking and baking; there was a roadside calvary; then a manor's sprawling outbuildings, and ahead the gray concrete of a castle's tower on a hill, with the town walls of Tillamook glimpsed at the edge of sight when a gust parted the fog for a moment. A fisherman had told them there would likely be an onshore breeze most mornings. The view would be better from the castle where they'd be guesting. . . .

And I'm sharp-set for breakfast.

They did an excellently good veal-and-potato pie here, and fine things with seafood you couldn't get in the Clan's home territory.

The baron's young son dropped his pony back from where the talk had turned boringly to trade. His father's men-at-arms and crossbowmen rode on the left side of the road, and the four Mackenzies who'd come with Rudi on the right, and behind it all the wagons and the clansfolk from Sutterdown who were wrangling them. He angled back towards the fascinating strangers and gave a would-be-regal nod.

"The best of the morning to you, young sir," Edain said.

That was polite enough, and Mackenzies didn't call anyone *lord*—even the Chief herself herself, *the* Mackenzie, much less some foreign kid in strange clothes. The boy was dressed in a miniature version of his father's green leather-and-wool hunting garb, down to the arms in the heraldic shield on the chest of his jerkin—a round cheese one-half sinister, with a Holstein head dexter, a crossed sword and crossbow below. He also had a real if boy-sized sword; otherwise he looked like any tow-haired and freckled seven-year-old.

"You guys sure talk funny," the lad said seriously.

"And sure, *we* think you northerners are the ones who talk funny," Edain replied, exaggerating his lilt and winking.

The youngster laughed, but Edain *did* think that; the Portlanders' accent was flat and a little grating to an ear accustomed to the musical rise and fall the younger clansfolk put into English, and the nobles here sprinkled their talk with words from some foreign language in an absurd, affected fashion.

The boy threw a look at their kilts and plaids and bonnets; Rinn Smith and Otter Carson had painted up too, with designs on their faces in black and scarlet and green and gold—designs of Fox and Dragon, for their sept totems. Not from serious expectation of a fight, but to play to the

Clan's image and look fierce for the outlanders. Rinn thought it impressed outlander *girls* no end, often onto their backs in a haystack, to hear him tell it, but then he was a boaster who'd have worn himself away to a shadow in the past couple of weeks if everything he claimed was true.

And he's not traveling with his girlfriend.

"And you wear weird clothes, too," the nobleman's son went on. "Even weirder than Bearkillers or the people from Corvallis."

"They are strange there," Edain agreed gravely. *Though not so strange as you Portlanders.*

"You've been to all those places?"

"To most of them. The wagons have come direct from the Clan's land, but the young Mackenzie and we have been wandering with our feet free and our fancy our only master for weeks now, and only joined them these last days."

Pure sea-green envy informed the look he got. "Cool! I'm going to go to be a page at the Lady Regent's court in a couple of years, in Portland and Castle Todenangst and places. So I can learn to be a squire and then a knight and stuff. That'll be cool too."

Edain found himself grinning; he'd come into the wide world himself now and seen some of the wonders of it, but to the lad this little pocket of farm and forest by the sea *was* the world, just as Dun Fairfax had been to him at that age. More so, because he'd had Dun Juniper just an hour's walk away, with all its comings and goings, and the Mackenzie herself dropping by to talk with his father. This place was a backwater.

The boy drew himself up then, consciously remembering his manners.

"I'm Gaston Strangeways," he said, left hand on the pommel of his miniature sword. "Son and heir of Baron Juhel Strangeways—Lord Juhel de Netarts, guardian of County Tillamook, with the right of the high justice, the middle and the low."

"It's an impressive array of titles, that it is," Edain said, and they shook hands solemnly, leaning over in their saddles.

"And *his* father was a knight, too. Even before the Change. He died a year ago, the same time the count did."

Edain had suffered through hour after hour of tedium in the Dun Fairfax school from his unwilling sixth summer to glad escape at twelve, and some of the pre-Change history lessons had rubbed off.

"I don't think they had knights or barons or counts before the Change, the old Americans," he said. "They had lobbyists and presidents and consultants instead."

"In the Society," young Gaston said. "Granddad told me about the tournaments and things." Then he cleared his throat and went on formally: "Welcome to our lands."

Edain grinned again; toploftiness like that was irritating from a grown man, but funny when it was a kid.

"And I'm Edain Aylward Mackenzie," he said. "My sept's totem is Wolf."

The boy's eyes went a little wider. "You're Aylward the *Archer?*" he said breathlessly.

Then an accusation: "You're not old enough! The Archer fought in the Protector's War, and my *dad* wasn't old enough for that. *Granddad* fought in that war and he got his limp then."

"That's *my* dad you'd be thinking of," Edain said, a little sourly. "Sam Aylward, first armsman of the Clan. Well, he was until a couple of years ago."

Hecate of the Crossroads and Him called the Wanderer, hear me; now wouldn't it be a braw thing to travel far enough that people think of me when I say my name's Aylward! I love my dad, but it's like being a mushroom growing on an old oak, sometimes.

"Oh. Well. That's cool too, you've got ancestors. . . . Did the Archer make your bow? Can I see it?"

"He did that, and you can. Careful now! It's well oiled with flaxseed, but I'd not want to drop it in this wet."

Edain reached over his shoulder and slid the long yew stave free of the carrying loops. It was strung, and the boy tried to draw it after he'd admired the patterned carving of the antler-horn nocks and the black walnut-root riser. The young Mackenzie let him struggle with it, and there were chuckles from the rest of the clansfolk as the youngster handed it back and said gravely, "That's a pretty heavy draw." He looked at Edain as he returned it. "I've heard a lot about Mackenzie archers. Is it true you guys are witches and can make magic, too?"

"Well, I'm not much of a spell caster myself, beyond the odd little thing to keep the sprites and the house-hob friendly, or for luck when I'm hunting—"

"I shot a rabbit with my crossbow just last week. It was eating the cabbages in Father Milton's garden."

"Sure, and if the little brothers won't mind your gardens, that's what you must do. Also a rabbit is good eating."

"Could you teach me a spell for luck when I'm hunting?"

"Mmmmm, I think your Father Milton might not like you making luck spells, so you'd best ask him for a prayer to your saints, instead. We're followers of the Old Religion, which you are not," he said, touching the Clan's moon-and-antlers sigil on his brigandine.

Then he glanced aside at his lover, Eithne.

"Now, this one you'd better be careful of!" he said, teasingly solemn. "A priestess of the second degree! She can sing a bird out of the bough, and 'chant a cow's teats to give butter ready-churned, and blind a man's eyes with love by a rune cut on a fingernail. The fae themselves give her a wide berth, hiding beneath root and rock unless she bids them fetch her tea and spin wool for her, the which they do in fear and trembling before her power, so."

The boy looked at her wide-eyed and crossed himself. "Is that why you've got a *girl* along?" he said, loading the descriptive word with scorn. " 'Cause she's a *real* witch?"

The mounted Mackenzies all laughed. The four of them were every one younger than Rudi; old enough to travel and fight but not solid householders weighed down with responsibilities like the group by the wagons. Eithne stuck out her tongue at the boy, or possibly at Edain. She was eighteen too, a tall lanky brown-eyed girl with skin one shade darker than olive and long black braids falling from beneath her Scots bonnet. The clasp on that held a spray of feathers from a red-tailed hawk, to show her sept totem, and she had a round yellow flower tucked behind one ear, late-blooming coast maida.

"It's because otherwise the *boys* wouldn't know what to do, the dear creatures, without a *woman* along," she said, her tone mock-lofty. "Pretty? They are that, but dim. *Ná glac pioc comhairie gan comhairie ban*, as the Chief would say. It's a female's guidance you need when advice is given."

"Very true! That's why I've got Garbh with me," Edain said guilelessly.

The big rawboned bitch walking at his horse's heels should have looked up at the sound of her name. Instead she made a sound halfway between a whine and growl, stopping stock-still and looking westward, the heavy matted fur over her shoulders rising and her ears cocked forward.

"*Aire!*" Edain shouted, loud as he could. "Beware!"

He blushed furiously as his voice broke despite the sudden sharp stab of alarm, but the clansfolk stiffened at the danger call.

He had just enough time to flip off his bonnet and slap his sallet helm over his curls before *he* heard something. Something familiar as breathing: the *wshhssst* sound of arrows cleaving air, but this wasn't a practice ground back home, or a riverside thicket with an elk in it. Someone was shooting *at* them, and doing it while he couldn't see three times arm's length.

"Down!" he yelled, conscious of eyes turning towards him. *"Incoming!"*

Young Gaston was still on his pony, gaping. Edain kicked his feet out of the stirrups and dove off his borrowed mount, grabbing the boy as he did and hugging him to his chest, turning his back to the deadly whistle. Black arrows with red-dyed fletching went *smack* into the mud around him. There was a harder, wetter thwack as one struck flesh, and someone screamed, and a horse bugled pain and fear. Then a hard bang and something hit him between the shoulder blades, also hard. Pain lanced through him, but it was gone in a moment—the little steel plates riveted inside his brigandine had shed the point.

"Down and *stay* down," he shouted to Gaston, throwing the boy flat in the roadside ditch. "Garbh—guard! Stay!"

Then he had his own bow out, slanting it to keep the lower tip off the ground as he knelt. As he whipped an arrow out of his quiver, he was suddenly and wildly certain that someone out there was trying to *kill* him, and felt an indignation he knew even then was absurd.

A high screaming rose from the misty field west of the road, and spears and axes glinted through the fog.

"Haiiiii-DA!" they called, a rhythmic screeching. *"Haiiiii-DA!"*

His father had told him that it was the waiting beforehand that was the time of fear, and you were too busy for it when the red work began. It turned out to be not quite that way for him; he was aware of being afraid, but he didn't have any attention to spare for the emotion.

Most of the strangers' arrows hit the Protectorate men on that side of the road, or whistled past into the fields and fog. Then there was a roaring onrush of half-seen figures, running in to strike in the confusion.

Edain drew and shot and drew, shot and drew and shot again, the deadly fast ripple he'd been taught from infancy, something else he didn't have to think about, and the other Mackenzies were with him. His quiver was half-empty when a man in a helmet with a raven beak covering half

his face came at him no more than arm's length away, spear drawn back
for a thrust, a shield covered with blocky angular patterns in his other
hand. Edain dropped his bow and snatched for shortsword and buckler,
feeling as if he were moving through thick honey. . . .

The snarling tattooed face behind the mask's beak went slack with
shocked surprise as a horse floated by behind him with a flash of steel.

"Morrigú!" Rudi Mackenzie shouted in a voice like brass and steel as
he struck.

He swung the long blade in an arc that crunched into someone who
staggered back in ruin on the other side. His black horse reared, its milling forefeet smashing heads and shoulders as he called again on the Crow
Goddess.

"Morrigú! Morrigú!"

Edain had his own sword out now, and the buckler in his left fist. His
friends were with him and they rushed across the road, shouting their
totem war cries; somewhere he could feel part of his mind gaping in bewildered horror, but he was too *busy* for that, too busy howling and hitting, spinning and dodging and leaping over a hiss of steel and stabbing
as he came down. . . . Shapes loomed up out of the fog, a man swinging
an ax at a fallen crossbowman. Edain punched him with the buckler before he could look up and felt a shivery sensation as a jaw broke beneath
the steel.

There were shouts all around him. *Haiiiii*-DA; calls of *Haro!* and *Saint
Guthmund for Tillamook!* Farther off a church bell started to ring, and a hand-
cranked siren wailed from the castle's tower.

Then suddenly there was nobody within sight standing up except the
people he'd started with. A man sprawled in unlovely death at his feet,
dark eyes wide in surprise at the arrow in his chest. A broad-built broad-
faced man not much older than he was, very dark, with blood in his black
hair, wearing a jacket of sealskin sewn with bracelet-sized steel rings. A
short thick bow of yew and whalebone and sinew lay near his hand and a
dented steel cap not far away.

Edain stood panting and glaring around; Eithne handed him his bow,
and he checked it automatically before sliding it back into the loops.
He still had half of his arrows left. The fight had been too brief and too
brutally close-quarters to shoot them all away.

Rudi cantered up, the visor of his helm up, and the baron with him.

"They must have come in before dawn," Juhel Strangeways de Netarts said, and then swore lividly: "Satan's arsehole, with piles like fat acorns! They'll be all over the country between the bay and the hills by now, stealing and kidnapping—"

"So we'll cut them off from their boats, before they can get back with loot and prisoners," Rudi snapped. "Where will they have come ashore?"

"Over there," Juhel replied, pointing a little south of west with his red-running broadsword. "It's the best spot near here—where we pull up the boats—no water deep enough anywhere else short of Bay City. They'll have one of their schooners off the coast. They tow the landing boats down from the islands for longshore raids, damn them. It's a good idea to take their boats, but I have to rally my retainers and the militia! Otherwise we can't hit them hard enough to overrun them."

"Juhel, we Mackenzies will keep them busy. You get your people together and relieve us—get them ready, but for the sweet Lady's sake, don't take too long!"

He swung down from Epona's back and looped up the reins to the saddlebow; the horse followed him like a dog, but this wasn't the weather for playing at knights, nor were there many Mackenzies besides Rudi who could. Edain and the clansfolk fell in behind him, his friends and a round dozen from the wagons, led by a lanky man named Raen with the twisted gold torc of a married man around his neck; he was old Tom Brannigan's son-in-law.

"Who are we fighting, Chief?" Edain asked as their feet splashed through a slough.

Wish I'd painted up, now, he thought to himself. *It'd be . . . comforting, like.*

His father disapproved of the custom of painting your face for war, but few Mackenzies under thirty agreed.

"They're Haida," Rudi said absently.

Cold water sloshed into his shoes, and then they were on dry land again; he could sense a river to their left, and the loom of the low Coast Range beyond that, but their path was wet pasture. Fairly soon his knee socks were as sodden as his feet. They moved at a steady jog-trot, as fast as was practical in unknown country with dense fog about them, spread out in a loose triangle.

"Haida, that's Indians, right, Chief? From somewhere up north?" Edain went on; he liked to get things tidy in his mind.

The Indians he'd met had all been folk much like anyone else, just with different customs; the Clan got along well with the Warm Springs tribes, who were allies of the CORA and had always been friendly to the Mackenzies. That wasn't always the case everywhere. . . .

"A lot of them are Indians and that's where they got the name," Rudi agreed. "From the Queen Charlotte Islands. Their ancestors used to raid like this in the old days, too, for plunder and slaves—long, long ago, before white men came here. Great seafarers and boatbuilders they were, back then. And things were . . . very bad . . . where they live, I hear, after the Change. So they probably remembered the old tales. Now, quiet."

Traveling through a fog like this when there might be enemies at hand in any direction made your balls try to crawl up into your belly; sometimes he could see a hundred yards, sometimes barely well enough to place his feet, and it muffled sound and smell. He wished Garbh were still with them.

At first they found nothing; then a two-wheeled oxcart tumbled empty. The oxen had been speared, whatever was in the cart carried off. A child's body lay by one wheel, picked up by the heels and with its head beaten in against the steel. The child's mother lay dead beside it, her skirts rucked up around her neck, legs spread and a stab wound low in her belly to show how she'd died.

The Mackenzies stopped as if halted by an invisible wall. Edain felt his stomach try to rise as his eyes went round in disbelief; all the parts of the picture were there, but he couldn't force his mind to take them in—and he didn't want to. Eithne was making a sound deep in her throat, a growl that would have done Garbh credit. Rinn *did* bend and spew. Otter backed away, making protective signs with his left hand and shaking so badly that he obviously didn't think they'd do much good.

And maybe they won't, Edain thought, fighting blind panic and feeling the hair bristling on his neck. *A curse, a curse, seven times a curse just to see it!*

Rape was bad enough, a dirty profanation of the Mysteries, of the loving union between Lord and Lady that made all creation. But there were evil men in any people and such things happened sometimes, especially in war. To kill a woman's child and then force her and then kill her through the womb, though—he half expected Earth Herself to open up and swallow him and everything else male and breathing within a mile, down to the hedgehogs, and at a gulp.

The thought made him look down uneasily and shudder, but at least it distracted him enough to let his stomach settle.

Rudi winced and looked aside and began to speak, to wave them all forward, but Eithne held up a hand and stopped him. Her face was white and set as well, but in fury rather than fear. She moved forward and bent quickly to rearrange the dead woman's clothes. When she straightened again there was blood on her hand; the woman's blood, and the child's.

"Stand still!" she snapped as he and the other men began to back away. "We don't have time for nonsense! You first, tanist of the Chief."

Rudi bent to receive the defiled blood with a face like iron. Edain shuddered again as she touched his forehead and cheeks, then repeated it quickly with the other men.

"You who bear the Lord's semblance—avenge this His Lady's blood, and make Earth clean of it," she said. Suddenly her lips skinned back over her teeth and white showed all around her eyes. *"Kill!"*

She was an initiate and priestess; Edain was still simply a dedicant, but he knew the voice of the Mother when he heard it . . . and She was *angry*. There was blood and death in that sound, and his skin rippled like a restive horse's at the midnight magic in it.

Rudi nodded grimly. "Let's go, Mackenzies!"

They did. Rinn and Otter dropped back a little to trot beside Edain.

"Your girl," Rinn muttered, tracing a sign. "The Night Face has her. The Dark Mother."

"That means we'll win this fight," Otter said, snarling eagerly. "Good!"

Edain shook his head. The Mackenzie herself had stood as Goddess-mother at his Wiccaning—and Dun Juniper was the center of the Mysteries. Also his mother was high priestess of a coven. He knew more about it all than most young men his age.

"No, it means the other side's going to *lose* this fight," he said grimly. "That's not the same thing as us winning, boyos, and you'd better believe it. Nobody's safe when the Devouring Shadow shows up."

Rinn winced. "The manure's hit the winnowing fan for true."

Whether the kettle hits the pot, or the pot hits the kettle . . . Edain thought, but did not say.

"Lord Goibniu, shelter us with Your arm," Otter prayed; his family were smiths, and favored the Ironmaster. "Goddess Mother-of-All, gentle and strong, be gracious to Your warriors."

Fire showed through the murk. They stopped, fitted arrows to string, then moved forward at a walk. Mud squelched beneath his brogans, and the pleated wool of his kilt shed beads of wet as it swayed about his thighs. Edain took a deep breath and let it out, another and another; ground and center, ground and center.

Dad was right; waiting's hard. The fighting just past spun through his mind in a welter of foul images, like butchering time but with people, and then there was the horror near the cart. *Lugh Long-Spear, spare me to avenge that!*

The mud smell was starting to yield to that of burning timber, but the fog was thicker than ever close to where the river ran into the bay, like having wool pushed in your nose and ears. The firelight was like a candle seen through glass thick with frost.

"Good as a beacon," Raen said to Rudi, softly.

"Probably why they did it, to show their raiding parties the way back. The fog works for them, but not if they get lost themselves."

The Haida had scouts out, but the fog that had helped them hindered now. One loomed out of the dimness, started to level his spear, started to yell, a high thin sound. Rudi killed him with a snapping lunge to the throat and it ended in a gurgle. More yells came out of the fog, from the direction of the burning light. The raiders there knew something was wrong.

Rudi turned and vaulted into Epona's saddle.

"Hit them hard and keep moving," he said to the Mackenzie warriors. "They won't know how many we are if we don't let them have time to think, and by the time they do the Tillamookers will be here."

Then he filled his lungs and called, a great brass cry like a chorus of trumpets given words:

"We are the point—"

Edain drew a deep breath and joined in as the others took it up:

"We are the edge—

"We are the wolves that Hecate fed!"

"At them, Mackenzies! Follow me!"

A knot of Haida warriors loomed out of the fog, standing guard over a clot of several dozen locals, men and women and children bound and sitting on the ground; bundles of tools lay beside them—adzes and broadaxes and two-man saws and drills and the rest of what you used for working wood.

The whole party dashed forward. A sudden banshee wail from beside him made Edain start; Eithne had been quiet since they left the dead woman. Now she wrenched a spear away from one of the Sutterdown men as she gave that appalling cry, a snatch so hard and swift he yelled in turn from the pain of his bruised fingers as she dashed past.

It was what the Clan called a battle spear, six feet of ashwood with a foot of double-edged blade on one end and a heavy steel butt cap on the other. There was an art to using one. . . .

Eithne charged into the knot of guards with the spear blurring over her head like the fan of a winnowing mill, shrieking, face contorted into a gorgon mask of horror, striking with butt and blade edge and point, leaping and using the torque of the spinning length to whirl herself around in midair. The guards were taken by surprise; one died in an instant splash of red as the blade whipped across his throat, and another as the butt crashed between his brows with a smack like a maul splitting oak and his eyes popped out of their sockets. . . .

Too many of them for her to handle, Edain thought grimly, setting his feet and ignoring everything else. *Got to—*

The string of his longbow went *snap* on his bracer. A man about to swing a war-hammer with a head of polished green stone into the back of Eithne's skull went down as the arrow tore through his throat in a double splash. Another, another . . .

Dimly he was conscious of shooting better than he ever had before, even at Sutterdown at the Lughnasadh games just past, when he'd carried away the silver arrow. Not much distance, but bad light and moving targets—and some of the arrows were passing close enough to Eithne to brush her with the fletching, a shaft for every two quick panting breaths.

Things burned behind them: sheds and houses and the ribs of a fairsized ship on a slipway. Four big boats of cedar and fir were grounded bow-first on the mud nearby, shark-lean flat-bottomed things forty or fifty feet long, their prows carved in blocky angular depictions of ravens and orcas and hawks colored black and white and bloodred. Heads were spiked to the wood below their grinning jaws.

Edain was even more distantly aware that Rudi and the others were doing something . . . cutting the bonds of the first set of prisoners, and the men were snatching up their tools—a maul or a broadax made a weapon, if you were strong and full of hate.

The freed captives swarmed over the last of the Haida guards. But more raiders were coming in, driving people before them, often laden with huge bundles of their own goods; and then armed Tillamookers started arriving themselves in dribs and drabs, hunting through fog for the flames and the sounds of battle. Village militia with hunting spears and crossbows and farming tools, the town guard with glaives and pole-axes, a snarling scrambling brabbling fight amid burning buildings and ankle-deep mud and shoreside rocks that shifted underfoot as the fog began to lift. Some of the Haida tried to keep them off while others heaved to push the boats back into the water.

The core of them broke only when the baron came with his knights and their menies behind them, their fighting-tails of men whose trade was war; barded destriers, lances and men-at-arms and wet-gleaming gray chain-mail hauberks.

He remembered seeing Rudi racing down the beach with gobbets of mud flying out from under Epona's hooves, throwing torches into the Haida boats. Three of them were burning, black choking smoke as the oiled cedarwood caught. Then the last started to slide free, and there was a savage scrimmage around its bow. A Haida chieftain with a raven's wing on his helmet thrust a spear down at Rudi and Raen and Juhel de Netarts, and swords were scything up at men along the ship's side who clubbed back with oars and tried to row it out deeper. Raen fell back wounded and Rudi reached down to pull him out of the red-stained water, throwing him across his horse's crupper, and Edain put the last arrow in his quiver through the Haida as he thrust downward at Rudi's face.

A few raiders jumped into the water and swam into the bay, but the others threw down their weapons. . . .

Edain staggered as silence fell, suddenly aware of his chest heaving against his brigandine as he struggled to suck in air, and the stink of his own sweat mixed with the tacky iron smell of blood. Or what felt like silence fell; there was still the crackle of fire—and the shouts of men trying to put it out, and others from the wounded, and a great crowd of people. A Catholic priest came up with a wagon, the red cross on its side and a load of bandages and salves within, and a brace of women in plain dark dresses and wimples—nuns, they called them. They began setting up a field hospital. The baron's lady and his mother and a round dozen of others in cotte-hardis and ordinary women in double tunics pitched in beside them.

The people cheered the Mackenzies, waving scythes and pitchforks and spades, some of them dripping red; people were pounding him on the back, harder than he'd been hit in the fight.

And they cheered Baron Juhel and his men as well, and harder, holding up their children to see the good lord who would not leave his people to the terror from the sea. Rudi looked around, visibly thought for a moment and then dropped back from where he'd been riding at the baron's side. . . .

To leave the cheers for Juhel, Edain realized suddenly, blinking and feeling as if his mind were floating up from deep water into the sun. *Well, that's the sort of thing a Chief has to think about, eh?*

The sun *was* out now, burning away the last wisps of fog; he blinked against that, and the harsh smoke stung his eyes and made him cough, conscious of how dry his mouth was.

Juhel de Netarts had his plumed helmet off, hanging from his saddle-bow, and pushed the mail coif to fall back on his shoulders. The smile he'd worn as he waved to his people slid off his face, and though he was well short of thirty he looked a lot older.

"God's *curse* on them," he swore, looking up at the burned ribs of the ship on the slipway. "I put money I couldn't afford into this, and borrowed more against Lady Anne's inheritance, and so did a lot of her subjects, at my urging. We were going to send it far south—down the coast to the Latin countries, and deal for coffee and sugar and cochineal on our own, make Tillamook a real town again with its own traders, with jobs for craftsmen and cash markets for our farmers. Those bastards in Corvallis and Newport skin us on every deal, and the Guild Merchant in Astoria and Portland aren't any better. Now . . . now I don't know what the hell I'm going to do."

"Petition the Lady Regent," Rudi said promptly, dabbing at a long shallow slash on the angle of his jaw and holding a swatch of bandage to it. "Get Lady Anne to deliver it. Say if you get three years' relief of the mesne tithes from your barony, you'll promise to put all of it into rebuilding. She *wants* people like you to do well. It's good for revenue, and it gives *her* more bargaining power with the Guild Merchant as well. That should let you repair the shipyard as well as the rest of the damage—it's just wood that burned, mostly, and you didn't lose many of your skilled workmen or their tools."

"Thanks to you for that," Juhel said, and looked at him dubiously.

"They'd have gotten away otherwise, and taken a lot with them. But the Spider's awful tight with a coin. Happier taking it in than giving it out. Usually bleating about the tithes just gets you what the sheep gets at shearing time."

"Yeah, she's not what you'd call openhanded. But she knows you have to spend to get, believe me . . . and I know the Princess Mathilda, and that her mother listens to her."

Juhel grinned delightedly and clapped the younger man on the shoulder.

Ah, Edain thought. *And the tanist doesn't even have to come right out and say he'll urge the princess to advise her mother. What a Chief he'll make for the Clan someday!*

Rudi lowered his voice: "And if I were you, I'd be very careful. The Haida knew too much about just where and when to hit you. Something smells there, and not like attar of roses, either."

Juhel nodded, then walked his horse a few steps over to where the other Mackenzies were grouped. Raen's friends and kin from Sutterdown had laid out his body and those of three others; they weren't keening them, being among strangers, but they'd put the coins on their eyes and laid holly on their breasts, and were chanting softly:

We all come from the Mother
And to Her we shall return;
Like a stalk of wheat
Falling to the reaper's blade—

Otter and Rinn were a little way off with nothing worse than nicks and bruises, accepting basins of water, soap and towels and bits of food and mugs of beer from an admiring crowd that seemed to include a lot of teenage girls, starting to grin as the relief of surviving their first hard fight sank in. Eithne leaned on her spear, still white and tense, sweat like teardrops making tracks through the blood on her face.

"Lord who holds this land," she broke in, her voice with an edge like sharpened silver. "What will you do with your captives?"

There were about a dozen of them, mostly wounded, bound and under guard. Juhel looked at her oddly, and shrugged.

"Take off their heads and send them to Portland, I suppose, mistress," he said. "Easier than sending all of them."

"No," she replied. She pointed with the spear.

The whole length of it still glistened dark red as the blood grew tacky. Juhel looked at her . . . but over her head, rather than in the face.

I wouldn't like to meet her eyes right now, either, Edain thought as she went on, giving orders like a queen:

"Is it that there's an ash tree there, not far from your castle, tall and great?"

The nobleman nodded, and his look grew odder still and more sidelong.

"Put your men about it—about it in a circle, wearing iron and carrying spears and the emblems of your god. Bring your dead and lay them beneath a cairn with the blessings of your Mass priest. Then hang the evildoers from the tree in sight of the dead and leave them for three days and nights. Do that, and you'll have . . . luck, luck for you and your land. Do that, or bury them living at a crossroads with a spear driven in the earth above."

"Ahhh . . ." Juhel swallowed, crossed himself and looked aside, shivering a little.

Rudi gave him a nod, short but sharp, and the baron drew a deep breath.

"I suppose we might as well hang them now. Sir Brandric! See to it! And the rest, as well."

"A pleasure, my lord. Very much a pleasure," the tall grizzled knight who commanded the garrison of Castle Tillamook said, and stalked off barking orders and grinning.

Eithne's knees buckled then, as if something—or Someone—withdrew a hand that had worn her like a glove. She shook her head as Edain tried to help her, then almost fell. When he caught her in his arms the eyes rolled up in her head and she went limp; somehow he'd been expecting her to be heavier, but it was the familiar slender form he picked up, though her head rolled against his shoulder. Cold fear worse than any he'd felt in the fight clawed at his gut as he bore her over to the aid station the nuns had set up, letting the spear fall to lie in the wet trampled grass.

One of them bent over the pallet he laid her on, pushed back an eyelid, felt her forehead and took her pulse with professional briskness. He showed her how to unbuckle the brigandine along the side and draw it off.

"Just stress and exhaustion, but a bad case of it," the nun said, clucking her tongue and drawing blankets over her. "A young girl's got no business doing this! She'll be fine with sleep and a good meal—just a few little cuts and scratches and some bruising here. Now, if you're not going to help, young man, get out! *She* won't be waking for a good many hours, and I've got urgent cases to see to."

Edain blew out his cheeks in a whistle of relief and backed away; they *were* busy here, and he would be as useless as an udder on a bull.

Rudi and the local lord had dismounted, holding their horses' heads not far away as they spoke.

"Remind me never to piss your people off, Rudi," Juhel said with feeling.

He looked at the spray of dead where the Mackenzies had struck out of the fog with surprise and terror at their backs; bodies in the mud with gray-fletched arrows in them, or tumbling gashed and bloodless in the cold seawater. He shook his head.

"Dad fought at the Battle of Mount Angel back in the Protector's War, and evidently he wasn't exaggerating."

While he spoke, a crossbowman with his arm in a sling came up leading a pony Edain recognized. Young Gaston was on it again, looking none the worse except for some dirt and bruises. Garbh trotted at his heel, then dashed over to Edain and gave a single bark as if to say, *The job's done.*

The baron's heir gulped a little at some of the sights around him and went paler, but sat his pony proudly beside his father. Juhel looked at him for a moment with a quiet and tender delight that went oddly with the blood-splashed armor and sword, and put his hand on his shoulder.

Then he looked at Edain and smiled. "I've thanked Rudi," he said. "But I haven't thanked you yet, Master Aylward. I saw you save my son. That was bravely done, and done for strangers."

Edain felt himself blush to the roots of his hair, and shrugged awkwardly as they shook hands.

"It's a poor excuse for a man who won't fight for his host, or help out a little kid caught in a battle," he said shortly. "Besides, I didn't notice these Haida buggers telling me they wouldn't hurt me if I were to kindly stand aside."

Rudi grinned. "He's a good man to have your back," he said, and clapped Edain on his. "And that's a fact."

Juhel laughed. "I don't doubt it. Fought with you before, has he?"

"No," Rudi said. "This was your first real fight, eh, Edain?"

The younger Aylward nodded, and the Chief's son went on: "But I *thought* he would be someone I wanted with me if it came to one. Now I know it."

Juhel's brows went up. "If that was your first fight, I'd hate to see what you'll be like in ten years! But you *did* save my son; you put your back between him and those arrows. Name a reward, and if it's mine, it's yours. In honor I can't do less."

Edain drew himself up despite the burning tiredness that made him want to crawl into the nearest haystack and sleep for a year.

"I didn't do it for that, sir," he said. "I'll take your thanks, and that's all that's needed—the gods and the Three Spinners will see to any reward."

Juhel looked bewildered, and Edain cursed himself as he saw the beginnings of offense. For a fact, he didn't understand how an Association noble's mind worked. Outsiders didn't understand Mackenzies, and that was a fact too.

"There *is* a gift you could give him, Juhel, and one he'd value highly, though he'd never ask for it," Rudi said.

He was grinning again, like a fox for all that his totem was Raven.

"What's that?" Juhel said. "Horses? Weapons? Gold? Land, even?"

"Better than that. Write a letter to his father, telling what he did—and that he wouldn't take anything for it, either. I'll deliver it."

Edain stifled an impulse to shuffle his feet. His father wouldn't say much, just smile to himself and nod. He blushed again and fought not to grin.

"I will write, then," the baron said. He looked at the son of the Mackenzie chieftain, a long considering glance. "Your people don't have princes, Rudi, do they?"

Rudi looked a little impatient as he replied: "I'm not even really a lord, Juhel; just the Chief's tanist. My mother's Chief, and I may be after her—if the Clan wants me, and for as long as they want me. No, no princes."

"That may be a great pity," Juhel said thoughtfully, then looked around. "Now, I'd better get to work."

* * *

Ingolf raised his brows as the story came to an end; silence fell, save for the low crackle of the fire and the howl of the blizzard outside.

Well, I guess there is a reason Rudi picked the kid. Though from the sound of it, maybe his girlfriend would have been just as good a choice . . . no, too spooky.

Edain yawned enormously, breaking the quiet that had followed his tale.

"Yeah, even if we can sleep in late tomorrow, we'd better get some rest," Rudi said.

Edain nodded, mumbled something, and slept with sudden finality. Ingolf drifted off next; his last sight was Rudi dropping a careful handful of sticks on the coals.

* * *

Rudi Mackenzie knew that he dreamed. But the dream was different . . . this time he was a viewpoint, detached.

Same place, he thought.

The little overhang was still there. The trees weren't, though a few charred stumps still showed where they'd burned. Great gullies scarred the mountainside instead, the mark of torrential rains long-gone; the only other vegetation he could see was a few stems of some thorny brush, and those were dead. A white-gray light pervaded everything, but he couldn't see all that far. The air held no haze—it was painfully clear—but somehow he had a sense that it was *thick* with a crushing weight. Thick and hot, very hot, like a sauna just at the edge of your ability to bear, so that rocks and clods glimmered in the middle distance.

A body lay under the overhang, dressed in a seamless overall of some odd silvery stuff that merged into boots and gloves of the same, and into the base of a helmet like a glass bowl. The face within was a sunken-eyed mummy's, desiccated into the texture of leather and an eternal snarl of yellow teeth, gray-white hair still stubbly on the scalp.

The dream seemed to last for a very long time. The slow heavy wind blew; now and then a piece of rock would flake off the barren mountainside and skitter downwards. Nothing else happened. Nothing else ever would.

"Huh!" He woke with a start.

"Last up, Chief," Edain said cheerfully, and handed him a bowl full of the oatmeal.

Cold sweat prickled under his arms and at the back of his neck where his hair lay on the skin. The horrors of the dream faded, leaving only an overwhelming sorrow; it was as if he felt another's grief, and that too large for a human mind and spirit to contain. Then that lifted too, as he shook his head to clear it. The little shelter was dark, just a little red glow from the fire . . . and a trace of cold grayish light down the improvised bark chimney.

"Storm's passed," Ingolf said, wolfing down the thick fruit-studded gruel. "But it's four feet deep out there, I'd say."

"Higher with the drifts," Rudi agreed. "Best we make as much distance as we can. Snow's bad, but this time of year it could warm up and melt right up to the saddle of the pass—and that would be worse."

CHAPTER TWELVE

ROVER TERRITORY, EASTERN OREGON
APRIL 15, CY23/2021 A.D.

Joseph Kuttner's single eye gleamed in the light of the fires as he sat in the folding canvas chair. The Rover chiefs squatted across from him, all hair and eyes and teeth and a strong outdoor stink of badly cured leather and horse and sweat, and of lanolin from the sheepskin cloaks some of them kept around their shoulders against the evening chill. Sparks flew upward into the huge star-flecked dome above, and the gnawed bones of a roasted sheep littered the ground.

"You want us to chop some CORA folks for you?" one of them said, grinning. "What for y'want that? We'd do for our own selves, if them western bastards come on our land."

He spit into the fire, a brief hissing sound. Kuttner nodded politely; he was very glad a dozen Cutters stood behind him, fully armed. These new nomads of the sagebrush country weren't former Eaters like the savages you found east of the Mississippi . . . not quite. They *were* nearly as dangerous to outsiders; a little less likely to attack, but much more effective if they did.

"I want them dead because one of them gave me this," he replied, touching the scar that traversed his empty left eye socket.

That brought more grins, as he'd expected. It was motivation they could understand.

"And they're enemies of the Prophet and His Son, and so of the Ascended Masters and the Unseen Hierarchy."

A few of them nodded; the mission was going well here. The Rovers' extreme poverty was a major reason. It wasn't that the land here couldn't yield a reasonable living, given how few and thinly scattered the dwellers were. What they lacked were the tools and the skills to make them, or anything much to trade for them in more fortunate areas. The Church Universal and Triumphant *was* willing to supply them, for allegiance and fighting men rather than for profit. It wouldn't be the first time that readiness to seek out the folk who'd had the most trouble recovering from the Change had aided the sacred cause.

What was that old-world expression? He searched his memory. *Ah, "rice-bowl Christians." But from that comes true faith, in time.*

"They're soulless pagan idolaters, minions of the Nephilim," he amplified. "Nine of them, and they'll be traveling with a large wagon and many good horses."

They *all* nodded at that, with eager greed. This was a hard place to scratch a living, even by Montana standards. Men who didn't grasp at anything they could with both hands hadn't survived here.

"And there will be CORA men as well, probably—from Seffridge Ranch. Rancher Brown's cowboys."

That brought more scowls and muttered curses, but a little apprehension as well as anger; they recognized the name of the holding, and of its lord. Kuttner made a gesture with one hand, and a Cutter came forward with a bundle of shetes. The fine steel glittered in the firelight as he laid them out with their hilts towards the four chiefs, and the brass pommels glowed.

"Two dozen good shetes. And many fine bows, and many arrows for each. If you kill them, the Church promises two slaves who understand bowmaking . . . for the most deserving of you, of course."

The chiefs glanced at one another, calculating who would get the most, and how it would affect their own balance against one another. Making horn-and-sinew horseman's bows wasn't a skill that was common around here, and such weapons were precious beyond words, even more than fine-forged swords. Many of their men made do with javelins, or carefully preserved pre-Change hunting bows. Those were good of their kind, but they seldom had a draw weight sufficient for modern war. Deer didn't wear shirts of steel, or even cured bullhide.

They didn't kill you if you missed, either.

One of the ones who'd been stubborn about the Church's preaching leaned forward. "Tell me more about the Prophet," he said. "If'n he can hand out gear like that, maybe God *does* favor him."

* * *

SEFFRIDGE RANCH, SOUTH-CENTRAL OREGON
MAY 7, CY23/2021 A.D.

"Well, that's a relief, Chief, and no mistake," Edain said, looking back at the mountain peaks.

It was the moment just before dawn, when a few stars still lingered in the western sky. That was cloudless, but the mountains there were snow-capped all along the horizon, like a jaw full of white fangs pointing at the heavens, high enough to catch the ruddy light before groundlings could see the sun rising. The great peaks of the Three Sisters were just visible at the northern edge of sight, eighty miles away and more beneath the endless darkling blue.

"I'll not be arguing with you the now," Rudi Mackenzie said.

The younger Mackenzie was smiling as he grumbled, and his pride was obvious. They'd come through a crisis—not an earth-shaking one, but they could have died if they hadn't acted swiftly, and it had been a hard slog afterwards.

"Still, it was interesting," Rudi went on.

Ingolf groaned: "Too much like *nearly freezing to death again* for my taste, and to hell with *interesting*."

"Where's your sense of adventure?" Rudi asked with a snort.

"It died with a Sioux arrow through the gut about seven years ago," Ingolf said, genially enough to take most of the sting out of it.

"It wasn't *that* cold," Rudi said aloud.

To himself: *And I'm not that much younger than you, my friend. And I'm in charge.* Then: *And there was that dream . . . I don't know Who sent it or what it meant, but I do know it frightened the squeezings out of me.*

"Cold enough to get you and your friend out of your kilts," the east-erner went on. "For a while."

Rudi and Edain were back in the pleated skirtlike garments, and had their plaids pinned at their shoulders.

It isn't that I really mind *wearing pants,* Rudi thought. *It's just that I'd rather not unless there's a good reason.*

Garbh plodded at her master's heels with her tongue hanging out, oc-casionally raising her shaggy barrel-shaped head to sniff with interest.

About the way I feel, Rudi thought.

Not near the end of his tether, but it was good to be down out of the high country, and next time he went that way he intended to wait until June.

They walked on southeast down a gentle slope, through open forest of ponderosa and lodgepole and jack pine, tall straight trees but more slender and less close-packed than the fir woodland on the western slope. It was interspersed with grassy meadows bright with golden-orange blan-ket flowers and nodding lilac-colored mariposa lilies; pine and strong-scented sage filled the cool thin high-desert air, stronger than the scents of leather and sweat. The snow was gone, but at better than four thou-sand feet May wasn't what you'd call warm; it got a little less chilly as the sun cleared the horizon and sent long fingers of light through the trees.

"At least our packs are a lot lighter," Rudi said cheerfully.

"That's because we're about out of food," Edain teased.

"Where's your sense of direction?" Ingolf asked Rudi. "Not as dead as my sense of adventure, I hope."

"It's been years since Mom and I visited out here, and we came over Highway 20 through the Santiam Pass and then down the railway from Bend," Rudi said. "But . . ."

He closed his eyes for an instant and called up the terrain, half maps he'd seen, partly his teenage memories of the visit, partly a picture those made in his head. They'd crossed the old Burlington Northern tracks yesterday evening, so . . .

". . . that was Bedpan Burn back there, I'm pretty sure. Silver Lake Road should be a little east of here. That'll take us right south to the ranch."

They pushed on. Then Garbh stiffened, pointing her nose south and making a small muffled sound just as they reached the cracked and frost-heaved pavement of the old road; the breeze was from that direction too. Rudi flung up a hand. Something was crashing through the brush ahead of them. They all melted behind trees and reached over their shoulders for arrows. Then they relaxed when they saw it was a red-and-white steer, gaunt with winter, all legs and horns. It faced them and snorted, then went back to grazing on the fresh new growth; the beast was a little thin, but too well conditioned and too used to humans to be feral stock.

"We're close," Rudi said, and the others nodded.

You couldn't leave stock wandering on their own for long, not with wolf and coyote, bear and tiger and mountain lion around, not to mention rustlers and horse thieves. This was the time of year ranchers started moving herds up towards the higher country, as the snow pulled back into the mountains. They passed more cattle and sheep as they walked, and saw riders pacing them on the edge of sight. Probably one had dashed on ahead to alert the camp, which was all to the good. You didn't want to surprise people, especially not people with bows and protective attitudes towards their livestock.

A little farther and they smelled woodsmoke, with an overtone of frying bacon and brewing chicory. Rudi cupped his hands around his mouth as they walked on through brush and onto the edge of a wide opening with only scattered trees.

"Hello! Hello, the camp!" he called.

Calling out like that was considered good manners hereabouts. He did it again:

"Hello! Hello, the camp!"

Dogs barked and voices rose; Garbh started to growl back, then quieted at Edain's whistle and stayed close to his heel, apprehensive and aggressive at the same time with the stress of being in a strange pack's territory—her kind weren't so different from human beings, in many ways.

There were a fair number of folk around the fires there, tending gear or getting ready for the day or striking tents; three covered buckboard wagons were parked nearby, and plenty of hobbled horses nosed at the ground. The humans included both sexes and all ages down to infants, all dressed in drab sensible leather and linsey-woolsey and sheepskin. A woman spun wool with a spindle and distaff as she watched a half dozen toddlers; that was less efficient than a spinning wheel, but you could do it on the move and do something else that didn't need hands at the same time.

Three men already in the saddle cantered over and pulled up with casual ease, leaving the reins lying loose on their mounts' necks. One wore a mail shirt, and the other two had breastplates of cowhide boiled in vinegar and strengthened with chevrons of thin steel splints painted brown; they all had curved swords at their belts, full quivers over their backs and round shields at their saddlebows marked with the intermingled S/R of their ranch. The man in the mail shirt had a horse tail mounted on the top of his helmet as a crest as well.

None of the three men had drawn swords, but they all had their short, powerful horn-and-sinew recurve bows in their hands and a shaft on the string. They drew up a fair distance away, and kept their eyes moving to make sure there weren't more strangers hidden in the trees.

"Howdy," their leader—the one with the mail shirt and the horse-tail crest—said. "You folks know you're on Seffridge Ranch land? Mind tellin' where you're from, and where and what your business might be?"

Rudi nodded. "Hello. We two are Mackenzies from over the Cascades," he said. "And our friend here is from out east—far east, from beyond the mountains, not from Pendleton," he added. *CORA and Pendleton don't mix well.* "We're here to see Mr. Brown."

The cowboy's brows went up; he was a leathery man of about thirty, with sandy-colored stubble on a suntanned face and blue eyes already cradled in a network of wrinkles.

"*You* want to see the *Rancher* his own self?" he said, sounding dubious. "I'm line boss here in this section. You got something to say, say it to me."

Behind him, one of the men muttered: "Not even saddle tramps."

Rudi nodded, concealing his amusement. People on this side of the mountains attached a lot of importance to your horses, and they looked down on men who traveled far afoot. He liked horses well enough himself and considered Epona one of his best friends, but he thought the attitude ridiculous.

"Mr. Brown is expecting us," he said. "Who we are is between him and us, sure, and our business likewise. No offense, but he wouldn't be thanking you for asking too many questions. If he thinks we're wasting his time . . . well, in his own house he'd be able to deal with that the way he thought best, wouldn't he?"

The cowboy gave a brisk nod, which set the horse tail on his helmet bobbing.

"He's had a good deal to do with Mackenzies before, I know that," he said thoughtfully, eyes narrowing. "And he's got a fair passel of guests to home right now, all of 'em foreign."

Then he came to a decision, and called over his shoulder: "Cody! Hank! Tommy! Git over here! Rest of you, there's plenty to do. We got eight hundred head to move."

Cody looked enough like him to be his younger brother and probably was; Hank was even younger, but dark and thickset; Tommy was about sixteen, a slender redhead. They were armed and equipped like the first three; so was every man here and a fair number of the women.

"These folks are here to see the boss. Tommy, you get back to the homeplace and let him know. Cody, Hank, cut them out horses and take 'em on down to the house."

The three travelers stood and watched the ranch hands break camp. Most mounted up and moved out to get their herds moving north into the old national forest. The rest finished dousing their fires and policing up their gear, ready to resume their slow journey up to the summer pastures where they'd live until fall. One young girl came over shyly and gave them each a buttered biscuit with a piece of bacon in it. A few of the others looked dubious, and he caught a mutter of, "Witches."

Cody and Hank brought them saddled horses. They seemed to be watching as the three mounted, and half hoping they'd do so with a clumsy scramble. Rudi smiled, put a hand on the cantle and vaulted easily into the saddle, feet finding the stirrups. They followed the old road, riding off the broken pavement to spare the hooves; the potholes had been filled in roughly to keep it passable to wagons, but dirt was easier on the horses' feet.

After an hour or two the two young cowboys were chattering merrily, and asking questions about the strangers' gear.

"Them longbows don't look too handy," Cody said dubiously.

"The dead pine," Rudi replied conversationally, nocked a shaft, drew and shot in one supple motion, before the cowpony he was riding had time to crab.

You *could* use a longbow from horseback, particularly when the target was directly to the left; it just wasn't easy. *Snap*, and then an instant later the shaft was quivering like an angry wasp in the trunk of the dead ponderosa pine a hundred and twenty yards away, while birds flung themselves skyward from it in alarm.

Cody gave him a look and cantered his horse across the slope to retrieve the shaft. He tried tugging it out, then gave up and dug at it with the point of his knife. When he came back he was shaking his head ruefully.

"OK, mister, you can shoot with that beanpole there," he said. "My daddy went west with the Rancher in the War of the Eye and he told me about Mackenzie longbows . . . still, I'd say a saddlebow is handier."

He raised his own weapon, copied from pre-Change recurve hunting bows, to illustrate what he meant; it was around four feet long, with flat-section laminated limbs that curled forward at the tips.

"It certainly is, when you're riding," Rudi acknowledged. "The longbow holds up better in wet weather, though."

Ingolf shook his head. "Not if you're careful about varnish."

"And that doesn't matter as much out here, where it don't rain all the damn time like I hear it does over the mountains," Cody added.

They spent a pleasant hour talking bows, horses and hunting as they traveled. Then the men drew rein and looked southward as they came out of the last of the forest, where it trailed off into the occasional stunted juniper amidst grass and sage and wildflowers.

Cody smiled, obviously expecting them to be impressed. "Quite somethin', ain't it?" he said proudly.

Ahead was open country, and they looked down onto a plain of sagebrush and bunchgrass green with spring and splashed by yellow bee-plant. It was cut by a small river lined with cottonwoods, running westward towards a stretch of marsh. Water glinted in the diversion ditches that irrigated fields of dark alfalfa and a patchwork of other crops; cattle and horses and sheep and long-necked alpaca moved over the broad pastures beyond under the eye of mounted herders.

"That's the homeplace," the cowboy said, waving at a clutch of buildings, toy-sized in the middle distance. "There aren't many so fine."

A little village clustered there around the low-slung fieldstone ranch house, amid a wider setting of corrals, bunkhouse, paddocks and big barns of old-style sheet metal and newer ones of sawn boards; the square stone tower at one corner of the big house was probably new, too. John Brown's holding had been a good-sized spread even before the Change, and afterwards he became one of the movers and shakers of CORA, the Central Oregon Ranchers' Association. He'd annexed several smaller ranches that didn't have good natural water, and as much of the old national forest as he wanted to claim and had the men to hold.

Couple of hundred people, more or less, Rudi thought. *Pretty much what one of our farming duns has, or a Bearkiller strategic hamlet, or a knight's-fee manor up in the Protectorate. Though there may be nearly as many out at the line camps this time of year.*

That wasn't many for tens of thousands of acres, but the bones of the earth were closer to the skin here than they were in his lush homeland west of the mountains, and Brown had taken in as many townsfolk as he could feed after the Change. The cowboy clucked to his mount and they all moved forward again. Half a dozen more riders were on guard; two came up to escort them in, one of them with a light lance bearing the rancher's sigil on the pennant.

"They say Bend is a lot bigger," Cody went on. "But I say you'd travel plenty and find nothing better than this!"

Ingolf blinked, caught Rudi's eye, and lifted a brow.

Yeah, it's not much of a muchness, the Mackenzie acknowledged with a slight shrug. *But sure, if they want to get excited over it, let's not be a wet blanket about it, eh? And it's probably a nice enough place to live. I don't like big cities myself.*

There was no wall around the settlement, but all the houses were stone, with fireproof tile or sheet-metal roofs; all the windows could be closed with steel shutters that had narrow slits for shooting arrows, and angle-iron posts set in concrete stood ready to carry tangles of barbed wire if need be. You could see how the masonry improved from the earlier houses to the later ones as hands gained skill, but they were all built thick and strong. The snout of a Corvallis-made catapult peeked over the top of the tower.

People were finishing breakfast or already at work, but they stopped to watch the strangers ride in. The smith was a brawny brick-thick man in a leather apron and sweat-stained shirt beneath; he and his assistants paused while he plunged a white-hot knife blade into a quenching bath before they came out to wave. Many of the other folk came out also, from saddlers' shops and bowyers' and a big open-sided shed where carpenters were putting together something complex—probably a pivoting hay lift.

"Mackenzies!" the smith called, sounding happy to see them, a white grin splitting his sweat- and soot-streaked face. The man went on: "I trained in Dun Carson!"

Rudi reined aside and leaned over to shake his hand; it was hard as something carved out of cured leather, and strong even by the young clansman's standards.

"Cernunnos and Brigid bless you, then, friend," he said.

"Goibniu strengthen your hand," the smith replied; it sounded a little odd in the flat twanging range-country drawl.

Now that Rudi looked, there was a mask of the Lord of Iron over the hearth, together with the crossed spears and cow horns—not as conspicuous as the patron deity of smiths would have been in a Clan settlement, but there. He made a reverence to it before he rode on. Most of the people here were Christians—there was a small Protestant church, and an even smaller Catholic chapel. He hoped it didn't cause the smith any trouble, but it probably wouldn't. Even a generation after the Change, metalworker's skills were still rare enough to be very valuable, and the CORA charter allowed freedom of religion.

Along one enclosure paced a great black mare, looking like another species amid the rough-coated ranch quarter horses. Epona whinnied indignantly when Rudi rode by with only a wave—John Brown, Rancher of Seffridge, was an old friend of the family, but he might get a bit huffy if Juniper's son stopped to greet his horse first. There were other western horses there as well, Epona's two daughters, and a clutch of sixteen-hand warmblood destriers that dwarfed the smaller range breed and outweighed them by a third or more. He didn't recognize them, though the four dappled Arabs his twin half sisters rode for serious business were familiar.

Rancher Brown stood to meet them on the veranda that wrapped around the old stone ranch house, a leathery man in his sixties with thinning white hair and skin wrinkled like a relief map but still erect and strong.

"You fellas get on back to the herd," he called to Cody and Hank. "Tell Smitty I know these folks and was expectin' 'em. And don't any of you go flappin' your lips about it."

Then he beamed at Rudi and came forward to shake his hand after he dismounted.

"Not that it'll matter, seein' as Smitty and his crew aren't coming back down for quite some while. You're looking all growed-up, boy," he said.

"This is Edain Aylward Mackenzie and Ingolf Vogeler, friends of mine," Rudi said. "And you're looking the same as ever, Uncle John."

He'd been sixteen the last time the rancher came west of the mountains on CORA's affairs, but Brown and Juniper Mackenzie had done business from the first Change Year, and they'd fought the Protector together even before the War of the Eye.

"And you're a liar," the older man said with a wry smile. "Mirrors still work, boy. Come on in, all of you. All your other friends are here."

All two of them? Rudi thought, a little puzzled. *And they're my sisters . . . well, half sisters . . . what are the twins up to now?*

The big living room held leather-upholstered furniture, racked weapons on the walls and a bearskin rug and more sheepskins on the floor; there was a mounted cougar head over the wide stone hearth. The twins were there, grinning their sly little *fooled you, ha-ha* grins, but they weren't alone by a long shot. Mathilda and Odard had the grace to keep their faces straight. A thin inconspicuous man he recognized as some sort of hanger-on to Odard was there too, and a warrior-monk from Mount Angel, a dark close-coupled man with swordsman's wrists.

Yes, he was there that night . . . his name's Ignatius. That's nine, he thought, his mouth thinning with anger. *Well, now I know where the destriers came from.*

He looked at his half sisters. They saw his face and did a creditable imitation of what he thought of as their aunt Astrid's elf-lord-with-a-pickle-up-the-ass expression of hauteur.

"Let me guess," he said heavily. "You didn't have to tell *her*"—he looked at Mathilda—"so you could get her in on it without *technically* breaking your promise. And Matti, you heard something from your mother, so you could tell them"—he nodded to Odard and his servant—"what you'd heard from *her.*"

Mathilda smiled and mimed clapping. "And nine is traditional."

The twins nodded seriously at that.

Father Ignatius spoke before Rudi could ask: "The abbot guessed," he said succinctly.

Mathilda went on: "It *will* give you a better chance, Rudi. And this is important. The Prophet thinks so . . ."

Ritva and Mary nodded vigorously. "We ran into a CUT preacher in Bend, and he started a riot we got sucked into. Not a nice bunch."

Mathilda gave them a quelling glance and continued: ". . . and so does your mother. I don't know about the Prophet, but I've always taken Lady Juniper's ideas seriously."

He nodded, touched despite his irritation. *And nine . . . that many aren't really more conspicuous than five, but another four good sword arms might make the difference in a tight spot. It's luck and the whim of the Trickster either way. Judgment call.*

There wasn't much sense in pitching a fit; he had no way of stopping Mathilda from following him except to turn back himself.

Of course, when and if we get back . . . Oh, sweet Mother-of-All, what if I come back and she doesn't?

"You realize *your* mother will kill me?" Rudi wasn't quite sure whether he was serious or not. "If something happens to you, she'll kill me *slowly*."

I like Sandra, but . . .

She'd saved his life when he was her husband's prisoner as a child during the War of the Eye—saved it several times, in fact. And she'd always been kind to him when he was visiting afterwards, and he'd learned a good deal from her. The problem was . . . he wasn't a kid anymore. With Sandra, you never knew. Was she capable of acting nice for twelve years as an act of calculation, just to get on your good side?

Oh, yeah. She's capable of it, no doubt about it. But would she be after doing it the now?

Sandra's daughter looked a little daunted, and then brightened—probably thinking that it would be the better part of a year before she saw her mother again, or more.

"That's the least of your worries," Mathilda pointed out. "For now, at least. Mom's back in Portland or Castle Todenangst." A grin, half-ironic. "And even the Spider's reach has limits."

Of a sudden, Rudi threw back his head and laughed. It *would* be a year, and he was still young enough for twelve months to seem like a long time.

"Well, when you're right, you're right," he said; her smile warmed him. "And Matti—I'd have done exactly the same thing in your place."

He turned and introduced the others. Odard had seen Ingolf before, and met Edain once or twice, and was smooth as ever, but when he and Vogeler shook, their forearms clenched a little as each took a squeeze. Rudi hid his smile at that—two strong men taking each other's measure, a bit like two strange dogs bristling and stalking around stiff-legged and then sniffing each other's behinds. The more so as Ingolf was a tried fighting man, and Odard just enough younger to be extra touchy about the fact that he wasn't.

"Pleased to meet you again, Sheriff Vogeler," Odard said when they'd finished.

He worked his right hand a little. That was a mark of a certain respect, and so was the form of address; Association nobles didn't always admit that the titles of eastern sheriffs were comparable to their own . . . and Odard was technically a baron now himself, while Ingolf was a younger son and landless wanderer.

"Pleased to meet *you* again, Baron Gervais," Ingolf said, impeccably polite.

He didn't flex his hand. That might mean he'd won the little unspoken exchange—he was bigger and heavier-boned, after all—or it just might mean that he had six years more experience and was better at hiding things. Or both; probably both.

Behind them, Rudi saw the three young women exchange a glance and roll their eyes skyward ever so slightly. He knew exactly what they were thinking: *Men.* That made him cock an ironic eyebrow at them.

Girls have their own way of playing who's-the-boss; if we do it like dogs, they're more like cats, he thought. *It's sneakier, usually, but it's the same game, sure. And they can play our way if they want.*

He shivered slightly, inwardly, at a memory. Tiphaine d'Ath had told him once that she even had an advantage at it; she skipped the preliminary strutting and chest-beating flourishes men expected and just killed whoever she thought was a threat. Of course, that had its drawbacks too; it made her hated almost as much as she was feared. Let the fear weaken, and the hate would become active.

There was a *reason* for the rituals; they let men settle their positions without fighting to the death every single time.

Rancher Brown had caught the byplay between the two younger men too, and snorted softly; with him it was probably that he had nearly seven decades of perspective, and was an old alpha dog who was sensible enough to let the sixty well-armed youngsters who followed his banner do his growling and sniffing for him.

"Come on in."

The breakfast table was still set in the dining room, though it looked as if half a dozen people had already eaten. Mrs. Brown was there, a quiet middle-aged blond woman a fair bit younger than the rancher—his first wife had died not long after the Change when some medicine she needed to live ran out. The current Mrs. Brown's children were there, down at the end of the table, two girls of eight and ten and a boy a couple of years younger than Edain.

The rancher's wife smiled as the newcomers loaded their plates with flapjacks and huevos rancheros and bacon and sausage and buttered muffins and toast from the lamp-warmed hot plates on the buffet. There was a—small—jar of maple syrup on the table as well. Rudi used it sparingly; the stuff had to be imported from the Willamette, and he suspected that its presence was in honor of the guests in general and of him specifically.

Everything was still good; he murmured the invocation and pitched in. Mrs. Brown smiled at him.

"You always were a good eater, Rudi. It's a pleasure to see a young man enjoy his food."

He grinned back at her; after crossing the still-frigid Cascades on foot and living mostly on hardtack and jerky while he did it, he certainly *was* going to enjoy a meal like this. Ingolf and Edain were putting it away with methodical pleasure too.

"It's a pleasure for a young man to eat it, too, Aunt Mabel." Then to the rancher: "I notice Bob isn't here."

Brown nodded at the mention of his eldest son, born before the Change.

"The boy's out getting a horse herd ready to drive east. Saddle-broke, young 'uns four to six. 'Bout a hundred and a bit."

Then he shook his head. "The boy?" He made a *tsk* sound and gave a rueful chuckle. "I'm gettin' old. Bob has a boy of his own who'll start shavin' in a year or three."

Rudi raised a brow. "Taking a herd east? Boise?"

Brown smiled slowly. "Well, maybe. Maybe not, too. General Thurston in Boise *is* paying pretty good for saddle-broke four-year-olds . . ."

"But New Deseret is paying even better?"

"Reckon. Leastways that's what their man promised; their war with this Prophet fella isn't going so well. And the Saints generally keep a bargain once they've made it. Can't always say that about Thurston, if he gets a hair up it about how you're in the way of his restorin' the US of A, which to his way of thinking means truckling to him."

A glint of anger showed through Brown's facade. "And this Prophet bastard out Montana way, he sent a man around not too long ago, tellin' us not to help Deseret, tellin' us like we were his hired hands. Talked trash to some of our people in secret, too, preachin' and tryin' to set them against their Ranchers."

And it's sure Rancher Brown is a bit ticked, if he's selling that many horses, potential breeding mares as well as geldings . . . Rudi thought.

"What did you do?" the young Mackenzie asked, using the plural to mean the leaders of the CORA.

"Told him to stop. When he didn't . . . well, we give him what he asked for."

"Which was?" Rudi said, willingly playing straight man to the grim oldster.

"He asked for *earth and water*. Said it was symbolic, a way of acknowledging we'd take his Prophet for bossman and that everythin' here would obey him."

"So you gave him earth and water?"

"Plenty of both down at the bottom of that old well, I'd say. After we dropped him in headfirst."

Odard laughed outright, and made as if to applaud. Everyone else at least smiled, except Mrs. Brown, who winced a little. Rudi didn't find it particularly humorous, but he wasn't unduly shocked either. An ambassador who tried to play politics against his hosts that way forfeited protection and could expect to get a spy's treatment. Brown went on:

"After that, we decided we'd sell New Deseret anything they could pay for. The Saints' money spends as good as anyone's; they're good neighbors from all I hear—better than Boise. If they use what we sell 'em to keep this Prophet busy out Montana way, the more power to them."

"And we're heading east, ourselves," Rudi said. *What did Aunt Judy say . . .* He remembered, and muttered it: *"Gevalt!"*

"Figured you were," Brown said. "Even if your sisters didn't say much.

Well, I got that letter from your mother, and more I don't need to know."

He nodded towards the twins, who smiled with identical smugness.

One of them said, "We picked up all the gear we'll need in Bend, too. A big wagon, tents, extra weapons, and everything else, paid for out of the Dúnedain account at the First National branch there."

"So if you were to head east with the herd . . ." Brown said delicately. "Well, that would be a help to Bob and the boys, a whole bunch more blades and bows. Comin' back, that won't be so hard; they can move faster."

And we'll be on our way, Rudi thought. A little rest and a good meal brought the excitement bubbling back and forced down homesickness. *On our way to the Atlantic!*

"It's a favor, and that's a fact," Rudi said, and leaned over to shake Brown's hand again, to seal the bargain this time.

After that the Browns tactfully left. Rudi looked around the knot of his relatives and friends and almost-friends and sighed.

"All right, first things first, then," he said. "You all want to come with me?"

A chorus of nods. Rudi went on:

"We'll be going a long hard dangerous way, then. Someone has to be in charge, and that one is me. This is not some game; I *have* to get to this Nantucket place. Ingolf I need for a guide, and because he's got the experience, sure. Everyone else is there to help us get there and back again. All that means I'm in command, and Ingolf is my number two. Do you understand what I'm saying, now?"

"Yah," Ingolf said. "In rough country, there's got to be discipline, by God." A grin. "And besides, you're young but you learn quick."

The twins nodded—in chorus. *By the Threefold Morrigú, am I going to be able to take having them in my sporran for a whole year?* Rudi thought ruefully.

Odard shrugged. "You're better qualified for it than me," he said cheerfully. "Ingolf is too. If I'm going to do something this crazy, I want it to work, by Mary and all the saints."

"Good," Rudi said, ignoring his own doubts—half the battle was *sounding* confident. "The next thing to remember is that everyone pitches in. Nobody's a nobleman on this trip . . . or we all are, whichever. Right?"

Odard's nod was a little slower still this time; Rudi judged that he hadn't considered all the implications of Adventure, particularly the part about scrubbing out pots with sand and latrine detail.

"And Odard, your man there isn't going to do your share of the chores, either."

The slanted blue eyes blinked at him. "But of course, Rudi."

*   *   *

CASTLE TODENANGST, WILLAMETTE VALLEY NEAR NEWBERG, OREGON
MAY 6, CY23/2021 A.D.

Juniper Mackenzie spread her hands. "Your message was the first I knew of it, Sandra."

They weren't exactly friends, but then they weren't exactly enemies anymore either, and they had known each other a long time now. She made a gesture.

"By the Ever-Changing One, by the Maiden, the Mother and the Hag, I swear it. May She turn her face and heart from me if I lie. I didn't even *suspect* it. Neither did Rudi, as far as I know—and he doesn't lie to me. According to the message John Brown sent me, Rudi was surprised himself when he showed up at Seffridge Ranch and found Mathilda there, the creature."

Across the polished malachite of the table, the shoulders of Portland's ruler slumped a touch.

"I believe you," she said quietly, and laid her fingers on an open letter. "That's what Mathilda says . . . and *she* doesn't lie to *me*. I almost wish I didn't believe you. Then I'd have someone to be angry with. Besides that little idiot herself!"

Her fist tightened on the lustrous green stone. It was a small fist; they were both petite women. The force behind it was nothing to sneer at, though; Tiphaine d'Ath and Conrad Renfrew flanked her on either side, symbols of the power that awaited that subtle mind's orders.

"And I can't even send an army to bring her back," Sandra said bitterly. "It's too late. Any force big enough would be too slow, and any fast enough would just make her conspicuous without being big enough to protect her."

Juniper had brought nobody with her except her man Nigel, and that partly because she'd known he would simply refuse to stay behind when she put her head in the lioness's mouth.

And sure, she might *have believed a written message. But coming here makes it certain.*

"I'm worried for Rudi, too," the Mackenzie chieftain said gently. "Worried sick. And I love Mathilda as if she were my own. If it's any consolation, I fear for her as well."

Sandra's brown eyes met her green. "He isn't your only child."

Juniper's brows went up. "Sandra, do you think that I would mourn Rudi less because I have Eilir and Maude and Fiorbhinn? That they're . . ." She hunted for a word. *"Spares?"*

"No," Sandra said softly. "But your whole life wouldn't be a waste if you lost him. Mathilda is the one thing I can be entirely proud of. What have I worked for, if not for her?"

Then she shook herself and put on briskness. "What can we do?"

Juniper nodded respectfully. "Not a great deal, except keep this as quiet as possible. But news *will* get out, especially now. Mathilda . . . I'm afraid Mathilda has made this considerably more dangerous. She is conspicuous all by herself, and even more so when she's not *here*, if you take my meaning. People are used to Rudi disappearing about his own business for a while, and Dun Juniper is more out of the way to start with."

"We *will* keep it as quiet as we can," Sandra said. "And there's something else we can do."

At Juniper's inquiring look, she went on: "Get ready for the war."

Juniper nodded soberly, then looked east. "And pray for our children, Sandra," she said. "We can do that, too."

CHAPTER THIRTEEN

Rudi Mackenzie opened his eyes and poked his head out into the dry chill. The sun threw a crimson band along the eastern horizon even before it rose. A rim of purple rose above that; stars faded there, but they still glittered in a frosted band towards the west. The camp was stirring. He made himself swing out of his sleeping bag, despite the cold rime on its glazed leather covering. Quickly he pulled out the coat and boots he'd stuffed down in it, and drew his plaid around his shoulders blanket-wise. From what he'd heard, this country east of Picture Rock Pass got very hot indeed in summer. But it was nearly five thousand feet up here; winter hit hard too, and relinquished its hold reluctantly.

Once he had the boots and sheepskin jacket on, the twins and Edain joined him, and one of the cowboys who was a dedicant. They crossed their arms and bowed heads to the sun as it rose over the eastern horizon, turning the crimson band to gold. Then they raised their hands with palms to the sky and chanted together:

> *Rising with the Sun*
> *Spirits of Air*
> *My soul follows Hawk on the ghost of the wind*
> *I find my voice and speak truth;*

All-Father, wise Lord
All-Mother, gentle and strong
Guide me and guard me this day and all days
By Your grace, with harm to none;
Blessed be!

He smiled as he spoke the familiar words. Partly that was because they *were* familiar, and always brought a feeling of comforting contact with the Powers. More of it was the sight of the vast land opening out to the eastward, rolling like the waves of some great frozen sea or rising here and there into a flat-topped mesa. Sagebrush covered it, silvery gray and coated with hoarfrost; the crystals sparkled for a single instant as the sun cleared the far ridges, turning the whole expanse to a field of diamonds.

Thank You for this, he added within himself in the moment of silence that followed.

Beside him Edain sighed and murmured, "Now that's the Spirit of Air, and no mistake."

The twins nodded, and they all glanced at one another, brought back to the light of common day. Over a little way Father Ignatius and Mathilda and their coreligionists—who included Ingolf and a half dozen of the Seffridge Ranch folk—were finishing their own morning devotions:

Queen of heaven, rejoice, alleluia.
For He whom you did merit to bear, alleluia . . .

Greasewood crackled as the fires were stoked up, and the companionable smells of scorched frying pan and sizzling bacon filled the air.

The party from the Willamette ate together, a little apart from the rancher's men. It was Odard's turn to cook breakfast, though Rudi had put the flat iron pot with the biscuit dough into the ashes when he finished his turn on watch late last night. The tops were nicely brown when he wrapped a corner of his plaid around his hand—it *was* a useful garment—and lifted the lid.

Everyone in their group crowded around to get their share. They had fresh butter—the ranch folk had a couple of milch cows along with them. They were scrawny-looking by Willamette Valley standards, and didn't give much milk, but they did produce enough for the ingenious little wheel-powered barrel churn in their chuck wagon to work. Odard added passable hash browns, beans that had also cooked overnight with some dried onion, and bacon. As they settled down around the fire Bob Brown came over and squatted on his heels.

The rancher's son was taller than his father, a lanky man in his thirties with hair somewhere between brown and sandy and dark blue eyes, holding a tin mug of the chicory-root brew people east of the mountains insisted on calling coffee; it smelled delicious and tasted vile, in Rudi's opinion. Bob accepted a biscuit and bit into it appreciatively.

"Not bad," he said. Then he looked at Rudi and shrugged a little. "And you were right: all your friends here *are* good enough to stand a watch."

Ingolf shrugged. "Only natural for you to want to see what we could do before you relied on us," he said.

Rudi shrugged in turn and finished the last piece of his bacon, fighting down a slight resentment; he'd come close to quarreling with Bob Brown about it, before Vogeler stepped in.

He's right . . . they were both right, he thought. *Just because I knew doesn't mean he knew, and it's not something you take chances on. I should have realized that right away and not gotten my back up over it. All right, Mackenzie, make a note.*

Aloud he went on: "It makes the math easier anyway. Glad you're happy with our performance."

Bob stirred his sugar-and-cream-laced chicory with a twig, sipped at it and gave Rudi a shrewd slanticular glance before he squinted out at the plain to the east. His eyes had more lines beside them than a man of his age from the Willamette, a face that spent a lot of time looking into dry winds full of grit and alkali dust.

"I'm not what you'd call real joyful about anything right now," he said. "This is the last of the CORA ranches we're riding over now—and the rancher here doesn't use this pasture much; too many rustlers, even when there's water."

He pointed his chin towards the small creek and pond at the base of the rise they had camped on. The horse herd was around its edge now, switching their tails and drinking, and it looked pretty and pastoral. There were even a few Russian olive trees trailing branches over the water. The little waterway filled only seasonally, and the water had a slight but unpleasant soapy taste. It was drinkable . . . sort of. You could wash in it, if you didn't mind an itchy film on your skin afterwards. They all had; it was likely to be the last opportunity for a while.

Bob went on: "Folks east of here, the Rovers, the best you can say is that there aren't many of them. Well, that and that they fight one another a lot. What else you can say is they're mighty poor, and they're thieves and cutthroats. Taking a hundred twenty prime head of horses through is like waving a lamb chop in front of a hungry kai-ote. It's like to take the chop and your hand too—and be gone before you've really noticed."

It took a moment for Rudi to realize that the rancher's son meant *coyote*. He'd always rather liked the clever little song dogs, but he could see his point—they did go after sheep, and they'd be a much bigger problem out here than they were in Mackenzie territory.

"Why are the people here out-of-the-ordinary dangerous?" Odard said curiously. "Aren't they ranchers like you?"

Bob bridled at that, like a Bearkiller A-lister mistaken for an Association baron by someone from too far away to know the difference.

Mary—or Ritva—cut in hastily: "Water," she said. "There just isn't much dry-season water here you can get at without deep pumps. No hay either, so you can't keep more stock than the winter pastures will support. We Dúnedain have had problems escorting caravans around here—but most trade with the east goes up the Columbia and Snake, or right across on the old Highway 20 through Burns, well north of this part. It's worse here."

Bob nodded. "We CORA folk bounced back fast, but they kept on going down a lot longer 'round here before they hit bottom, what with their pumps and such gone. Mostly they don't even have homeplaces anymore; they just follow their herds from one patch of grazing to another and pray there's water. Roving around, that's why we call 'em Rovers."

Unexpectedly, Father Ignatius spoke.

"My Order has had some missions out here, bringing windmill pumps and doctors. Not with any great success. The . . . wandering bands . . . are still very bitter. Not entirely without reason. Nobody shared much with them in the bad years. What they really want now is weapons."

Bob looked a little uneasy. Ranches like his father's had snaffled off the best of the refugees from Bend and Sisters and Madras, men and women with skills that had been hobbies or luxuries before the Change and were suddenly very important indeed. They'd also done very well out of their contacts with the Mackenzies and the other Willamette communities—Juniper had reminisced about that to her son, how she'd traded bows and arrows for cattle the very first Change Year, and for providing bowyer training later.

"Someone should put this area in order, then," Mathilda said decisively. "It's wasteful and breeds trouble to have lawless zones like this—or like Pendleton, come to that. CORA is part of the Meeting, so we should all do something about it."

She sounds very sure of herself, Rudi thought with a quirk of his lips as he wiped his fingers on the gritty soil and then dusted them off. *But then, she always does.*

And she was usually right. The problem was that she was just as convinced on the rarer occasions when she was wrong. That was annoying but tolerable in a friend. Rudi suspected it would be much more of a problem in a ruler who wasn't really accountable to anyone else except God and, theoretically, the pope.

The rancher's son cleared his throat. "Be that as it may, we still got to get the herd through here, so nobody up to Bend or Burns will notice and tell General Thurston in Boise. Bet that Prophet fella has spies there too."

Father Ignatius smiled wryly. "He does, my son. Unfortunately the Order's information is that he has had missionaries preaching to the wanderers east of here, as well."

Bob finished his chicory and turned the cup upside down. "Yup. Which means we should all suit up from here on out. Riding in armor ain't what you'd call comfy but it beats getting an arrow through the gizzard all to hell and gone."

* * *

"Annwyn take it!" Edain said. "Fetch, girl! Fetch the sodding thing!"

He sounded frustrated enough to cry. Garbh cantered over and bent her head to gently draw the practice arrow out of the gritty, rocky dirt beside the sagebrush and trotted back proudly with it held in her mouth. Edain bent in the saddle to retrieve it. He wouldn't cry, of course, but his face was red and angry; that showed easily, with his fair complexion.

It was probably even more embarrassing that he had to practice near the CORA men, who'd grown up shooting recurves from horseback.

"Better this time," Ingolf said.

Rudi nodded to himself, sitting his horse nearby. It *had* been: a near miss. Which was surprising; Edain was a champion shot with the longbow, and this last year he'd given Rudi hard competition at the butts. Only to be expected from Sam Aylward's son, of course, which made it the more puzzling he was having so much trouble learning this.

Ingolf went on patiently—he made an excellent teacher, and he was at least Rudi's equal with the shorter recurve horseman's weapon.

"Look, you're first-rate with that yew pole of yours, but this is different. You've been practicing shooting on foot all your life, right?"

"Since I was about six," Edain said proudly, the flush dying away. Awkwardly: "I'm just not used to *missing* all the time, is what."

"Yeah, you're scary with that longbow on foot, kid. But what you know is getting in the way of what you've got to learn—I've been doing this since *I* was six. You're not going to get it in a day or a week."

The sagebrush-clothed plain stretched around them, but the silver-gray brushes were thinner than any they'd seen before, interspersed with patches of glittering alkali salts, some of them still muddy. A few miles behind them were the steep canyon-scored eastern escarpments of the Steens Mountains, green with aspen and juniper higher up. The rocky slopes of the Bowden Hills were growing—slowly—on the eastern horizon. High overhead a red-tailed hawk folded its wings and stooped at a rabbit flushed out of cover by the oncoming caravan. Plumes of dust rose towards the arching blue dome of the sky, kicked up by hundreds of hooves and the wheels of the two wagons.

"Take a minute and watch," the easterner went on, lifting his own saddlebow. "Look, from what I've seen with a longbow you draw like this, past the angle of your jaw and below it."

The long draw was the way to get the best out of a yew stave. He shifted his string hand upward three inches and slightly forward.

"Now, with these short recurves you have to draw *to* your ear. The limbs come back and the string lifts off the section towards the tips as they straighten out and then bend the other way—a nice sharp C, not a shallow curve like your bows. Believe it or not, the bowstave gets longer that way; that's how you can shoot a long arrow from a short bow. Try it."

Edain did, and sweat burst out on his forehead as he forced himself to overcome training that went far below the conscious level.

"I feel awkward as a hog on ice," he grumbled.

"Again," Ingolf said. "You just have to get used to shifting methods back and forth."

Edain did it again. As he did, he tried to set his feet as he would shooting a longbow from the ground. The problem with *that* was that the horse he was on interpreted it as a command and wheeled sharply to the right, dust and bits of gritty yellow-brown rock spurting from under its hooves. It also snorted and looked back at him, as if to say, *What do you think you're doing?*

Ah, I see the problem, Rudi thought.

The young Mackenzie was a fair horseman; the Aylwards could afford to keep a riding horse, being well-to-do by the Clan's standards. But those standards didn't include a class of landowners with dependents to do the work and the leisure to master mounted combat, the way Bearkillers or Ingolf's folk did. Mackenzies were smallholders, farmers who might ride horse or bicycle to battle but who got down and fought on foot.

Edain brought the animal under control and started to try again, his square face grimly intent. Sweat streaked the white dust and brown-yellow stubble on his face; two days ago they'd been taking an icy plunge in Mustang Lake, which memory was too pleasant to recall in this hot dry saltbox.

"Clamp down with both your thighs evenly," Ingolf said patiently. "Stand a little in the stirrups when you do it. That's a range-country horse and he's trained to it."

The lesson went on. There wasn't much else to do as the horse herd and Rudi's party made their way slowly eastward. Even in the spring flush the grazing here wasn't much, which meant a hundred and twenty horses—not counting the riding and draft animals—had to spread out and spend a lot of time eating. The cowboys told a joke about a jackrabbit that starved to death hereabouts because it forgot to run between one blade of grass and the next.

With excruciating care, Edain did everything the way Ingolf had told him to. This time the arrow went *shnnnk* right into the base of a brush fifty yards away. By his banshee whoop, it had even been the one he was aiming at.

"Keep practicing," Ingolf said.

"That I will," the younger man said. He waved a hand around at the arid emptiness. "It's not as if I had anything else that needs doing, eh?"

Rudi nodded, and gave him a smile and a slap on the shoulder as he legged his horse up to a canter. *I'll make him self-conscious if I practice around here,* he thought.

He was giving Epona all the rest he could, so he was on her daughter Rhiannon; the five-year-old needed the exercise too, being more full of monkeyshines than her mother. Mathilda and the others were wearing light armor and practicing as well; Odard's man Alex was throwing raw-hide disks to skip and bounce along the ground as they galloped by and shot, since he was good with a crossbow but no archer at all.

Hope he brought along a couple of extra crossbows, Rudi thought ironically. *Not likely to find replacement parts out here.*

Some of the score of Rancher Brown's hands along on the trek were practicing archery as well; it didn't take many to keep the horses moving. Rudi gave them a glance as he reined in next to the others.

"Not bad at all," he said.

Everyone nodded. They were all young, but they had been trained by professionals from childhood.

"Strange they're such good archers," Odard observed. "Most of them are barely even middling with the sword, and they're mere dubs as lancers."

"Not really strange," Rudi said. "It's the same reason they're such good riders. What they do to feed themselves in peace is training for war, you see. They spend most of their working lives in the saddle watching their stock. The bow's a tool for them too, for hunting or guarding the herds."

Mathilda spoke thoughtfully: "Mom and the Grand Constable are a bit worried about that," she said. "About the trouble it might cause in the long run. There's a lot of cowboys, not many in any one spot but a lot in total, because there's a *lot* of ranching country out there."

Mary and Ritva nodded silently. One of them took a small jar out of her saddlebag and they both applied the greasy-looking lotion within to their faces and necks and hands. Mathilda took it with a sigh and began to do likewise.

"This stuff smells and feels like someone dragged a dead sheep through a field of wilted flowers, and then bottled it," she said.

"Lanolin with lavender extract," Ritva or Mary said. "Believe me, it's better than what the sun and wind out here do to your skin. This is from a shop in Bend."

Bob Brown came trotting over and heard the last remark. "The Rovers use butter instead," he said, grinning. "Or sheep's-wool grease. You could try that. . . ."

Mathilda shuddered again. Rudi took the jar and began to apply the lotion; he didn't like the feel or the smell either, but it helped. He wasn't quite as blister-by-lamplight as his redheaded mother, but it was close, despite his blood father, Mike Havel, being a quarter Indian. He didn't tan even as well as the twins, and the drying wind made his skin feel as if it were about to split over his cheekbones.

"Ride a bit with me," Bob said to Rudi.

The two men turned their horses aside; as he did so, Rudi caught Mary's eye—or Ritva's—and let one eyelid droop for an instant. The rancher's son pointed to their right, southward, as they ambled away from the main party. A rocky eminence stood about two thousand feet above the level of the plain.

"That there pimple is Lookout Butte—Buckskin Mountain, some call it."

Then he pointed directly east. "The old Whitehorse Ranch is that-away, less than a day's travel. That's where we're supposed to meet the buyers from Deseret and turn over the herd. There's good water there, wells, but pretty deep and not too much of it. The Rovers use it, but not usually this time of year—more in summer, when things dry up farther out. The Saints probably plan to head back east through Blue Mountain Pass afterwards; that's about another twenty, twenty-five miles. Or maybe south over the old Nevada line. I didn't ask and they didn't tell me."

Rudi looked at the older man. "You're expecting trouble?" he said crisply.

"Hope not. But if there *is* trouble, that's where it'll be. The Rovers would rather steal horses than silver, but they wouldn't mind stealin' horses *and* silver and the gear from my bunch and the Deseret folks too, right down to our socks, you see what I mean? Not to mention our scalps."

Rudi looked slowly around the circle of the horizon. "They've been tracking us," he said.

" 'Course they have," Bob growled. "Herd this big, I might as well be wavin' a sign says, 'Rob me.' Or 'Kill me and lift my hair and *then* rob me.' Only that wouldn't be as dangerous as throwin' up a dust trail, on account of the Rovers can't read."

"Thanks for the heads-up," Rudi said. "If it comes to a fight, we'll do our part."

"We ought to scout ahead, but I don't like splittin' my people. We'd be shorthanded if they tried something tricky, like cutting part of the herd out after dark while another bunch made noise. Any of your folks you'd recommend?"

"I figured you'd ask that. Send the twins," Rudi said without hesitation. "For a quiet sneaky skulk, they're the best there is."

"You sure?" Bob said.

Rudi grinned. Cow-country people weren't as odd about girls and what they should do as Protectorate folk, but they weren't Mackenzies or Dúnedain or Bearkillers either.

"You can come out now," he said, in a normal conversational tone.

One of them rose from behind a sagebrush that grew on the edge of a shallow gully, one small enough you'd swear it couldn't have hidden a jackrabbit. Rudi could tell she was breathing fast—she'd had to duck into the depression and run crouched over—but she hid it well.

"Shit! *Jesus!*" Bob said.

Then he swore again as he looked over his shoulder and saw the other twin raise her head over a rock and wiggle her fingers too, with a smug little *can't catch me* smile.

"Maybe you know what you're talking about, Rudi."

"Maybe. And we should get Ingolf in on this. He's got a lot more experience running a war band than I do."

Bob looked at him. "Not all that many men your age admit they've got anything to learn."

"I'm young," Rudi said, putting on the air of a man making a great concession. "But I'm not stupid . . . I hope."

*   *   *

"There it is," Mary—or Ritva—said.

Rudi, Ingolf and Bob Brown lay on the ridge, about a hundred feet above the level of the plain. The ruins of Whitehorse Ranch lay a little less than a mile to the east, with steeper heights rising beyond above the clump of dead cottonwoods and maples. Rudi watched, occasionally raising his binoculars, and fought back a sneeze from the pungent desert herbs crushed under their bodies.

There were people there now, using the roofless buildings and their half dozen wagons to make an improvised fortress; a dark banner hung limp in the warm dry air over one of the vehicles. Horsemen prowled around the laager, with no more order than a pack of wolves . . . and no less. As they watched a dozen of them suddenly set their horses forward at a gallop, raising a plume of dust. Steel twinkled within it as they rose in the stirrups and shot, then wheeled away again. The field glasses showed long spears leveled among the wagons, and the flash of bolts as they shot back—crossbows rather than archery, he decided.

"How many of the Rovers?" he asked thoughtfully.

"Around ninety, assuming all the ones we saw this morning are here," one of the twins said.

Bob had a pair of binoculars too. "Make that around eighty-nine," he said. "One of 'em just dropped out of the saddle and they're carryin' him away looking limp. It surely is a war party, right enough—no stock but their remounts, no women or kids or wagons, just some packhorses and a couple of tents."

"That's your buyers forted up?" Rudi asked.

"Yup. See the flag? A golden bee on dark blue—that's New Deseret."

"There can't be many of them," Rudi said regretfully; if there were, the little attack just now would have cost the Rovers more.

"Nope," Brown agreed. "About as many as we got to start with, no more. Less now."

He looked up at the sun; it was about noon. "I'd say the Rovers hit them at dawn, maybe snuck someone up to cut out their horses first. The Mormons're good enough in a tussle from what I hear, but they're farmers and townsmen mostly, and their ranchers 'n' horse soldiers are all out east fightin' the Prophet. This sure isn't a place for a farmer's fight."

Rudi looked over the little battlefield, and the endless rumpled landscape around them. Brown was right, and he felt uneasily self-conscious about it. He'd never come so far east . . . and he'd never been involved in a fight this size, either.

Ingolf squinted at the Rovers. "So there's the nine of us, twenty-one of your men, Rancher, and maybe fifteen or so in the wagons down there—and they don't know we're here."

"But we've got some heavy horse," Rudi pointed out. "We bought Ingolf the gear for it too"—he nodded to the older man—"and you were already fine with a lance. If we could get in range for a charge, we could spatter them."

Bob Brown shook his head. "Hell, I was in the Mount Angel fight in the war," he said. "I remember how the Protector's knights cut us CORA folk up. It was like trying to outbutt a mean old bull. But that was in the Willamette, where we couldn't run far. You try that here, they'll just run—and then when those big horses of yours are tuckered from a-haulin' all that iron around, they'll shoot you full of arrows."

"Like wolves with an elk." Rudi sighed. "So much for *that* idea."

"Wait a minute," Ingolf said. "Bob's right *if* they can run away. But back in the Sioux War, there was a time when . . ."

He went on, giving the details and then pointing out the features below—the hills, the water, the wagons and ruins, how far a horse *could* run. . . .

"Oh, now that's a lovely plan, sure!" Rudi said, watching it take shape in his mind's eye.

"Lovely if it works. Four-to-one odds just purely don't leave you much to fall back on if things get fucked," the heir to Seffridge Ranch said dubiously.

"But we'll have to be quick; they're going to get overrun down there before sunset," Rudi said.

"Well, dip me in shit and roast me with nuts if it isn't our only real chance," the rancher's son said ruefully. "Can't just go home and tell Dad, 'Sorry, the Rovers done kilt all our customers.' "

Then his eyes went back to the ruins. "Be tricky timing, though. If it goes south, we're in it up to our asses."

"Never yet been in a fight that didn't have some risks," Ingolf said. "I wouldn't try it if there weren't those hills in back, but that makes it a chance worth taking."

CHAPTER FOURTEEN

"I hope this is worth it," Odard said, slapping each palm against the vambrace on the opposite forearm to make sure it was seated firmly, and then pulling on his mail-backed gauntlets.

"You have to help your friends," Mathilda said, as she bloused her long tunic of titanium mail a little around her sword belt. "And your friends' friends. And we need their help getting farther east after Rancher Brown's men turn back, unless we want to try swinging far south and tackling the Colorado Rockies by ourselves."

"Point," the Baron of Gervais said.

Rudi grinned as his head emerged through the neck of his brigandine; he pulled out the bottom of his coif and tossed his head so the lower part of the mail hood would lie on the shoulders.

"And it's a nice day for a fight," he went on. "No clouds, not too hot . . . Someone give me a hand here?"

Edain did; putting on full lancer's armor was always a bit awkward. Mathilda met Rudi's eyes and gave him a grave nod as she fastened the flap of her coif across her mouth, then lowered the conical helmet with its splayed nasal bar onto her head and buckled the chinstrap. A plume of black-dyed ostrich feathers rose from the peak, traded from hand to hand at incredible cost from the deserts of the southwest where the birds ran free.

"Well, I'm off to do my bit, then, Chief," Edain said. "Wings of the Morrigú shelter you."

"Horned Lord with you," Rudi replied, clapping him on the shoulder. "And may the Wolf fight by your side."

Edain started towards his horse, then turned his head to say, "And thank Him and Her and Father Wolf too that I don't have to use that bloody saddlebow!"

The lancers' horses were ready; they'd armed them before themselves, with chamfrons to cover their heads save for the eyes and nostrils, and peytrals of steel plates mounted on padded leather backing on their chests and necks and shoulders. Epona whickered greeting; the chamfron went *clink* on the mail that covered Rudi's upper arm as she tried to nuzzle him. Her eyes rolled behind the ridges of steel that protected them as she snorted and stamped a foot eagerly.

She knows what the gear means, just as I do, Rudi thought. *But she likes it more than I.*

He settled the sallet helm on his head—a low dome of steel that came down to the angle of his jaw save for the open space before his face, and flared out to protect his neck. A smooth curved visor with a narrow vision slit slid up under his hand, shading his eyes like the bill of a cap.

Twin sprays of raven feathers stood in holders at each temple. Thin lines had been graven in the steel, and filled with black niello, in the likeness of more feathers; the visor came down to a slight peak. On this trip he wasn't supposed to advertise *who* he was, but he could still show *what* he was.

His thoughts went grimly on:

Epona just doesn't like people, except me; she wants to hurt them, the way they hurt her before we met. We're old souls to each other, I think; we've met in past lives, or in the Summerlands. But I don't enjoy killing men. It's necessary, sometimes, that's all.

He leaned against the saddle for a moment, closed his eyes, and murmured under his breath, "Dread Lord, Father of Victories, Storm-rider, Wild Huntsman, aid us now. Dark Goddess, Morrigú of the Crows, Red Hag of Battles, to You I dedicate the harvest of the unplowed field of war, and the blood to be spilled this day on Your earth. Be You both with Your children; and if this is my hour, then know I go most willingly to You."

Sometimes the regard of the Powers could be as warm as a lover's embrace or a summer's wind lying in new-mown hay; but most often They came in the Aspect that you called. Now he felt as if a wind were blowing, blowing along his spine and into the spaces of his head, cold and bitter from a place of ice and iron and bones. Then he swung into the saddle and picked up a lance from the seven that leaned against the wagon.

Father Ignatius had the band's Catholics gathered about him for a moment. Rudi could hear their voices following his:

"Lord Jesus Christ, have mercy on us. Come to the aid of us Christians and make us worthy to fight to the death for our faith and our brothers. Strengthen our souls and our whole bodies, Mighty Lord of Hosts, God of Battles. Through the intercession of the Immaculate Mother of God, and of all the saints, we humbly beg this of You. *Deus lo vult!* Amen."

Then the monk swung into the saddle and rode over. He smiled and hefted the next of the eleven-foot ashwood shafts, looked critically along the length, and gave the nod of a workman satisfied with his tools.

Their eyes met, and Ignatius smiled. "Serious business, Rudi. It's always well to start it with a prayer."

"Right you are, Father," Rudi acknowledged.

The twins and Mathilda seemed to think so too. Odard was cool and detached, making sure his gear was just so.

"This is a damn good plan, Ingolf," the baron said. "If it works, I owe you a bottle of wine." He laughed. "And if it doesn't we'll be too dead to drink, most likely."

Odd, the Mackenzie thought. *I wonder what it's like to be Odard? You can hunt and drink and spar with a man, and laugh at his jokes and play poker and talk about girls, and still you wonder what the inwardness is like, when he talks to himself in his head.*

Odard went on: "They won't have ever dealt with real knights, this far east."

Rudi nodded; that *was* the plan. Unfortunately there were only seven of them fit to carry a lance—himself, the twins, Matti, Ingolf, Odard, and the soldier-monk.

Ingolf looked down at the kit he was wearing—much like Rudi's, a brigandine supplemented by mail collar and sleeves and breeches, with plate greaves on his shins and vambraces on his forearms. He'd stuck to his own kettle helmet, though.

"I'm not used to wearing this much armor," he grumbled. "Boy isn't either."

"He'll get used to it," Rudi said. "And you're already pretty good with a lance. Full armor doesn't make that any different."

"Just safer." Odard laughed, slinging his long kite-shaped shield over his back by the guige strap and swinging up into the saddle. "Safer for you, and more dangerous for the other guy."

His voice was muffled behind the mail coif; he tossed the lance's length of ashwood and steel overhead and twirled it like a baton until it made the air whir and the pennant crackle—a flamboyant and mildly dangerous trick that took good timing and enormously strong wrists.

"Stop showing off, Odard," Mathilda said sharply. "This is a fight, not a tournament with barriers and rebated points. I don't want to get that thing in my back because you slipped."

"Your Highness commands," he said, bowing his head and chuckling again before he put the lance at rest.

Over with the Seffridge Ranch folk Bob Brown gave Rudi a thumbs-up. The horse herd was safely penned in a box canyon, with Mrs. Jason and her daughter—who usually managed the chuck wagon—watching them. The cowboys were well equipped, for light horse; Bob and four others had short mail shirts, and the rest steel-strapped leather breast-plates, and they all had good round shields and bowl helmets. They'd all slung an extra quiver to their saddlebows, too; you ran out of shafts fast in a serious fight, and the man with the last arrow was likely to be the one who rode home. The youngest of them was looking mutinous, and leading a train of several packhorses with panniers full of bundled arrows.

Rudi rested the butt of his lance on the toe of his boot and nodded. The rancher's men formed up in a rough column of twos and trotted away eastward, their hooves a growling rumble on the hard alkaline dirt. Dust followed them as the sound faded away; there wasn't any way around that with so many horses.

But we want them to be seen. Let's see, they've got a mile to go, he thought. *Of course, we seven don't want to be seen. . . .*

Ingolf looked up at the sun. "Nothing shows up at a distance on a clear day like a bright lancehead," he said, and flipped his down and buried the point in the mud of a drying puddle for an instant. "Everyone, get it muddy."

Everyone did, though not eagerly in some cases. "Hell of a thing to do to good steel," Odard grumbled.

"You can wash it soon in blood, hopefully," Mary pointed out, as she unhappily followed suit.

Vain as peacocks, Rudi thought affectionately as he looked at his sisters . . . and Odard. *Or as cats.*

"And I said *stop showing off,* Odard," Mathilda added sharply. "The point is to kill them, not make them applaud our chivalric brilliance."

"Point taken," Odard replied.

"Let's get going," Rudi said, as the Baron of Gervais reluctantly daubed the bright-polished steel in the puddle.

They did, straight eastward rather than a little north of east as Bob and his men had done. That put them on course for a gap between two high rocky hills or low mountains; the one on the left had the remains of an old radio tower on it, and the one on the right a name, Red Mountain, from the ruddy sandstone of the cliffs. Seven horses put up a good deal less dust than twenty; the plume from the rancher's party was bigger still because half a dozen of his men were dragging clumps of sagebrush behind them on their lariats. Feint to distract, then strike to kill . . .

The CORA men said the Rovers were wild and undisciplined to a fault, but that might be prejudice speaking. Hopefully not. Ingolf agreed; from his tales, the Sioux were the same way.

Mathilda was on his left. "I hope the Mormons who were supposed to buy Rancher Brown's horses hold out till we get there," she said, leaning closer. "It would be sort of futile to do this if they were all dead already."

"Thanks," he replied with a grin. "I didn't have worries enough to occupy my mind the now!"

Edain and Alex would be seeing to that. He forced aside worry for the young man, and even for the thought of having to tell Sam Aylward that his boy had died so far from home. That Sam would be so brave about it made the thought worse, not better.

It'll either work, or it won't, he told himself. *And if it does . . . well, my totem is Raven, but maybe Ingolf's is Coyote. It's a trick worthy of the Trickster!*

* * *

"Hssst!" Edain breathed quietly.

Hooves clattered on rock and gravel. Two Rovers passed by below at the bottom edge of the hill and stopped by the rough stone circle of a well. If they saw his horse and Alex's back in that ravine . . .

They both lay motionless, letting their war cloaks hide them, gray-green fabric with sagebrush twigs stuck through the loops. He could see fairly clearly through the gauze mask of the hood; the Rovers looked up the slope for an instant before they heaved the heavy timber cover off the well and threw in a leather bucket on the end of a lariat. His hand closed on the grip of his longbow, and he could smell the acrid sweat beneath his brigandine, strong even with the overwhelming smell of dust and creosote-like scents baked out of the bushes. The two horsemen were only fifty yards away; an easy shot.

At fifty yards, I'd be certain—haven't missed a shot like that since I was a kid. Father Wolf, totem of my sept, strengthen me now! Don't let me flinch!

The older Rover was a man in his thirties, bald or shaven-headed, with a long dark brown beard tied into two plaits with leather thongs, and a bucket of javelins slung across his back. The younger was about Edain's age; the yellow hair on the front of his head was cut down to stubble, with a patch at the back grown long enough to braid. The bearded man had a boiled-leather breastplate over a ragged shirt and threadbare jeans tucked into rawhide boots; the blond youngster wore only a breechclout and a bracer on his left arm, his sinewy feet bare in the molded leather stirrups of his mustang's saddle, but he carried a good recurve bow and had a quiver over his back. Both had shetes at their belts, and round shields and leather helmets sewn with plates of metal slung at their saddlebows.

The younger man kept watch while the older hauled up water hand over hand, carefully holding the bucket so the horses could drink without spilling much.

"I hope those farmers got some pretty gals along," the young man said.

"Hey, what'll Sandy say about that?" the other asked.

"She'll say, 'Thank you kindly,' if I bring her a Mormon gal to do the camp chores and help with the baby," the young man said.

Then he clutched boastfully at his crotch for a moment. " 'Sides, I got plenty. I ain't a wore-out old man like you who couldn't get it up with a rope tied to it."

"Yeah, the sheep all run when they see you comin', Jimmie," the other man said dryly. "Rams and ewes both."

They both laughed as they swung back into the saddle. The older Rover went on: "Me, I want their gear. My kids could use some blankets and coats, and my ol' woman needs a new cookpot pretty bad since the patch come off the old one."

Edain gave a silent sigh of relief as the two men cantered off northward, disappearing behind the bulk of the hill.

"Let's go," he hissed to Alex, then saw with a start he was already halfway to the crest.

He followed, placing his feet carefully; the last thing he wanted now was to start a rain of pebbles and rocks. Even the quiet *snick-snick* of the arrows in his quiver sounded as if some malicious redcap or boggart were doing a heel-clicking tap dance on his back. At last he reached the crest overlooking the ruins where the Mormon expedition had camped.

"They're still holding out," he said, licking his lips and then spitting to get the bitter-sour taste of alkali out of his mouth.

"As your master said they would," Alex Vinton replied.

Edain scowled at him. "I'm a Mackenzie. We don't have *masters*. Rudi's my *Chief*. And *my* father was first armsman of the Clan for sixteen years."

He glared, leaving the *as opposed to body servant and bum-kisser to the by-blow of some gangbanger-turned-lord* unspoken . . . for now.

"No offense, no offense," the older man said soothingly. "Let's get on with our work."

The two lay behind a greasewood brush atop the ridge behind the ruins of Whitehorse Ranch; the sun was halfway down the sky towards the west, still baking spicy medicinal smells out of the herbs and bushes. Edain cautiously raised the precious pair of field glasses he'd inherited from his father, making sure they wouldn't catch sunlight and betray the position.

The Rovers were prowling in closer to the wagon-fort; he saw fire-arrows flick out and stand in the tilts of the prairie schooners. Ordinary arrows snapped at the men who stood to throw buckets of water at the spots where the burning ones hit. A dozen Rovers rode in close, and there was a scrimmage along the northern edge of the laager, figures doll-tiny even through the glasses.

"They're something determined," Edain said thoughtfully. "Both sides."

"Your first battle?" the man from the Protectorate asked.

"No," Edain replied shortly. "Second, more like—one real fight, some skirmishes." Then he went on: "Look! Half of the Rovers are drawing off to that well north of here to water their horses. Let's go!"

They headed downslope; their own mounts were hidden in a short ravine at the rear of this hill. Garbh paced beside him, silent but bristling all over, lips peeled back from her long yellow teeth. He tried to walk as quietly as he could, but rock rattled and slid as they went crouching down the juniper-strewn slope.

"Uh-oh!" Edain said. "It was a feint—*run!*"

They were approaching the south side of the improvised fort, a section of crumbling mud-brick wall flanked by wagons on either side. He was still just high enough on the hillside to see the forty or so Rovers who'd ridden out towards the well suddenly turn their horses as one, an eerily uniform motion, like a flock of birds wheeling. They broke into a gallop back towards the north side of the laager, screaming like a grindstone on metal as they came, and shooting as fast as they could draw bow.

A bellowing war cry rose to meet them from within the encampment: "*Come, ye Saints!*"

Edain could see men rushing to that side of the laager. He could also see that they weren't all going in that direction, and someone who'd stayed behind on the south side was leveling a crossbow at him.

"Friends!" he shouted. "We're friends . . . *oh, sod all!*"

The last came as he threw himself flat, to the *tunng* of a crossbow shot and the *shunk* of a bolt hammering into the dirt far too close to his nose. Someone hadn't believed him.

On the ground he could also feel hooves hammering, the vibration coming up through the palm of his right hand; and they were also far too close. Garbh spun around, snarling like ripping canvas. Edain did too, coming up to one knee, feeling the gritty soil bite at his bare kneecap above the knit stocking. Two mounted Rovers were coming at them, less than a hundred yards away—the ones he'd seen at the well. One had a javelin in his hand, cocked back to throw; the other was raising his bow. The points of spear and arrow looked uncomfortably sharp, and all aimed at *him*.

And they weren't just targets; they were men he'd heard talking and joking and concerned about their children. . . .

Suddenly he was calm as his right hand went back for an arrow; somewhere far away he knew his blood was racing and his bladder felt too full, but it didn't matter.

Nock shaft, he heard his father's voice say. *Tilt the bow so the tip doesn't catch on the ground when you're kneeling. . . . Don't look at the arrow, just where it's going to hit. . . .*

The string went *snap* against his bracer. The arrow flashed out, flying almost level with the short range and heavy draw, just at the instant the other man loosed as well. The blond young horse archer threw his arms up and pitched over the back of his rough-coated pony as the arrow went through his chest without stopping, leaving a double splash of red along the way. In the same instant something punched Edain in the pit of the belly, hard enough to knock most of the wind out of him.

"Ooof!"

He looked down. A broken arrow was on the ground, still moving, the point curled back on itself where it had slammed into his brigandine. He wheezed and struggled to get air into his lungs.

Tunnng.

Another crossbow—Alex's, this time—and it missed; the javelin man was already ducking in the saddle and the bolt went *whhhpptt* through the space he'd occupied an instant before. Then it was the young Mackenzie's turn to dodge—aside, in a dive that left him rolling as the pony flashed by and the throwing spear buried its head in the dirt where he'd been.

He came erect again in time to see a bolt from the laager hit the surviving Rover's horse just behind the shoulder. That was either fantastically good shooting, or the Hunter's own luck; the horse took three steps and dropped limp as a wet rag hitting the floor on washing day. The bearded rider who'd wanted blankets for his children and a cookpot for his wife shot forward, landed on shoulder and neck in an audible snap of bone, and rolled until he lay still jerking and twitching in a cloud of dust. That sank around his body as his heels drummed on the ground.

"Come on, friends!" someone yelled from the laager. "Come on!"

"We're coming, so don't bloody well be shootin' at us this time!" Edain shouted back.

He ran, the bow pumping in his left hand and his kilt swirling about his knees. Alex ran beside him, trying to work the lever in the forestock that cocked his crossbow at the same time. Garbh dashed ahead, then cleared the bed of the wagon ahead with a long smooth leap, like some hairy salmon migrating upstream past an obstacle. Edain and his companion followed her with a scramble nearly as swift if considerably less graceful.

Two men confronted him—no, one a girl a bit younger than he was, in an impractical-looking denim dress that reached to her calves and a headscarf under a straw hat, but holding a businesslike crossbow in her arms. The man was older, with an odd-looking fringe of beard about his jaw but his cheeks and upper lip shaved. He wore a pot-shaped helm and held a glaive—a giant knife on a six-foot pole; the blade glistened with a liquid coating of bright red, and there was more spattered across his bib overalls.

"You're a man!" the girl blurted, staring at Edain's kilt and then his still mostly beardless face.

"And you're not," he snapped, suddenly conscious of how dry his mouth was.

"Thank you, strangers—" the man began.

Garbh snarled again, and they all looked up in dismay. The wagon laager was roughly oval in shape with its long axis running east–west. The northern face was only twenty yards away, and it suddenly changed shape. The Rovers had managed to get half a dozen lariats around one of the wagons there and then backed their horses together to drag it out of position.

It swiveled away and then fell over on its side, like an opened door; two-score of mounted warriors boiled through. The defenders tried to stand them off with pikes and glaives and short chopping swords, but there weren't enough of them, not nearly enough, and everything was dissolving into a mass of rearing horses and shouting screaming men who stabbed and slashed and clouted at one another. He could see a Rover dodge under a thrust from a pike shaft, then lean far over in the saddle and swing a light ax with dreadful skill in an arc that took off the pikeman's hand at the wrist. The hard *tock* of steel in bone came through the roaring brabble of the fight.

"Right, then." Edain grunted, taking stance in the archer's T, feet at right angles. "Twenty yards, clout shots."

After struggling with the unfamiliar recurves on horseback, some straightforward shooting Mackenzie-style would be a pleasure . . . almost. And he could hit a squirrel's head to spare the flesh and hide, nine

times out of ten, at this range. The yew stave bent in a smooth flexing motion. Not much armor to worry about either; most of them didn't even have a boiled-leather breastplate. He could as well have been using hunting broadheads as bodkin points.

Snap.

A horseman looked down in astonishment at the gray goose fletching that stood against his breastbone, and toppled forward.

Snap.

Another screamed as a shaft pinned his thigh to the saddle and punched on through that into the horse's body, breaking a rib along the way. The wounded animal turned and went bucking off across the plain, tossing the man like a rag doll in an ill-natured child's hands until he fell and let out all his blood onto the thirsty gray soil through the severed femoral artery.

A Rover with a metal-strapped leather cap spurred at him. Edain pivoted on his left heel as he drew.

Snap.

The clothyard arrow banged off the helm, turned by the acute angle at which it met the piece of old highway sign laced to the bullhide. The head left only a bright streak in the metal, but a shaft driven by a hundred and fifteen pounds of draw weight hit *hard*. The rider dropped shield and shete and sat dazed for a moment. Then he screamed—briefly—as Garbh lifted off the ground, her jaws wide. They closed on his face as the bodies went down in a thrashing tangle. He tried to tear the big half-mastiff bitch loose with frenzied strength, and did, but a lot of the face came with her.

Nock . . . .draw . . . aim . . . loose . . .

Snap. Snap. Snap—

The attack was blunted before his quiver was half-empty. Someone behind the scrimmage around the overturned wagon shouted an order in an unfamiliar accent and waved a pole with two horsetails sprouting from either side at the top. The Rovers who could turned their mounts and galloped off northward. Some of them shot backward as they went; none of the fighters in the laager seemed inclined to reply. They lifted the wagon back onto its wheels and shoved it into place instead, and then slumped or saw to their wounded or drank wearily from canteens, too tired even to wonder at the pair who'd turned up here in the back end of beyond and in the middle of their battle.

"Not many of them left here," Alex murmured to the young Mackenzie.

He thumbed another bolt into the firing groove of his crossbow and held the weapon business-end up. Edain nodded, a quick slight jerk of the head.

"Heel!" he called.

The bitch slunk to take station behind him, still growling low and bristling, licking at shaggy jaws that dripped red. There looked to be about a dozen still on their feet within the laager, but many of them had bandages showing blood. More wounded were lying on blankets, with a medico of some sort working on them and a couple of walking wounded as helpers. Edain winced a little as a man shrieked for his mother and bucked against the hands holding him down while the arrow spoon went in after a barbed head—either they didn't have morphine or they were out of it.

A round dozen more lay with blankets over their faces. A few near where the breakthrough had happened weren't covered yet. Aylward's son gulped quickly and looked away, then made himself look again. Back when he'd been about ten he'd gotten a close-up view of a man who'd tripped while drunk and fallen face-first into the business part of a threshing machine, and that had given him nightmares for years. These were worse. At least back at Tillamook there'd been other people to clean up afterwards.

The older man he'd seen first came up, with the girl. He wasn't as old as Sam Aylward's sixty-plus, as Edain had thought at first; a closer look put him at a very, very tired forty. There *weren't* many people around as old as Edain's father. Which meant this one had been about Edain's own age at the Change. That was an odd thought.

And when I am his age, will anyone be left who can remember the old world the way Dad does? That's odder still, when you think about it. Though I'd rather think about that than what a man looks like with his ribs showing like a rack of lamb at butchering time.

The stranger seemed to be waiting for someone to speak, but Alex Vinton preferred to stay in the background when he could. The archer shrugged, returned the arrow on his string to the quiver, and extended his hand.

"Edain Aylward Mackenzie, of Dun Fairfax and the Clan Mackenzie," he said formally, and touched the wolf tail that hung from the back of his helmet: "My sept is Wolf."

The man's hand was strong and calloused, by work more than the sword. He blinked at Edain's clothes. The younger man had learned what outlanders thought, and went on with a slight sigh.

"This is a *kilt*—" he began.

The girl flashed a smile. "We know what kilts are," she said. "We just haven't seen anyone *wearing* them in a while."

He nodded at her, pleased, and touched the horns-and-moon emblem on the breast of his brigandine. "This is the Mackenzie sigil."

The other man collected himself. "I'm Bishop Joseph Nystrup, of the Church of Jesus Christ of Latter-day Saints, and the Republic of New Deseret. This is my daughter Rebecca. Many thanks to you, strangers. They'd have broken in that time if not for you and your friend. But I'm afraid you've leapt onto the deck of a sinking ship here."

"You're the ones who are after buying horses from Rancher Brown, eh?" Edain said, glancing at Rebecca.

Even then, he was tempted to try a smile; she was about his age, with blue eyes and a thick yellow braid down her back and a comely snub-nosed face with a dusting of freckles across her nose and cheekbones. The haunted look in her eyes stopped him, and he nodded grave thanks to her instead.

"Yes. Are you one of his men?" Nystrup answered eagerly.

"I'm from farther west, but my friends and I are traveling with his son. We're thirty strong altogether."

"Do they know about these Rovers?" the man asked anxiously.

He wasn't like any bishop that Edain had seen before—for one thing, he was in denim overalls—but he supposed customs would be different this far from home. The Mackenzie smiled grimly.

"Oh, they know," he said. "And if you'll look north, you should be seeing Rancher Brown's men the now."

They did, scrambling up on the bed of one of the wagons and looking through the singed and tattered canvas of the tilt. The Rovers were mostly gathered around the well to the northward, about a double bow-shot away, with a few little clumps sitting their horses around the laager at a respectful distance but ready to dart in.

Suddenly the main knot of them boiled like a kicked-over ant heap. With his binoculars he could see—just—how many of them were pointing a little west of north. He swung his gaze that way and saw the plume of dust.

With a grin, Edain handed the field glasses to the bishop. Garbh jumped up beside them and barked at the distant figures, a woof with a bit of a growl in it; the doggy equivalent of: *We sure showed them, didn't we, boss?*

The older man fumbled a little with the focusing screw and then exclaimed, "Those are Rancher Brown's men?" Edain nodded, and the man from New Deseret went on: "There must be more of them than we thought! Perhaps enough to destroy these agents of the Adversary!"

"Not so many in that lot right there," Edain said with a grin. "But that's not the only arrow in the quiver."

Which reminded him he'd shot off a dozen from his. Reluctantly, he jumped down and began collecting them. Many of them were still in bodies, and he'd never pulled a shaft out of a man's gut before.

I've tweaked their nose, Chief, he thought. *Now it's time you kicked them in the arse, eh?*

CHAPTER FIFTEEN

"So, so, wait for it, girl. We don't arrive before the dance starts," Rudi crooned to Epona.

"It's all in getting them to stay still long enough to hit, when you're fighting wanderers like the Sioux or these Rovers," Ingolf said, adjusting the chinstrap of his kettle helmet.

Epona tossed her head again as if in agreement, with a clatter of bridle fittings against the chamfron and peytral. The hills lay on either side of them now. Rudi squinted over his shoulder at the westering sun, glanced aside at Ingolf's imperceptible nod, and then waved a hand forward.

"Let's go."

They all set their horses moving, down from the saddle between the hills and along the old gravel road; nobody had done any repairs since the year he was born, but it was still passable in this dry climate. Gear clattered and clanked, hooves crunched, and the taste of the desert dust was sharp and salty on his lips. They turned left—north—when they hit the flat, and picked up the pace to a walk-trot-canter-trot-walk. The big horses couldn't keep that up all day the way cow-country ponies could, not carrying the load of steel they were, but it was only about five miles to the old ranch buildings. Everyone would arrive fresh enough for a charge or two.

The road ran north, with a low plateau two or three hundred feet higher a mile or so to their east; if Rudi had been in charge of the Rovers he'd have had lookouts there, but it looked like they were as sloppy-undisciplined as the CORA men said they were. And this effort would be two or three gangs of them working together; none of them would know where all the others were.

"Uh-oh," he said, looking slightly off to the right. "Look there, where the road turns east, north of the hills. Right on the way we have to go."

Everyone did. Ingolf's eyes were the next keenest. "Looks like horsemen. Say five or six."

"There's a well there, according to the old maps," Father Ignatius said.

"Getting right up their ass without their noticing was a long shot," Odard said in a resigned tone.

Rudi's lips thinned as he nodded. *It would have been nice, though,* he thought.

"Bet you they don't notice who we are for a while," Ingolf said.

"We certainly don't look much like Rovers!" Rudi said, with a toss of his helmet to indicate their armor-clad bodies and big steel-barded horses.

Ingolf grinned, a hard expression. "Oh, you'd be surprised. People see what they're expecting to see, mostly, and nowhere more so than in a battle. I could tell you . . ."

The Rovers were watering their horses; at first they just glanced up. It wasn't until they were within a hundred yards that the first of them pointed and yelled.

Then they leapt into the saddle, reining around and spattering every which way, shooting as they went. Arrows went by with nasty *vvvvwpt* sounds; one ticked off the curved surface of Rudi's sallet, a painful whack even with steel and padding between it and his scalp. Several of the Rovers rode right back east towards the main gang; the others just headed anywhere that wasn't blocked off by hills. The quarter-horse mounts they all rode had acceleration like jackrabbits, and they left trails of dust with a speed the bigger western horses couldn't match. Rudi shifted his weight backward and Epona—after a moment's reluctance—slowed.

Ingolf had an arrow sticking out of his brigandine. He pulled it free and looked at the bent point with an expression of mild interest that Rudi had to admire.

"I think it popped a rivet," he said. "There's something to this sand-wich armor you folks make. I don't think my old mail shirt would have stopped it nearly so well."

"It's a good thing it was long-range, even so," Rudi said.

Ingolf nodded, then called loudly, so that everyone could hear: "Keep it down to a canter. If your horse gets blown you're dead."

Rudi nodded in turn; he was relieved that nobody in their party had been hurt, or wounded beyond the bruise-and-scratch level. But even the best harness didn't always stop a hard-driven shaft. If the arrow that had banged off his helmet had been three inches to the right it would have punched on through his face and the brain behind it, and he'd have been riding with the Dread Lord on his way to the Summerlands.

Another mile and they could see the ruins of the old Whitehorse Ranch and the wagon laager there. Just north of it the Seffridge Ranch men were skirmishing with the Rovers; the distant twinkle of arrows went flicking through the clouds of dust, and then the longer flash of bared steel as saber and shete and ax swung. War cries came faint with distance, the catamount shrieks of the Rovers and the yipping, whoops and bark-ing, "CORA! CORA!" of the rancher's men.

"Looks like the cowboys are retreating," Ingolf said. "Yeah, the Rovers're trying to work around their flanks."

Then the scene changed in an instant; most of the enemy pulled out and galloped southwest towards Rudi's party, warned by the dust plumes and the fugitives from the skirmish at the well. Their rush was led by a standard of two horsetails on a pole. It fluttered in the wind, streaming out with the speed of the sudden attack. A few remained be-hind to hold the rear guard as Rancher Brown's retainers went forward in turn.

"Things certainly change *fast* in a fight out here," Rudi said, proud that his voice held nothing but interest.

"Yeah," Ingolf said, and his mouth quirked up at the corner. "I re-member being surprised about that myself. Richland's like your home territory—lots of trees and ridges and such. But the Red River country is more like this—well, flatter and with grass instead of sagebrush, but the principle's the same, you know? There's usually room to run away . . . but not the way we've arranged it."

Rudi nodded. *Right,* he thought, taking in the field of battle. *Between those people in the laager, the hill behind it, us, and Bob's men, we're three sides of a triangle and they can't get out, just like we planned.*

"Good," Ingolf said on his left. "Got 'em boxed."

"It spares our horses if they come to us, too," Mathilda agreed.

Only an experienced ear—and a young, keen one—could have picked their voices out of the rumble and clank, creak of leather and rustling chinking clatter of harness, and through the steel and liner of the helm and coif.

Of course, there is one thing . . . Rudi thought, and then spoke aloud:

"Of course, we've got people who *outnumber* us four to one boxed." He grinned. "But with a military genius on either side of me, what can go wrong?"

Someone male wearing a coif with a flap covering the lower face— which meant Odard—answered: "Well, that's why you have a fight, isn't it? To find out what the hell can go wrong."

Rudi ignored that and went on, louder: "Canter until we're just out of bow range; then hit them hard."

Epona had a good smooth rocking-horse motion in a canter, not like some horses that could pound your guts loose with it. He tugged at the strap that held his round shield over his back, brought it around and slid his left forearm into the loops. Then he reached back with his right hand and lifted his lance out of the tubular leather socket, holding it loosely with the point well up; the tapering length of ashwood surged and dipped with the motion of the pace and the streamer fastened below the point began to thutter and snap. Epona tossed her head and snorted again; he could see the great red pits of her nostrils flare through the holes in the chamfron, and she mouthed in eagerness, a little foaming slobber running down the metal and leather of the bridle.

Closer, closer . . .

The Rovers in front rose in their stirrups and drew, those who still had arrows in their quivers. The rest waved their blades and screeched; it made a blinking ripple along their line as the whetted metal caught the sun. Dust smoked behind them in a cloud that hid everything beyond. They came on fast, to ride over this little band of strangers they outnumbered so greatly, to cut them into hacked meat and return to the real fight with the enemy they knew.

"Morrigú! Morrigú! *Charge!*" Rudi shouted.

He'd inherited a baritone version of his mother's voice, and the belling shout carried through the noise of hooves and harness effortlessly as the band responded. In the next instant he used the edge of his shield to snap his visor down.

"*Morrigú!*"

Black wings vaster than worlds beat at the corners of vision for a moment, and he heard a song like the slow implacable strength of glaciers that grinds rock to dust. The sunlit plain with its sagebrush and patches of white alkali vanished into a world of gloom, lit only by the bright strip of vision through the slit.

His voice sounded like something in a bucket now, lost in the thundering rumble as the horses rocked forward into a gallop. He brought his shield around to cover his body between the rim of his visor and the metal-shod arch of his saddlebow. Epona was the fastest here, even if she was carrying more weight than some; lance points came down on either side of him, pennants streaming and snapping backward, then fell to the rear as he forged a little ahead. His comrades turned into a blunt wedge pointed at the shapeless swarm of the Rovers.

Arrows flickered by, half seen. One banged off the chamfron over Epona's face, startling a snort out of her. Another slammed into his shield, punching through the sheet-metal cover and standing humming in the double thickness of bullhide and plywood beneath. It rocked him back in the saddle for an instant, and felt like a sharp rap with a hammer. The evil quiver of it ran into his hand through the grip.

With it came that little fillip of astonishment you always felt, that someone was trying to *kill* you. Then everything seemed to slow down, as it usually did in a fight—as if he were in a universe of amber honey, or the floating movements of a dream, with noise and danger and death something infinitely distant.

He slanted the lance down to the level over Epona's neck where her head pounded up and down with the convulsive effort of her gallop. A man on a pony was just ahead, wide staring blue eyes and a shock of sun-bleached blond hair and a young faced spotted with zits, dropping his bow and reaching for the shete at his belt and trying to dodge all at once.

Too late. Rudi clenched thighs and braced his feet, hand and arm clamping his lance against his side at the last instant, putting nearly a ton-weight of galloping horse and man behind its narrow foot-long point.

Epona swerved on her own to help place that point exactly where it needed to go.

Thud.

The massive impact slammed him back against the high cantle of the war saddle, his whole body feeling as if it flexed like a snapping whip . . . or as if only the armored shell that surrounded him kept parts of him from flying off and his spine breaking in two. The lance head crunched through meat and bone and out the other side of the Rover's body in a double spray of red and another from his mouth and nose, flipping him into the air as his pony ran out from under him. There was a dragging weight for an instant, then a hard crack as the lance shaft split across. Epona stumbled slightly, and gathered herself again.

Rudi clubbed the stump of the lance down on a head shaven save for a roach at the back. Wood cracked, or bone, or both; he couldn't tell which, but he let the broken shaft drop and swept out his longsword. He kept his head moving from side to side; a helmet hurt your peripheral vision and one with a visor killed it dead. Something coming at you when you couldn't quite see it could turn that literal really fast.

Dust and screaming men and wounded horses sounding like women in a bad childbirth, and a flicker of steel half seen. He brought his shield up and around, slanting it above his head without blocking his vision. An ax filed down from an old tree chopper bounced off its curved surface and he stabbed beneath the shield's lower edge, across his own body from right to left. The ugly soft-heavy resistance meant that the point had gone into a belly, and he twisted his wrist sharply as the speed of the horses dragged it free. The Rover already stank beyond belief of sour milk and rancid butter and old sweat, and the wound added to the smell as he shrieked and fell away.

An enemy to his right cut skillfully at his sword-side leg with a shete while he was occupied, striking hard enough to bruise his calf even through the spring-steel greave that covered it, then froze for an instant with his mouth in an O of surprise as the curved slashing blade bounced away, vibrating in his hand and almost cutting into his own horse. Rudi smashed a backhanded cut at the man and sent him reeling away as the heavy knife-edged blade raked his shoulder and arm. A spray of blood followed the yard of edged metal, casting red drops through the air in a looping spray.

"Morrigú!"

Another Rover had been unhorsed and tried to roll under Epona's belly with a long knife. She used her speed and armored breast to knock him down, and then stamped on him as she galloped over, deliberately and hard. Rudi didn't have time to pay attention to the popping, crunching-crackling sound that followed as the man's body was caught between those pile-driver hooves and the hard, hard ground, but some part of him knew he'd remember it later. He caught flickers of movement to either side: Rovers going down with lances in the chest or belly, cow ponies bowled over by the massive impact of the barded destriers and rolling right over their riders often as not. Then the swords were out, and the charge slowed into a melee.

"Morrigú!" he screamed again, stabbing and hacking and keeping Epona moving. *"Morrigú!"*

Ugly steel-in-meat sensations flowed up his arm, and the harder crack of an edge meeting bone. Epona aided him with hoof and teeth and battering weight, as if their bodies were one.

"Red Hag! Red Hag!"

A medley of war cries joined his: "Haro! Holy Mary for Portland!" and "Richland!" and *"Lacho calad, drego Morn!"* and "Face Gervais, face death!" all blending into a single stuttering roar under the sudden scrap-and-anvil sound of battle.

Ingolf's shete took half a face away, then cut back into a thigh. Mathilda hung back at Rudi's left, the big kite-shaped shield with its blazon of the Lidless Eye in crimson on black covering her from eyes to ankle, sword moving in economical chops and thrusts at anyone who tried to engage him. Odard slammed his sword into the back of a skull, nearly died as he tried to tug it free, then abandoned it and snatched the war-hammer that hung at his saddlebow and swung it in an arc that ended with a gruesome popping as the serrated steel head struck a rib cage. . . .

Then the standard of the two horse tails was near Rudi. A young man bore it in his left hand and a war-pick in his right—cut down from an old pickax, spike on one side and narrow hammerhead on the other. Beside him was another Rover with a good steel helm shaped like an old-time football helmet, and metal-and-leather armor on his body. That and the fine shete in his hand probably marked him as the chief of this band. A red beard streaked with a few strands of gray and powdered with dust fell down his chest. Ritva and Mary came in at him from the other side, one with the sword, the other thrusting overarm with her lance from behind.

The chief banged the lance head up with his shield and cut at the shaft in the same motion, cunningly aiming behind the metal lappets that guarded the wood for a foot below the business end. There was a crack and the top two feet of the weapon went twinkling away. The shete looped up in a backstroke that beat down the other twin's sword thrust in a shower of sparks, and then the press swept them away. Rudi's knees and balance set Epona at him; the banner bearer's horse was in the way, but the destrier's shoulder set the lighter pony back on its haunches with a thudding smash. The Rover chief pivoted his mount with effortless skill to avoid the rush and come in on Rudi's unshielded side.

The black wings beat behind Rudi, invisible, more solid than stone and vaster than worlds. He felt as if his blood had been replaced with something that scalded and froze at the same time, like boiling acid. Somewhere an eerie keening wail sounded, and he knew it was from his own throat. The shete floated out towards him, aimed at the vulnerable underside of his jaw. He ducked his head and cut at the Rover's thigh; the plate of metal-rimmed steerhide shed the blow.

Bang.

The shete glanced off the upper part of his visor, and then slid from the curved surface of his helm. Weight carried it upward, and the long point of Rudi's sword darted out like a frog's tongue striking for a fly. It went in under the chief's armpit, broke the links of the patch of mail there and ran another three inches into flesh.

Behind the wire-grid face mask of the Rover's helm his eyes went wide and shocked at the sudden agony. His shield arm dropped useless to his side. Rudi stood in the stirrups and brought his longsword up and around and back until the point tapped his brigandine over his own kidney, then down with all the lashing power of arm and shoulders and gut. Hard leather and thin metal parted under the knife-sharp edge of the heavy blade, and the chief was galloping away shrieking, with blood spouting from the ruined arm that hung by a few shreds of flesh and gristle and armor.

Beside him Mathilda sent the bannerman reeling back with his face laid open and teeth showing through the flap; she let her shield fall by the guige strap and used her freed left hand to wrench the pole with the horse tails away from its wounded bearer, brandish it overhead and throw it down in the dust.

The Rovers were brave men, but they'd never met true heavy horse before; nobody had reinvented it yet in their part of the world. It took them a few moments and more than a few lives before the survivors realized how terribly vulnerable they were to that ironclad violence at close quarters. The sight of their chief's fall and the loss of the horse-tail banner broke them; they turned and scattered, leaving their kin on the ground and a small herd of horses running with empty saddles.

Suddenly Rudi had no targets within arm's reach; he pushed his visor up with the edge of his shield to gain better vision, and the world opened out before him. His sword sank . . . then rose again with frantic haste at a glimpse of motion behind him, something long and looping spinning through the air.

Epona whirled at the shift in his balance, as cat-nimble as a roping pony at a roundup despite her size and weight. One of the Rovers had used a lariat as soon as he had the room for it. The braided rawhide had settled down around Mathilda's shoulders, clamping her arms to her sides and her shield to her body. She was half out of her high saddle already as Rudi slashed with reckless speed. The good steel of his sword was still knife-sharp, and the pull of the leather rope kept it taut. He grunted as the weight of the awkward cut leftward and back pulled at shoulder and arm; he had to risk wrenching a muscle to keep from cutting Epona on the neck as he recovered, and the edge did touch the barding lower down.

The Rover didn't stop, but he was still looking at the severed length of rope when Bob Brown cut him out of the saddle with a sweep of his stirrup-hilted saber. His eyes went blank as he slumped and fell.

"Howdy," Brown said, grinning at the two of them, his weathered face speckled with someone else's blood. "Do I know you folks from someplace?"

Rudi rested the longsword across his saddlebow and nodded back, panting like a bellows and feeling as if his armor were squeezing him to death; he had been beyond the world for a while, and the return always came hard, hard. The dry air cut the death-stink a little, but his gauntlet and steel-clad right arm were running red, and it was soaking into the padded arming doublet below. He slid his shield onto his back by the strap.

The Rovers were scattering for real now, in panic flight and not as a tactic, like beads of mercury under a hammer; some of them were far enough away already that they were trails of dust turned reddish by the setting sun rather than men and horses. Brown's men were after them, their quivers refilled from the packhorses, shooting them down as they fled.

"Now, that was one *good* plan, Mr. Vogeler," Brown went on. "It actually worked the way you laid it out, which in a fight is somethin' of a prodigy of nature. You can dance lead any hoedown I'm at, far's I'm concerned."

Ingolf shrugged. "Worked the last time I tried it," he said. "Worked even better this time." To Rudi: "These western-style lancers of yours have real punch, if you can get them into position."

"I'll remember that," Rudi said, as he checked to see that none of his band were badly hurt.

The cowboys definitely had a few down, and more wounded, but they weren't carrying nearly as much ironmongery as his folk.

It's needful, he knew, as Brown's retainers drove their ruthless pursuit to the edge of sight.

We have to frighten the Rovers down to their toenails to make them leave us alone; if the ones still alive aren't afraid enough, they could try another attack.

It still wasn't to his taste, any more than finishing off the enemy wounded was. That was needful too; the Rovers weren't a civilized foe who dealt in ransoms and exchanges, and the hate between them and the settled ranchers farther west was bitter. It was a blood feud; if you let enemies crawl away and heal today they'd kill you or your kin or friends a week or a month or a year or five years down the road.

Odard had dismounted to recover his sword; he limped as he came back to his horse, swearing softly and leaning against its side instead of swinging back up.

"Are you all right?" Mathilda asked her liegeman sharply; she'd unhooked the flap of her coif, and it dangled beside her sweat-wet face.

"Got a whack on the knee from something," he said, wiping and sheathing his blade. "It's not broken, but I'm going to buy some plate poleyns after this, and damn flexibility. It's a good thing those Rovers couldn't run away, though. We'd never have caught them in a long chase."

Rudi wiped his own sword clean, carefully making sure nothing was left to get under the guard and rust unseen, then sheathed it with a hiss of metal on leather and a steel-on-steel *ting* of quillions against the guard at the lip of the scabbard.

Ingolf snorted. "If they'd had time to get their asses in gear and room to run, they'd have pecked us to death like crows mobbing a hawk," he said shortly. "How would you go about beating eighty men you can't catch and who can shoot at you from sunup to sundown?"

Rudi's canteen seemed to be missing; he took Mathilda's with a grateful nod as she extended it, washed a mouthful around and spit to clear his mouth of the thick gummy saliva. He'd cut the inside of his mouth against his teeth at some point, and he was just now conscious of the sting; the gobbet was tinged with pink. Then he drank deeply of the water, blood-warm and salt-bitter and delicious.

Mathilda was looking a little wide-eyed at the consequences of their plan, and crossed herself twice. There were nearly three-score bodies scattered over the rolling sagebrush plain between the wells and the wagon laager; this was far and away the biggest fight either of them had ever seen. Buzzards were circling overhead already. More would come as soon as the first felt safe enough to glide down; they watched one another for that, and the ripple could bring them in from hundreds of miles away.

He handed the canteen back and gave her armored forearm a slight squeeze as she took it. Their eyes met, and he felt a momentary warmth, as he saw himself thanked God for. Ignatius crossed himself as well, touching his crucifix to his lips afterwards. Rudi could hear him murmuring beneath his breath:

"*Ora pro nobis . . .*"

One of the twins was near him; she was saying something in Sindarin, a Dúnedain prayer of thanks for the shelter of the Lady's wings and the Dread Lord's spear. He nodded agreement and added his own silent gratitude.

And men were coming out from the wagons. Rudi saw Edain among them, and broke into a delighted grin; Odard nodded calmly to his multitalented manservant Alex. A middle-aged man was walking with Edain, and beside him a pretty girl in a dress with a crossbow in her arms.

No, Rudi thought a moment later.

He scrabbled at the chin fastener of his helm with his free hand, pulling the confining weight of the sallet off his head and hanging it from the saddle horn, then tossed his head to let the air at his damp hair; the shock was almost like cold rain, and wonderful.

Not a pretty girl. She's young, but she's a woman, and beautiful.

* * *

Edain waved to Rudi as his chief sat easily with his raven-plumed helm on his saddlebow, looking like the young Lugh as the dry evening wind cuffed at his long red-gold hair. His own smile soured just a little bit as he noticed Rebecca staring at the horseman with her jaw dropping slightly and her eyes wide.

Well, that's *not fair or right!* he thought, then gave a rueful chuckle. *He does look like the young Lugh come again in glory. I look like a farmer who's good with a bow . . . which is what I am.*

"I hope it's not going to be like this all the way to the coast, Chief," he called. "That was just a bit more lively than comfortable."

CHAPTER SIXTEEN

Two hours after sunset Rudi pushed the beans and salt pork around his plate with the spoon, then made himself eat; you had to, even after a battle. He hadn't had much appetite, but it was unwise to be careless of Her gifts. The Saints had buried their own dead, and they were very quiet as they went about their chores; the scents of cooking food competed with the faint iron-and-sewage smell of spilled blood and violent death, despite everyone's efforts at cleaning up.

If they hadn't had so many wounded and been tired beyond exhaustion, it would have been better to move camp a bit. The Seffridge Ranch men had packed their chests of bullion, turned over their horses and were ready to head west anyway, anxious to get back to the CORA territories before the Rovers recovered from the drubbing they'd been handed. It gave the camp a lonely feel, though Bob Brown had said he'd be around to say good-bye.

That's what this trip is going to be, Rudi thought, looking around at the faces of his friends.

Apart from us, it's a series of meetings and partings. A bit like being a ghost, flitting through the life of the land without much touching it.

A voice started up from the Saints' part of the encampment, half chanting in a strong carrying tone:

". . . Why am I angry because of mine enemy? Awake, my soul! No longer droop in sin. Rejoice, O my heart, and give place no more for the enemy of my soul. Do not anger again because of mine enemies."

Rudi sighed at the chorus of "Amen!" That was not bad advice, even if it was from a different path than his.

He made himself eat, concentrating on the physical sensations, the smoky taste of the food, the *chink* of the spoon against the tin plate, the cool slightly metallic tang of the well water in his cup, even the bruises and stiffness and the pain in his right calf, refusing to let his thoughts chase their own tails. The others looked fairly glum too, apart from Ignatius, who had his usual steady calm, and Odard, who was in quiet good spirits apart from the occasional twinge in his swollen, bandaged knee.

He whistled tunefully—Rudi recognized the song, a nice bouncy one called "The Bastard King of England"—as he worked over the edge of his longsword with a hone mounted on a wooden holder. The damascene patterns in the steel shone and rippled in the firelight as he ground down on a spot where the edge had nicked on bone or a piece of harness. Rudi looked over at Mathilda, where she sat beside him with her arms around her knees and her chin on them, staring into the low flicker of the greasewood fire, and put his emptied plate aside.

"Second thoughts about the trip, Matti?" he said quietly, as he unpinned his plaid and folded it blanketlike around his shoulders; the temperature was dropping fast in the thin air of the high desert.

"No . . . no, not really," she said, her voice equally low. "It's just . . . I don't like killing men. I'll do it when I have to, yeah, and I won't get all sick about it like the first time, but I don't *like* doing it."

With a sniff: "I'm not like Odard."

"Odard doesn't like killing; it's not that he's got a taste for blood. He likes *fighting*. There's a difference," Rudi observed.

Of course, he thought, *I like fighting too. The difference is that I really don't like killing; I'm not indifferent to it, even when it has to be done. I hope I don't ever become so, sure.*

"I don't like fighting *or* killing." Her mouth quirked, and she added: "Despite having had Baroness d'Ath teaching me how all my life."

"Well, you don't like girls the way Tiphaine does, either; some things are just the way the gods make you," he said with something just short of a chuckle.

Mathilda smiled, but there was duty in it as much as amusement. "Really the problem is . . . well, I'm feeling guilty at how Mom must be feeling."

"Hey, you're Catholic—of *course* you're feeling guilty," he teased. "You see the advantage of the Old Religion? Praise and blessing, we don't go in for guilt. Or prolonged virginity, either," he added slyly.

This time her grin at the chaffing was genuine. "Licentious pagan!"

"Uptight beadsqueezer!"

"Tree hugger!"

"No, that's the elf wannabes," he said, and they shared a chuckle. "We Mackenzies may *worship* trees, yes: hug them, no."

"But I really am feeling guilty about hurting Mom this way," Mathilda said, the smile dying away from her face. "She must be going out of her skull. I know she doesn't try to keep me wrapped in padding like an egg . . . but I know she really has to *make* herself not do it, too. She's always afraid for me, even if it's just a hunt or a tournament. Now she's got real *reasons* to be afraid. I could have bought it today, and we'll be taking risks like that for a long time."

"Then why did you do it?" Rudi asked, more to help her than to satisfy his own curiosity; self-knowledge was never wasted.

"I'm . . . not really sure," Mathilda said; she picked up a stick and prodded at the fire; something crackled, and a trail of sparks drifted upward. After a half minute she went on:

"I mean, yes, I'd miss you like hell, and yes, we're *anamchara*, so I've got an obligation to you, but I'm heir to the Protectorate and that's a duty too. I think . . . the real reason I'm guilty about it is I think deep down part of it's that I wanted to punish Mom. Or part of me does, and it sneaks up on me, so I do things that hurt her without really meaning to."

"Oh?" Rudi said. "Well . . . you know, she's always been pretty good to you, Matti. And to me, for that matter. Even back during the War, when I was a prisoner."

"Yes." She hesitated. "But . . . Rudi, sometimes I think that she's not a good *person*, you know? She . . . I know she's done some . . . questionable things. And a lot of the time, when she does *good* things she does it because it's . . . efficient, expedient. Not because it's *right*. And Dad . . ."

She shrugged. They didn't talk about her father. He didn't know how much she really knew about Norman Arminger, who'd been a tyrant's tyrant even by the brutal standards of the first Change Years; how much she knew, how much she knew but didn't let herself know, and how much she'd carefully avoided knowing.

"Matti?"

She looked up, probably not seeing him as more than a dim outline after staring at the red-yellow flicker over the coals for so long.

"OK, I'm not going to run a moral checklist on your parents for you."

Because you'd defend them and then we'd just get into a screaming fight. Once was enough for that. OK, what can I say that's true and tactful both?

Aloud, he went on: "But keep one thing in mind—your mother raised *you*, you know? And she raised you to think about this stuff and worry about doing the right thing, sure and she did. And *you* turned out to be a pretty good person. So that's got to count for something, eh?"

The smile she gave him was warm, and a hand followed it; they closed their fingers together for a moment.

"So what you're *really* afraid of is that you'll end up turning into your mother, right?"

She squeezed his hand again, gratefully. "Yeah, I am. Especially if I'm going to be Protector. Maybe *that's* what I'm running away from, do you think? I have to do the job, but can I do it and still be *me*?"

"Yeah, maybe that's what you're afraid of. But you don't need to be, *I* think." He winked. "I mean, and aren't I your conscience, so? Just the thought of me looking at you with sad-puppy disappointed eyes and my lip starting to tremble and perhaps a tear running down my cheek would keep you on the straight and narrow."

She freed her hand to punch his shoulder and snorted. "*Thanks,* Rudi. That makes everything all right . . . I don't think."

"*De nada.* I mean, we're *anamchara;* what are soul friends for? And freeing you of guilt is a lot more fun than giving you funeral rites if you fall in a foreign land."

The snort grew into a real laugh. She opened a bag of dried peach slices and cranberries and walnuts and offered it to him, and they sat in companionable silence for a moment; she leaned against his shoulder, and he spread the plaid around them both.

"I'm feeling a little guilty about my mom, too," he said after a moment.

"Hey! She *wanted* you to go!"

"No, she knew I *had* to go; declining an invitation from the Powers is *not* a good idea. That's not the same thing as wanting me to go at all. She's going to be worried every day until she sees me again. So will Dad . . . my stepfather. And Signe over at Larsdalen will worry about the twins."

Though not much about me, he reflected; his father's widow had never stopped thinking of him as a threat to her own son's inheritance.

"Life's complicated." Mathilda sighed.

"Well, that's an original thought you're having the now."

She poked him in the ribs with a forefinger, hard, then settled back against his shoulder looking across the coals and the ring of light. Outside it, in the darkness beyond the wall of wagons where the piled corpses of the Rovers lay, coyotes snarled and yipped at their feast. A wolf howled somewhere in the distance, scout for a lobo pack; that breed were more wary of men than the song dogs. They and the buzzards would bide their time until the living two-legs left.

Rebecca came over into the circle of firelight. She gave a little start as Edain stepped into it behind her, with his bow in his arms and Garbh at his heels.

"All clear, Chief," he said to Rudi, giving her a studiously absent nod. "Nobody out there but the coyotes."

Rudi grinned at the younger man. "And *your* hairy brother, a minute ago."

Rebecca sat, curling her feet under her; there were dark circles under her eyes. "His brother?" she said.

"He's a Wolf, so all wolves are his brothers . . . sort of," Rudi said. "I'm a Raven. It's our septs, the totems."

"Oh," she said, obviously uncomprehending.

"Sort of an initiation thing," Rudi said.

He cocked an eye at Edain where he sat by the fire, pouring himself a cup of the chicory with elaborate unconcern; Garbh lay beside him, laying her head on her paws with a long sigh.

"Edain just got told what his sept would be two years ago. Not that anyone ever had much doubt; his dad might as well be Father Wolf himself."

The young woman's eyes lit with real curiosity; a relief from her worries, too. She hugged her knees and looked at the other Mackenzie.

"Told?" she said. "How does that work? Your parents tell you, or something?"

"I got told the usual way," Edain said shortly. "Nothing special. A vision in a dream."

Rudi's voice took on a solemn tone: "Why don't you tell her about it, Edain?" he teased. "It's not polite, getting someone curious and then clamming up."

"Yes, I'd love to hear," Rebecca said.

Edain shot Rudi a look, then sighed and shrugged. Rudi nudged Mathilda as she raised an eyebrow. Sotto voce, he murmured, "This always slays me."

"Well," Edain began. "Well, ah . . ." He sighed. "It happened like this, pretty well . . ."

* * *

Edain Aylward Mackenzie, as yet of no sept, woke under the tree. He was stiff and chilled despite the cloak wrapped around him, good warm wool from his own family's sheep and his mother's loom.

"Oh, damn all," he said. "I'll have to do this *again*."

Then he looked up at the tree. It was a Douglas fir, its top a hundred feet above against the gray sky of spring . . . except that it was a *lot* taller than that now, a towering column like a living mountain. And so were the rest. And those snow-topped peaks over to the east weren't the Cascades. He took a deep breath of air clean and fresh as a Beltane morning, scented with water and rock and familiar fir sap. A jay flitted by, screeching, but farther off in the woods he caught a glimpse of something huge and hairy, with legs like pillars and great curled ivory tusks and a trunk raised to trumpet. . . .

"Well, I *am* dreaming." Though it felt oddly lucid, more *real* than the usual dream. In fact, it felt more real than waking life. "Now to see what sort of vision I get . . ."

A wolf came trotting like a gray-brown shadow between the great trees, an occasional twig crackling under its pads. Edain accepted that for a moment, until he realized the great wedge-shaped head of the gray beast was on a level with his own, standing. He felt a surge of . . . not quite alarm, not quite joy . . . that died before it could do more than tighten the skin over his gut.

The wolf sat down, yawned, and scratched behind one ear with a foot larger than the man's.

"Typical," the huge carnivore said. "Isn't that an Aylward all over? Can't imagine *important* without *big*. Subtle as a hay fork in the goolies, the lot of you."

The voice sounded normal—deep and a little growly—but the giant wolf wasn't moving its lips; the words just *appeared* somehow. Edain's mind noticed the detail the way a drowning man's hand flails for a stick. The alternative was gibbering.

"Moving my lips?" it said, though the young man hadn't spoken. "Like this?"

Suddenly the thin black lips *did* move, peeling back from wet yellow-white teeth that looked to be as long as his fingers, drooling a little . . . and all of it was inches from his face. The growl beneath the words sounded like it came from the animal's chest, all right. It also sounded like rocks churning when a spring freshet roiled a mountain stream.

The air was cool, but Edain could feel sweat start trickling down his flanks. He kept his face blank, and crossed his arms with a creditable imitation of calm.

Good idea. This way he can't see my hands shaking.

The growling stopped, and a long pink tongue hung out over the fangs. The wolf's ears cocked forward; Edain had an indefinable sense that the amber eyes held approval.

"Moving me lips would be just too bloody stupid, wouldn't it?" the wolf . . . the Wolf . . . said. "This isn't being done by fookin' Disney, y' know."

Edain was vaguely aware of what Disney had been—some illustrated books had survived. He hadn't expected Wolf to talk about something pre-Change. Come to that, he hadn't expected the Father of Wolves to have an accent like his own father, either. The beast snorted.

"Well, it's your mind and memories we're using, innit? Let's get on with it."

The great black nostrils ran over him, quivering, from head to foot. He felt the warm breath of it on his skin, and the slightly rank doggy odor.

"Right." Wolf pronounced it *roit*. "There you are, then. You're Wolf sept and I'm your totem."

There was a moment of silence. "Well?" Edain said to fill it. "What now?"

"Now wake up, sod off 'ome, and get back to work. Your dad's got the Three Oak Field to plow and he's not as young as he was once."

"That's *it*?" Edain said, stung out of wonder to amazed anger as the wolf started to swing away. "I come all this way—"

"You're still under that tree not two miles from Dun Fairfax, you thick little burke—"

"—and it's 'fine, you're a Wolf, now back to the spring plowing'?"

The wolf looked at him. Edain swallowed suddenly. The yellow eyes were like endless wells into times deep beyond deep, ancient with years where the birth and death of trees was like the flicker of autumn leaves in the wind. Suddenly he *knew* where he was.

This wasn't just a forest. It was *the* Forest, where the forever trees grew. The wood of the times before, that stood when man first made fire or cracked flint. It towered still in the world beyond the world where the shadows of things that had been lingered, casting their own reflections spiraling back into the waking world.

Father Wolf cocked his head to one side. "Bit slow on the uptake, lad, but you're gettin' there," he said in that infinitely familiar Hampshire-and-army drawl. "Now, if you're done, I'm busy."

"Busy?" Edain heard his voice squeak hatefully, something he'd thought he'd shed two years ago. "You're *busy*?"

The great wolf's nose wrinkled again and he raised his head, as if scenting far-off winds. "Lots of new packs getting started."

A deeper sniff, after a pink tongue the size of a small bath towel swept over the nose.

"Even back in your dad's little island, now that you lot aren't scarfing everyone else's share of dinner. All to the good, that, but . . ."

Father Wolf sighed; *that* sound seemed to come from his actual chest. ". . . but they need looking after. Would you believe it, some of them have been fucking *dogs*? That's not right nor natural. It's going to be hard graft getting things fixed up proper again without floppy-eared bastards running about holding their tails wrong."

The amber eyes glared at him. "Now you're mine, don't let me hear anything like that about *you*, boyo."

"No, sir," Edain heard himself say. "Not that way inclined, anyhow."

"Good. Now, like I said, I'm busy, so you can bugger off back. Give my regards to Sam. He doesn't know it, but I've been keeping an eye on him; tell him to remember that night on Mount Tumbledown and the Argie with the shovel."

"But aren't you going to . . . to . . ."

The yellow eyes met his again. "Look into your eyes while you bury your hands in my ruff and I impart some bloody immortal wisdom that will transform your soul?"

A snort. "My arse. Doesn't work like that, lad. Be thankful you didn't get Coyote. *That* sneaky little shite would keep you here talking until your fur fell out and you'd be none the wiser for it."

Edain stood, speechless. The wolf sighed again.

"All right. I'll tell you the rules, now that you're Wolf. Hunt clean. Look out for your pack, your mates; stick by your pack leader and back 'im up. Don't go looking for a fight, but fight like a mad bastard for your kin if you have to, and seven times over for the pups and the nursing mothers."

"I already knew all that! That's *it*?"

"I couldn't tell you unless you knew. What more do you want—'keep your pelt clean and cover your scat'? Or I could piss on your ankles to mark you if you want."

The wolf scratched again, stretched, yawned cavernously, then turned to go.

"You'll do, boy. You'll do," he said over his shoulder, and trotted away.

* * *

"Wow," Rebecca said, looking at him wide-eyed. "That's . . . that's some dream!"

"Yes," Edain said moodily, prodding at the fire with a stick. "I get to meet the Father of Wolves, and he's like my dad on a bad day. Bollocks."

She suppressed a chuckle and turned to Rudi. "And you're a Raven, you say? Was it a dream for you?"

Silence fell; she seemed to sense it after a moment, looking from Rudi to Edain and then to Mathilda's slight trace of well-concealed fear.

"No," Rudi said softly, looking inward at his memories. "Raven . . .

Raven came for me when I was still young. And not in a dream; He came to me by the light of common day."

They all looked up when Ingolf walked back into the circle of fire-light; a tension broke that Rudi hadn't noticed until it was gone. The older man looked grimly satisfied, and Bob Brown was with him.

"Bingo," he said, crouching down to put himself on the same level as the others. "Thought I'd find something like this."

The big easterner had a shete in one hand and a medallion on a leather thong in the other.

"CUT," he said, holding out the blade.

It showed a rayed sun etched into the blade near the hilt. Then he offered the medallion on the palm of one calloused hand.

"And CUT."

Mathilda straightened up with a sigh and leaned forward to look; Rudi did likewise. The medallion was marked with the same symbol, in silver and gold on a turquoise background. Rudi took it and tilted it towards the firelight; the workmanship was excellent, with the slivers of semiprecious stone skillfully joined with hair-fine seams, and the surface of the metals rippled and polished.

"The CUT hand these medals out to ranchers and bossmen who give the Prophet earth and water," Ingolf said grimly.

Bob Brown grunted. "Wondered how them Rovers got such nice blades. They don't have a smith to bless themselves with—who'd work for 'em out here in Lower-ass-end Township of Crotch-scratch County if he could get a bunk at a decent ranch, or in a town like Bend? They don't have enough to buy much gear honestly, either. My father will want to know about this."

Bishop Nystrup came up. "Do you mind if I join you, gentlemen . . . and ladies?" he said.

"Sure, and you're always welcome at our fire," Rudi said gently.

The older man was looking ill, as well he might with half the party he'd led west dead or hurt. One of the latter was apparently his son, as well; Rudi had the impression his daughter wouldn't be helping out with his work in normal times. The bishop took the medallion in turn and sighed.

"Even here?" he murmured.

"Yeah, even here, Bishop," Ingolf said.

Rudi leaned forward and made his voice firm yet friendly as his mother had taught him, pouring strength into it: "And even here, you'll find that you have more friends than you thought. This Prophet has a gift for the making of enemies. He's made foes of my folk, and we'd barely heard of him before his murderers came on our land, the creature."

"Ours too," Mathilda said decisively.

Odard nodded agreement. "Those, ah"—he stopped and glanced at Father Ignatius—"bad, wicked, depraved people are going to pay for my new poleyns, one way or another."

"And the Dúnedain have a quarrel with him as well," the twins said, in chorus.

For once that unanimity seemed unintentional, and they looked at each other with exasperated expressions—identical ones. Then Ritva went on:

"Fighting the current Dark Lord is standard operating procedure, for us. *Dyel!* They're like cockroaches—squash one and another one scuttles out of the baseboards."

The Mormon bishop tried to smile. "I thank you, my friends. But nine young people, however valiant and skilled . . ."

Rudi grinned, a charming expression. "Bishop Nystrup, I think you'll find we're more than a clutch of young wanderers."

His brows went up.

Father Ignatius cleared his throat. "Yes, they are," he said. "Or rather they're a very wellborn and influential group of young wanderers."

Odard preened, slightly but unmistakably. Mathilda shot him a warning glance, then another at Rudi with a question in it, and nodded soberly.

"I'm . . . heir to an influential position in the Portland Protective Association," she said carefully.

"And I am a knight-brother of the Order of the Sword of Saint Benedict. You may have heard of us," Father Ignatius added.

Rudi drew a deep breath. Sometimes you had to take a risk. "My name is Rudi . . . Artos . . . Mackenzie," he said. "And this is—"

* * *

"What was it that you wished to say?" Father Ignatius said.

The *it is very late* was left unspoken. Mathilda swallowed.

"I'd like to confess, Father," she said.

"Now?"

"If it's not too much trouble."

Ignatius looked at her. "There is always time for a soul in distress," he said. "Come then."

He led them to a campfire a little way from the others. Mathilda sat down on one side, hugging her knees. The Benedictine priest sank and sat cross-legged on the other.

"Bless me, Father, for I have sinned."

"When was your last confession?"

"Four weeks ago, in Castle Todenangst, with Father Donnelly. Just before Mass."

"Then you have not been neglecting the sacraments, but it *is* time."

"I want you to communicate me, Father, if you would."

Mathilda Arminger kept her eyes from the half-seen figure across the campfire from her in the darkness, wishing she had the screen of her familiar confessional booth between them. She waited in awkward silence; at least, it felt awkward on her side, and at first. Then it began to feel peaceful, with the crackling of the flames and the slow upward drift of sparks. When he spoke, it was as if the moment had unfolded itself.

"What are your sins, my child?"

"I killed a man today. Possibly three but certainly at least one. I mean . . . it was war, and self-defense, and they were attacking people who'd never done them harm and I had to stop them or they'd do worse . . . but I did it. I ended a life and felt it run down my sword. Perhaps I sent a soul to damnation, and anyway there's a family grieving for him—perhaps children with no father. And he probably thought that he was doing what he had to do."

"Yes," Father Ignatius said, nodding.

His voice was . . . not quite casual, but normal and friendly, without the hieratic tone that some priests had on occasions such as this.

"Do you regret it?" he went on.

"Well, I'm not sure. I think . . . what's bothering me is that I regret it for my sake rather than his. I mean, it had to be done—but I wish I didn't have to do it. If I want something to be done, shouldn't I be willing to do it with my own hands? But it makes me feel . . . sort of dirty. I keep seeing his face."

"Good," the priest said. "Taking life can never be wholly blameless, even if it is the least of possible evils we must choose between. That it is ever necessary is a sign of the burden of sin that we bear, that this whole fallen world bears. If you live, you will one day be required to weigh lives and deal out death in judgment, as surely as you did today with steel."

"I know, Father. That's part of what's bothering me now."

"It should. But don't become too focused on your own subjective feelings; that is the temptation of a sensitive soul, and it turns self-examination to self-indulgence, to scrupulosity. A sin is wrong not because it makes you feel bad—though it should—but because it is *wrong*."

"What can I do to feel clean again?"

"You can do nothing, but God can, if you let Him. Remember always that God so loved the world—so loved *you*, not the princess but Mathilda Arminger, the young woman who exists here in this place at this time—that He gave His only begotten son to suffer and shed His blood and die for *you*; and for exactly this, to lift the weight of sin from your soul. Turn your thoughts to Him, to the Sacred Heart of Jesus, and He will take away your burden."

Mathilda felt herself smile. "Thank you, Father. That helps."

"Good. As your penance, say the Five Sorrowful Mysteries. As you do, also fix your mind on the men you slew, and remember also that Our Lord died for *them*. And remember that He blessed the centurion, knowing what that man's work would be."

A moment's pause, and Ignatius went on. "And the other thing that troubles you, my child?"

Mathilda started, then gripped her will in both hands and went on: "It's Rudi."

That calm waiting silence went on again. A coyote howled in the distance.

At last she said, "I've been having . . . well, impure thoughts about him. Fairly often. It's happened before, but never like this, not just in passing."

"Ah." This time the hint of a smile. "And have you welcomed these thoughts?"

"Well . . ." Mathilda forced herself not to wriggle.

It's better and worse than Father Donnelly. Father Ignatius is young enough to understand. And he's a Changeling like me, or nearly. But it's more embarrassing because he is young enough to understand.

"Well, I try not to."

Ignatius nodded. "That is all you can do."

Another pause, and she went on: "It's a bit different now. I mean, we've been like brother and sister all these years, and this . . . sort of changes things. I don't know why it's just now. I've been, ummm, noticing boys for quite a while! And Rudi's, well, he's a witch; you know how *they* are. I guess it's because Mom and I talked about us maybe marrying. I'm not sure if I love him, love him that way, but I sure think I *could* if I let myself. It may be just *because* we know each other so well. And . . . well, he's so damn pretty. And I keep imagining us together, you know, not just . . . well, I keep thinking about children and a life together and stuff."

Ignatius surprised her with a chuckle. "My child, are you confessing to longing to know Rudi Mackenzie in a carnal manner *after* you marry him?"

"Ummm . . . sort of. Yes, with the thinking part of me. The other part's just . . . longing, when I let it."

"Then you have not sinned, not even in intention. It isn't Satan who gives you such feelings, you know. The worst the Deceiver can do is tempt you to misdirect them. He can mar even the highest things, but he creates nothing."

Mathilda blinked in surprise. "But . . . are you saying that God wants me to marry Rudi?"

"Not at all, my child. That may or may not be possible; there are matters of State, which you must consider as part of the duty your birth has laid on you. *That*, thankfully, is not a priest's to decide. And there is the difference in faiths, which does concern your spiritual directors. But the desire itself is pure."

"Then what *does* God want me to do?" she said in frustration.

"He has told you that, Mathilda Arminger. He has said it very plainly: 'Be ye perfect.' "

Mathilda shivered. "I don't have the makings of a saint, Father."

Ignatius's voice turned sharp for an instant: "Oh, yes, you do, my child."

He gestured upward to the dome of stars. "When all this beauty is past and all Creation is a story that has been told, *you* will endure—either a horror beyond conception, or a radiance of glory such as we can scarcely begin to imagine. *That* is the *makings* that God put in you!"

Mathilda looked upward herself, and then nodded slowly. It was a humbling thought, when you looked at it that way.

"I, well, I've never had a vocation. I thought I did for a while when I was younger, but I didn't, really."

"Not a calling for the life of a religious, no," Ignatius agreed. "But He does not give us each the same cross to bear. Your nature and mine are different, and so we seek Him by different paths, but we are both loved by God and called to His perfection."

"Father, thinking about the perfection of God scares me silly. How can I be perfect, just being . . . me? It's not just being on the throne someday, though that scares me too. I know that'll always be like a fight in the dark, no matter how hard I try, and I'm afraid of it twisting me and making me someone who can't trust or love anyone or anything. But being with Rudi all this time, the things I want, a home, babies, they just don't seem in the same . . . the same *league* as, well, perfection."

She made a wry face. "I mean, they feel so *animal* sometimes. Not in a bad way, but it's a lot like a mare with a foal, or a mother cat with her kittens."

"*Now* you are verging on the sin of pride! Lying in His mother's arms and nursing was good enough for Our Lord! God has given you these desires—including your desire for Rudi—and He gives us carnal love for a purpose, for mutual delight, to produce children, and the sanctification of the soul. Cast yourself headlong on God's love, begging His grace to help you in the perfection of the nature He gave you. To love another so deeply that we seek union with the beloved, by that to bring an immortal soul into this world and care for and shape it . . . that is to imitate God Himself in His splendor!"

They waited together for a moment more. "Now make an Act of Contrition, my child, while I pronounce the words of Christ's forgiveness."

While the young priest spoke the words of absolution, Mathilda recited the formula:

> *I am most heartily sorry*
> *That I have offended Thee*
> *And I detest all my sins*
> *Because I dread the loss of Heaven*
> *And the pains of Hell*

But most of all because
They offend Thee, my God
Who are all things good
And deserving of all my love
I firmly resolve
With the help of Thy grace
To sin no more
And to avoid the near occasions of sin.

"Amen," they finished together, and she signed herself.

She always found confession comforting, and always tried to keep herself mindful of the importance, but it rarely struck her so strongly as it did this night, with the fallen of battle not a thousand yards away and the memory of the Death Angel's shadow, Azrael's wing brushing across her eyes.

I'm not sure exactly what I'm sorry for, but I sure feel better, she thought. *Thank You, Lord.*

Ignatius took his kit from his baggage and they walked a little way into the darkness; others didn't notice, or looked politely aside if they did. He lifted out the white surplice and red stole and donned them; as he did he seemed to change somehow. Mathilda knelt, and he lifted a wafer from the ciborium. It seemed like a snowy sunrise in the darkness of the wilderness as he raised it.

"*Ecce Agnus Dei,*" he said three times. "*Ecce qui tollis peccata mundi.* Behold the Lamb of God, behold Him who takest away the sins of the world."

She took the wafer on her tongue.

"*Corpus Domini nostri Jesu Christi custodiat animam tuam in vitam aeternam.* May the Body of Our Lord Jesus Christ preserve your soul for everlasting life."

CHAPTER SEVENTEEN

"Yes," the scout-commander of the detachment of the Sword of the Prophet said, sketching in the wet sand beside the pool. "The misbelievers and their general are heading south and east, towards Goose Valley—you see, here, north of Wildhorse Lake—they may push on into the hills south of the flats, to trace the old irrigation canal and repair it. The western pagans are keeping on eastward with the Mormon infidels; they should meet Thurston's force, or come very close."

The one-eyed man smiled, looking east and west over the encampment at the bottom of the canyon. There wasn't much to see; the horse lines were scattered up and down the rocky cleft wherever there was water within digging range, usually in clumps of cottonwood and willow. The men were even less conspicuous in the shadow cast by the narrow rock walls; a soft murmur of chanting came as some repeated the teachings in chorus, and the sound of oiled stone on steel as others touched up the edges of shete and lance and arrowhead. There was no smell of woodsmoke as there would have been with ordinary levies, no matter what the orders were; only rock and dust and the peppery-spicy scent of crushed sage and greasewood.

The commander of the detachment nodded eagerly at the scout's report; he was a youngish man, well short of thirty, shaven-headed and scar-faced.

"See how the Ascended Masters guide the lifestreams!" he said. "Your mission and mine, High Seeker, are now fully compatible."

Kuttner suppressed an impulse to grind his teeth. *His* authorization from the Prophet's son overrode ordinary military commands, or it should. There were times when he wished very much that the Prophet would establish clearer lines of authority below his own level, instead of letting disputes fester until they had to be referred to him . . . or to the Son.

And the Prophet speaks so seldom now, and so . . . oddly. . . .

He shook his head. *The Son has given you a mission. Let's get on with it. And when the Prophet discards his mortal envelope to rejoin the Masters, things will change.*

Kuttner looked up again, and a man on the rim of the canyon waved down, stooping behind a boulder to be invisible from the outside.

* * *

Ritva Havel and her sister lay behind a ridge of rock. Their war cloaks covered and concealed them; perhaps not as thoroughly as elven ones woven in Lothlorien, but enough to make them effectively invisible beyond a few yards if they didn't move. The thin tough cloth with its loops full of grass and twigs and the gauze masks also provided welcome shade on what was turning into a hot day. In the high desert anything that broke the sun made a big difference.

There had been fresh horse dung down on the road that ran below and a mile west of this ridge. Someone had come by, even in this emptiness. Chances were they would again. Shod hooves, to boot. Which meant civilized men, or at least the more capable and therefore dangerous type of savages.

The stretch of river valley ahead of her—the maps called it Goose Valley—ran from southeast to northwest, with an old graveled road down its center. It had been cultivated once; you could still see the outline of the square fields, and new marshes where the irrigation canal had burst its banks, and a few small clumps of burnt-out houses. She didn't know why whoever had lived here had left, but even this far into the interior things could have been very bad right after the Change. The thought was dispassionate; she'd grown up in a world where ruins were simply part of the backdrop of life. The death of the world that had built them was only a little more real to her than the Fall of Gondolin.

Insects buzzed and occasionally burrowed in and bit; conquering ants bore a beetle off in triumph across the ground in front of her face from right to left. Dry sage gave off its spice-and-sneeze scent, to mingle with sweat she could feel trickling down her neck and flanks, and the smell of the dusty earth and pebbles beneath her. With the sun overhead there wasn't much danger of her binoculars giving them away either . . . though since there apparently wasn't anyone to see them, that was a bit moot. Still, they kept motionless as the sun crept up the sky behind them and then down westward ahead.

Think rock. Think root. Let the wind flow through you.

A maddening itch on the instep of her right foot came and went. A long-eared desert hare hopped by, stopped for a moment to stand upright and wrinkle its nose at the dry air, then went on its way. A few minutes later a coyote came trotting along its trail, then caught their scent when the wind changed. It shied violently sideways with a little spurt of dust before turning and loping away.

Ritva smiled to herself, a bit from the expression of bug-eyed alarm on the beast's face and a bit smugly as well. When you could fool a song dog into coming within arm's reach, you were *hiding*, by Manwë and Varda!

That was how Aunt Astrid and the others insisted on training Rangers, and they were quite right, though some outsiders thought the Dúnedain were too sneaky and patient to be real warriors.

Very faintly, she snorted and thought: *Canuidhollin.* Rangers just didn't go in for the two-masses-of-farmboys-in-steel-shirts-with-pikes style of head butting. She was sure the Fair Folk had never been quite that stupid; they'd had to contend with a much higher grade of Dark Lord than you found nowadays.

Though this Prophet guy seems to show some promise.

Antelope ran across the deserted fields; birds rose from the marshes and the dead trees. Then . . .

"Mmm-hmmm!" Mary said.

"Lots," Ritva replied; speaking quietly rather than whispering—whispers carried farther because of the sibilants.

There was dust coming from the north; individual trails, and behind it a plume—several dozen wagons or fifty or sixty horsemen, she estimated. And eagles and hawks, hanging in the air above them; they always did that out here when humans were on the move, hoping for birds and small animals spooked into the open. One plunged as she watched, coming up with something wriggling in its claws.

And let that be a lesson to you, she thought. *That's what comes of breaking cover 'cause you're nervous.*

The trails of dust turned into horsemen. Ritva turned the binoculars with extreme care; the sun was getting lower and nothing gave you away at a distance like a glint. They looked like anyone's light horse—except that everything they wore was *exactly* the same; same short chain-mail shirt, same stirrup-hilted saber, same model of saddle, same five-pointed star tooled into the leather of the bow cases in front of their right knees.

About a dozen of them, Ritva thought. *No, twenty.*

They were obviously scouting the line of march; they poked into every clump of trees, over to the riverbed to the westward, and every ravine in these hills within range of the road.

Of course, to be really sure they should push foot patrols up into these mountains. The ones behind her were a tangled dome two thousand feet higher than the valley floor. *But if they did that, it would take weeks.*

After a while more khaki-colored dust showed to the north, and a little after that an iron *tramp-tramp-tramp* of booted feet and the *trrrripp-trrripp-trrripp* of a marching drum and the squeal of a fife.

Ah, not fifty or sixty horsemen after all. Five times that number of men, but on foot, and some wagons. Lots of tools on the wagons, picks and shovels and wheelbarrows . . . bet those are sacks of cement, too.

At the head went the banner, a golden spread-winged eagle on a tall pole clutching arrows in one claw and an olive-wreath in the other, with the old American flag beneath, carried by a standard-bearer with a wolfskin cloak whose head topped his helmet; he was flanked by drum and fife. The men behind were in armor of steel hoops and bands, and they carried big oval shields and six-foot javelins; the points of the throwing spears moved like the ripple of wind on reeds to the earthquake tramp of their marching.

Yeah, Boise, Ritva thought.

She'd never been to the city, but she'd been on their territory, and there was a lot in the Mithrilwood files. A good well-stocked filing system was one of the marks of those reckoned mighty among the wise.

As the soldiers halted and began digging in their marching camp—six-foot earthwork, ditch and palisade—the sisters began to work their way backward. They were too far away to be seen easily, but even so they moved with exquisite care. Now that the Boise troops weren't moving, they might take the time to check the hills, or at least all the points that conveniently overlooked their camp. You never knew. . . .

A pebble turned beneath a hoof, and Mary hissed. Both young women froze. Icewater ran from Ritva's lungs to her bladder, and her body tried to twitch in reflex fear before she stilled it. Slowly, slowly Ritva turned her head within the loose hood of the war cloak.

Two men had ridden up the dry creekbed behind them and a little south. They were in thick clothes of the type you usually wore under armor; the cloth was mottled with gray and olive green as well as dark russet, so it took a moment to realize that it was a uniform. They wore hoods over their heads as well, baglike ones with only a slit for the eyes. In fact . . .

Pretty much like the ones in Sutterdown last year. Uh-oh. *Cutters. The Prophet's men.*

The men swung down from their mounts and dropped the reins to the ground—which meant very well trained horses. They were lightly equipped: daggers, point-heavy slashing swords worn over their backs so they wouldn't rattle, quivers, horseman's bows—about what the twins were carrying. And presumably they were on the same mission as she and Mary, which was a bit of a giggle when you thought about it.

Ritva made her breathing long and steady and slow, and felt the flutters in her stomach go away. Fear worked both ways—if you suppressed the physical symptoms, it calmed your mind. Dealing with people who wanted to kill you was never *really* a giggling matter, particularly if they had any chance of actually doing it. Rudi and Odard had boasted about the fight in Brannigan's inn, in a classy modest way. But then they were males, and therefore idiots about some things.

She glanced over at Mary, and caught the almost imperceptible single shake of the head. *No.* Her own nod was as quiet. Not worth the risk.

The two Cutters came up the slope towards the crest line, the last dozen yards on their bellies, moving slow and steady. When their heads rose above the peak of the ridge it was with glacial slowness; one brought a monocular to his eye, shading it with a hand to make sure it didn't flash in the setting sun. He spoke softly; his comrade dropped back until he was out of the line of sight, brought out a pad and began writing and sketching. They kept it up for a little while, and then the one with the monocular dropped down too, looked at the paper, and nodded.

Then they just waited. Perforce the twins did too; Ritva felt something crawling up her pant leg, and moved her hand down *very slowly* under the war cloak to kill it. Mary didn't move, but Ritva could feel her disapproval.

Well, it wasn't your sensitive bits it was going to sting, she thought. *It had too many legs. They have centipedes around here! And scorpions, I think!*

The sun faded westward and the wind blew colder, colder than the warm rock beneath her. The white and gray of the sagebrush desert turned colorful for an instant, red and umber and sienna, and the mountains to the north and east blushed a pink that faded and changed tone instant by instant.

Then the light went that clear gray color you got in dry country just as the sun was dropping below the horizon—the hour between the dog and the wolf—and then it was dark. Stars frosted the sky as the last purple died from the sky westward, fading into being one by one.

Farewell, Father Sun. Mother-of-All, I greet the stars that are the dust of Your feet, and . . . ab . . . Help!

Something howled far away; hard to tell, but she thought it was a lobo rather than a coyote. The two Corwinite scouts were simply darker spots. It took all her concentration to see when they finally started to move. Only a clink or two and one very slight rattle of stone on stone marked their passage—if she hadn't known they were there, she would have missed it in the general night noise.

When they got to their horses one of the beasts snorted. The enemy scout made a shushing noise and spent a moment gentling it; she hoped it hadn't scented her horse or her sister's, and that the two wouldn't answer in kind. They were well trained, but horses had their own purposes and tended to forget things. Then the beat of hooves on sand sounded as the enemy walked their mounts away down the arroyo.

Which didn't mean they were safe. The two Cutters could be fully aware of them and just off to set up an ambush. In fact . . .

There was enough light to speak Sign. Ritva pushed her hands through the slits in her war cloak.

Should we get ahead of them and . . . ?

The gesture that followed was one the Dúnedain had come up with, and involved shooting, slitting and bashing motions in one quick writhing of hand, fingers and wrist.

I don't think so. Let's trail them instead.

Carefully!

The Cutter scouts looked like they were keeping to the high ground east of the valley. And they apparently knew it; all the twins had was a map copied from a pre-Change *National Geographic* and what they'd seen on their way up northward—and they'd taken the road most of the way. Navigating through rough ground you knew well was difficult in the dark. Trying it when it was strange country was a guarantee of getting hopelessly lost—or blundering into the enemy's main force.

The only way we're going to trail these yrch *is to get ahead of them,* Mary said.

Ritva hesitated; that was risky. But it was important to know where the enemy had come *from.* She raised her head and whistled softly; a few moments later her Duélroch and Mary's Rochael came trotting up. They slid into the saddles and turned west, down into the river valley, over the road and into the abandoned fields. Those were tall with brush and weeds, and rows of trees beside long-unused irrigation ditches, but the mounts were Arabs and agile as cats . . . thousand-pound cats with hooves, of course.

They signaled their mounts up to a slow canter, keeping their eyes wide for threats to their legs—once they had to crow-hop over a big disk-harrow that had been sitting and rusting and growing a coating of vine and stalk since before they were born. A barn owl went by overhead, a flash of white in the darkness and a screech as it dove through the night to carry off something small and furry spooked into motion by the riders.

"That's enough," Ritva said softly, peering to see the black outline of the heights against the star-shot blackness of the sky.

Mary nodded; one of the advantages of being identicals was that they agreed on most things. This *was* far enough ahead that they could cut back into the hills eastward, given that they'd moved faster. At the edge of the broken ground they left their horses standing in a hollow with the reins looped up; that took *really* good training.

Hold, Ritva Signed.

It was the two Cutter scouts they'd seen. The twins stopped in the shadow of a stand of scrub pinyon pine, their war cloaks turning them into shadows within shadows. The enemy were feeling more confident now, walking along leading their horses. The twins turned their heads slowly, slowly, keeping their eyes moving. Ritva still felt herself blink when four more stepped out from behind a steep fold of striped rock.

Uh-oh, Ritva thought, clenching her teeth. *We must be inside their screen.*

Mary Signed: *Might as well go forward as back. We need to get some hard information on this crew.*

Which was true, but still unpleasant. They waited again, while the men they'd followed disappeared behind that tall fold. Their eyes found a course—from one boulder or patch of scrub to another, points that would screen them as much as possible from the lookouts they couldn't see but knew were there. Walk slowly, pause . . . then down on your belly and crawl like a snake . . .

And catch the damned war cloak on thorns. Careful, careful. Nothing caught the eye like a flutter.

As they moved they watched for the betraying movements and noises. Setting out a string of guards around your camp was all very well, but you had to check on them regularly—otherwise someone could sneak in, practice Sentry Removal and then get away again without being detected. You had to make sure the sentries were just being quiet, not lying there cooling to the ambient temperature.

The officer who did the rounds was quiet enough, but they caught his motion—his helmet was glossy, not dull matte, and it showed in the moonlight. Ritva felt her own pulse and counted, drawing her breath in steadily and evenly as the sentries were checked.

He makes his rounds every fifteen minutes, she Signed. *And the lookouts are there . . . there . . . there . . . and there.*

Mary nodded agreement. *Another ten minutes, and we'll go through below that boulder. Maybe we can get out past them that way later. In the meantime, let's go look at what all these sentries are guarding.*

It was snake-crawling all the way now, imitating a clump of brush. From pool of darkness to darkness, halting five minutes for every one they moved. The wind was in their faces, what there was of it, so dogs wouldn't be able to scent them, if the Corwinites had any. At last they were in the darker blackness beneath the great rock. Ritva raised her head, fractional inch by fractional inch.

There.

A long narrow cleft in the rock, east–west mainly but with serpentine wriggles, stretching out of sight on her right, and probably opening up to the river on the west. Black cottonwood trees along the sandy bed of the arroyo, and an occasional thicker clump that was probably a spring; the moonlight turned everything to shades of gray and silver, but the *thickness* of leaves was still apparent. And the low red dots of banked campfires scattered down it, bright to their dark-adapted eyes. A slight smell of woodsmoke, too, and cooking, and the stamp and whicker of horses.

Let's see, Ritva thought. *Eight men to a fire . . . that means somewhere around two hundred all up.*

She got the binoculars out. The horse lines were well hidden, in along the sides of the canyon, but she could see men hauling buckets of water to them, and bags of cracked grain fodder.

Enough horses for every man and a fair number of remounts . . . that's a wagon, light two-wheeler. They're traveling without much baggage.

For most of an hour they lay on the lip of the gorge, carefully noting the details. The Cutter soldiers did the things soldiers usually did—sharpening blades, tending armor, sewing things and patching things and oiling things and putting new laces in things, eating stew or beans out of communal pots and flat wheat cakes cooked on griddles. They also seemed to do a lot of praying, in a manner which involved kneeling in ranks and making gestures in unison; presumably they were leaving out any chanting or singing.

Then . . .

A face sprang out at her in the binoculars for an instant: a middle-aged man, forty or more, not big, not small . . . but with a patch over his left eye, and a long white scar diagonally across it. Mary hissed very slightly beside her. Ritva memorized the face; part of her noted that the man certainly had luck, to have survived that. Someone had cut him across the face with a sword, and hard enough to nick the bone. He turned away and walked into the darkness; two other men followed him, with the indefinable air of someone listening to a superior.

One by one the fires were covered by earth and the men lay down, wrapped in blankets and pillowed on their saddles. They also set up their walking sentries, close in and by the picket lines where their horses were tethered, and relieved the outflung ones on the heights around.

Good, Mary Signed. *There's one we missed, see?*

Ritva nodded. *And right on our way out.*

That was the problem with making yourself invisible. If someone missed *you,* you could miss *them.* Particularly, you could miss them until they *didn't* miss you.

This was going to be awkward. Her hands moved again.

Can we get past them on the sneak?

I don't think so. Not going this way.

Ritva bared her teeth behind the gauze of her war cloak's mask. They weren't here to fight, and she didn't like to fight unless she had to anyway, and if they couldn't do it quick and quiet they were unpleasantly dead. Her eyes went along the path they'd have to take, past the big boulder, then over the ridge. . . .

Yup, she Signed mournfully. *Sentry Removal. No choice.*

Dúnedain training involved a lot of Sentry Removal, and they'd taken the Bearkiller version before they left Larsdalen for Mithrilwood.

It wasn't precisely like combat. Killing people was relatively easy—which went both ways, unfortunately—but doing it very suddenly with complete silence and nothing visible beyond a few feet was another matter. Human beings were surprisingly tough that way; just stabbing or hitting them rarely did the job fast enough and often involved a lot of shouting and screeching and clanging. It was even more difficult when they were wearing armor.

They turned and crawled, waited while the Cutter officer did his rounds of the sentries, then moved forward right afterwards to take advantage of the maximum time before he came back.

The Corwinite scouts were well-placed, about ten yards apart and turned so each covered the other's back, each lying behind a convenient rock with a leg drawn up so that they presented a smaller target but could spring erect quickly. And each had his recurved bow ready with an arrow on the string.

Can't shoot them, Ritva thought.

An arrow made noise, not much but enough on a still quiet night like this, and it usually ended in a scream even if you hit something eventually fatal. Both the men were in three-quarter armor, back-and-breast of over-lapping plates of waxed leather edged with steel, leg guards like chaps, mail sleeves. That didn't make them invulnerable to bodkin-point arrows from an eighty-pound bow, but it did make a quick kill even less likely.

Certainly can't run up to them and fence. Two swords now, two hundred in a couple of minutes after the first sound of steel. And I don't like the way those two sit and wait—I'll bet by Elbereth Gilthoniel that they know which end of the sharp pointy edgy cutty thing to pick up. Wild Hunter, give me a hand here, will you?

Her hands moved in minimal gestures. Mary's war cloak moved slightly as she worked underneath it, but no more than the slow cool breeze might ripple a bush. Then she crawled away, with the same stop-and-start rhythm as before, while Ritva waited, filling her mind with the image of a leaf drifting downward. Calm . . .

They were close enough now to see the sentries turn their heads, and Mary stopped whenever their eyes started to swing around in her direction. If you timed it right that made you the next thing to invisible; when it was this dark, a good war cloak just couldn't be told from a natural lump of dirt and vegetation. Ritva's right hand went to her waist. Not to draw a blade; instead she slid out a weapon made of two lengths of ashwood, each two feet long, joined by a short length of fine alloy-steel chain.

With deer, the stop-and-start tactic could let you get close enough to touch them, or slit their throats, as long as they didn't scent you. Human senses were less keen but they could make up for it with wits. A good lookout memorized all the bushes and outcrops near his post. When one turned up where it shouldn't . . .

Her sister was out beyond the two Cutter sentries now. One of them—the one farthest from Ritva's motionless position—stopped his steady back-and-forth scanning and turned his head with a sharp snapping motion. The first time as if he didn't quite know what he was looking for, the second in a whipping arc as he noticed something that *shouldn't* be there.

Mary came to her feet in a smooth twisting arc that spun her like a discus thrower. Her buckler was in her hand, gripped by the rim; she'd stripped the rubber gasket from around the rim a few moments ago and slipped the hand grip out of the hollow side.

That left her with a shallowly concave steel disk a foot across, very much like what the old-timers called a *Frisbee*, two pounds of it with a knife-sharp edge all 'round. It flew from her hand in a long smooth arc that bisected the Cutter's face below the brim of his helmet with an audible but not-too-loud crunch.

You could cut through a two-inch sapling that way, or chop a horse's leg out from under it. There were old practice stumps in Mithrilwood with a *lot* of crescent-shaped slots in their surfaces.

As the man dropped, limp as a puppet with cut strings, some very distant part of Ritva's mind knew she'd wince over that sound for a long time to come. The rest of her reacted automatically, hitting the quick-release toggle of her war cloak and charging on soft-soled elf boots with a tigress precision that hardly rattled a rock. The other Cutter had whipped around to see his comrade die. He drew and shot with lightning speed; the arrow might even have hit Mary if she hadn't thrown herself flat again the instant the buckler left her hand.

He didn't waste any time when he saw or heard or felt or sensed Ritva coming up behind him, either; he dropped the bow and turned the reach for an arrow to a snatch at the long hilt of his shete. That brought his hand down across his body to his left hip, which was convenient.

Once you'd snuck up on a sentry, you had to *do* something with him. If he was stronger than you—which a man would be more often than not—it required something more than brute force to *remove* him. The weapon she carried gave her a five-foot reach; the quick flick of her right wrist and arm swung it in a blurring circle towards his neck. The chain link struck flesh and the other handle swung around to go *smack* into her left palm. Her wrists crossed and wrenched apart with a savage economy of motion and all her shoulders and gut behind the explosive power. The handles and chain multiplied it like a giant nutcracker . . . and back home they practiced this move by swatting flies out of the air on summer afternoons.

There was a crackling, popping, yielding sound like stiff wet things giving way—which was exactly what it was, and which echoed up her hands and arms in a way that made her bare her teeth in distaste. The man's eyes bulged for an instant, and then he collapsed, not quite as limp as his companion but not doing more than kicking and gurgling a little before he went quiet.

Aunt Astrid called it "using leverage."

Ritva frowned as she crouched beside the corpse and its heels drummed on the hard earth one last time. There were times . . . there were times when she wondered if there was something *wrong* with Aunt Astrid.

She passed a hand over her eyes and over the dead Cutter's, and touched a finger to the earth and to her lips. To take life was to understand your own death—that the Hour of the Huntsman also came for you; the sign acknowledged that, and that they would all lay their bones in the Mother's earth and be reborn through Her.

Of course, there's Uncle John, she thought, as she joined her sister in a quick silent dash downhill towards where they'd left the horses. He *doesn't use* leverage, *much*.

Little John Hordle's idea of Sentry Removal was to sneak up—he was astonishingly quiet for such a big man—grab the sentry's chin in one huge red-furred hand and the back of his head with the other and give a sharp twist so that the unfortunate was looking back between his own shoulder blades.

Aunt Astrid called that "crude, just *crude*."

* * *

Two days later Ritva hid behind a hillside rock a hundred and fifteen miles farther south and west, struggling to control the impulse to shoot.

Why do they keep following *us?* she thought. *It's not* reasonable!

She could see six of the Cutters below them, trying to track the twins over an expanse of bare rock. It was ninety yards' distance, and she *could* kill at least a couple of them. . . .

The problem was that then they'd know they were on the right track; also they'd start shooting too, of course. She and Mary had doubled back on their own trail to see if they were still being tailed, and here the *irritating* pursuers were.

Don't be angry, she thought. *Anger is first cousin to fear. If you make decisions because you're scared, you'll fuck up.*

Under her breath, a movement of lips rather than air, she recited one of Little John's training mantras to herself:

> *I must not lose my temper.*
> *Temper-temper-temper is the bum-killer.*
> *Temper is the little mistake which leads to you lying*

On the ground wondering Oi! What's with all this spreading
    pool of blood, then?
I will permit it to pass over me and through me.
And when it has gone past the other bugger
Will be the one bleeding.
Only I will remain, wiping off me knife.

Calm returned. One of the Cutters was on foot, quartering back and
forth over the gravel and sandstone, trying to find a place where hooves
had scored it. He wouldn't have much luck; they'd led their horses over
this bit, then come back barefoot and wiped out every sign of their passage that they could detect—even sweeping up a lump of horse dung.

The dart of her will beat on the men; she hoped *they* could feel it as
she murmured a binding spell. At last one of them straightened up and
looked around at the rocky hillsides. Then he threw his helmet down and
kicked it, shouted an order at another Cutter, who went and fetched it;
and then they turned back on their own trail.

She slumped behind the rock, breathing deeply, feeling her heart
slowing down from its pounding roil.

I was not *scared,* she told herself. *I was just . . . peeved.*

* * *

And it's weary by the Ullswater
And the misty break-fern way;
Till through the crutch of the Kirkstane pass
The winding water lay—

The song seemed to soothe the little clump of horses, or at least make
them less determined to browse among the thin scatter of green brush in
the tumbled rocks at the base of the hill, where water collected beneath
the dry gritty soil. Rudi waved his lariat and got them moving back towards the main herd, keeping an eye out for their wild kin—they'd had
problems with mustang stallions trying to cut the mares out.

These interior lands had an eerie emptiness to someone who'd grown
to manhood in the lush valleys west of the Cascades. Life of hardy types
adapted to the dryness and the alternation of savage heat and deep cold

throve here, but sparsely; little handfuls of burro, mustang, bighorn sheep, feral cattle scattered across endless miles, wolves and cougar less common still, with even jackrabbits and coyotes not something you saw every minute. They'd seen nothing of humankind besides the ashes of an old campfire near water now and then. This country had been thinly peopled before the Change, and most of the survivors had moved elsewhere in the generation since. The few who remained were wandering hunters, solitaries or single families or tiny groups who shunned outsiders.

He grinned to himself as he took up the song again; one of the little feral mustang studs had tried to cut out Epona, and gotten kicked into next Tuesday for his trouble. The big black mare got along better with horses than with most human beings, but she wasn't one to permit liberties either way.

The horses were moving well back towards the main herd when he finished:

> *And she sang: Ride with your brindled hounds to heel*
> *And your good gray hawk to hand;*
> *There's none can harm the knight who's lain*
> *With the Witch of the Westmoreland!*

He broke off as the head of the Mormon party rode up; he'd noticed that some of the old songs made the bishop a bit uneasy, grateful though he was.

"Thank you again for helping us with the horses," Nystrup said as he reined in by Rudi's side. "That alone will mean a good deal to my people."

Neither of them talked about anything larger or more political, though Rudi knew the older man was nourishing a desperate hope of aid from the free peoples of the far West. Rudi had advised him to send an embassy, and given a letter of introduction, but . . .

I wish I could go back to arrange it, he thought. *But I can't. The Powers have given me a task. And Matti's recommendation . . . her mother is probably so angry she'd string the messenger up rather than promise them help, sure.*

"A little honest work never hurt anyone," the Mackenzie replied politely, wiping at his face with a bandanna as he rode. "And we're not there yet, to be sure."

The sun was strong but the air temperature only a little on the warm side of comfortable—the part of northern Nevada they were passing through was six thousand feet up, and didn't get really hot until August. Even then it would be a crisp, clear dry heat.

Sparse grassland and silvery sagebrush rolled on every side, studded here and there with the darker green of dwarf juniper on a hillside. A golden eagle wheeled high overhead in majesty, across a pale blue sky that was clear from horizon to horizon. It was probably waiting for rabbits or other small game startled up by the horse herd. Insects buzzed and rattled, and a long-tailed spotted lizard stared at him with beady eyes for a second and then whipped off behind a sage.

A herd of pronghorns had been edging closer most of the morning to get a look at the horses and wagons—the little beasts were incorrigibly curious—but now they took fright and fled at better than sixty miles an hour, white rumps flashing, faster than anything on earth except a cheetah. Occasionally one would bounce up out of the herd's dust cloud, rising as if it had landed on a trampoline.

Maybe they're just running and jumping because they like it, Rudi thought, watching them with pleasure. *Well, I do occasionally myself, so why not them?*

They'd acquired that speed when there *were* cheetahs in North America, fifteen thousand years ago; to them the returning grizzlies and wolves and the spreading tigers weren't anything they had to worry about except from ambush. But there were cheetahs again, rumor said, down on the southern plains, escaped from private hunting preserves in the aftermath of the Change along with lions and a dozen other types of game. In time they'd work their way north, adjusting to the harsher winters as they went.

And when the cheetahs arrive here, the pronghorns will be ready. As Mom says, that sort of thing shows how thrifty the Powers are at getting us to work their will, will we or no.

Hills rose to the east and north, white stone scored by gullies and spattered with the wide-spaced green of ponderosa and pinyon pine on their higher slopes. There wasn't much motion right now, apart from the fleeing antelope with the Y-shaped nose horns, and a fat desert tortoise calmly burying its eggs a little to the north. Then a flicker of something showed in a ravine, and a click and rattle of stones followed, faint with distance. His eyes narrowed, and his hand began a motion towards the bow cased at his knee.

"Someone coming," he said to the Mormon.

"Where?" Nystrup said, startled.

"Up there . . . ah, it's my folk. My sisters, to be precise."

The twins came riding from the higher ground northeastward, their horses picking a way down the rocky slope. They were wearing war cloaks, which made them look like bushes on horseback with the tufts of greenish yellow grass and sprigs of sage and juniper stuck through the loops that studded the garments. That meant they'd been doing a sneak on foot somewhere to the eastward during their scouting mission. . . .

And that they found something important.

They drew up and nodded at the bishop and Rudi; the rest of the party from the Willamette drifted over as well.

"There are people ahead of us," one of the two said, her face dusty and drawn and tired. "Two different bunches of 'em, both about a day's ride out northeast."

The other took up the tale: "One of them's mostly on foot, heading south along the old gravel road. Say three hundred on foot, fifty on horseback, and packhorses and mule-drawn wagons for baggage. Over to you, Ritva."

Ritva—or possibly Mary—continued: "The others came in from the east a couple of days ago and they've been waiting since—camping cold, small fires for cooking and doused immediately, not much smoke and no noise. Two hundred, all mounted, with a remuda herd and some light wagons. They're holed up in a canyon overlooking the trail heading south up this valley to that old lake. . . ."

She pointed south. Bishop Nystrup nodded and supplied the name: "Wildhorse Reservoir."

"Right."

She pulled a map out of her saddlebag, and they all dismounted to look at it; the twin weighed the corners down with rocks, and drew her dagger to use as a pointer as they knelt around the square of waxed linen and held their horses' reins.

"They're holed up *here* except for their scouts. They've got *good* scouts. The other bunch aren't bad but these guys are *good.* We had to do some *Sentry Removal*—"

He could hear the Dúnedain italics and capitals in the words.

"—and they nearly caught us. Hiding is harder out here."

Rudi's brows went up. "You're sure they *didn't* backtrack you?"

"We holed up for a whole *day* watching our trail, Rudi. No, we lost them in some lava country; we saw them turn back. But it was a bit hairy, and they'll be on their toes even if they didn't make us."

"They will?"

"They're short a couple of sentries."

Mary—or possibly Ritva—broke in: "And then we found tracks, men and horses both, near here, just now. Three miles north of here, but that's close enough to spot our dust trail, with binoculars. Maybe two days old. Shod horses, so they're not locals. About six of them, I think. We waited in ambush on their trail, but they must have come out east a different way. Almost certainly more Cutter scouts. So they've made the main party here."

"Describe the ones you saw."

"The ones on foot've got the old American flag in front and they look like soldiers—infantry with some mounted archers for a screen, and a four-piece battery of field artillery. Boise regulars, we've seen them before. We Rangers escort caravans that far east now and then."

In the terminology that Boise used, the men they were talking about were part of the Army of the United States. Everyone else called General-President Thurston's regime after its capital city; he preferred "USA." In fact, he insisted on it. . . .

"The ones hiding up are pretty much like the Prophet's men from Ingolf's descriptions, composite leather and metal armor, sort of reddish brown stuff. Medium horse—bows and swords and light lances. Flying a flag of dark red with a golden-rayed sunburst."

Ingolf nodded. "Not just Cutter soldiers. The Sword of the Prophet, out of Corwin—his personal troops. Well trained, and they all really believe the horseshit the Church Universal and Triumphant peddles. Very bad news."

Rudi pursed his lips. "That's not a good sign, a unit of them all this way west of New Deseret," he said to the bishop, who looked as if he were sucking on a green persimmon.

"No," he said shortly. "But we're thinly spread out, most of our towns are on rivers or irrigation canals. If they came in from the south, or through one of the sparsely settled areas . . ."

He shrugged. "But why should it concern us, Mr. Mackenzie? The others are clearly Thurston's troops, and he's no friend to us. We should try to avoid both."

"Are you at war with Boise?"

"No . . . no. Not *now*. But we have had . . . clashes . . . in the past."

"Then you should *get* friendly with Boise," Ingolf said bluntly. "And they with you. Or the Prophet will pile your heads in a pyramid next to theirs."

"One thing at a time, Bishop Nystrup," Rudi said calmly, nodding.

The older man fell silent and Rudi looked at the map. Three lines converging on a spot . . .

"What's Thurston doing sending troops down here? I mean, I know he claims the whole continent, but it's a bit outside his usual stomping grounds."

Nystrup's daughter spoke up unexpectedly; she was some sort of aide or secretary to the bishop as well as his child, but usually rather quiet because it was an irregular thing, a wartime emergency measure and a sign of how hard-pressed they were. Now she said, obviously consulting a mental file, "There's good water at Wildhorse Lake, and at least a thousand acres of pretty good land that could be brought under the furrow near it. And a lot of underused grazing. Enough land for a big village, maybe two medium-sized. He *could* be planting a colony. We considered putting one there, before the war started."

Ingolf cut in: "From what I heard while I was there, everyone in Boise has to serve in the army for three years when they turn nineteen, and then they get land or a workshop or something when they muster out, if they don't stand to inherit one. They tried hard to get *me* to enlist while I was passing through there—I ducked out by night—and they offered me land at the end of the hitch. It would have been tempting, if I hadn't had places to go."

A grin. "Haven't had that damned *dream* since I met you, Rudi. You don't know how good that makes me feel!"

Rudi nodded absently. *The new farmers build his country's strength and they'd be loyal to Thurston, too, probably,* he thought. *Smart.*

Aloud: "So that's why a column from Boise might be heading south."

"Not just a column," one of the twins said. "The flagpole has a golden eagle on top."

"That's either Thurston himself, or a very high-ranking panjandrum of his," Ingolf agreed.

Rudi looked at Bishop Nystrup. The older man nodded. "Thurston is . . . hands-on, they used to say."

Rudi nodded. "Now . . . if I had a couple of hundred of the Prophet's horsemen, what would I be doing here?"

Ingolf spoke. "Something important. They wouldn't be risking elite troops like this except for something major."

"It's not likely that two forces are this close by accident," Mathilda said thoughtfully. "And when one's hiding and the other's not, that's pretty obvious—the Prophet's men are here to attack the Boise force. Which is another argument that someone important is heading it up."

"The false Prophet is at war with us, but not with the United States of Boise. Yet," Nystrup said. "To attack them would be reckless, even for the madman of Corwin."

"Who *is* a madman, eh?" Rudi pointed out. "And possibly possessed by something that's no friend to humankind. But certainly crazy at least, and given to doing crazy things."

"One more thing," one of the twins said. "We got a look at what we think is the Corwinite commander. He's a pretty ordinary-looking guy."

She looked at Ingolf, her tilted blue eyes considering. "Except that he's wearing a patch over his left eye. Didn't you mention you got the one who was holding you prisoner that way?"

"Yeah," Ingolf said, his tough battered face flushed.

Interesting, Rudi thought. *That's a killing rage, if ever I saw one. And Ingolf isn't a man governed by anger, usually.*

After a long pause, the easterner went on: "Still, we should go south with these folks. No sense in running into the Prophet's men earlier than we have to, and we've got places to go."

Rudi shook his head. "But along the way, things to do. We go north, and we save this General Thurston by warning him, that we do."

＊　＊　＊

Epona pawed the roadway, where a little gravel had survived the rare but violent summer thunderstorms of twenty-two years. Rock rattled off her steel-shod hoof, and a puff of khaki dust went up around it as she stamped. Rudi crooned soothingly and ran a hand down the black arch of her neck, muscle like living metal under the gleaming coat. He thought he saw a twinkle of metal northward; that might be a Boise scout giving them a once-over. Well, they *wanted* to meet them. . . .

"Think the Mormons will be OK, Chief?" Edain asked, looking back over his shoulder at the dust cloud fading towards the south.

Rudi shrugged. "They'll be better off than they would with two hundred Cutters hunting them," he said. Then he smiled. "Rebecca in particular, eh?"

The younger man flushed beet red under his tan. "She's a nice girl, Chief, but she was a bit busy and grief-struck for dalliance, nor I so stupid as to try it. And there's that religion—Horned Lord and Mother-of-All, it's strange!"

"All in the point of view," Rudi said tolerantly. "Many paths."

"Do you think they were after the Mormons, then, Chief?"

"Either them or General Thurston," Rudi said. "More probably Thurston. And in either case, I'm thinking it would be a good thing to thwart them, so it would."

Everyone in their party looked a little tense, in their various ways. None of them were wearing armor, not even the brigandines or light mail shirts that they usually did on the trail; the shields and helms and lances were all back with the wagon and their remounts, in an arroyo and being watched by Odard's man Alex. The rest of them sat their best horses and tried to look peaceful—they had their swords and bows, of course, but you could scarcely expect travelers to have anything less.

Ingolf edged his horse closer. "You sure about appealing like this to General Thurston?" he said quietly. "I never saw him when I went through Boise, but he's got a major reputation as a hard-ass, and his people certainly looked that way to me."

"No, I'm not *sure*, exactly. Though they say he's a law-abiding sort, not one who chops off heads on a whim," Rudi replied cheerfully.

Mathilda nodded. "On the other hand, from what Mom and Lady d'Ath and Count Odell told me, as far as he's concerned, he's president pro tem of the United States, and everyone else who claims authority within the old borders is bandit scum who deserves hanging."

"Well, he's not the only one with that delusion," Ingolf said dryly. "Every second bossman out East called himself president back in the old days, from the stories my father and uncles told. Some still do—the Boss-man of Des Moines lists it right after *governor of Iowa* when he's being formal. Ours in Richland doesn't bother anymore."

"Not so much of that backward nonsense in the Willamette," one of the twins said pridefully. "We've got sensible, modern titles, like the Bear Lord or the Chief of Clan Mackenzie or the *Hiril Dúnedain*."

"Or the Lord . . . Lady . . . Protector," Odard said. "And barons and counts." He glanced slyly at Father Ignatius. "And sovereign bishop-abbots, of course."

"The mayor of Mount Angel is elected by the people," Ignatius said, frowning. "The abbot-bishop conducts the Order's business, not that of the secular population."

Which means running outposts across half the northwest, Rudi thought. *And the mayor listens most attentively to what Dmwoski tells him, to be sure.*

"There's the Faculty Senate in Corvallis," the other twin said judiciously. "They're weird. But not as weird as having a *president,* like something out of the old days."

Everyone nodded. "We *are* out in the backwoods here," Rudi said. "Let's remember to be diplomatic, even when they're being odd."

"I'm always diplomatic when heavily outnumbered by armed strangers," Odard said with a small dry smile.

"Prudence is a virtue," Father Ignatius said. More thoughtfully: "I wonder how long the ghost of the United States will haunt men's minds? As long as Rome's did in Europe in the last Dark Age?"

They turned their horses north and shifted a little forward. Ingolf leaned close to Rudi while the clatter of hooves covered his voice.

"Is that why Odard's always so polite and diplomatic?" he murmured. "As far as he's concerned, we're armed strangers who outnumber him?"

Rudi blinked. "Hadn't thought of it that way," he replied, equally quietly, then put it out of his mind; he had more immediate worries.

Though it fits him uncomfortably well, the creature. Have to think about that sometime.

Mathilda's horse shifted over towards him as they waited. "Rudi . . . *anamchara,* why are we *really* doing this?"

Rudi sighed. "Partly because I think if the Prophet wants to kill Thurston, we want to preserve him," he said. He hesitated a minute and went on, very softly: "And to be sure . . . the Powers have sent me on this journey. But I'm not altogether Their puppet. Or so I like to think."

The Boise scouts came in sight. They were a file of eight light cavalry spread out in a fan centered on the road. All of them were well equipped with saber at waist, bow cases at their knees, short chain-mail shirts and flared bucket helmets modeled on the old army's style; the armor was covered with mottled camouflage cloth. Their swords stayed in the sheaths, but they were riding with arrows on the string, and they swung out to check the open country on either side of the western party with professional thoroughness. Rudi held up his open hands in the peace sign; the others sat their horses, trying hard to radiate harmlessness. Father Ignatius smiled benignly and signed the air as the strangers drew closer.

"Peace be with you, my children," he called.

Their leader was a wiry dark woman about thirty, the only female in the squad, with a set of chevrons riveted to the short sleeve of her armor. She reined in half a dozen yards from Rudi once the surroundings had been searched and looked him over; first with businesslike appraisal, and then with a different sort of glance.

"And with your spirit, padre." Then: "All right—you, the tall, blond and handsome one," she said dryly, letting her bow rest on the horn of her cowboy-style saddle. "*Who* the hell are you guys, and *what* the hell are you doing here? You're sure as shit not locals."

Her eyes took in their gear. Rudi knew she'd be seeing the quality of their horses and details of weapons and clothing, and also that they couldn't have gotten this far without more mounts and transport and equipment than was showing.

"We're travelers from the far West, from beyond the Cascades," Rudi said, putting calm and warmth into his voice—his mother had helped train it. "And we've got urgent news for your commander."

"For the president, eh?" She looked at him, then turned in the saddle. "Smith, tell Captain Valier we've got some wanderers who want to talk to the bossman. Rojas, take my binoculars, get up on that hill and keep an eye out for company. There may be more of them than they've mentioned."

"Sergeant!" they both barked, and turned their horses to obey.

The rest sat watching the comrades, while not neglecting their surroundings either; not exactly hostile, but extremely businesslike. The infantry came into view, marching like a giant spear-tipped centipede behind the eagle and the flag of the Republic. . . .

Rudi took in the hoop-and-strap armor, the heavy throwing spears and big oval shields, and then the officers, one to each eighty men, with the sideways crests on their helmets and vinewood swagger sticks in their hands. . . .

"Bet I know what General Thurston's favorite historical reading is," he said softly.

"Yeah," Mathilda replied, equally sotto voce. "I recognize it all—*Osprey Men-at-Arms 46, Roman Army from Caesar to Trajan.*"

Other volumes of those illustrated histories were a staple of military education in the Willamette; he supposed he shouldn't be surprised they were used elsewhere, too. And wasn't Thurston supposed to have been a soldier before the Change, an officer of the old US Army, trained at West Point? Not all that many of them had survived.

They mostly died trying to feed people and keep order, Rudi thought. *Well, against Fate even gods cannot contend, much less even the best of men.*

Doubtless Thurston had studied a lot of military history. There was a battery of field artillery along with the troops, six dart casters and shot throwers, which wasn't something you expected out here—the mechanic arts weren't as advanced in the far interior. Or so he'd thought . . .

The scout sergeant motioned them off the road, and they reined aside politely. The standard-bearer passed, and then the first block of soldiers; Rudi whistled silently to himself as they didn't even glance aside.

"Now, that's *discipline,* by God," Odard said from his other side.

The Boise cavalry sergeant waved to the small group of horsemen that followed the block of infantry. One of them spoke to a signaler, and a bugle blatted. The entire column came to a halt—a step and a stamp and a short harsh shout, and every man was waiting like a statue. Another blat and they relaxed, reaching for their canteens or turning to stare at the strangers.

Rudi could hear a couple of them speaking softly to each other.

". . . use the rest, by Jesus."

The other answered, in a mock-childish falsetto: "What are soldiers for, Daddy?"

The first grinned and poured a little water from his canteen into his hand before rubbing it over his dusty face. He made his voice deep and gruff as he answered: "To hang things on, my son."

Well, they're human after all and not machinery, Rudi thought; then he made his face solemn and straightened in the saddle as the command group approached.

That's him, he thought.

Lawrence Thurston was a tall man, about Rudi's height and built much like him, lean but broad in the shoulders. He wore the same armor as his men on foot; it looked adaptable that way. His helmet crest was transverse, but dyed in stripes of dark blue, red and white, and he carried a round shield marked in the same colors.

When he pushed back the hinged cheek pieces of his helm and then slung it to his saddlebow Rudi saw the face of a man in his fifties, with some gray in his short sable cap of hair and hard blunt features, broad nose and thick lips. His skin was the dark brown that the pre-Change world had miscalled black, a shade that reminded Rudi of Will Hutton, the Bearkiller ramrod until last year. He rode with straightforward competence but not a natural horseman's seat, and his mount was a strong-bodied brown gelding, good without being in the least showy.

"Right, western Oregon," he said, looking them over.

His knob of a chin turned towards Mathilda and Odard. "You and the boy there are from Portland, the group that's resurrected King Arthur and the Round Table, right?"

Mathilda bridled at the words and the clipped tone. "We're Associates of the Portland Protective Association," she said curtly.

The twins smiled sweetly, and Ritva spoke before he could ask: "And we're the cuckoos who live in the woods and think they're elves," she said politely. "Though really that's just a scurrilous rumor and a narrow, bigoted stereotype."

"*Mae govannen, cáno,*" Mary added: *Hello, General* in Sindarin.

"*Mae govannen,*" the general replied. "A secret language is sometimes useful."

"And Edain and I are Mackenzies," Rudi said.

Some men—and women, for that matter—had *baraka,* a force of personality that made them hard to resist; it was a gift of the Powers, and Thurston had plenty. Rudi had more experience than most with it, and set his mind like a wall. His voice was dry as he went on: "You know . . . kilts . . . bagpipes . . . witchcraft . . . pagan gods."

The dark eyes considered him levelly for a long moment; then, unexpectedly, he smiled.

"OK, I've spent *my* life trying to resurrect the United States. I don't think that's insane . . . but I'll agree it's obsessive," he said; there was a trace of a soft drawling accent in his voice, overlain with decades of Idaho. "The Scottish discarded the kilt for all but ceremonial reasons in the First World War because they used too much cloth. Trews were logistically more supportable. And there's no finer sound than bagpipes in battle. As to the rest, 'Congress shall make no law respecting an establishment of religion, or prohibiting the free exercise thereof.' That's from the Constitution of the United States, which is *your* Constitution, too. Well met, all of you."

Then Thurston's eyes narrowed as he looked at Ingolf. "I recognize *you*," he said. "My intelligence people debriefed you last year. Got a fairly wild story, along with some useful stuff on the eastern states and some even better information on the Prophet."

Ingolf nodded. "I didn't mind telling them what I knew. It was the pressing invitation to stay that had me doing a flit. Reminded me too much of Corwin."

Thurston shrugged. "I can always use more good men—and so can the country."

Then he turned back to Rudi. "I thought I placed your faces. I know *who* you all are, too; there's been a hell of an uproar out there in the West lately."

Mathilda winced, and Thurston noted it with a quick flicker of his eyes. He went on: "Why shouldn't I spank you and send you home to your parents?"

"Sure, and I didn't think you *recognized* our parents," Rudi observed.

And it's a wee bit impressive you know who we are. Has anyone taken a photograph of me?

There were cameras around, though not many, but they were large and distinctive and he didn't remember posing for one since before his voice broke.

Or does he have men keeping files on us, complete with sketches? Then after a moment: *Not a bad man, really, I think . . . but very focused.*

"I didn't think that you recognized the Portland Protective Association's sovereignty either," Mathilda observed.

"I don't recognize your parents," Thurston said. "Not as legitimate governments. But swords have a certain weight in themselves these days, and when I'm not in a position to immediately restore the nation's authority, I have to make tactical accommodations with de facto regimes. I could gain a fair bit of goodwill by handing the young lady there back to her mother."

A bleak smile. "I've had messages to that effect from Portland. Very *emphatic* messages, carried by men with titles that would be imposing if they weren't so funny."

"I'm the heir," Mathilda said quietly. "It's not that many years from now that I come of age, either, and I'll be the Protector then. You wouldn't win *my* goodwill that way . . . and I may live and rule a long time."

"A point," Thurston conceded. "On the other hand, if you get your fool neck chopped on this stunt, and I could have prevented it, your mother will be . . . very unhappy with me, for as long as we both shall live."

"And, well, that weight which you truly say swords have is why we turned out of our way to meet you," Rudi added blithely.

He let the accent he'd learned from his mother grow a little stronger as he went on:

"There are two hundred heavy swords waiting for you the now not ten miles away. Heavy and *sharp*, sure, and two hundred men to carry them, and every one a long ungainly dreadful *bachlach* thinking on you with dark and ugly intent, the creatures. The Church Universal and Triumphant's men—the Prophet's Cutters in person."

"Unit of the Sword of the Prophet, out of Corwin," Ingolf added. "Guardsmen commanded by a High Seeker."

Thurston's face changed, though most observers would have been hard-pressed to say exactly how. Rudi decided it was as if a buried playfulness had withdrawn further into the forged-iron core of the man.

"Is that so?" he said softly. "I suggest we all get off our high horses and talk about it." Then: "Captain Thurston, we'll take a short rest break here."

"Mr. President!" barked a young officer who looked like a younger edition of the Boise ruler, then strode away shouting orders.

Thurston went on over his shoulder: "Sergeant. The map and table."

"Got it, Captain," a man behind him said.

Rudi dismounted and let Epona's reins drop; she'd stay still, unless he called her. The others tethered their mounts to convenient bushes, and they crowded forward. The man who'd called Thurston a captain came back with a folding table covered in cork, then set it out and pinned a map to it, a modern one block-printed on rather thick cream-colored paper. He was fair-skinned under his tan, with a graying blond buzz cut and blue eyes in a nest of wrinkles, and otherwise enough like his commander to be his brother.

"Captain?" Rudi said quietly.

Thurston considered him for a moment, then gave a very slight nod of acknowledgment.

"Captain was the rank I held on March seventeenth, 1998—Army Rangers, Seventy-fifth, out of Fort Lewis near Seattle. Sergeant Anderson was with me before the Change."

For a moment the ruler's eyes were distant, looking down the road of years.

"Our team was one of the ones sent out to find out what the hell was going on. . . . He'll acknowledge my self-promotion to general-in-chief and president pro tem when we retake Washington and hold national elections."

"Yes, sir, Captain," the man said stolidly.

"Sure, and we all have our nonnegotiable points," Rudi said gravely.

And the old Romans had a man next to a triumphant general who whispered, "Remember, you are human," in his ear. Not a bad idea.

Then the Mackenzie traced the road they were on with a finger, down southward towards the old reservoir. "They're making camp here—the most of them, with a net of scouts flung out. . . ."

He looked at Ritva, and Mary quickly tapped the locations, describing each lookout post in detail.

"Only two hundred?" the general mused.

"It's an ambush," Ingolf pointed out.

"And surprise is the greatest force multiplier left, now that nuclear weapons don't work," Thurston agreed, rubbing a finger on his chin. "But why would the Prophet's men be on my territory? They're fully occupied with their war against New Deseret, according to my reports."

Rudi coughed into one hand. "Ah . . . as it happens, we were traveling with some folk from there, for safety's sake. *But . . .*"

His finger moved on the map again. ". . . we were heading east, so, well south of here. The Cutters wouldn't have seen us. The Deseret folk are still down there, on their way to home. We spotted the Cutters and turned north to warn you."

Mathilda spoke: "If you know anything about the Prophet—and you're closer to him than the Protectorate is, General Thurston—you'll know he's insatiable. If he gobbles up the Saints, you're next. Why haven't you helped them?"

And it's not tact that you excel in, is it, Matti? Rudi thought.

Thurston stared at her, his face bleak. "Young lady, I don't approve of theocracies—the Prophet's, *or* New Deseret's. Granted they aren't murderous lunatics like the Unawhacker, but there's the principle of the thing. They've been offered help, if they rejoin the nation and accept separation of Church and State."

Well, there's the little thing of the delayed elections in Boise, Rudi thought, but did not say aloud. *That collection of two-score graybeards you call the Senate and the House of Representatives haven't been chosen by anyone since before I was born, from all I hear.*

"In any case, they're here *now*," Rudi said. "And I understand you claim this territory. In the immediate rather than theoretical sense, that is."

"I do," Thurston said shortly. "Let me think for a moment, please."

He took a turn, boots scrutching in the dirt and rock, armor rattling. A few of his officers tried to speak to him, but he waved them curtly aside. The soldiers waited, leaning on their four-foot shields or their long javelins, a few munching hardtack crackers or chewing stolidly on board-tough strips of jerky.

Then the black general nodded as if to himself. "We'll go see about the Cutters. And then we'll see about you youngsters."

After a moment, he went on softly: "And perhaps we can also find out who told the Prophet's men I was coming this way."

Sure, and I wouldn't want to be that *man when our good General Thurston finds out,* Rudi thought.

He'd known a fair number of very hard men, good and bad, starting with his own blood father and Mathilda's dreadful sire, and he suspected he'd met another here.

"You're walking into their trap?" Mathilda asked, curious.

Thurston smiled. "It's only a trap if you don't know about it."

Rudi nodded to himself as Ingolf chuckled. "And if you know it's a trap, it's still a trap . . . for the other guy."

And that's something to remember.

* * *

The Boise wagonmaster had taken over the Conestoga with a nod of approval at the vehicle's state as he added it to the column's baggage train, but nobody had objected to the westerners getting their fighting gear out. The infantry marched in their armor as always, but the camp auxiliaries had put on light mail or studded-leather jackets too.

"I'm thinking this will be a footman's fight," Rudi said, thoughtfully shrugging to settle his brigandine and resting his longbow over his shoulder. "At least on our side."

"Couldn't we have an earthquake or a bit of a stampede or a flood, something of that order instead?" Edain asked. "It's a bit soon after the last fight for *my* taste, to be sure."

"It's in total agreement I am," Rudi said sardonically. "But I doubt the *Prophet* agrees."

Edain sighed. "That's the thing, Chief, innit?" He looked at the ground, and then the sky. "And I wasn't *asking* for a flood or earthquake, understood?"

Everyone was acting nonchalant, which was surprisingly hard when you expected homicidal lunatics to attempt your life at any instant. The high hills pulled back on the right, but to the east they were still close to the road. Rudi sang softly in Gaelic as he walked:

> Oh, fhàg mi ann am beul à brugh
> M'eudail fhein an donngheal dhubh . . .

"That's your mother's language," Mathilda said.

She recognized it easily enough, but didn't know more than the odd word or phrase most Mackenzies dropped into their conversation now and then. Those were rote-copied from Juniper just as so many imitated her accent, and others imitated *them*. Often badly and to her exasperated annoyance, though it had grown natural enough to the second generation, who'd picked it up from their parents just as they did any other part of their native tongue.

"What's it mean?" she went on.

"Ummm . . ."

Rudi thought hard; his mother's mother's birth speech was a splendid one for song and poetry and flights of fancy, but not especially easy to translate. It had always been the secret way he and his mother spoke together, at least until his younger half sisters Maude and Fiorbhinn picked it up as he had, sung to them in their cradles.

Aloud he went on: "It's a song about a brown-haired girl. . . ."

Mathilda grinned at him and tucked one seal-colored lock under her coif with its covering of lustrous silvery-gray titanium mail. "Keep going!"

"I'd render it more or less like . . .

> I left yesterday in the meadow of the kine
> The brown-haired maid of sweetest kiss,
> Her eye like a star, her cheek like a rose;
> Her kiss has the taste of pears."

He hadn't seen her blush often lately. She did now, and clouted him on the shoulder. Since he was wearing a padded doublet with short mail sleeves and collar under the brigandine torso armor, it was more symbolic than anything else.

"You're just missing all the Mackenzie beauties dazzled by your looks and lineage," she said dryly, after clearing her throat. "Well, *I'm* no light-heeled witch-girl to be charmed onto her back with poetry."

"Alas," he said, rolling his eyes at her with a theatrical sigh. "What a pity. It's such a *nice* strong shapely back that it's a true pity it sees so little use."

Then they both laughed; though Rudi acknowledged to himself there was a *little* truth to his *anamchara*'s accusation. There were only three women on the expedition, after all—and two of them were his sisters, while the third was a very good friend and determined virgin.

I hadn't thought about it till recently, but it does look like this is going to be a mostly celibate trip. Lady of the Blossom-Time, have mercy!

On her other side, Odard smiled thinly with his helmet under his arm; then his blue eyes narrowed over Rudi's head, and his handsome dark face stiffened slightly.

"I think I saw something move," he said softly.

Rudi saw something else; the heads of officers beginning to turn, and then carefully not doing so.

"Yeah," he said. "Nice one, Odard."

Ingolf gave a sigh. "You know," he said, "I usually don't go looking for a fight. But I would *really* like to meet Mr. Kuttner again. Maybe deal with his other eye . . ."

When the attack came, it was a surprise even though expected. The first arrow went *thock* into a shield even before the rattle of steel horseshoes on gravel reached them. A trumpeter went down, in the clump of men around the flag of the Republic; a few more fell along the line.

Then the whole formation turned left in unison, going from a column headed south to a three-deep line facing east with a deep shout of "*Oooh*-rah!" The big oval shields snapped up, the first rank vertical, the next slanted back, and the rest raised in an overlapping roof. Rudi blinked in amazement even as he ducked behind the corner of the wagon, with more arrows whistling overhead or going *thunk* into the vehicle's body and cargo or *punk* into the drum-taut canvas of the tilt or bouncing off the steel frame like ringing metallic rain. He'd never seen anything like that dragon-scale maneuver.

Like the unfolding of a tree into leaf but a thousand times faster, or a bird's feathers bristling, he thought.

At close range some of the arrows punched through the thick leather and plywood of the shields, and a few more men fell. One went between Ingolf and him as they peered around the wagon, and they both drew back.

"Something smells," Ingolf said tensely. "That's a goddamned stupid move, and the Cutters aren't that kind of stupid."

Rudi nodded. The horsemen in the russet-colored armor weren't trying to turn the formation's flanks; they were coming straight down the rough slope at the part of the Boise line ahead of the command group, shooting as fast as they could. Then they switched bows for lances—done with formidable speed—and bored right in, their formation a blunt wedge.

The knights of the Protector's Guard couldn't break that line with a balls-out-hair-on-fire charge, Rudi thought. *Not even Bearkiller A-listers. Not without artillery in support or something.*

And the Boise field pieces were going off now with a series of loud metallic *tunnnngggg* sounds. Four-foot arrows punched out in blurring streaks, nailing men to horses or smashing through two and three at a time, ignoring armor as if it were linen, ripping off limbs or slicing open bodies. Then a globe of stickfire hit, turning one rider and his mount into a pillar of flame and splashing burning napalm in all directions. Horses screamed, but the men never broke their chant:

"Cut! Cut! Cut!"

The Boise officers shouted all together: "Ready . . . first rank pick your man . . . pilaaaaa—throw!"

The formation opened out a little as the front rank cocked their heavy javelins back. Then a hundred muscular arms did throw, at point-blank range and within a second of one another. The Cutter charge stopped as if it had slammed into a massive glass wall, invisible but hard. Horses went over, pitching forward in complete somersaults or tripping, and more behind them reared screaming as they tried to avoid the gruesome pileup. Rudi winced as he heard leg bones snap; he always hated the uncomprehending agony of the poor beasts. They had more sense when men left them alone. . . .

"Ready . . . second . . . throw!"

The second rank lofted their throwing spears into the heaving mass, and then the third, and then the first rank used their second javelin. The volleys kept punching out until the spears were gone.

"Companies . . . charge!"

The Boise soldiers moved in unison again, to a huge crashing bark of: "USA! USA!"

Each sword hand snapped down to the hilt of the stabbing blade slung at each right hip, and then flicked it out and forward in a movement beautiful and deadly and swift. Then they smashed forward into the Prophet's men, swarming at them like ants—punching with the bosses of their heavy shields at the horses' faces, clubbing with the edges at the legs of mount and rider, holding them up to turn the strokes of the long shetes. And stabbing, stabbing . . .

The Cutters' trumpet wailed from higher up the slope. Every horseman who could turned his mount and spurred out of the melee, while the Boise infantry slaughtered those who couldn't.

"The Prophet's Guard don't run like that," Ingolf said.

Rudi's skin prickled, with a nervousness that had only a little to do with the edged iron flying about. Then something caught the corner of his eye. Pure instinct moved him: he turned on his heel even as he drew the clothyard shaft past the angle of his jaw and shot. One of Thurston's guard threw himself aside with a yell as the fletching brushed his neck.

The general wheeled just in time to see the spear drop from another's hand where it had been driving for his back. Surprise froze him an instant, and then he snatched at his own sword as the would-be assassin plowed into the ground face-first in a clatter of strip-armor with an arrow driven up under the flare of his helmet. Sergeant Anderson was already between them, sword and shield ready; Rudi could see his mouth working in soundless curses as he looked around at the other guards.

Rudi had drawn and loosed again before the first man struck the ground, conscious that Edain had gotten off his first shaft less than a second later than his. Another man among the guards pitched backward with a Mackenzie arrow standing in his face, and then a third went down—the bodkin points of two arrows driven through his armor and into gut and chest. His target had been a man near the general; that one struck as he spun, slashing open the assassin's throat to make three death wounds before he had time to collapse.

Then Rudi threw down his longbow and flung his hands in the air; barely twenty seconds had passed since the first shaft left his string.

"Peace!" he cried, pitching his voice to cut through the roar of noise around him. "They were trying to kill your general! Peace!"

An instant later Edain did the same, and the others of their band froze very still; there were probably a dozen weapons trained on them, and fingers trembling on triggers or ready to loose strings. Rudi felt a wash of cold liquid fear in his gut until Thurston himself bellowed, "Hold!"

The last of the Cutters were out of range, sped on their way by bolts from the Boise fieldpieces. Thurston stared down at the body lying so close to his feet and then clashed his unmarked sword back into the scabbard. Men were beginning to shout and turn as word spread from one individual to the next—most had had their eyes fixed firmly on the retreating enemy.

"Silence in the ranks!" Thurston bellowed.

And a sort of silence *did* fall; even through his own fear Rudi admired the discipline of it.

"Officers, get your men in hand. *Now!*"

The beginnings of chaos died. A long moment later Thurston waved a couple of aides aside and walked over to Rudi; they'd been only a hundred feet apart. Two men followed him, the others who'd been saved from blades in the back by a ripple of Mackenzie archery. Rudi's eyes skipped over them; both had transverse crests on their helmets, and as they took them off . . .

Yes, they're his close kin, from the looks. Their skin was lighter, toast-brown rather than near-black, and their short hair loose-curled rather than woolly, but otherwise the cast of features was the same. *Sons, from their years—one's a bit more than my age and the other's about Edain's.*

Thurston halted within arm's reach. Their eyes met for half a minute or so, and then he extended his hand. Rudi shook it.

"That was damned quick work," the Boise ruler said. "You saved my life there, you and your man . . . and saved my sons, too," he went on, confirming Rudi's guess. He glanced at them. "Martin, Frederick . . . Captain Thurston and Lieutenant Thurston, respectively."

Martin was the older; he extended his hand too, and then Frederick did as well. The younger son was grinning.

"Pretty fancy shooting," he said, and touched Edain's longbow with a finger. "That yew tree didn't die in vain!"

His older brother was more sober. "And how the *hell* did the Prophet get men into the presidential guard detail?" he snapped.

His father made a quelling gesture. "We'll have to find out. They were ready to strike without a chance in hell of escaping, too . . . and at a guess, this whole attack was aimed at giving them an opportunity. Goddamn, I thought the Change at least got rid of suicide killers. Wish we'd taken one alive."

He turned back to Rudi: "I now owe you two a considerable debt," he said. "Enough for an escort to the New Deseret border, no questions asked—but this area's not safe, with the Prophet's cavalry loose in it. We'll return to Boise. You need to do some planning and I need to do some investigating. Maybe some of the Cutters know what's going on."

A glance back at his frozen command group. "And that *was* some fancy shootin', given the angles and the time you had."

A few yards away, a Boise officer who'd been questioning a wounded Cutter swore and jerked his head back. The man had bitten off his own tongue, and spit it at the questioner in a spray of blood as he bent to hear an answer. He was laughing with a thick gobbling sound when a soldier jammed a spearhead through his throat; then he choked, kicked and died.

"What shall we do with the others, Mr. President?" an officer said, white-faced with shock at the assassination attempt but too disciplined to babble.

Thurston removed his helmet and sighed, rubbing a hand across his dense cap of tight-kinked hair; he looked his age then. "We're heading back to Boise. We'll take them along. They can talk, or they can join the infrastructure maintenance battalions. Have their wounded treated as soon as ours are OK."

Then he looked over at Rudi and Edain. "I've got some good archers," he said, to the younger Mackenzie this time. "But none like *that*. I could use a longbow corps; maybe you could teach some of my men if you're interested in a job. . . . What's so funny?"

The last was a snap that dampened the smile on Edain's face. Still, he was a free clansman of the Mackenzies, and he spoke boldly.

"I was just thinking of how my father trained *me*, General."

At his raised brow, the young man went on: "When I was six, he gave me a stave cut to my size. I'd hold it out until my arm ached . . . and if I let it droop then he'd wallop my backside. I learned to hold it as long as he liked . . . so then he gave me a thicker stave. When I got a real bow, I practiced an hour a day and longer on weekends, and that's not counting archery classes at school; I learned to care for my string, my bow, my arrows, to cut my own feathers and fletch my own shafts. I practiced shooting in calm, breeze, and strong wind, at still marks, moving marks, targets on the flat and in the air, and dropping fire on hidden ones, and all of them while I was standing . . . or kneeling . . . or running . . . or jumping."

Thurston looked as if he'd like to interrupt, but Edain continued: "Even shooting blindfolded at a target that rattled! Not to mention hunting. I dropped a running buck through thick brush at a hundred paces the year I turned thirteen, and he said I just *might* make a bowman worthy of the name. At sixteen I nailed a squirrel to a tree at the same range and he allowed that sure, I'd gone and done it. And *that*, General Thurston, sir, is how you make a Mackenzie archer!"

A couple of Thurston's soldiers looked alarmed at his insolence, even busy as they were. The general's own frown gave way to an unwilling grin, and his younger son matched the expression.

"Well, that put *me* in my place. Sometimes I'm *still* not used to the way some things take so long to learn these days."

Rudi nodded to himself. *He'd* noticed that about people who'd been fighting men before the Change. Evidently guns had been easy to learn well, easier even than a crossbow.

"Wait a minute," Thurston went on. "What's your last name, son? The real one, not the Mackenzie part."

"Aylward."

"You're Sam Aylward's kid?" Thurston said. "Well, no wonder."

"You know my father, sir?"

Edain sounded half-glad, half-disappointed—he'd been living in that shadow all his life, and here it was a month's travel from home. Rudi sympathized; he knew what it was like to have famous parents. In his case it was worse; his were legends on both the spear and cauldron side.

"I met him in 'ninety-one," Thurston said, animated for a moment. "On a mission in the Gulf. And then he dropped in to Fort Lewis back in 'ninety-eight, just before the Change . . . and I heard of him afterward. Aylward the Archer, eh? No wonder, then. Wish to hell he'd ended up with me and not the flakes . . . er, the Mackenzies."

"You know, I love my dad," Edain muttered, as the lord of Boise turned away and began a rattle of orders to his waiting subordinates. "But there are times I get bloody sick of hearing about Aylward the Archer."

"Cheer up," Rudi said, slapping him on the shoulder. "Think of all the years *you'll* be Aylward the Archer."

From his expression, Edain was—and then suddenly his face fell as he realized that would mean his father wasn't around anymore.

CHAPTER EIGHTEEN

I t was an hour or so until sunset and the Boise road still headed northwest, though they'd turn east to enter the city itself. Shadows were
beginning to fall around them, though the upper parts of the town
walls and their towers were still brightly lit in the middle distance, and
the white and scarlet fabric of the three tethered hot-air balloons that
hung several thousand feet above was even brighter. Higher still light
flashed briefly from the canopy of a glider.

"It's all so . . . tidy," Rudi said, looking around and blinking in the
bright summer sun. "Not a board loose or a building unpainted or one
poor gasping weed left to propagate its kind."

Truck gardens occupied most of the land this close to the city, watered by canals and spinning windmills. There was a scattering of barns
and sheds, and things like chicken coops and pigpens adding their pungencies to turned wet earth and compost, but not many houses close
to the city proper—as usual, people close enough to walk out from the
walls lived inside them. The pleasant tinkle and chug of running water
sounded, and plenty of folk were out tending the vegetables and berry
bushes and small orchards of apples and peach and cherry with hand
tools and horse-drawn machines, or harvesting greens and early roots.

Many stopped to wave or shout greetings as the soldiers went by, and some of the closer ones stared at the obvious foreigners.

"So very, very, very *tidy*."

Rudi spoke with a mixture of mild scorn and grudging admiration. Mackenzies were farmers, and good ones, and that meant that they worked very hard indeed and admired hard workers and a neat job. But they stopped when they'd done enough to get the job done; it wasn't as if there was ever a scarcity of things that needed doing about a croft, and if you had any time to spare you spent it on dancing or a festival or a little fancywork like carving a god-post. Around here . . .

"You noticed?" one of his half sisters said dryly.

"Who could be missing it?" Rudi replied, his tone equally pawky.

"Yeah, you're riding along a road and you drop an apple core here and three people scold you and point to the waste bin," Ingolf confirmed.

"They don't feed apple cores to their pigs?" Edain said, puzzled.

"Yeah, but you've got to put it in the waste bin *first*. The *official* waste bin. That's the Approved Procedure. And if you think this is neat and tidy, wait until we get into town. The punishment for drunk-and-disorderly is going around sweeping the streets up after the horses and oxen, with some sergeant kicking your ass while you do it."

The suburbs here around the modern city had been torn down with a thoroughness Rudi had never seen anywhere, even the foundation pads of the houses broken up; a last few metal-frame buildings were being disassembled as they passed through, with bundles of girders lowered to the ground by cables and stacked on big ox-wagons to be hauled away for smithies and forges and fortress construction. The manicured look of the gardens was a *little* unusual. The walls ahead, though . . .

"Mount Angel is stronger," Father Ignatius said stoutly.

"It is that. On the other hand, it's also on the top of a four-hundred-foot hill," Rudi pointed out. "The which is a pimple in a plain of exceeding flatness. This is not."

Boise was on the east bank of its river; that ran in a blue band north–south, with three bridges crossing it and mountains rising not far beyond. The walls weren't just tall. Old high-rises had been built into them and infilled with concrete as well. Rudi was used to the giant structures of the ancients, but most of them were dead. Seeing them worked into something as natural and modern as the outer curtain wall of a fortress-town was eerie, and it gave the defenses an odd alien angular look.

Traffic was thick on the road; carts with farm produce, everything from baskets of eggs cradled in straw to burlap sacks of potatoes and casks of wine and flats of early lettuce and green onions and radishes; bigger wagon trains with trade goods in bales and bundles and barrels; people on foot and horseback and an occasional flock of sheep or herd of cattle. They all pulled aside for the general's party; news of their coming had been flashed ahead by heliograph and semaphore-telegraph stations, running from hilltop to hilltop.

"Yeah, I wouldn't like to try to storm it," Ingolf said.

Rudi's eyes flicked ahead to Thurston. There wasn't much of a fuss over the ruler's arrival; he'd seen that the man didn't like pomp. As he watched, two riders came out of the gate and down the cleared lane to meet them, saluting briskly.

"Mr. President," the first said.

He was in uniform too, but a blue one with NATIONAL POLICE sewn on the shoulder, a plain-looking man in his thirties with a short-clipped mustache. The younger man beside him was in the camouflage cloth of Boise's army; his helmet hid his hair, but from the freckles and pale complexion Rudi thought it must be as red as his own mother's. The first man looked at Thurston, his eyes flicking to Rudi and the others.

"They're cleared," the ruler said. "I know they're most assuredly not out to kill me . . . which is more than I can say for my own guards."

That brought a wince. "I thought you should know, sir, we found out how those men were infiltrated into the guard detail. We and Military Intelligence."

"Interservice cooperation. Wonders never cease," Thurston said dryly. "Go on, Commander Lamont."

"They were *supposedly* rotated down by Colonel Winder in Lewiston."

"Supposedly?"

The younger man beside the officer of police spoke up. "Three men were sent. Someone intercepted them on the way here, presumably killed them, and substituted ringers. Ringers who looked fairly similar and had extremely well forged papers . . . well-briefed ringers, too."

"They couldn't have hoped to keep that up long," Thurston said thoughtfully. "This isn't a very big country, not yet. But it nearly worked. Get me a report on procedures to make sure this doesn't happen again by ten hundred hours tomorrow. And start working on the real question."

"Sir?" the two officers spoke almost in unison.

"Why do they want to kill me? Even if it worked, the vice president would take over—and Moore would declare war on them immediately. Which I'm now going to do anyway. So there's no upside for them, and they didn't even try to hide the fact that they were involved. Get to work on it. *Why* is always more important than *how*, in the long run."

They saluted and turned away. Rudi cleared his throat.

"Your guards aren't with you for long, then, sir?"

The ruler of Boise nodded. "Candidates for our OCS—Officer Candidate School—spend some time in my presidential guard detail. It gives me a chance to evaluate them."

Father Ignatius spoke: "Someone knows an uncomfortable amount about your security precautions, General. Specifically, the Prophet does."

"Yeah, padre, they do," Thurston said.

His eldest son broke in. *Martin*, Rudi reminded himself, as the man spoke.

"Sir, perhaps it would be better if you went to the Old Prison for now. It's easier to secure the perimeter there."

Thurston chuckled. "Captain, the day I lock myself up to avoid assassins, you may move for my impeachment. Besides which, given what happened . . . what if I'm locking the potential assassins up in there with me?

"It's not actually a prison," he went on to the others, nodding southward. "It was, once, long before the Change. Good solid stone-built compound, and we've improved it since, a couple of miles south of town."

"The . . . guests . . . then, sir?" his son went on. "The sixth regiment is there—more than enough for security, and I'll vouch for them."

The general-president's eyebrows went up: "You weren't commander of the sixth, last time I looked, Martin, just a junior officer." Then to his guests: "Any takers?"

Rudi shook his head. "No, thank you, sir, if it's all the same." He smiled. "I've a fancy to see this town of yours."

"I should see to the sixth myself, then, sir," Thurston's son went on.

"You're *still* not regimental commander."

The younger man grinned. "No, sir. But I *am* in command of B Company, Sixth Infantry Regiment, and it's not fair to let my platoon leaders and company sergeant carry the can this long. Particularly with so many new men."

"Very well."

"Give my regards to Mother, sir."

"And mine to Juliet, Captain."

Thurston's elder son turned his horse aside, followed by a pair of others. The tall gates on the other side of the bridge were open; a squad did a neat maneuver as they rode through the gloomy thickness of the wall. Rudi looked around as they rode eastward towards what looked like an interior citadel, with a big building with a gilded dome catching the setting sun not far from it.

Much was what you'd expect from any modern city; pre-Change buildings modified to new uses, or new ones built to infill empty spaces that wasted precious space within the fortifications. Ground floors were stores or workshops with their proprietors living above, though less spilled onto the sidewalks than even Corvallis's strict laws enforced. There was a public library, and a fair assortment of houses of worship: Catholic, varieties of Protestant including some he didn't recognize, a Mormon temple of some size and a small Covenstead that had him smiling at the sign of the Triple Moon.

Thurston's younger son pointed out features—the big silo-shaped granaries where blindfolded oxen turned capstans that raised barley and wheat by geared screws, the waterworks and sewage plant with the attached bio-gas plant that provided illumination and purified sludge for the farms, the railroad station. . . .

The clothes on the people were very old-fashioned, though, even in new cloth: jeans and T-shirts and jackets, knee-length skirts and even the odd collar and tie. People moved briskly, as Corvallans did, but without the animated knots of impromptu argument you always saw there. There were no street musicians or beggars as there would be in Portland or Newberg or Astoria in Association territory, and no rickshaws, though plenty of bicycles and pedicabs. And none of the street shrines and little touches Sutterdown had.

Plus there were a *lot* of uniforms. And big, colorful posters on four-sided hoardings at crossroads. The process was stone-plate lithography; he'd seen examples in Corvallis advertising this and that, and in Portland for tournaments and saints' days and proclamations from the Regent. The themes here were quite different. . . .

One he saw nearly every time showed five figures—a muscular soldier in the harness of a Boise regular, shield and sword in hand, an equally muscular male farmer or laborer with a spade, a woman with a pruning hook, another in a white coat with a test tube and a mother holding an infant. They all glared forward with square-jawed purpose, striding together in unison, and a legend beneath read in big block letters:

WE'RE BUILDING AMERICA WITH OUR SWEAT!
DEFENDING IT WITH OUR BLOOD!
DON'T GET IN OUR WAY!

Others exhorted people to buy Reconstruction Bonds, whatever those were, or to attend night schools, whatever *those* were—he suspected they weren't much like a Mackenzie Moon School—or most frequently of all to vote in the Regional Representation Referendum, whatever *that* was. The visual images all had that characteristic style although they were obviously by many different hands; even the idealized farm cottages managed to look muscular and determined, somehow.

He wasn't all that surprised. Most communities he knew had their own underlying unity of style. You could tell Mackenzie artwork, even when it was something as utterly practical as a wooden lever and stump for breaking flax—there'd be a little knotwork on the end of the handle, or a Triple Moon.

"And what would a Regional Representation Referendum be, General? I understand the three words, but put them together and it's a mystery."

Thurston was deep in thought. His younger son answered instead:

"Whether we should elect a new Congress and Senate, locally, since we can't exactly do it nationwide. Fa . . . the president just realized a while ago that the ones we've got are all going to die of old age pretty soon."

Thurston snorted and gave him a pawky look, but seemed to come out of his brown study.

Rudi judged his moment after they passed through another wall into an inner citadel, taller and stronger even than that around the outer city, with more of the high-rises built into it. The echoing dimness of the entranceway made good cover for his words as he murmured, "General . . . your ghost would make a most fitting banner for a war of revenge. They tried to kill you, but they'd lose even if they succeeded and double if they failed. There's more to that plot than the bit Edain and I foiled."

Thurston gave him a hard grin. "You noticed? Yeah . . . and you're not just a pretty face, are you, Rudi Mackenzie? I've been wondering about that. Where's the upside for him? And I *will* be making a declaration of war—if this isn't a *casus belli* I'm Jane Fonda."

"Who?" Rudi said.

"A witch from before the Change—and not in the complimentary sense of the word."

The citadel had a broad parade ground of good concrete several acres in extent, enough that the column of three hundred men didn't crowd it. The flat ground was surrounded by barracks and stables, armories and workshops and offices, plus a number of what looked like pre-Change houses with tiny stretches of lawn and garden.

"Major Winters, you may dismiss the column to quarters," Thurston said.

There was a bark of "Halt!" and "Left face!" then "Stand easy!" and "Dismissed!" The bulk of the troops filed off.

Thurston handed his horse's reins to a soldier in fatigues of rough gray homespun and raised a brow as his thirty-strong guard detail remained braced to attention.

"Excuse me," he said to Rudi. "I've got business to deal with, unless I miss the signs.

"Major?" he went on.

"Mr. President, the men of the guard detail request notification of the penalty you have in mind."

Boise's ruler raised his other eyebrow. "I've identified the security breach, Major, but if any further information requires disciplinary action, rest assured you'll be informed."

The officer saluted and did a neat about-face before marching off. Watching Thurston's face, Rudi wasn't in the least surprised when the guards remained.

One corner of the Boise ruler's mouth quirked up very slightly. "I think I heard the order to dismiss given."

"Sir!"

It was the tall grizzled sergeant named Anderson; he'd been so quiet Rudi had almost forgotten his presence.

"Yes, Sergeant Anderson?"

"Sir, the men feel that some field punishment is in order."

The quirk in Thurston's mouth was almost noticeable this time. "Dick, are you telling me that the men are *demanding* a punishment?"

"Sir, as your guards—"

"I've seen some strange forms of insubordination in my time, but this is about it!"

Thurston's voice was a growl; his face was like a carving in dark wood as he looked at the rigid brace of the troops. The countenances framed by the brims and cheek pieces of the helmets were equally blank.

"Sergeant, give me a hand here."

Methodically, Thurston undid the snaps and buckles of his hoop armor. He handed the pieces to the noncom; when he'd finished not much of the man was visible. Rudi smiled to himself in silent applause as the general stalked out in front of the double file of guards.

"All right . . . pila . . . *present!*"

Each man flicked his throwing spear into the overarm position.

"*Ready!*"

The long javelins cocked back.

"Now, if there are any suicide assassins left in this presidential guard detail, *take your best shot.*"

Thurston stood with his arms spread, then slowly turned in a circle. Silence followed; even the men and beasts moving about the big parade ground on various errands seemed frozen in place.

"All right then," Thurston growled. "You young idiots, if I didn't think you were trustworthy, I'd have had you disarmed. No punishment for the assassination attempt. Personnel security review isn't your responsibility. For this indiscipline, one week confinement to barracks and one week's stoppage of pay. Now *slope spears* and *dismissed,* damnit! I want a bath and I'm hungry. I'm too old for this shit and my wife's got supper cooking."

As they marched off, he turned to Rudi and his companions. "You're all invited. Sergeant Anderson will arrange your quartering . . . after he stows that armor."

* * *

We know the Sun was Her lover
As They danced the worlds awake;
And She lay with His brilliance
For all Their children's sake.
Where Her fingers touched the sky
Silver starfire sprang from nothing!
And She held Her children fast in Her dreams.

There was a glory in that forest
As the moonlight glittered down;
And stars shone in the wildwood
When the dew fell to the ground—
Every branch and every blossom;
Every root and every leaf
Drank the tears of the Goddess in the gloaming!

There came steel, there came cities
Wonders terrible and strange,
But the light from the first-wood
Flickered down until the Change.
And every field, every farmhouse,
Every quiet village street
Knew the tears of the Goddess in the gloaming!

Now the Sun comes to kiss Her
And She rises from Her bed
They are young—and old—and ageless
Joy that paints the mountains red.
We shall dance in Their twilight
As the forests fall to sleep,
And She whispers in our ears the word remember!

Rudi let his hands fall as the soft-voiced hymn ended and the sun sank below the battlements to the west. Edain and the twins did the same and they stood in silence for a moment, heads bowed over crossed arms, then looked at one another and smiled.

As they turned to go back down the stair from the fortress wall he adjusted his bonnet with the spray of raven feathers in the clasp over his left eye; you had to spruce yourself a bit for dinner with the ruler of a foreign land, for form's sake and the Clan's credit. Dressing up for a Mackenzie was simplified by the fact that everyone wore kilt and plaid, except for a few older or pregnant women who preferred the arsaid. You just changed from the everyday ones into the ones you kept for festival, added a few fancies and you were set.

In his case the fancies included a leaf-green Montrose jacket with worked silver buttons down both sides; cravat and ruffled jabot; a *sgian dubh* with a hilt of silver and black bone tucked into his right knee sock; silver brooch at shoulder and silver buckles on his shoes wrought in curling knots picked out with turquoise. And a formal sporran, tooled black leather edged with badger fur rather than the rather battered and scruffy article he wore every day, which usually held odds and ends like a lump of wax and spare bowstrings or a half-gnawed hardtack biscuit.

Edain's outfit was a slightly scaled-down version of Rudi's, made by his mother's careful hands from the shearing of the sheep and the pulling of the flax on—and she was a loom mistress second only to Juniper Mackenzie among the clan. The main difference was that his formal coat was dyed a dark russet with Saint-John's-wort—Melissa Aylward called it his *calm jacket*.

Ritva followed his eyes and snickered. "And you were saying there were a lot of uniforms around here," she said. "At least they're *different* uniforms. Mackenzies are always going on about how free they are and how they can do just whatever suits their fancy and it's true—as long as they fancy a pleated skirt and a blankie over the shoulder. All in the Clan tartan."

Rudi raised one brow and took in their identical clothes; black pants, belts, jerkins with the silver tree-crown-stars. . . .

"Hey, that's *family*," Mary protested, tossing her golden hair. "Besides, these aren't uniforms. They're *outfits*. Say what you like about the Dúnedain, we've got *style*."

They turned and went down the spiral stairs to the parade ground. The risers ran widdershins—Kerr-handed, they'd said in the old days, after a clan that were mostly lefties—to pin an attacker's shield arm to the inside.

The others were waiting for them at the bottom; Father Ignatius had simply put on a clean robe, and Ingolf was in his usual good plain eastern-style roll-necked sweater and long coat. The two from Portland, however . . .

"Sure, and it's blinding them you'll be," Rudi said dryly.

Odard and Mathilda had both brought suits of the latest Court fashion, suitable for a banquet at Castle Todenangst or the High Palace in Portland. Tight hose, tooled shoes with upcurled toes sporting little silver bells, tunics with long dagged sleeves dropping down from the elbows, jeweled belts and dagger hilts. Odard's outfit was even particolored, wine red on the left and dark indigo blue on the right, not counting the golden fleurettes along the hems and seams; a spray of peacock feathers flared backward from the livery badge at the front of his roll-edged hat with the dangling tail. Matti was a little more somber in brown velvet, but the heraldic shield on her chest had the lidless eye picked out in genuine rubies and jet. . . .

Rudi flung up a hand. "Aieee!"

Odard snorted and examined with satisfaction the little golden chains that held the snowy linen of his fretted cuffs.

"You're just damned jealous, because you're stuck with that skirt and blanket," he said. "I return your envy with the lofty, pitying compassion suited to a Christian gentleman of good birth and coat armor."

Rudi grinned and told him where he could put his sympathy. "With a hay fork," he added.

"Peasant," Odard said genially.

They walked towards the house where the ruler of Boise lived. It was an unremarkable building, substantial but not grand—redbrick and white trim and shutters, two stories tall with dormered windows on the roof, of a type that had been old before the Change and often copied since. There wasn't much sign of pomp about it, save for the Stars and Stripes over the door and the two sentries in polished armor on either side. They snapped to attention with a clank and stamp and rustle, rapping their spear butts on the flagstones of the veranda.

"Come in, please," a soft voice said from inside as the door opened. "I'm Cecile Thurston."

They blinked against the incandescent mantles of the gaslight in the hallway, amid a clean smell of wax and floor polish and faint appetizing cooking odors; a black-and-white cat stared at Rudi and the others with the usual cool insolence from halfway up a staircase. The woman greeting them was tallish and in her forties, in a dress with a full knee-length skirt, her long hair light brown where it wasn't gray.

"But you can call me Cecile," she said, giving a sudden brilliant smile aimed at him and Edain. "I know what you did for Larry."

It took him a moment to realize that Thurston was *Larry* to this comfortable-looking woman. There wasn't any physical resemblance to Juniper Mackenzie—Cecile Thurston was three inches taller, for starters—but she reminded him of his mother a little.

They all shook hands and made introductions. Young Frederick Thurston was there, in a neat green uniform; and two girls of about seven and twelve, who turned out to be named Jaine and Shawonda. Both were staring at him—the older particularly, with her eyes virtually bulging.

Oh, and I hope that's not going to be awkward, Rudi thought. *Sweet Foam-born One, none of your jokes, now!*

He knew the effect he had on a lot of females, and liked it very much—when they were of age. Crushes by youngsters ranged from a boggart-level nuisance to a full-blown pain in the arse. Then Odard and Matti saved the moment by bowing—the elaborate leg-forward, hat-off, bent-knee flourish an Associate used with a lady of high rank who was also their host.

Cecile Thurston smiled. "My, that's impressive!"

Mathilda chuckled. "Theoretically I should curtsy, but it always looks absurd when you're wearing hose yourself."

"You could all probably use a drink," Cecile said. "Come on into the living room and let me take your coats . . . well, cloaks . . ."

The living room had a good rug, sofas and tables and upholstered chairs—most of it looking like modern work but made to late pre-Change patterns, which gave it all an old-fashioned look. The two young girls' stares turned considering as they took the whole party in; they reminded him forcefully of his younger half sisters Maude and Fiorbhinn. Particularly the younger, Jaine, who looked somehow as if a whole lot of crackling energy would burst loose any moment and make her slightly frizzy dark hair stand out in all directions, despite her careful grooming and clean frock. The elder girl was quieter, with a round face and an unfortunate spray of pimples.

"I bet you're a prince from foreign parts," young Jaine said to him after a moment of awkward silence. "You *look* the way a prince should."

Rudi grinned. "Not quite," he said. "My mother's a Chief, and I'm sort of . . . an assistant Chief."

"Oh," she said. "Like a prince is an assistant king, I guess . . ." Then she brightened and looked at Mathilda. "Are you a *princess?*"

"Well . . . yes, actually," Mathilda said.

Rudi judged she was taken a little aback at princesses being rhetorically classed with unicorns and dragons and other exotic creatures of mythology. After all, princess was simply her job description, and not even one she'd asked for or wanted all that much.

Jaine frowned. "I thought princesses had to be beautiful? You're sort of pretty, I guess, but . . ."

Edain choked over a sip from his wineglass. Rudi managed to smooth his face into polite impassivity before he caught Mathilda's wilting glare. *She* knew he'd had to swallow a laugh.

"And don't princesses wear beautiful long dresses with jewels and stuff like that?"

Mathilda nodded solemnly. "Sometimes I do. But I'm traveling and they're too heavy and the skirts catch your legs and you can't move your arms very well in one. And all the buttons!"

Rudi smiled a little to himself, and saw Odard smoothing away an identical expression. Evidently he'd also heard Matti when she went into full *it's like being in irons* rant on the cotte-hardi.

"Oh," Jaine said, sounding a little disappointed. "I thought it would be fun to wear dresses like that. But," she added generously, "what you've got on now is cool too. Sort of like what people on playing cards wear."

She frowned. "Why've you got the Sign of Evil on your chest, though?"

"Ah . . ." Mathilda looked down. "It's hereditary. It's not the Sign of Evil. It just means that the Throne is supposed to be all-seeing to detect enemies and evildoers."

Jaine turned to Odard: "You're not a prince either, I guess? You're not as handsome as he is, but you're *dressed* like a prince."

"I'm a baron," he replied helpfully. "That's sort of like—"

"A wicked feudal oppressor!" Jaine said delightedly, clapping her hands together. "I've read about that in school. Do you have a castle and a *dungeon?*"

"A castle, a small town, six manors—four held for knight service by my vassals, two in demesne—ten villages and a hunting lodge," Odard said.

"And dungeons? With racks and rats and straw and guys in black hoods and stuff?" she said with gruesome relish.

"No. The High Court of Petition and Redress doesn't like that sort of thing these days. And I'm not all that wicked or oppressive . . . all my peasants would leave if I were, and then where would I be?"

"Broke, and earning your own living," Rudi said. "And that wouldn't suit you at all, at all, Odard."

And you can't hunt runaways with dogs anymore, he thought.

Odard's father had been an enthusiastic hunter of runaway peons, with a pack of sight hounds trained to kill, and a busy torture chamber. Though to be fair, *that sort of thing* had been over before Odard's voice broke; it had been part of the settlement at the end of the War of the Eye that anyone could move if they wanted to. It was amazing how the Portland Protective Association's standards of management changed once the implications of "voting with the feet" sank in.

The interrogation continued relentlessly: "What do you do, then, if you're not being wicked and oppressive?"

Odard was looking a little bewildered; children were more strictly kept in the Protectorate. He probably hadn't had much to do with kids in his own household since he was one himself.

"Ah . . . I keep the garrison up to scratch, drill the militia, keep order, collect the taxes, see the demesne farms are managed properly and the tithes paid, preside at sessions of the court baron, throw out the first baseball of the season . . ." Odard said.

"Oh," Jaine said. "Boring stuff, like Dad does."

Her brother cleared his throat. "Excuse her," he said. "We don't get that many foreigners here."

"We're all Americans," his mother said soothingly. "Have a canapé."

The word was only vaguely familiar to Rudi; evidently it meant things like bits of liver paste and capers and caviar on crackers. At home Mackenzies would have called it a nibblement; Sandra Arminger referred to them as petit fours or, when she was being obscure, faculty fodder.

Jaine's older sister cut in with a question for the twins: "And you two are elf-friends?"

There were bookcases on one wall of the living room, across from the fireplace. Rudi's eyes flicked in that direction. Yes, a set of what Aunt Astrid insisted on calling "the histories," and looking well-read.

"Well, we sure would be if there were any elves around to be friends with right now," Ritva said.

"Provided *they* liked us," Mary said pedantically. "Which we can't tell, really. Who knows? They might be all snooty and condescending."

Seeing disappointment, Ritva went on: "But we do live in a flet and *talk* Elvish. Well, Sindarin, not High-Elvish. That's for special occasions."

Both the Thurston sisters looked interested. "Say something in Sindarin!" Shawonda exclaimed.

"Ummm . . ."

The twins looked at each other, cleared their throats, and sang a few verses instead—they had pleasant sopranos, as well trained as you'd expect in a Dúnedain, and they were very good at two-part harmony. Mackenzies liked to sing, but Astrid's Rangers couldn't say, "where's the outhouse?" without a chorus sometimes.

It was Rudi's turn to nearly choke on his wine, and he saw Mathilda flush with annoyance—she had a catlike obsession with propriety, sometimes. It sounded pretty—Elvish always did—but rendered into what Dúnedain called the common tongue the song would have gone:

> And into that dusty den of sin
> Into that harlot's hell
> Came a lusty maid who was never afraid,
> And her name was—

Aunt Astrid had pitched an absolute fit when they translated that one, a couple of years ago, and another when they started singing it in taverns as they passed through and rumors started spreading about what the lyrics actually *meant*.

Songs just didn't get more luridly gross than "The Ballad of Eskimo Nell."

"That's beautiful," Shawonda said, and sighed. "And are you on a *quest*?"

This one would be prime Ranger bait, back home, Rudi thought. *She'd be off to the woods in a flash.*

Aunt Astrid's bunch attracted that sort of romantic the way cowpats did flies. To be fair, they did a lot of good work to earn their keep.

"Well, we're not qualified to quest for rings or anything like that," Ritva said solemnly. "We're still young and just finished our *ohtar* training three years ago. You have to be twenty-one to be a *Roquen*, a knight. Mostly back home we find lost livestock or children, and track down man-eaters or bandits or fugitives, and guard caravans or explorers going into dangerous country."

"It's sort of like being a town watchman . . . a policeman, you say here."

"But with more trees and lots and lots of venison."

"And squirrel stew and wild greens."

"We'd *like* to do a quest, of course."

"We're working our way up from minor things," Mary continued.

"Like questing for Bilbo's pen and inkstand," her sister specified.

"Or Galadriel's tea strainer."

"Or Arwen's hand-lotion pump."

"And right now, our klutzy big brother's magic sword—he's always losing things. Dumb-blond syndrome."

"But *you're* blond. Blond*er*. His hair is sort of red and blond but yours is just yellow."

"Yeah, but we're girls, which makes up for it."

Shawonda laughed; then her mother pointed through an archway. "You two go help get the first course out."

To Rudi and the others: "I'm sorry, but they're very excited—I know they can be a bit of a trial at times."

"Not at all," Rudi said, as Mathilda and Odard murmured much less sincere disclaimers. "They remind me of my sisters . . . my mother's younger daughters, not the Terrible Two here."

"They remind us of us," Mary or Ritva said.

"Now you're getting *nasty*," Mathilda said dryly.

"They remind me of *my* sister," Edain said, and then grinned, suddenly looking a lot less adult than his nineteen years. "But sure, and I won't hold it against them."

Rudi looked at the mantelpiece. There were a few framed pictures there. One showed a much younger General-President Thurston in the uniform of the old American army, standing with his arm around Cecile; she was holding a baby in the crook of one arm. The picture was in color, and it had an archaic sharpness to it.

His brows went up in surprise. "You and your husband met before the Change, then, Mrs. Thurston . . . Cecile?"

"Just before—we were married in the spring of 1997," she said. "Martin arrived in a hurry . . . and he's been that way ever since!"

"But then . . . I thought General Thurston was sent out of Seattle? You went with him?"

She shook her head and smiled, fond and proud. "No. He came back for me and Martin."

The smile died. "We were hiding in the cellar of the colonel's house. That was after the mutiny, and things were . . . very bad. The MREs were all gone and I would have had to go out to look for food in a day or two. And there he and Sergeant Anderson were."

Rudi glanced at his friends. They were looking as impressed as he was, even Edain, who was a crucial few years younger. They'd all heard the stories. The only people who got out of most big cities alive after the Change were the ones who ran, and ran *fast*, before things went totally bad; the only exception they knew was Portland, and there Mathilda's father and his bullyboys had burned large sections down and driven most of the survivors out to die.

Going back into the hell of Seattle for someone a full month after the Change must have required a trip all the way around Robin Hood's barn, and the Horned Lord's own luck. He mentally revised his *one tough bastard* estimation of General Thurston upwards a notch.

Then Cecile went on: "And here's Larry now."

The front door opened again; Rudi caught the draft of cooler air, and the crash and thump of the sentries. Thurston senior's voice came, muffled as if he were talking over his shoulder.

". . . and have the mobilization orders on my desk for signature by oh nine hundred tomorrow, Major. Staff plan seventeen-C."

Thurston's younger son turned at the words, quivering a little like an eager hunting dog; he was just the age to long for his first war. His father visibly forced the scowl off his face as he came in and greeted his guests. Cecile handed him a cocktail of the type Rudi had turned down in favor of wine; in his experience hard liquor just before a meal stunned your taste buds. The ruler of Boise looked as if he needed it, though.

He gave them all a nod, then turned to Father Ignatius. "Did you mention you were an engineer, padre?"

The priest signed assent. "We all study the basics, sir," he said. "The knight-brethren are actually more often in command or advisory positions, you see. We have to be able to lay out a fort or build a siege engine. Or plan a town or an irrigation system and pumps."

"You might like to take a look at some of our stuff while you're here, then."

"I'd appreciate it, sir," the priest said.

He was as calmly polite as always, but Rudi noticed a flare of interest in the dark eyes. Rudi wasn't surprised that Thurston would know a man's interests . . . and not surprised that he had no small talk, either.

"It's a pity we didn't get more of your missions out here," the general went on. "We could have used them."

Ignatius nodded. "But there are others who need it far more," he said. Then a rare charming smile: "You've done too well to need us."

They went into the dining room and the meal came out: potato-and-leek soup first, then a rack of lamb—nicely and slightly pink in the center—with a plum-honey-garlic glaze, scalloped potatoes and steamed new vegetables. Those were welcome. The salad of early greens was much more so; Rudi forwent the dressing. Traveling usually meant living on a winterlike diet of bread and salted and smoked meats, with vegetables dried or pickled or in jars. It was good to taste seasonal delicacies like fresh tomatoes again. The bread was excellent too, less crumbly than that made from the Willamette's soft wheat—Portland's court ate something similar, from flour imported down the Columbia from the Palouse country.

At last the dessert—peach pie—was finished and the younger children sent off with a minimum of protest.

"Excellent dinner," Odard said courteously, as they moved back to the living room for coffee and liqueurs. "My compliments to the cook."

"Thank you," Cecile Thurston said, showing a dimple as she smiled. "You're looking at her."

Mathilda looked a little less surprised; but then, she'd spent part of many years at Dun Juniper, where Rudi's mother always did her share of the kitchen chores.

"You're in a bit of a fix," Thurston said bluntly, when the drinks had been poured. "What the hell were your folks thinking, anyway?"

"A fix? That I knew before I left," Rudi said wryly. "And if we told you exactly why we were heading east—well, it makes sense in our terms, but I doubt you'd be agreeing."

Thurston raised an eyebrow. "Heading for Nantucket? Yeah, I've gotten some rumors about the place, and if there's some hint about the Change I sure as *hell* would like to know. And there was our friend Ingolf's not-very-complete story to add spice. This isn't the time, though, with the fighting getting worse."

Rudi spread his hands. "Sir, when would it be this *right time*? There's been war and rumor of war from here to the Atlantic since the Change, and I don't expect it to much improve before I'm old and gray, so."

"According to my intelligence people, it's pretty damned bad east of here—the Prophet's boys beat the Snake River Army—that's one of New Deseret's main field forces—east of Pocatello, and it'll be under siege soon. Then they'll head for Twin Falls . . . which is entirely too close to *my* border. There's fighting down in what used to be Utah, too. It's all coming apart and there are raiding parties everywhere: Corwinites, deserters from both sides, freelancers and mercenaries and general road-people bandit scum. It'd be a poor payment for saving my life and my boys' to send you into that."

The companions exchanged sober glances. "That all went to hell in a handbasket woven lickety-split," Ingolf said. "New Deseret was holding up pretty well when I went through last year."

Thurston held out a broad palm and turned it as if it were a seesaw on a pivot, at first slowly and then with a snap.

"They spread themselves too thin and let the Cutters get inside their decision curve. Walker—he's the Prophet's main commander—is a bastard but a smart one, and he managed to mousetrap a lot of their infantry down south. Sort of a replay of Manzikert . . . a battle about a thousand years ago. He was army before the Change. After that he kept them rocked back on their heels and their coordination broke down. When the balance tips, things go from slow to fast real fast."

Ingolf gave a grunt and a nod, the sort you did when somebody said something you knew was true by experience. Rudi looked at him.

"Yeah, the general's right. It's like fighting one-on-one with someone who's about as good as you are; you know how that is."

Rudi made a gesture of acceptance. "Back and forth until someone makes a mistake . . . and they get hurt and then they can't recover and then it's all over but the last strike?"

"Yeah, that's about it, on a bigger scale. If you don't have a margin for error, error kills you."

Everyone else in his group signaled agreement. None of them had fought in a real war except Ingolf, but they'd all been in skirmishes and fights on a more personal level.

"Will you help them now, Larry?" Cecile said, surprising Rudi a little; she'd been very quiet during most of the dinner, and he'd pegged her as the type who did her consulting in private. "I *told* you we should have intervened last year."

"Yeah, I will," Thurston said absently, looking up at the ceiling. "I'd have done it earlier, if they hadn't been so damned *stubborn*."

"Stubborn as you, Dad?" Frederick Thurston said.

"Just about. I should have softened my terms and they should have realized how deep the shit they were in was earlier. But if I hit the Prophet's men *now*, they'll still be weakened from taking out New Deseret and they won't have had a chance to consolidate. If we get lucky, we might be able to break them and take Montana and Wyoming too. And this assassination thing will keep the politics simple, thank God. They screwed up and I'm going to . . . ah, take advantage of it."

Then his eyes snapped back to the present. "But it's going to be a pain in the ass for you people. I regret that—I owe you seriously—but there's nothing I can do about it. I do suggest you stick around Boise for at least a little while, to see who jumps where. I'll let you have the best intelligence I can on developments."

The conversation went general after that; the Thurstons saw them to the door later. The big central enclosure of the citadel was only half-darkened; there were crescents burning on the towers around it, and gaslights around the perimeter, and guards walking their rounds. Still, it had the sad slightly chilly horses-and-woodsmoke smell of nighttime in a fortress, and it was easy enough to halt everyone in a place where it was impossible to be overheard.

"Something smells," Rudi said bluntly.

Nobody looked like they disagreed. "That was the most counter-productive assassination attempt I've ever seen or heard of," Odard said thoughtfully.

"Guaranteed to produce just the wrong results if anything went pear-shaped," Edain agreed. "So unless these Cutter people are stupid—"

"They aren't," Ingolf said flatly.

"By no means," Father Ignatius said. "Wicked, and I would say almost worshippers of evil in some senses, but extremely efficiently so for the most part."

"Then there's something crooked going on," one of the twins said. "Someone's angling for the Boromir Award."

"By which you mean treachery, in the common tongue," Mathilda said with heavy patience. "Is it really important to us? We're just passing through."

"We want to keep *alive* while we pass through, or we'll be staying—six feet under," Ritva said.

"There is that," Rudi said. "They were trying to kill *us*, too. And the assassination . . . it would probably have worked if we weren't there. But then what would they have gained, with Thurston and his sons dead? They aren't his heirs anyway, are they?"

"No," Father Ignatius said. "There's a vice president, Colonel Moore, who is an old friend of the general's and beyond suspicion. And a competent man."

"We need to get a bit of a grip on what's going on here," Rudi said. "Since we're guests . . . or at least it wouldn't be the wisest thing to leave right now, as it were."

CHAPTER NINETEEN

The practice ground occupied the clear space just inside the city wall, paved with blocks of asphalt cut from old roads. It was mostly deserted with sunset only a half hour off. Mostly . . .

Edain unstrung his bow and held out his hand. Six of his arrows were neatly grouped in the bull's-eye and one more had been pushed three inches out by a backdraft; none of the others had come close to matching that. The sight made him a little nostalgic; it had been years since he did much shooting at a beginner's target like that.

"Here!" the Boisean cavalryman who'd proposed the match said, and slapped green bills into his hand.

He did it hard enough to sting, if Edain's hand hadn't been covered with calluses as thick as his own. As it was, there was a dull *thock* sound.

"Many thanks," Edain said, as several of his comrades followed suit. "And sure, anytime you feel like shooting a few again . . ."

Garbh rose and came over, looking up in his face and wagging her tail slightly because she sensed his enjoyment. He'd been raised to know the value of a dollar, mostly because it represented sweat and sore muscles, often his own, and partly because even near Dun Juniper clansfolk didn't use coined money much, still less the paper kind. Bets like this were just for fun, though; found money you could waste without being guilty about it, like a prize for winning a game at a festival.

The infantrymen who'd been watching laughed, slapping one another on the back, which produced a series of *tonk* sounds as hard palms hit steel armor; then they started collecting *their* bets from the horsemen of the cavalry troop who'd shot against him, or who'd bet on those who did. It had been natural enough to fall in with them; they were all conscripts doing their term of service, and close enough to his own age.

Their grins were the reverse of the cavalry's sulks. The remaining cavalry*woman* smiled, though; she was Rosita Gonzales, the sergeant who'd greeted them back on the road. And *she'd* seen him shoot before, for real, at that.

"Notice *I* wasn't putting any money on you losing," she said.

"Why am I not surprised, Rosita?" he said, batting his eyelashes theatrically. "Would a lady as brave, beautiful and skilled as yourself be anything but wise? Now, if I could spend some of these fine winnings on a drink for the both of us, that would set the flower crown of spring upon my happiness, so it would."

She snorted laughter. "Yeah, try to butter me up. I'm too old for what you've got in mind, kid! Or you're too young for me."

"Now, why would you be thinking I had something in mind?" he said.

" 'Cause I know guys your age are hard-ons with legs and you *always* have something in mind."

"Not more than every thirty heartbeats or so. And you're *not* too old for anything you choose," he said.

Sincerely, since she was short of thirty and comely if you liked women wiry and dark and muscular. Which he did; being nineteen, he liked them almost any way except elderly or unripe or wolverine-trap ugly.

"Keep smiling like that and I'll lose my resolve to be good, so I'm off." She paused to rumple Garbh's ears, which the mastiff permitted, having been introduced. "See you later."

Edain shook his head and put the folded bills in his sporran, watching her depart—or at least the part working in her rather tight black leather riding breeches—and sighed.

"Christ, man, how'd you get Iron-ass Gonzales so friendly?" one of the foot soldiers said.

"Not iron, I'd say; just pleasantly squeezable, from the look of things," he said, strolling over to retrieve his arrows. "Not that I've had the opportunity to test the notion, alas."

"Ah, I always thought she liked girls. Maybe it's your *skirt* she likes."

"Which would show good taste," Edain said. "For it's true I like both the wearing of the kilts and the kissing of the girls myself."

Which got him more laughs; he snorted and slid the unstrung longbow into the carrying loops.

"No, it's me winsome charm and the archery that wins the ladies, and I don't doubt it'll work here in the big city too."

"You wish. It's pretty good duty otherwise, being stationed here in the capital, but with all the goddamned army swinging dicks around you can't get laid without paying for it, and even *that's* expensive as fucking—you know what I mean—hell. Two-fifty a day and your keep is good money out in the sticks, someplace like Lewiston, but it doesn't go too far here in Boise."

There were half a dozen of the soldiers, and they were all friendly now.

Now that I've earned them all a week's pay or more, he thought.

Most of them came from little farms and villages that didn't sound all that much different from Dun Fairfax, if you allowed for the fact that they were Christians of various sorts—Protestants and Catholics and Mormons, he thought, though he wasn't altogether clear on the differences and none of them seemed to be much bent out of shape about it either. He'd been nervous and out of place in General Thurston's house, but these lads he understood right off.

"Thanks for the tip on the bets," one of them said; he was a towhead named John Gottberg, and the file closer, which meant roughly a corporal. "I heard about the thing where you and your bossman saved the president's life, but most of those donkey dongs were just in from road patrol and hadn't got the word."

He extended his hand towards Garbh—cautiously, which wise men did, with a dog who weighed a hundred and twenty pounds and came up above their waist.

"Friend!" Edain said.

She sniffed politely but didn't radiate anything beyond tolerance.

"She's a bit of a one-man dog," Edain said.

"Best kind. Hunting dog?"

"Hunting, guard . . . raised her from a pup, that I did."

"Nice to see the burro bangers taken down a bit," said a freckle-faced redhead called Kit Mullins, returning to the discomfiture of the cavalry. "Fuckers think they're hot shit 'cause they come from ranches and ride around. We're the backbone of the army, by God. It's us who stand and take it and dish it out when the metal hits the meat."

That made the first one thoughtful: "Maybe Iron-ass really likes your looks; she didn't tell *them*."

"And maybe she made a bit on side bets," another said.

Edain shook his head. "It's Rudi she'd really like to meet. The Chief has a way with the girls and that's a fact."

"So, this guy Rudi you're traveling with, he's your king or something out west? They say you've got kings and knights and weird shit like that out there."

"No, he's the Chief's tanist," Edain said. "Ummm . . . by Chief I mean the head of the clan, the Mackenzie herself herself. She presides over the Clan, and he's her . . . understudy."

"So it's *like* a king, or what do they call it, a crowned prince?"

"Not in the least! The Chief's the Chief because the clan assembled hailed her—many's the time over the years—at the Beltane festival. And we hailed Rudi, too, as tanist, just now. And we'll hail him as Chief too, when his mother dies or steps down, free and open for all to see, and any benighted ijeet who wants turnips and cowpats thrown at him could stand up and ask for the same."

"So hailing, *that's* like an election?"

"A bit. Everyone makes speeches and we all argue ourselves blue and we have a show of hands. And then there's games and a lovely great feed, and singing and dancing and music and drinking and sometimes a bit of a punch-up on the sidelines."

"Sounds like quite a party!"

"It is that. It's supposed to be very Celtic, which is what they called clansfolk in the old days. And Beltane bowers . . . the girls like the blossoms. Puts them in the mood to worship the Goddess, as it were. And speaking of parties, what do you say to a few beers?"

"Hey, mostly, 'Hello, my dear beer!' " Gottberg said.

Edain checked the fletching of the last arrow as he slid it back into the quiver. He caught the glances the squad gave one another, and this time kept his look of innocent friendliness without letting the grin show. They *were* a lot like the lads back home, which meant they were always ready to put one over on an outsider, friendly or not.

"What do you say we do a little pila practice?" Gottberg went on, elaborately casual. "And low man buys the first two rounds? It's not too different from throwing a hunting spear. . . . I'll bet you use hunting spears sometimes. . . ."

"Oh, sometimes, but mostly bows. I'm not much with spears . . . I wouldn't turn down a sporting bet with you lads, though."

They walked over to the pila targets, shapes of tight-rolled matting on wooden posts. Those at least resembled men with shields, which was good. He'd never yet fought an enemy or hunted a beast who was round and colored white and red in concentric circles. They weren't very far away—only about twenty yards—but then the heavy javelins were short-range weapons. The pila were piled in neat tripods with the big oval shields stacked against them and the helmets hung by the chinstraps. The young men put the helmets on and clipped their cheek pieces in place before picking up the shields and javelins.

Good, Edain thought. *Practice the way you're going to do it for real, or as close as you can.*

Thoughts like that always sounded a bit like his father's voice.

"Two throws each," the file closer said. "Kit, get a couple of spares for Eddie here."

It took a moment for Edain to realize he was an Eddie, locally. While he struggled with the thought, the Boisean noncom took a step forward, shield up. The spear went back and then *forward* in a long blurred arch. There was a *thunk!* as it sank through the center of the target and into the wooden pole within. The second matched it, a handbreadth lower down. Both sank as the long iron shanks behind their points bent.

"Now that's clever," Edain said. "So they can't throw them back at you, eh?"

The file closer nodded. "And if it goes into a shield, whoever's holding it has to throw it away or spend time trying to pull the pila out. You want to go next?"

"Oh, I'll wait and see how the rest of your lads do," Edain said innocently.

Or he thought it was innocently; Gottberg was a little older than the rest of his file, a bit older than Edain himself, and shrewd.

Most of them were *nearly* as good as their corporal. When they'd finished the twelve throws, only four spears had missed or glanced off, and most of the ones that hit were solidly planted through the wicker or in the central pole. The Boise soldiers knew their business, and they had the strong limber bodies of well-fed young men who'd worked and trained hard all their lives.

They'd most likely all inherited keen eyes and steady hands too; even in fortunate areas like this, not many weaklings had lived through the Change and its aftermath to breed more of their kind.

I can't lose either way, Edain thought. *If I'm last man, I buy them more beer and they get talkative. If I'm not, I get more respect . . . and they'll be more likely to speak freely, eh? And I hate to lose; so may Cernunnos guide my hand!*

He hefted the spear he'd been handed, which had a much-dinted shaft and an iron shank that looked as if it had been straightened any number of times. It was a practice weapon; well balanced, but probably a little off center. And it was as heavy as a battle spear, or nearly, which was *not* meant to be thrown.

"Ground and center, ground and center," he murmured to himself.

Edain was wearing his brigandine, which was fair, but that was a hair less hampering than the cuirass of steel bands and hoops that was their equivalent. He didn't use the solid face-front step-and-throw method the local men did; that was designed for use with a great twenty-pound shield in your left hand to balance you. Instead he took a half sideways skip forward and put all his body into it with a snapping twist. Throwing something this heavy that far took real effort; his breath hissed out between clenched teeth.

Good!

The throw had the smooth heavy-to-light *flow* that said it was going where it should as it left his hand. It arched higher than the others had . . . and then his lips moved in a silent curse as it wobbled in flight.

Thunk.

The long pyramidal point of the spear clipped a little twist of osier from the wicker figure's notional head as it went by, and then banged into the asphalt a half dozen yards farther on.

"Not bad," Gottberg said, taking off his helmet and scratching vigorously. "Most newbies can't even get a pila to go that far."

The redhead named Kit looked at him narrowly; he'd be the one buying the first two rounds if Edain wasn't. "I thought you said you only used bows?"

"No, I said I *mostly* used bows," Edain said; grinning. "Sometimes we use spears—hunting boar in thick country, when you want something heavy at close range. Aren't you glad I didn't put money on it, eh?"

Several of the others laughed. Kit smiled, if a little sourly. "Here," he said. "Try this one—it didn't bend and it's better than those old clunkers from the practice bin."

Edain caught the tossed spear with a smack of palm on wood. It *was* a better weapon; he could feel it in the swoop and sway as his arm rocked back under the impact. He made a half bow.

"*Nár laga Ardwinna do lámh,*" he said formally.

He didn't speak the old language—only a few scholars did, and Rudi and his mother and his sisters Fiorbhinn and Maude, of course—but he'd learned a few of the Chief's sayings, as most people in the Clan did.

"May the Huntress never weaken your hand," he repeated in English.

Breathe in, breathe out, and . . . throw.

Shunk.

This time he speared the target through the inner edge of the shield. Not the best throw—just good enough to win him next-to-last place.

Kit sighed. Edain held out his hand. "We're low men on the pole, so let's split those first two rounds," he said.

The redhead shook the outstretched hand. That won him more acceptance than he'd hoped for. The file shed and racked their armor at the gatehouse barracks. Edain did the same with his brigandine and bow and quiver, though it made him feel a bit naked so far from home and among strangers.

"Let's get that beer," Gottberg said. "And something to eat."

"They don't feed you?" Edain asked, surprised. A lord usually did, at least keeping table for his full-time warriors.

"Sorta-kinda." Kit grinned. "It's on the list of Soldier's Superstitions."

At Edain's raised brow he went on: "We all get it on a printed sheet when we're called up, with the rest of the paperwork. It's sort of a list of things soldiers believe. Like, 'It is very unlucky to get a spear in the guts on a Friday.' "

Gottberg went on: "The one he's thinking of is, 'When the sun rises in the east, it is a sign that we shall have stew for dinner.' "

"Mystery meat stews with desecrated vegetables. And they *say* the stuff with it is beer. I say the quartermaster's horse has something bad wrong with its kidneys."

"We'll go to the Fife and Drum instead. That's where a lot of guys go off duty. It's a bit pricey but not too bad and it's all fighting men."

"I'm not much of one for brawling in taverns."

"Oh, they don't brawl there. Because—"

* * *

The city of Boise was an orderly, law-abiding place, like the rest of the United States governed from there. People mostly liked it that way, and those who didn't tended to meet the National Police and then either dance the hempen hornpipe on air or spend many sad and stressful years working under extremely unsympathetic management in the National Infrastructure Reconstruction Battalions.

The Fife and Drum tavern was orderly and law-abiding too, usually, but the National Police didn't go there. Nor did the military police, nor did officers, and it wasn't a place where a civilian would last long either.

The loud raucous sawdust-floored atmosphere reminded Edain of some places he'd seen in Corvallis, student hangouts around the university. The smell was the same—gaslights, cooking food, beer. There was a little more sweat, and the voices were harder, somehow, and there were a lot of battered weapons and hacked shields on the walls, down to one made from a pre-Change traffic sign with a spear that looked like a kitchen knife on a stick beside it.

It was more orderly than those Corvallan pubs, though; off along one wall were a series of booths in which most of the patrons were scarred middle-aged men with quiet gimlet eyes. Some of them were smoking pipes or cigarettes, or chewing wads of tobacco, habits that were nearly extinct elsewhere.

Young soldiers who wanted to fight and break things went to other places, establishments where noncoms didn't go either. They came here when they didn't want their dinners dropped into their laps by the arrival of flying bodies.

"He's all right," Gottberg announced to the room, and the stares at Edain's kilt and general foreignness turned less hostile; Garbh's hair lay back down on her shoulders. "And he's with us. And he's one of the guys that saved the boss."

"Is that Sergeant-major Anderson over there?" Edain said with interest as they grabbed a table.

It was big enough for everyone if you didn't mind a little jostling; Garbh lay down at his feet, too disciplined to wander, but letting her nostrils wrinkle with the fascinating mix of scents.

"Yeah, and you don't stare at him. He's *Sergeant-major Anderson*. The top NCO. That makes him a lot more important than most officers."

"Most officers lower than major," Kit said. "Or maybe colonel."

"Oh, I don't know," Gottberg said. "Lieutenants have their uses."

"Yeah, they're useful when it comes to stopping a spear that might've hit someone who works for their living."

"Oh, I dunno," Gottberg repeated thoughtfully. "I mean, the boss's kids, they're both pretty useful. Only what you'd expect, though." ·

A waitress came out with glasses and big pitchers of beer. Edain sampled his.

"Not bad," he said. "Nice and crisp. A little lighter than they brew it at Dun Juniper, where you eat it with a spoon, but well hopped."

"Hey, traveling the way you do, you must get to see a lot of different types of booze," Kit said enthusiastically.

"Some. More often, it's many different types of bad water."

"Tell me," Gottberg replied. He cast an eye at some of his men. "You can get the galloping shits that way . . . unless you're careful about purifying the water. *Right?*"

"Ah, hell, Corp, we never have to do that back home."

"And back home your mama still holds your cock while you pee, right? Jesus, what is this, an army or a nursery school?"

"You're starting to sound like Sergeant-major Anderson, Corp."

"Nah," Gottberg said, but he looked cautiously over his shoulder when he did it. "You haven't heard me talk about how great things were in the *old* army, have you? You know, the *real* US Army, where they had *real* soldiers, with *guns*."

The young men all laughed, a bit uneasily. The food came out—starting with corn on the cob, a rare treat in the Clan's territories, where maize grew reluctantly. Spareribs in hot sauce followed it, and grilled pork chops with sage and onion stuffing, mounds of fried potatoes, steamed cabbage and carrots, brown bread and butter; plain food and plenty of it, and more beer along with it. Everyone said their varieties of grace—including one that simply went, "Good God, good meat: Good God, let's eat!"—and then all of them dug in with thoughtless voracity.

"Ah, that's better than I've had in a while," Edain said, pushing back his plate and wiping his mouth. "Saving your top man's own table, and that was seasoned with nervousness, for me."

Crackling and crunching and slobbering came from under the table, where Garbh enjoyed the bones; her jaws were more than strong enough to crunch them like stalks of celery, except that they had roast marrow in the center, which explained the ecstatic slurping sounds.

"Apple pie and ice cream all round," Gottberg went on to the plain middle-aged waitress. "Hell, Judy, bring the bucket, and make it chocolate!"

Her brows went up. "You boys just win a lottery, or sack the Prophet's palace in Corwin, or what?"

"Nah, we get *him* in a month or two, and I'll buy a plow team with my share. We won a bet today. Found money and it's burning a hole in my pocket."

More serious work with fork and spoon followed. The talk turned to politics; Edain kept mostly quiet but kept his ears pricked.

"So we replace those useless old farts with another bunch of old farts just a bit younger," Kit said. "Hell with it. Why do we need 'em? And who's going to run against the boss for president? That would be like trying to take God Almighty's job."

That brought a laugh, but one soldier went on seriously: "Well, God bless him, but the boss *isn't* going to be around forever. I mean, you wouldn't know it the way he keeps up in the field, but he's an old man too—nearly sixty. I mean, sixty . . . how many people do you know last much past sixty?"

The hard young faces suddenly went a little uncertain. Edain recognized the feeling; people got the same way back home, thinking of what Clan Mackenzie would do without *the* Mackenzie. She was the Goddess-on-Earth, the one who'd brought their parents or their grandparents alive through the Change and given their world its shape and meaning.

Still, they had Rudi ready to take over the job. . . .

"We should elect him a new vice president, a younger guy. The boss can have the top job as long as he wants . . . understand, I've got nothing against Colonel Moore, but . . ."

"I figure he's OK, but he's as old as the boss. We should elect Captain Martin vice president," Gottberg said firmly, scooping more of the walnut-studded ice cream onto his plate.

It took Edain a moment to remember the ruler of Boise's eldest son; they must mean Martin Thurston. Who was about Rudi's age or a little more, come to think of it.

Gottberg went on: "That way if . . . well, you know . . . it'll be like the boss wasn't really *gone*."

"Yeah," Kit said. His eyes turned a little hooded. "I remember my dad telling me about how the boss found him and Mom and some others hiding out in an old warehouse near Nampa—this was just after the plague, you know, when it all went to hell?—and he said, 'Come with me if you want to live,' and they did. And they got a crop planted in time."

One of the rest of the squad nodded. "And if we pick Captain Martin, then when the boss *is* gone, we'll have someone closer to our age in charge. Christ, I get so fucking *sick* of those old geezers who never shut up about things before the Change. It doesn't *mean* anything! I'm not talking about the boss, of course. Just the rest of them. Like *my* old man."

"Yeah," Gottberg said. "If I have to hear another story about how wonderful it was to sell, what did they call 'em, elstronics, for a living I'm gonna puke. Besides . . . when I get out of the army, I'm going home and then when my father's ready I'll take over the farm. I know that ground—know it through my hands and feet, know what every inch of it can do. I'm the oldest son, so I'll get it when Dad wants to sit by the stove and rest; that's fair, that's right. I figure it's the same with the country—why not?"

Edain ventured a comment: "This Captain Martin of yours, he's had his hands on the plow handles, then?"

Gottberg nodded. "I figure Captain Martin's got to know the Chief's job the same way I know our farm. It's not like he's some goof-off; he's been doing jobs for his dad for years now, running a company in the sixth, helping start new villages—he talked the folks up north in Moscow into rejoining the country, too, the way I hear it, even if he was just in charge of the escort on paper."

"Yeah, that's true," Kit said. "And Martin Thurston's . . . he *understands*, you know? Nothing against the boss, but sometimes he doesn't think like us. I've heard Captain Martin talk and I've talked to guys in the sixth regiment. They say you can always go to him with a problem and he'll see you right—he'll stand by a friend no matter what. And he's a young guy, like Joe says, he's got his pecker up, he's got big plans for the country. Time to do something new, like his dad did when *he* was young."

"You'll hail him tanist, then?" Edain asked. "Vice president, I mean."

"Well, there's some bullshit rules about it," Kit said. "I don't see why we've always got to get our panties in a twist 'cause of something written way over on the other side of the world back when."

Gottberg put down his spoon, his blue eyes narrowing. "Fuckin'-A. And those Cutter loonies from Corwin, they tried to kill him—snuck killers into the guard detail! Kill him *and* the boss and his brother too! I've got nothing against Colonel Moore, but he's even older than the boss, like you say. If those scumbags hadn't been shot in time, we wouldn't have anything of the boss left."

That brought a growl all along the table. Men sitting at others close enough to hear nodded; a couple of them gave Edain a thumbs-up gesture, probably having heard who it was who saved their ruler.

Rudi will be interested to hear this, Edain thought.

Politics lost its charm; someone began to sing. The Boise men didn't have as much training as so many clansfolk would, and it was odd to sing without women's voices, but they had some catchy tunes.

They liked "March of Cambreath," and he did it twice so they could get the words; the "How many of them can we make die?" chorus was really popular. Then they started in on their own war songs. Soon the whole room was hammering mugs and fists on the tables and bellowing:

> *Yanks to the charge! cried Thurston*
> *The foe begins to yield!*
> *Strike—for hearth and nation*
> *Strike—for the Eagle shield!*
> *Let no man stop to plunder*

But slay, and slay, and slay,
The God who helped our fathers
Fights by our side today!

Edain turned down an invitation to follow them to a *sporting house*, whatever that was. He didn't know what the conversation had meant, not wholly, but it did give him a bit of a feeling for the place, and Rudi was better than he at putting the bits and pieces together.

* * *

"Yeah, that toadsticker you use is dangerous one-on-one," Martin Thurston said. "As long as you've got room to give ground."

Rudi nodded and settled back in the big chair; he felt loose and relaxed after the sparring and the shower. The officer's mess of Boise's citadel was a comfortable place, with leather furniture and good paneling, and a discreet bar. It also stood on the sixth floor of an old high-rise, the Williams Office Building, built into the new citadel wall, which gave it a magnificent view of the state capitol—national capitol, according to the residents—when the heavy steel shutters with their arrow slits were drawn back.

There were a few other officers and their guests there, but Martin and Juliet Thurston were getting a deference that was just a *shade* more than the man's official rank would account for. Particularly from the younger men.

"That saber *you* used is fairly nimble, too," Rudi said. "You gave me a few uncomfortable moments, if you know what I mean. A more subtle weapon than the shete, I would say."

"Just plain and simple better . . . as long as you're not trying to clear brush with it. Shetes are so point-heavy all you can really do is make like a woodchopper. The easterners dote on the damn things, though, I suppose because their dads used the original-article machetes to get through the Change and the dying time."

"I've a man in our company from the east who uses a shete very well."

"Vogeler? The tall fella? He looks like things would stay down if he hit them with a club, much less any sort of sword."

They grinned at each other, two big men who'd taken each other's measure with the tools of their deadly trade.

Though I have less sense of the man than I would expect, Rudi thought, sipping again at his drink. *Usually you get a feel for the mind in the head when you test the sword in the hand.*

His foster father, Nigel, said that it was hard to lie with a sword.

"Yes, he's got wrists like a bear, anyway," he went on aloud. "Even so, the shete is slow."

"The saber's faster," Martin agreed. "But it's a cavalry weapon. Not suitable for our infantry tactics . . . and speaking of cavalry, do you have any stallions out of that mare you ride? I'd pay gold for one of them in our stud."

"I can believe it, sure. Unfortunately young Ahearn is in stallion heaven back home, improving the breed throughout the Willamette Valley. And outside the Clan's territories, it's often enough I'm paid in gold indeed."

He raised a brow. "Which makes me sort of an equine pimp, I suppose. . . ."

The young Thurstons joined in the laugh, before Martin went on: "Pity. That mare's the best piece of horseflesh I've ever seen . . . well, we depend mostly on our infantry, and short swords are our weapon of choice for the foot. Though in a one-on-one duel, I'd still take a longer blade. But for fighting in ranks . . ."

"I know the short blade's dangerous, close in," Rudi said. "Many of my people use them. A line of them, with those big great shields of yours, that would be more dangerous than is comfortable to contemplate."

"Iron discipline and the short sword, that's what makes good heavy infantry," Martin replied. "In fact—"

"Oh, God, honey, you're not going to go into the glory-of-the-legions thing again, are you?" his wife said.

"Sorry, darling," the young man said with a quick smile.

Juliet Thurston was . . . the word *sleek* came to Rudi's mind. Partly that was the glow of early pregnancy—about four months along, he thought—but most of it was a general catlike smoothness, not least in her long blond hair, and the way she curled into the red leather of the couch. She was pretty otherwise, too, long-limbed and well curved, with an oval face framing bright blue eyes. They seemed guileless.

And they're not, sure, Rudi told himself.

The mess steward came by; she chose a fruit drink of some sort; Rudi and her husband took another whiskey-and-water each. He took a sip. It was good, with a smooth burnished taste he wasn't used to, probably from something else besides barley in the malt.

"Tell me about your mother," Juliet said. "Judging by the little we hear from the far West, she must be quite a lady."

"She is that!" Rudi said enthusiastically.

And I miss her, he thought. *I miss everyone.*

"She's elected, you say?" Martin asked.

"Hailed, every Beltane," Rudi said. "I suppose someone else could stand and ask for it at the same time, but there wouldn't be much point, and someone might throw things . . . not sharp or metallic or *pointy* things, but even so . . . though now and then a Jack-in-the-green does."

"Jack?" Juliet said.

"Sort of a licensed fool . . . one of the merrier parts of our religion. A Jack does outrageous things and it doesn't count."

"She didn't mind you standing for . . . what did you call it? Tanner?" Juliet said.

"Tanist," Rudi said, noting a quick glance between the two. "Much like your vice president, I think."

"Sensible," Martin said. A smile: "Though perhaps sending you haring off across the country in the middle of a war isn't."

Rudi shrugged. "It's necessary."

Juliet sighed. "I wish we didn't have to fight the Corwinites," she said. "But we do."

"Since they tried to kill me and Frederick and Dad, yeah," Martin said dryly. "But you're right, honey, that's going to be hard. And not just the fighting. The reports are there's a great big mob of refugees headed this way."

"I hope it won't interfere with mustering your war levy . . . no, it's *mobilization* you call it, isn't it?" Rudi said.

Martin nodded crisply. "You'll find that *nothing* can interfere with our mobilization," he said proudly. "In fact, we're making arrangements for the refugees to help with the harvest, while our reservists are under arms. Speaking of which, I should get going."

"Don't go," Juliet said after her husband had shaken Rudi's hand and walked briskly out. "You were going to tell me about your mother."

* * *

"Fascinating," Father Ignatius said sincerely.

He absently wiped the sweat from his forehead; the summer morning was warm.

"How many cubic feet of hydrogen, did you say?" he went on.

"Couple of hundred thousand," the engineer replied. "That's not counting the central hot-air ballonet that we use to help with altitude control."

The *Curtis LeMay* was nearly three hundred feet long, crowding the arched sheet-metal expanse of the hangar, but nearly all of that was the great orca-shaped gasbag—from bluntly pointed prow through swelling midsection to the cruciform stabilizer fins at the rear.

The glider and airship field was well north of Boise proper, though it had probably been suburbs before the Change, and the land around showed the snags of burnt-out ruins and some trees still living to mark the sites of gardens.

Tawny hills rose northward, fading into blue distance as they climbed towards the forested mountains, with a crest line at about eight thousand feet. An occasional ranch house speckled them. Just south was *still* a suburb, or at least the outside-the-wall residences of wealthy men, often surrounded by barriers of barbed wire or concrete blocks, with gardens and stables around the big houses within.

The field itself had an X of runways as well, and a long ski-ramp launching mechanism with counterweights and hydraulic rams that could snap gliders into the air to catch the updraft over the hills. The winged craft were kept in a series of hangars salvaged from the old municipal airport; a larger one housed the airship and several uninflated balloons. There was a smell of metal and sharp acidic chemicals and paint and shellac, as well as the more usual scents of people and horses and vegetation.

"Do you find that the power-to-weight ratio is sufficient, Major Hanks?" the monk asked.

The military engineer looked at him. "You are an unusual young fella," he said.

The Boisean was in his late forties himself, lean and with a crew cut of stiff, grizzled brown hair. Ignatius spread his hands.

"I received a classical education . . . the pre-Change sciences, or at least some of them," he said.

"Wish more did," Hanks said. "The young guys I get off the farm nowadays, you just can't convince some of them machinery can't be treated like a horse. I guess it comes of growing up without anything more complicated than their mom's sausage grinder."

An orderly came up and gave them both cups of hot herb tea—the stove was *well* away from this area. Things didn't explode the way they had once, but that didn't mean hydrogen wouldn't burn.

A lot of it catching all at once would burn very hot and very fast.

There were vats alongside the walls of the blimp hangar, where zinc shavings and sulfuric acid combined to generate the lifting gas as needed. Technicians were uncoupling the hoses that ran from those to the gasbag as he watched, coiling them away neatly. Others pulled ropes to open broad slabs of the roof, to make sure none of the gas lingered inside.

Everything about the air base was neat, almost fanatically so, the grounds swept, every piece of wood painted and every metal part polished or oiled or enameled. Ignatius profoundly approved, as a soldier and an engineer and a monastic as well. Physical things were like time—both belonged ultimately to God; sloth and waste were a form of stealing from Him.

"Well, we've got twelve pedal sets on either side," Hanks said, returning to the cleric's question and pointing upward. "Set up recliner-fashion, that gives you maximum output."

Ignatius nodded, following the finger. The airship had an aluminum-truss keel along the bottom of the sharklike gasbag; that made it semirigid. The gondola below was covered in thin doped fabric, for streamlining, but enough panels were unlaced for maintenance that he could see the spiderweb scantiness of the interior structure as technicians made their final checks and fastened the sheets once again. Idle now, a twelve-foot propeller stood at the rear, behind a long wedge of rudder.

"The rudder is worked from a wheel at the prow of the gondola. She carries twenty-four pedalers, and another six reliefs who act as the deck crew—you can see their positions at the rear there, like a semicircle—plus the captain and second in command."

Ignatius smiled to himself. Hanks had *not* answered the question. The engineer caught the smile and shrugged.

"Well, in a dead calm, they can get her up to about the speed of a trotting horse."

"And against the wind?"

The engineer shrugged again, and smiled himself, a little bitterly. "You go up or down trying to find a wind going in the right direction. Or anchor and wait it out. Trying to fight a breeze in this thing is like trying to hammer a nail through a board."

Ignatius raised his brows. "Not very difficult, you mean?"

"Only the nail's made out of candle wax."

They shared a chuckle, and Hanks went on: "That's the downside. The upside is that you can stay aloft a lot longer than a glider can. Less speed and control than a glider, but a hell of a lot more than an ordinary balloon. If only we had a goddamned *engine* . . ."

Ignatius nodded. He recognized the engineer's bitterness without sharing it. The man had grown up before the Change, and like many such—particularly those who'd worked much with machines—he *resented* the limitations of the new world with a savage passion.

God must have His reasons for it, Ignatius thought. *Though it would have been interesting to have such possibilities open. . . .*

He didn't voice the thought; it would be futile, and would serve only to further disturb the middle-aged engineer's soul. Instead he asked a technical question about the gearing. Hanks brightened, and they talked ratios and aspects and hollow-cast driveshafts for a few happy moments.

Outside an observer keeping an eye on the wind sock shouted, "Clear!"

Hanks strode away, and Ignatius stepped back politely; the ungainly craft had to be brought out quickly, lest a cross-wind catch it and smash it up against the edge of the big hangar's doors. The ground crew were all hefty-looking young men, and they tallied onto the long metal-tube skids beneath the gondola and simply walked the craft out into the open by main force, before hooking a long cable onto a ring at the front of the gondola. It stood bobbing at head height as they tallied on and pulled until the *LeMay*'s nose was close to the base of a tall metal pole.

"Crew aboard!" Hanks shouted.

Most of the crew were women, which surprised the monk for a moment. Then he took a long look at their builds underneath the gray overalls as they scrambled up the rope ladders. Every one of them was slender and wiry enough to be assembled out of steel cables and springs.

Ah, he thought to himself. *Maximum leg strength with minimum overall weight per pound of leg muscle. This is an instance in which a female's relative lack of upper-body mass is an advantage rather than a hindrance. Interesting.*

Also very interesting to watch; he'd sworn celibacy, but found inner disinterest much more difficult. He sighed and closed his eyes for a second, praying for strength.

"You interested in a ride, padre?" Hanks called.

"Thank you!" he said eagerly. *After all, it's not as if I'm deliberately looking.*

And while he'd been aloft in balloons and gliders once or twice, he'd never been up in a powered craft. It would be like a little hint of the fabulous days of old. His grandfather had been a helicopter pilot in a place called Vietnam, and the old man had lived through the Change, lived long enough to tell stories of marvels to a young boy then named Karl Bergfried. He had never seen his grandmother, though it was her inheritance that gave the slight umber tone to his skin and the tilt to his dark eyes.

The boat-shaped open gondola dipped and swayed beneath him as he kirted up his robe and climbed carefully into it, stepping onto the aluminum treads of the central catwalk. The crewmen—crew-women—were settling into the seats and pedal sets on either side, strapping themselves in. Their positions left them facing backward, and he noticed that a few wore crucifixes. Not an ounce of spare weight otherwise, though there were clips above each position for a bow and quiver, and a bundled parachute strapped ready.

Hanks sat behind the wheel, his feet on rudder pedals, and a board with control levers and dials beside him.

"Water ballast, emergency valves, ballonet superheat and venting," he said, indicating them. "Altimeter—that's from a small airplane—airspeed indicator, rpm on the propeller shaft, main cell pressure, reserve tank pressure. We can switch the torque on the main shaft to a compressor that takes hydrogen from the lift cells and pumps it into metal tanks just above the keel. It's more economical than venting if we have time."

"Fascinating!" Ignatius said again, his eyes taking the instruments in greedily.

"No, when we hit clear-air turbulence, *that's* fascinating," Hanks said cheerfully. "So what say you strap in too, eh, padre?"

There was a seat on the other side; Ignatius took the suggestion. Hanks turned his head.

"Bosun, drop keel weights three through fifteen!"

The noncom went down the walkway, stopping at every second square of flooring to raise it and flip something underneath. Solid thumps sounded from underneath the gondola, and the blimp bobbled very slowly upward until it hung at twice a man's height from the ground.

"Lead ballast," Hank explained. "It counterbalances our fixed weight. We drop some of 'em at the beginning to set basic load for the trip, so we've got neutral buoyancy at about ground level. The rest are for emergencies, and the side ballast—"

He pointed to aluminum water tanks along the rail.

"—is for ordinary maneuvering. We try to avoid valving gas or dropping ballast as long as we can—hydrogen isn't cheap."

Then, louder: "On superheat!"

One of the crew fiddled with something amidships. There was a thump and a muffled roar as a compressed-gas burner went on. That made him itch a little, until he reflected that if it leaked at all, hydrogen leaked *up*.

And only a mixture with air is really dangerous, he told himself stoutly. *And I do have this parachute.*

The hot air went up a tube into the central body of the gasbag above. As the hot-air ballonet expanded the outer skin creaked a little inside its netting. A sensation of *lightness* put a grin on Ignatius's usually solemn face; the ground was beginning to slide away beneath them. The anchor cable rose off the ground and ran up the mooring pole; then it dropped away as Hanks pulled a lever.

"All ahead full!"

"All ahead full!" the bosun cried, in an alto roar.

There was a mass grunt as the crew pushed at the pedals, fighting the inertia of the system—it was as light as possible, but Ignatius did a quick mental calculation and realized that it must still mass a fair bit in absolute terms. The big propeller at the rear of the gondola started to turn, slowly at first and then shifting into a flickering circular blur. Wicker and rope creaked and metal complained as the thrust surged through gondola and keel and pushed the gasbag against the resisting air.

"We're under way!" Ignatius said in delight, feeling the slight but definite force pressing him backward in his seat, and suppressing an impulse to bounce up and down in it.

It was a little like being in a pedal car on a railroad, though the feeling was statelier than that alarmingly fast mode of transport. Buildings sank away to toy size below him, and people to scarcely more than dolls—as marvelous now as the other two times he'd seen it. The air grew cooler. . . .

"Damn! Double damn fucking hell!" Hanks barked.

"What is the problem?" Ignatius asked.

"Wind's out of the east and we're going backward. But we're still rising . . . yup, that's better. We're getting some forward movement now."

The *LeMay* turned northeast, struck an updraft and soared, then curved around the city as the crew settled into a steady pumping rhythm.

Looking down, Ignatius was shocked out of his happy technical preoccupation. Roads pointed inward towards Boise from every direction, and they were crowded—crowded with columns of marching troops and baggage wagons. Sunlight glittered off spear points like morning on rippling water, and long plumes of dust rose from herds of stock driven along for provisions; wagon trains lumbered forward on rail and road with their beige canvas tilts strapped over bale and barrel.

White rows of tents were already going up in places, as regiments dug their marching camps. Cavalry patrols cantered about, tying the whole together. His lips pursed silently, and he gave a slow nod. The lack of frantic bustle in Boise itself had made him think the locals were taking their time about gathering their host.

I was wrong, he thought. Then with a slight smile: *Thank you, Lord, for a lesson in humility!*

Sometimes the harshest lessons were the most valuable; as a sage had said before the Change, in pleasure God whispered, in logic He spoke, but in pain He *shouted.*

"Yeah," Hanks said proudly, following his gaze. "If the Corwin crazies think they can fuck with us and get away with it, they can think again."

CHAPTER TWENTY

"Good-looking farming country, but too hot and dry for my taste," Edain said.

Rudi nodded silent acknowledgment, hearing the effort it took the younger man to sound casual. The Snake River plain was flat here, flat and rich with wheat and alfalfa and potatoes and orchards where the fruit swelled towards ripeness, wherever the irrigation canals from the old-time dams still stretched; silvery-gray sagebrush-filled fields had gone out of cultivation for lack of hands to work them or pumps to raise the precious fluid. Much still endured, tilled by the soldier-farmers whose earth-and-concrete walled villages dotted the land, grain turning gold under the hot sun, nearly ready for the reapers.

But the fields looked empty today, nobody at work, the livestock driven within the walls for safety or to the distant hills on the edge of sight northward. The gates of the farm-towns were tightly barred now, with families and older reservists anxiously atop the fighting platforms watching the army of the Republic march by . . . and their sons and husbands and younger brothers joining it, trickles that joined together to swell the endless river of green and brown and steel-sheen that passed, with a rumble of boots and wheels and hooves, a trail of dust and the strong smell of sweat and oil and metal.

Edain lowered his voice: "I'm a bit worried about Garbh, Chief. In a battle and all, a big one."

The big mastiff bitch looked up at her name, grinning and wagging her tail slightly, then going back to plodding in the dust.

"If it's any consolation, I don't think we're going to do any of the fighting. It'll be a spectator's position for us, like the watchers at a baseball game."

Cavalry patrols made their own trickle-plumes of dust at the limits of vision, with sometimes a blink of light off the edged iron of a lance head. A glider hovered high overhead, riding the summer thermals and occasionally heading northward to climb again on the updraft over the rugged country there; it bore Boise's USAF blazon. Nobody seemed to know if the Church Universal and Triumphant had any aerial scouts, and if they did they weren't here now.

Mounted couriers or ones on cross-country bicycles dashed up to the command party now and then. The refugees from New Deseret straggling along the sides of the road or off in the fields to either side told their own story, and had since the day's march began. Rudi felt his inwardness wince slightly as a mother sitting on the bundle that must be all her household's goods watched him pass with dull beaten blue eyes, mechanically jogging the infant that cried against her breast. Two older children sat beside her, and a white-bearded man who was probably her father slept on the hard dry ground limp with utter exhaustion.

Rudi saw his fellow clansman's eyes skimming over the refugees.

"Worried about Rebecca, too, eh?" he said—not teasing, but a real question.

"Well, we were friends," Edain agreed. "I'm sorry for all these folk, true I am, but it's different if you know someone in particular."

Another courier drew up with a spurt of gravel and dust from under his mount's hooves.

"Mr. President!" he said, saluting and pointing southeastward. "The Saints' command group is about half a mile that way, with a couple thousand troops following. They're in pretty rough shape, sir—a lot more of their civilians and a lot of wounded, and they say their rear guard pulled out of sight of Twin Falls three days ago. The enemy's snapping at their heels."

"Thank you, Corporal," Thurston said. "Please give my compliments to their commander—"

"Bishop Nystrup, sir. Civil official."

"To Bishop Nystrup, and tell him we'll be with him shortly."

Rudi saw Edain's ears prick up at the name. Ragged tent camps appeared, set up by the civilian refugees and the Red Cross from Boise, and shapeless masses of exhausted people lying where they could in pasture and fallow land. More crowded around a field hospital and the advance guard of the main Boise force, who were handing out buckets of water and big loaves of hard dark bread from wagons.

But they're not trampling the standing grain, Rudi thought with sympathetic approval. *That takes a special type of decency, it does, when you're hungry and hurt and fleeing for your life.*

Just then Edain's head came around, a swift movement like a hunting wolf's. He reined his horse aside and heeled it up into a canter, over to the field hospital, then leaned from the saddle and spoke to one of the helpers. When he came back, he was grinning, if a little lopsidedly.

"That *was* Rebecca! The Mother's hand is over her, and that's the truth!" A scowl. "They have some bad enemies, Chief. Those people aren't just hurt and hungry. Some of them . . ." He shook his head.

"Regiments . . . *halt!*" Thurston called, in a flat unmusical tone like angle iron hit with a hammer, as a dark thread grew visible on the road ahead.

The trumpets brayed, relaying the order down the long snake of men and animals that filled the old interstate for miles behind them. The marching regiments did halt, from the back of the column forward and in a ripple that brought the whole to a stop in less than a minute, without any of the collisions or stop-and-start you could have expected among ten thousand troops on foot and half as many horses and mules.

"Command group, follow me!"

They legged their horses into a canter, the flag beside the ruler of Boise flapping in the hot wind of their passage; nobody had complained at Thurston's whim of allowing the youngsters from the farthest west along, though they got the occasional glance. A group of mounted men sat their horses at the head of the troops ahead, beneath another banner—dark blue emblazoned with a golden bee. Rudi recognized the Mormon leader who'd bought the horses from Rancher Brown, looking . . .

Terrible, he thought. *And I don't think he recognizes me . . . just doesn't have the attention to spare.*

The bishop sat his horse among several other soberly clad bearded men, and a clutch of what were certainly soldiers and from their years most probably officers. They all wore olive-green uniforms and steel breastplates, mail sleeves, armguards, and round bowl helmets fronted with the golden bee. The armor was dinted and worn, and the square shields some carried were hacked and splintered, a few showing the stubs of arrows. Several wore bandages as well, some seeping red. As he watched one had to scrabble out of his saddle as his horse collapsed. The stink of dried sweat from them was powerful even by the standards of soldiers in the field, and their faces were thickly covered with sweat-runneled dust.

"Thank you . . . Mr. President," Bishop Nystrup said as Thurston drew up, his commanders and aides beside him and the golden eagle and Stars and Stripes lofting above.

He spoke humbly; and unless Rudi was wrong, it was a difficult task for a proud man.

The army behind him was still proud too, but it was beaten, even the unhurt. A ragged bristle of pikes stretched backward in clumps that were not really units, mingled with archers and crossbowmen and a single field catapult that he could see; you could sense the weary shuffle that had brought the broken companies this far. There were wagons full of wounded interspersed among those still walking, their moans and cries a soft threnody of pain below the sound of hooves and wheels on the broken gravel-patched pavement of old US 84. Supply columns from Boise were doing their best to feed them and take care of the injured.

"We'll do whatever we can," Thurston said, swinging down from the saddle and taking the man's hand as Nystrup clambered down stiffly. "And we'll do our best to get your people what you need."

"Thank you," Nystrup said again. "We've already gotten the food and medical supplies you sent, and . . ."

He fought his face to stillness. Thurston turned his own gaze aside for an instant, to let the man recover his self-command.

Nystrup swallowed. "Our rear guard has broken contact with the Corwinites, but they're close behind us."

One of the Mormon officers spoke. "We'd have had to turn and fight to keep them off the civilians within a day or two."

His eyes met Thurston's, sharing the same thought: *And been massacred to the last man.*

"Then we'd better coordinate our efforts," Thurston said, his face like brown iron.

"We're willing to consider your terms—" the bishop began again.

"My only terms are that we fight together to put down this madman," Thurston said, clapping him on the shoulder.

Startled, Nystrup blurted: "That's a change!"

Thurston shrugged. "I've made mistakes, but I try not to make them twice . . . and three times is excessive. I do ask for the military command, but we'll leave the politics for when that's been done. I intend to restore your people to their homes, and the US government won't ask for any territory—for anything that your people don't freely grant by their own unforced vote."

He spoke firmly, and loudly enough that both his own officers and the party from the east could hear him. Some of the Mormon military officers behind the bishop blinked in surprise at that, startled out of their exhausted dejection. A few looked suspicious; many glanced at one another, and there was a murmur as the words were repeated backward down the line.

Well, I've never heard a man confess a fault quite that smoothly, Rudi thought, letting one corner of his mouth quirk up. *Sure, and I'll have to make a note of that for future reference, unless the gods give me the gift of infallibility.*

And a few of the officers *behind* Thurston exchanged glances as well—doing it with a discreet flicker of eyes rather than any movement of the head.

"Let's get your wounded seen to, your troops fed, and your officers can brief me on what you've got available," Thurston said briskly. "There's a good defensive position about three miles east of here that would do nicely, and shelter these civilians until we can get them west and behind walls."

"Do you think the enemy will attack today?" Nystrup asked; his voice was calm now.

"No," Thurston said; several of the Mormon officers were shaking their heads in unconscious agreement. "Not today. But tomorrow, or the day after at the latest. They've got their peckers up."

His smile was broad and cruel. "That's the easiest time to trim them off."

* * *

"I don't like it," Rudi said quietly, as the sun came fully over the eastern horizon ahead of them.

I don't, for sure and all. Something . . . something makes me itch. Or gives me a wee bit of a chill on a summer day, and it's not just the prospect of a fight in it. A fight I don't mind, and I have the beginnings of a grudge against this Prophet fellow, don't I just, by the horns!

He stood holding Epona by the bridle a little way from Thurston's command group, behind the Boise line, his companions around him. The grumbling, rumbling clatter of white noise, voices and armor clashing and feet thudding, made it possible to speak privately if you wished. Garbh was lying with belly and chin flat to the ground, ears cocked, quiet, but bristling in rippling waves.

But Thurston himself seems confident enough. Of course, he'd be acting that way in any case, eh? And he's taken a liking to me, right enough, enough to let us hang around, and to tell me his thoughts now and then. Well, and so have I to him and his sons. A hard man, yes, but not so hard as he's been painted. I think he's seen all he's done as . . . needful, even when it hurt him to do it.

Mathilda spoke quietly beside him as she stroked the nose of her charger. "The game of thrones, the game of swords . . . I don't like what they do to people. The ones who have to play them."

Rudi looked over at her in surprised affection. "It seems your thoughts are running with mine again, Matti. Well, you may not be liking it . . . but our host yonder seems a natural at it."

Mathilda shook her head and leaned on her tall kite-shaped shield. "I like him," she said.

"Me too."

"And I was thinking of how much happier he'd be running a big farm and breeding horses . . . or maybe something like a sawmill or a bunch of riverboats or . . . he's got the gift for organizing; he reminds me of Count Conrad that way. Him and his lady and their kids, making a home, doing something . . . really useful, not just necessary, the way ruling is."

There was a wistfulness to her voice. Rudi nodded ruefully.

"I know what you're driving at." He hesitated. *Still, when better to say it? This probably won't be our last day before the Summerlands; but then again, it might.*

"I've been glad to have you along on this journey, Matti."

She gave him a quick glance, concerned; he could see her brown eyes narrow under the mail coif. At that he laughed.

"No, I'm not fey and hearing the screecher. I'd say so if I were." She relaxed in relief. "I am glad to have you with me, even though it's fair selfish of me. For you're my oldest friend, and you know my mind without my having to speak it all, and I yours, and that is a comforting thing."

She put an arm around him. "You are too, Rudi . . . remember that night at Finney's farm, back during the war, just outside Corvallis? I was so lonely, and so homesick, and you and Juniper were about the only ones who were nice to me at first. We were ten, and you told me I was your best friend then. You're still mine. And I'll tell you something else; I'm glad to be here."

He nodded, then grinned slyly. "And while then you were a skinny little thing with a scab on your knee, now you're easy on the eyes, sure, even in a hauberk and greaves."

She snorted and thumped her gauntleted hand on his arm. "Men!"

Rudi jerked his chin towards Thurston, serious again. "Still, someone has to stand between the farms and mills and those who would burn them and kill the folk or carry them off slaves."

She sighed wordlessly and turned her face towards the east whence the Prophet's men would come, as if to say: *From them.*

They were on a slight rise, with much dry pasture and a few wheatfields that were nearly ripe behind and more of the same ahead; this ground had been too close to the old border to be densely settled. The lay of the land let him see the way the regiments flowed out of their encampments to take up their positions with unhurried speed. Messengers waited, and others manned an arrangement of lever-mounted mirrors on tripods.

That's a cunning device, so it is, but it won't be useful for long, Rudi thought.

This soil was fertile but light, and it was dry—still a little cool with night, but you could tell it was going to be hot, too. It would come up like fine dust under hoof and boot. There was already dust from the light volcanic soil in the air; he could taste the slightly salty alkaline bitterness of it on his lips, and it made him want a drink from his canteen. He resisted the impulse until he looked over his shoulder and saw light water tanks on wheels stationed behind the battle line, along with the ambulances and supply wagons full of spare javelins and bundled arrows and stacked shields.

There was more dust ahead eastward, much more—a plume growing wider as he watched.

Odd, Rudi thought. *They could go around this army, sure and they could. Battle is like dancing, in its way; the partners really have to agree for it to happen. They may not send messengers and set out a time and place, but everything short of that, yes.*

Ingolf spoke quietly, squinting into the rising sun under a shading hand: "They're shaking out from column into line. Moving fast, too. A lot of horsemen in that army, more than the Boise folks have. Three, four thousand, maybe even five."

"Any knights or men-at-arms?" Odard asked with interest; he was in full lancer's panoply. "Thurston's people don't seem to have any, just light horse."

Ingolf shook his head. "There's the Sword of the Prophet—like the ones we saw at the ambush, nothing heavier than that. Most lighter, like those men of Rancher Brown's."

He kept his eyes eastward, blinking in the sunlight. After a moment: "They're going to overlap our line a bit. Could be a lot of them, or they could be dragging brush to make it look that way, trying to spook us out of position. This is good ground—rises a bit towards us, and we're closer to water."

Ignatius nodded somberly. "There will be much more dust before sundown. As the crops are trampled and destroyed . . . what a waste war is. Men sweated to plow and plant here. I hate to think of their children hungry, because the work of months is spoiled in hours."

Edain spoke: "It's a slight on the Mother, is what it is."

His voice went quiet. "Back home they'll be up early to get the last of the wheat in. Pancakes and bacon, and Brigid's crosses hanging in the kitchen. Folk'll be thinking of the festival, and the feasting, and getting the gear ready for the fall plowing, and maybe taking some elk if Cernunnos grants, and the Lughnasadh games. I took the Silver Arrow last year, second time in a row. Dad was that pleased."

The homesickness on the square open face turned to a reminiscent smile. "He said he'd never shot better at his best! And after he had a beer or two at the tent he sang that old song that he had from his grandfather and his grandfather had from *his* . . . you know it, Chief?"

"And hasn't he sung it at Dun Juniper, now and then?" Rudi said; it was good to speak of homey things for a moment.

And we'll all drink together
Drink to the gray goose feather
And the land where the gray goose flew!

The twins were silent for once; he gave them a curious glance, and there was a spark there. Rudi's brows went up; his half sisters were uneasy too, and more so than they should be, more so than anything he could point to and name justified.

Mathilda spoke up, her voice a little distant: "The sun will be in our eyes."

Ingolf nodded. "For a while. If it's a long battle, it'll be in *their* eyes. And it's the end of a fight that counts, not the beginning."

They all fell silent. A gap in the noise let them hear what Thurston was speaking to his officers:

". . . so this will be a meeting engagement; they'll push us hard, to see if they can keep barreling west. Let *them* advance to contact; we've got the good ground and they'll break their teeth on us. You'll hold the sixth in reserve, Colonel Moore, with the seventh and twelfth. Any questions?"

His eldest son spoke: "Sir, any more news on the enemy's dispositions? This isn't his whole field force we're facing, not from the look of the dust."

The elder Thurston shook his head, but Rudi could hear the pride in his voice at the quick accurate guess: "Nothing new, Captain. Half Walker's men are still encamped around Twin Falls, which is holding hard. The rest are facing us—about our numbers, say ten thousand counting the Saints who've joined us. They're heavy on cavalry; his foot are mostly in the siege works. Say half-and-half horse and foot on their side, so watch your flanks carefully. Anything else? No? Then take your positions, gentlemen. It's going to be a long day."

＊　＊　＊

Odd, Rudi thought eight hours later. *A whole battle, and I've not drawn blade nor bow, done nothing but watch and wait and move forward or back a little. And yet I still feel tired.*

Neither had Thurston touched his sword; in fact, he'd spent the entire engagement nearly motionless save for his eyes and the hands holding his binoculars, bending to consult a map, speaking now and then to send out his messages by flashing mirrors or courier. A few arrows stood in the shields of his guard detail, and a field-catapult battery was dug in not far away, lofting six-pound iron round shot and long javelins at the enemy whenever they came in range.

Right now it was an enemy they could hardly see; the world had closed in, gradually at first and then more swiftly as the armies churned talc-fine volcanic soil and the rising wind sent it over their heads in tawny drifts. The *sound* of combat rolled up and down the front line—voices human and equine shouting and screaming, the whistle of arrow and dart, now and then the *rattle-clang-thump* of close-quarter fighting building to a crescendo and dying away.

"Odd to hear more of a fight than you can see of it, and that in daylight!"

Several of the others made noises of agreement; the twins were ostentatiously playing mumblety-peg to show how relaxed they were, and occasionally coming too close to their own toes. Twenty or thirty yards ahead he could see the backs of the nearest Boise troops, three staggered ranks waiting on one knee with their shields propped up against their shoulders, a line that stretched out of sight to either side.

He knew there was another triple rank a little farther forward, but the dust-fog swallowed sight. The sharp edge of battle had swayed back and forth here; there were dead men and horses of the Prophet's forces lying, their blood drunk by the thirsty soil; no wounded, luckily, any such among the fallen Corwinites having been given the mercy stroke. The unfamiliar dry acrid-sharp odor of the dust drank most of the smells of death, but there was an iron-and-sewage undertone to it that was all too universal.

As he watched a trumpet call rang, relayed down the whole front. The resting soldiers stood, raised their shields and trotted forward. As they faded into the war-made fog the three ranks that had held the front for the last half hour came walking backward into sight; most were walking, at least. Their breath came harsh, eyes stood stark in faces darkened with a paste of dust and sweat, and the pungent musky smell of them was strong even through hundreds of feet of dry air.

Some were using their long javelins as crutches, some were helped along with arms over the shoulders of unwounded comrades, and a few were carried on shields used as stretchers. Mule-drawn ambulances dashed forward to take the wounded; the hale gulped water from the carts that followed and then sank into the same formation as the men who relieved them. Each file sent men back to pick up bundles of fresh pila for their comrades.

"That's a good trick, switching the ranks like that," Odard said thoughtfully.

"Yeah," Ingolf agreed. "Keeps the men fresh . . . well, sort of fresh. Fresher than the other guys, I'd bet."

Rudi nodded, though that hadn't been uppermost in his mind. It was true, though. Fighting was brutally hard muscle work, worse than digging earth or cracking rocks with a sledge, especially when you did it in armor. The man who got tired and slow first was nearly as helpless as a sheep held for the butcher's knife. With the difference that an enemy wouldn't take trouble to make it painless or apologize to your spirit.

What I was thinking of was how difficult that was to do, and no mistake! Just a bit wrong, and the enemy would smash you up while you were at it like a hammer on an egg.

Another light water cart came up to supply the command group.

"My turn," he said, and everyone handed him their canteens.

Thurston came over to the water wagon as the Mackenzie tanist filled his friends' canteens and put his own under the other tap; despite knowing that half of leadership was showmanship, Rudi was a little impressed at the casual confidence that showed.

"Disappointed?" the older man said.

He spoke through a mask of dust and sweat; even the red-white-and-blue transverse crest of his helmet was nearly khaki. His dark eyes still twinkled a bit.

"Not in the least," Rudi said, truthfully. "I'm not so in love with hand-strokes that it grieves me to miss a fight, and I don't enjoy watching men die. And I've learned a good deal from following how you managed the battle, sure."

The corner of Thurston's mouth curved up in a smile. "Maybe I shouldn't have let you. I might have to extend the nation's writ out west, someday."

"In your dreams . . . sir," Rudi said cheerfully, and they shared a smile.

"What's your appraisal, youngster?" Thurston said, a considering look in his eye.

"Well, you're beating them, so far. It's been like watching a man try to batter down a wall by running at it with his face, so."

Thurston nodded. "It's nearly over, though they may give one last hard heave; they've got an uncommitted reserve somewhere; I can feel it."

Thurston peered eastward into the dust, rubbing water over his face and then taking a long drink. "Damn this dust, though. It makes my gliders useless, and I had to land them back around noon."

"There's that airship of yours," Rudi said. "The good father was most impressed with it. Like something out of the ancient times, he said."

"Yeah, on a nice calm day close to home it's a world-beater," Thurston said. "The rest of the time, it's me trying to explain why I wasted the public's hard-earned money on it. Hanks is too damned persuasive and he makes like that pedaling platoon of his is a diesel engine . . ."

"It would be useful here now," Rudi said. "The airship that is, not the easel."

"Diesel—" Thurston began, then snorted laughter. "You know perfectly well what a diesel is—was."

The noise of fighting began to die down a little, enough so that you noticed how loud they remained. Thurston's voice was meditative.

"If they weren't so stubborn, it would have been over hours ago. They've got better infantry than I expected, and horse archers are always a pain in the ass, but they don't have a hope of breaking us and they can't go around us."

"Why not?" Rudi asked. "It's a spacious landscape you have here, to be sure. I was thinking just now that it was as if you and they had agreed to fight here."

"Go around?" Thurston's grin was feral. "Yeah, with fortified villages in it like raisins in a cake, and my army across their line of communication ready to corncob them. And they must have lost two, three thousand men today—they weren't expecting our field artillery, not a bit. I've kept it out of sight the last ten years—no big pitched battles where I really needed it."

"What will you do next?"

"I can beat them, but I can't catch them if they backpedal and don't want to fight; they've got more cavalry. So I'll just march towards Twin

Falls in battle order. Then they can either fight with the city as the anvil and us as the hammer—and get broken completely—or they can lift the siege and pull right out of the Snake River plain, losing everything they've fought for three years to get. After that . . . we'll see."

The general's head came up, looking westward towards his reserves. The dust made it difficult to see, and the huge roaring surf of combat cut hearing, but it looked as if men were moving. He waved Rudi aside and strode back to his subordinates.

To an aide, he snapped, "Get to Moore and find out what's happening there!"

A minute later the young man came galloping back. "Sir, Captain Thurston reports—"

"Captain Thurston? Where the hell is Colonel Moore, then?"

"Dead, sir. He went to contain an enemy breakthrough—stray arrow in the eye. Captain Thurston says that he had to shift the twelfth and four batteries of the artillery reserve to contain it."

Thurston grunted. "Sergeant Anderson!"

The tall silent blond man came forward. "Captain?"

"Go see what the hell is happening with Martin and why he's senior man there—or acting like it. Get back here soonest."

The noise to the front died down then, almost to silence. The wind rose slightly; Rudi could feel trickles of it on his neck, stealing down to leave tormenting bits of comfort in the greasy, itchy sweat that accumulated under armor. He filled his helmet before the water cart trundled off, and then dumped it over his head; it ran down into the padding beneath his brigandine and mail, a flush of delicious coolness. His friends were silent as he handed out the canteens, their eyes fixed eastward.

Dust parted before them, though everything was still blurred by a brown-gold haze. Through it the foot soldiers of the Church Universal and Triumphant could be seen, pulling sullenly back in a thick dark mass of large round shields edged with steel spear points. They parted in the center like a door opening.

Beyond that was a line of glittering metal points of light over red-brown . . . the lance heads of the Sword of the Prophet, three thousand horsemen strong. The line of light rippled and flashed as the butts of the lances were lifted out of the scabbards; it would be cold steel now, not long-distance play with arrows.

Thurston grunted as if he'd been punched in the belly. "Christ! Well, now we know where *their* reserve was. Courier! *Courier!* Get spare pila forward—"

Rudi stepped back as Thurston's voice rapped out in a string of orders and men exploded outward like a covey of geese spooked from a pond. Off to the north the dug-in artillery batteries were in a flurry of activity too, crews pumping like madmen to send water through the armored hoses to the hydraulic jacks that cocked their actions. More field catapults galloped up from north and south and deployed as he watched, and their loaders dashed back and forth to the ammunition wagons, staggering under loads of four-foot javelins and hundred-and-twenty-pound rope bags of round shot. Others broke out bundles of beehive—wickedlooking six-inch finned steel darts, needle-pointed and heavy.

His friends tightened girths and set their helms on their heads; you left that for the last minute if you could. Wearing a helmet for hours at a time gave you a headache, as sure as a blow from a mace.

"For what we are about to receive—" Ingolf said.

"—may the Lord make us truly thankful," Odard finished, then kissed his crucifix, tucked it back under his hauberk and crossed himself; Mathilda and the big easterner followed suit, and Odard's servant Alex.

"Lady of the Ravens, fold me in Your wings," Rudi murmured. "Antlered One, God of my people, You whose voice is heard on the mountainsides, lift Your hand over us. To both of You I dedicate the harvest of the unplowed field."

His skin was prickling as he stripped the cover off a shield to let the world see the antlers-and-moon blazon of Clan Mackenzie. Edain gave him a grim nod as he strung his longbow and then started working his right arm in circles, loosening the thick muscles; he looked very much like his father just then, which was comforting.

A silence fell along the line—silence save for the screams of those too hurt for anything but the rending of their bodies to have meaning. The dust drifted westward, and they could hear the low endless rumble of twelve thousand shod hooves striking the ground; hear it, and feel it through the soles of their feet, first as a low vibration and then a shaking like a stationary earthquake as thousands of tons pounded the flesh of the Mother in every instant.

Epona tossed her head and snorted, ears forward; the other horses shifted uneasily, and Macha Mongruad squealed in rage, the leather-backed steel plates of her barding clattering.

Odard thought having two destriers ready was being extravagant. I don't think so.

A human sound rose through the hooves. The Sword of the Prophet were chanting as the lance heads fell level: *"Cut! Cut! Cut! Cut!"*

The fighting men of the Republic replied, a long *Oooooo-rah* that rolled up and down the ranks, a deep snarling shout full of guttural defiance and threat. A sharp bull bellow of "Come, ye Saints!" from the New Deseret troops off southward.

"CUT! CUT! CUT! CUT!"

When ten thousand men shouted in unison it was less a sound than a blow, something that thudded into your face and made your chest sound like a drum. And it struck below that too, and made Rudi's lips curl back from his teeth.

He understood what it was to look into a man's eyes over a blade and know that one of them would die; that was how the Lord and Lady had made the world, as much as the leap of a tiger on a deer, or two buck elk locking horns in the spring. That was strength and speed, skill and luck and nerve against the same. Having a small city coming towards you with nothing but murder in its heart was something else again, and as impersonal as being caught in a mudslide . . . or lying strapped to the latest log in a sawmill.

"CUT! CUT! CUT! CUT!"

Thurston shouted to someone, loud enough to be heard above the stunning roar: "I don't care what they're doing; get the reserve up here *now*. All of them, and on the double!"

The catapults of the field batteries cut loose in unison with a multiple crashing of throwing arms against rubber-shod steel. Javelins arched out, twirling as their curved fins took the air, seeming to slow as they went, and the steel balls of the round shot. Men fell, their mounts fell—sometimes an entire file of three, where a six-pound steel ball traveling at four hundred feet a second hit the ground and bounced and broke legs like brittle sticks as it spun whirling forward.

The Sword of the Prophet came on at a steady hand-gallop, opening out around bodies thrashing and screaming and bodies lying still, closing again like a flood around a rock in a display of horsemanship that would have been beautiful if it hadn't been so frightening. The companions turned their mounts towards the front and raised their shields, barding and the kite-shaped lengths of plywood protecting them and the horses against the bale-wind of arrowheads whose farthest spray began to fall around them.

Ground and center, ground and center, Rudi thought; not trying to calm himself, but instead channeling the building fear and fury, until they opened doors in his soul.

When you did that *Someone* was always likely to answer. The world flashed for an instant into black outlines veined across with red, like the feather of a skeletal raven dipped in blood drawn across the surface of existence. Coolness ran across his skin, turning muscle and nerve to silk and fire, balanced and pure, moving to the beating heart of Earth that was his own pulse. Talons gripped all creation, and wings beat a wind whose dust was stars.

Doubt flickered out of him, like a candle flame's instant death in a gale. *This is* right, *it is,* he thought. *This is just where* They *wanted me to be.*

Arrows whickered up from the rear ranks of the Cutters, black against the tired fading blue of the afternoon sky, snapping down faster and faster as they arched over the huge blunt wedge. Rudi's mind saw their course through the air, the weft of a single great loom, each etched like a thread of diamond through the world. The lancers seemed like men without shadows as they charged into the setting sun, the heads of their horses driving up and down above the dust-mist that half hid them. The catapults switched to the canister rounds, the bundles of darts sweeping forward, spreading out like the claws of leaping cats as the bands that bound them snapped.

They crossed the arrows in flight, warp to their weft, and the world shook to the thump of the loom's heddle; the Weaver's face hung over it, ancient, terrible, sooty and single-eyed, scored with grief and anger huge enough for the death of suns. The massed grunt of the Boise footmen as they launched their spears made an undertone to it, part of the song the worlds sang. So was the endless flicker of their swords as they drew and crouched behind their big shields, shoulders tucked into the inner surfaces and strong muscled legs braced.

And the lances struck.

The sound went through him, *thud,* as if the massive impact had been in his own belly, snapping his teeth together in reflex. A crash, but the crash went on and on. Lances with a ton of galloping horse behind them struck through thick shields and steel-hoop armor, or broke and went pin-wheeling up into the sky in a blurring flicker. Men were bowled over by sheer impact, falling and sprawling stunned or curling under their shields against the stamping hooves; the whole front line vanished. Wedges of horsemen drilled in threes thrust into the gaps the lances and arrows had left; men stepped up from the second and third ranks, smashing with their shields, stooping for the hocking strike against the hamstring of a horse, stabbing, stabbing.

"They're breaking through!" Odard shouted, his voice crackling with excitement.

He snatched a lance from his servant Alex's hand and used it to lever himself into the saddle. Rudi put a hand on the cantle of Epona's saddle and vaulted into it. The Prophet's men had broken through, or at least chunks of them had. The Boise line kept stubbornly re-forming behind them, and then the Corwinite infantry charged again. All the neat forma-tions were gone, and it turned into a churning chaos of men who hit and stabbed and staggered forward and back, locked more closely together than lovers, sometimes stopping for a second by unspoken mutual con-sent to wheeze hatred at one another until they got back breath enough to fight.

Patterns, Rudi thought. *It's all patterns.*

So easy to see, with eyes that *could* see. Three or four hundred of the Sword of the Prophet were loose in the rear; they regrouped, like beads of water sliding together on a waxed board, and spurred their horses straight for the command group where the eagle standard of the Republic stood.

"Follow me!" Rudi shouted. Then a shriek: *"Morrigú!"*

They had just enough room to build up momentum as their lances dipped. The seven of them crashed into the side of the Cutter wedge as *it* hit the line of the presidential guard detachment. Rudi left his lance in a man's side and swept out his longsword; the motion ended in a cut across a wrist and the hand leaped free. . . .

Seconds passed. A catapult lay on its side, one wheel spinning and its crew gaping dead about the tumbled metal. A horse beat its head against the ground and thrashed as it tried to stand, but both its forelegs were smashed, splinters showing through torn skin. A man crawled away from

it, his face a mask of blood, patting the ground before him as he called,
"Thumper! Thumper, boy!"

The roar of combat died away abruptly; a long trotting line came up
from the westward, threw their pila, snapped out swords and charged in a
bristling unison like the hairs rising on an enraged boar's back. The combat
swept past Rudi, swept the others away from him, all but Edain standing
at his stirrup and glaring, his last arrow on the string. The eagle standard
stood canted to one side, the red and white and blue of the flag hanging
limp. Dust blew about them again, and the sun had touched the horizon
to the west, starting its slide below the plain. Heat held him like a vise,
and the hand of something more. The sword fell slowly to his side.

Rudi could see. And hear, as if the scene before him were only at arm's
length. Martin Thurston was on his knees beside his father, hand just
touching the broken Cutter lance driven up beneath his ribs. Men stood
around him, men with a numeral 6 above the crossed thunderbolts on
their eagle-faced shields; those same shields kept what happened from
view.

"You're *late,*" the president whispered, in a last attempt at gallantry.
Then a gasp, and: *"Medic!"*

With that he saw something in his son's face; his own went slack with
surprise.

"Why?" he said, the tone almost normal, despite the blood on his
lips.

"I had to," the younger man said. "You'd take my inheritance and my
son's—your grandson's—and give it to strangers. I can't let you do that.
Not even you, Father."

"Not . . . *yours,*" the wounded man gasped, as he began to struggle.
"Not mine, not yours!"

"You're old, Father. Old and out of touch, and I knew you'd never
understand. And—"

His hand moved on the wood of the lance shaft, driving the steel
head deep with a single strong wrench. The body in his arms stiffened,
tried to call out, then relaxed limply with blood on its lips. He pulled the
steel loose then, and laid it beside the dead man.

"I'm sorry, Dad. I'm so sorry," Martin Thurston whispered, as the tears
ran down a face rigid as a board. "I'm so sorry."

Seconds passed, and the son bent to kiss the father's forehead. *Patterns*, Rudi thought.

Only one man had been close enough to see, besides himself. Frederick Thurston stood not ten paces from him, his gaze slack and unbelieving. Rudi saw Martin's eyes on his brother as he rose from their father's body; they were black and bitter cold even as the rest of the face twisted with a terrible grief.

The universe moved, like a mountain balanced trembling on the sword blade of a god.

"Morrigú!" Rudi shrieked, breaking into the tense stillness of the moment, and clapped his heels to the destrier's sides.

A trooper of the sixth regiment went down beneath the pounding hooves; following at her dam's heels Macha Mongruad stamped on him, hard. Martin Thurston's mind might be in turmoil, but his reflexes did not sleep; he threw himself back with a yell, rolling in a back-somersault despite the weight of his armor. The tip of the longsword tore a tiny divot of skin and flesh from the tip of his nose as it passed, and snapped his head to one side. Then Rudi tossed it into his left hand along with reins and the grip of his shield, and bent in the saddle.

Rudi knew he was very strong. Frederick Thurston was a grown man in armor; to snatch him off the ground from horseback, and that at the gallop, was something he'd have thought beyond his reach. Now he did it, though every tendon from his right hand to his hips seemed outlined in blue fire for an instant. Then he was through; the young man he'd rescued from his brother seemed sensible enough to lie quiet across Epona's saddlebow for an instant.

As he circled around the rest of his companions gathered about him; the edge of battle was passing westward again, and the fight breaking up into clumps of men who hacked at one another or fled.

"We have to get out of here," he said bluntly, letting the young man slide to the ground. "Martin Thurston killed his father—"

"What?" Mathilda said, eyes wide.

"It's true," Frederick Thurston said, his voice shaking. "I saw it . . . he was wounded . . . Martin *killed* him. . . ."

"There's no time," Rudi said. "He'll want us all dead; he saw that I saw, and his brother too—"

Odard snapped his fingers. "That ambush we interrupted down south—the assassins—he must be working with the Prophet's men!"

Rudi flicked a glance westward. It was several thousand yards, but he could still hear the snarl of wrath that went through Boise's army as the news of their leader's death went from man to man.

"I wouldn't want to be the one to hold him to his deal," he said. "Not now that he's won."

"Yeah," Ingolf added, his lips tight. "He won't stay bought . . . uh-oh. Cavalry headed our way. Those Cutters who broke through aren't trying to get back to their own lines. Looks like they've got orders about us."

"We've got to split up," one of the twins said. "Into smaller groups at least."

Rudi nodded. "If they've got one dust trail to follow we're all dead. Meet at the rendezvous. *Fast.*"

Rudi had swung down out of the saddle and stripped off the barding from Epona and her daughter as he spoke; they didn't need fifty extra pounds.

"Right," he said, tossing Macha Mongruad's reins to the younger Thurston. "Fred, you'll go with Father Ignatius."

He met the cleric's eye, and received a short sharp nod.

"Everyone, *get going.*"

*   *   *

Baron Odard Liu slid out of the saddle as his horse collapsed, wheezing blood and froth as the arrowhead worked its way into the lungs. He was in the upper reaches of a defile, and he'd have had to let the beast go soon anyway, as the footing grew worse. Rock crunched and slid under his feet, and he turned with his shield up as the yelping cries of the pursuit echoed off the tall rock faces to either side.

Death tasted of salt and tears and sweat, and bitter alkali dust and the chill of morning. Awareness of it had been growing as they ran and hid and twisted through the hours of darkness.

No man could outrun an arrow.

Or his fate, he thought. *Still, I'd have liked to lay a few more girls in the clover and sing a few more songs before I went . . . at eighty, by preference, and on a throne. . . .*

"Sorry," he said to Mathilda Arminger. "I'll hold them as long as I can. Ingolf drew off a fair number."

Her face was stiff but unyielding. *Brave to a fault,* he thought, then scowled as she slipped down from her own mount.

"Now, please, don't spoil my gesture," he said. "I *would* like my last heroic stand to have some point."

"Don't be ridiculous," she said. "I can't climb that in a hauberk, and if I try taking it off, they'll be on us before I'm half done. Let's make it cost them."

He sighed. "How deplorably practical you are, Princess," he said. "Admirably courageous, though."

But then, whatever anyone called her father, nobody ever said he was a coward. And I don't think the Spider has nerves at all, just clockwork and levers inside. Whenever I regret my mother, it would be well to remember what poor Mathilda has to put up with!

There was a mouthful of water left in his canteen, and they shared it as the Cutters rode into the space beneath them. Two boulders and a dead cottonwood gave the three of them a little cover. He was a bit surprised to see Alex hadn't slipped off; the little man was reliable, but this was beyond the usual call of duty.

That must have shown on his face. "The dowager baroness charged me most particularly to keep you safe, my lord," he said, and turned away to cock his crossbow.

"Good man," Odard said. Then he looked at Mathilda. "By the way, I love you," he went on. Then at her shocked look: "Well, it may not be the opportune moment, but there may not be all that many more."

The Cutters had sent their horses to the rear and were standing crouched with their shields up. It was middling bowshot, but they were fairly well armored, and the ground wasn't too steep most of the way from the dry creekbed to his position. . . .

Their commander came out from his unit's shield wall and stood with hands on his hips. "I haven't got the time to shilly-shally," he called. "The High Seeker wants you alive; only the Ascended Masters know why. Give yourself up—and I guarantee your safety until you're turned over to my superiors. If you don't, well, I didn't promise to capture you *unharmed.* Just alive."

Odard searched for a suitable reply; Mathilda preempted him with a short pungent pair of words. The Cutter's tuft of chin beard moved as he grinned.

"I won't forget that, soulless Nephilite whore," he said coldly, and drew his shete. "Ready, you servants of the Light-bearer!" he called to his men.

The universe dissolved in silver light. When Odard could think again he found himself facedown, and even the dry gritty smell of the rock beneath his face made his stomach twist in nausea. He recognized the other sensations—whirling dizziness, stabbing pain—and didn't bother trying to stand up; getting your brain rattled around in your head wasn't like taking a nap, and nobody just sprang back to their feet and went on their way afterwards. The coif and padding had absorbed most of the force of the blow by Alex's crossbow butt, but enough had gotten through. . . . He gulped back stomach acid and glared at his servant's boots.

The older man held the crossbow on Mathilda and spoke: "Your Highness, I didn't promise the baroness to keep *you* alive at all costs, so please don't move. Even that armor won't stop a bolt at this range."

"Traitor!" she snapped.

"I'm a Gervais vassal, and you're not my liege," Alex said tranquilly. "Baroness Mary saved my life and my family's after the Change, and I'm going to keep her son alive whether he has the sense to agree or not."

"Kill me, then!" Mathilda spit, beginning to raise her sword.

"Oh, I won't kill you. I'll just shoot you through the shoulder . . . and I'm a *very* good shot, Your Highness. The Cutters won't hurt either of you. They'll even give you a good doctor. But you'll be laid out for months."

Slowly, reluctantly, her fingers opened and she dropped the blade. *Smart, too,* Odard thought with punch-drunk detachment. *God and the Saints, what a woman!*

Alex nodded and called out over his shoulder without taking his eyes off her, much louder: "Glastonbury! Violet God-flame! I have your safe-conduct passwords and two very valuable hostages, gentlemen!"

Odard let his head fall to the rock and groaned slightly. Obviously Mary Liu had been giving instructions behind his back again.

Mother, must you always interfere? he thought, and then let himself fall back into the waiting blackness.

* * *

Ingolf Vogeler laughed. "Haven't we been here before?" he said, as he looked at the drawn bows of the Cutters.

Near-ripe wheat hissed against his stirrups, the mealy smell earthy and dusty-sweet, infinitely homelike in a way that would fill him with bitter nostalgia if he let it.

Maybe I could have eaten enough crow to stay home, he thought. His spine stiffened, and he remembered Pierre Walks Quiet's voice around a camp-fire one night: *A man lives as long as he lives, and not a day more.*

He glanced over his shoulder at the walls of the village double-bowshot away across the flat yellow-blond field. He'd run all night and into the dawn. Almost made the village wall, almost made the hills be-yond. So close . . .

And I'm going to die thirsty and hungry and tired. Shit.

"The last time was a good ways east of here," he said. "It wasn't as good a day as you thought, or as bad as I did at first."

"Indeed we have met so," High Seeker Kuttner said. "Glad to see you again like this, Vogeler. Oh, so very glad to see you."

"Not seeing as much of me as you did the last time when you had two eyes, you pissant little Cyclops," Ingolf taunted, forcing a sand-dry mouth to speak and to smile.

He gave a silent sigh of disappointment as the gesture that had almost ordered the horse archers to shoot stopped unmade.

The commander of the score of Corwinite cavalry looked around anx-iously. Every third man of his troop was wounded, some with bandages still leaking blood, and foam streaked the shoulders and necks of their horses. Only two unsaddled horses followed on leading reins. He licked his lips and spoke: "High Seeker, there are enemy patrols all around us."

"They may not be looking very enthusiastically," Kuttner said, with a secret smile.

"High Seeker, we *must* break eastward now if we're to get through be-fore the Boise cavalry get their screen tight. What shall we do?"

Kuttner smiled more broadly. Even ready for death and raising his shete for the final rush, Ingolf found his stomach twisting a little at the cruelty in the expression. Killing this one would be a service to human-kind in general. His eyes flicked around; a dozen bows, but he *might* just live long enough to cross the ten yards and strike—

"What shall we do? What there wasn't time to do when this apostate escaped from Corwin," Kuttner said.

Then he spoke three words and moved his hand in a sign. Ingolf dropped his shete to his side. Incredulously, he looked down at it and told it to move. Instead the thick muscular fingers opened, and the weapon fell point-first to go *shink* in the gritty volcanic soil beneath the wheat; the golden heads waved around the leather-wrapped hilt.

Kuttner rode close, and slapped him casually across the face. Sweat broke out on Ingolf's skin as he strove to move.

"You have much to learn," he said. "Much to experience, Ingolf apostate. The Ascended Masters have called your name. It echoes through the Valley of Paradise and whispers in the Eternal Flame. The Prophet is dying, and in His passing He will require servants. And there is a drum you desecrated that needs a new hide to cover it. Come with me."

* * *

"*Lacho Calad! Drego Morn!*" Ritva shouted in unison with her sister.

There were four men in the Cutter patrol that came over the rise, pushing hard to catch the pair they'd been chasing for hours. Two died as the sisters shot, the arrows cracking into their breastplates and sinking halfway to the feathers; it was only thirty yards, and they'd carefully picked the ones with bows in hand and arrows on the string. The Cutters had all been in the battle yesterday, and the quivers of the other two were empty.

They charged without hesitation anyway, one leveling a lance and the other holding his shete up. Acrid dust shot up from the hooves of their horses, heavy with pebbles in this stretch where the flat plain met the northern foothills.

"Where did you two get that ambling crowbait?" Ritva shouted, as she legged her horse into a gallop towards them.

Which was unfair; Duélroch and Mary's Rochael had been standing idle all yesterday, and the Arabs had uncanny endurance to boot. On the other hand, fighting was the last thing on the Lord and Lady's earth you wanted to do *fairly*. The mares built speed with jackrabbit bounds despite the shallow slope they were climbing.

The two Dúnedain and the pair of Cutters closed with the shocking abruptness a combined gallop produced, but the Cutters' horses were laboring. She could see snarls of effort on the men's faces, and the marks of exhaustion. Then only a pair of pale eyes over the shield rim as the enemy braced themselves for impact, ducking down behind their shields against arrows . . .

. . . and the twins pivoted left and right, splitting to either side like water from a wedge and throwing themselves away and down in the saddle as well. Ritva took her weight on her bent left leg and pressed her face into Duélroch's flying mane for an instant. The lance head went through the space she'd been in; then she was back in the saddle as her leg uncoiled like a spring, bringing the mare up on her haunches to shed her hurtling forward momentum.

Or most of it; still on her hind legs, Duélroch had to crow-hop twice to keep from tumbling, with dust shooting forward from under her hooves. Then she landed and whirled, superbly responsive to Ritva's shift of balance. The Ranger's hand went back over her shoulder and she had the arrow drawn to the ear before the horse had fully settled again. It stood stock-still to the signal of knees and legs as she aimed for half a second, with the kissring on the string touching the chapped skin of her upper lip and the narrow pile-shaped arrowhead resting on the arrow ledge over her gloved knuckle.

The Cutters were frantically trying to rein their own horses in and around, but they'd only begun when the *snap-snap* of bowstrings on steel cut sharply through the whistle of the wind and the hammer of hooves.

Crack.

At less than twenty feet even the best armor wouldn't stop a bodkin point from a powerful bow. The leather plates over the Corwinite horse soldier's upper spine hardly even slowed it as it punched through and into bone. The man dropped limp as an empty sack, striking the ground and rolling twice, snapping the shaft of the arrow off.

Crack.

Mary's arrow missed the spine, smashing through just beside it and out the man's chest, transfixing the lungs but not the heart. He screamed and fell and dragged, one boot twisted in the stirrup; the horse stopped and looked back at him in puzzled alarm. Mary swung down out of the saddle and did the needful thing with her sword, putting the point behind one ear and giving a single sharp push; the man didn't resist, either too nearly unconscious or glad of the release from pain.

Then they freed the horses, stripping off saddle and bridle and slapping their rumps to set them off; they'd find water, and probably somebody would round them up eventually.

Mary grimaced as she came up, wiping and sheathing her sword.

"I hate doing that," she said, taking a drink from her canteen after they had both tasted earth and murmured the prayer.

"Me too, sis," Ritva said, thankful her kill had been clean.

Her hands fought to shake; suddenly she was conscious of sweat and itches and the heat of the noonday sun. Hot dry wind was cool on her sodden hair as she slung her helmet to her saddlebow.

"I think Rudi got cut off a little south of here," she said worriedly.

"*Mer,*" Mary said, agreeing. "But he might get ahead of them and circle north. Let's get to the rendezvous and see who made it."

They worked their way northward, towards a butte shaped like a camel's head and hump. Ritva's head came up as she caught the ringing stamp of a shod hoof on rock, and then she relaxed again and lowered her bow as Father Ignatius stepped out from behind a curve of stone. Edain came next, and then young Frederick Thurston. *He* looked like a man who'd been hit behind the ear with a sock full of wet sand, but not quite hard enough to knock him out.

But then, Ritva thought compassionately, *he's got it worse than us. He's seen treachery by his own kin.*

"Rudi?" Mary said sharply; he and the younger Mackenzie left the battlefield together.

Edain's sunburned face flushed. "We had a big clump of them on our heels so we split up. I managed to lose mine and get here." His lips thinned. "We've been waiting since."

Father Ignatius nodded and glanced at the sun. "Anyone who is not here yet isn't going to arrive," he said.

Then he pointed north, to a tall hill. "And there is a dust trail heading in this direction. At least a score of men."

Ritva winced. That meant either the enemy, or Boise cavalry . . . who might well now *be* the enemy; she didn't have enough of a feel for the place or the politics to know how openly Martin Thurston could hunt the ones who knew he'd killed his father.

If it's the Cutters, they caught someone and made them talk, she thought.

"What do we do?"

Ignatius smiled; it was grim, but confident. "We need to find the others . . . Rudi most of all."

"Head back towards the Prophet's men?" Mary said. "And . . . well, if they've caught him, they'll either kill him or take him east. That's a big piece of flatland and then hills east of here. We can't search it all."

"Not on the ground," Ignatius said. "But I think there is an alternative, God willing."

* * *

Ignatius looked at the leveled crossbows and raised his empty hands in a sign of peace.

"Give me a moment to speak, my sons, and then do as you will," he said.

The great curved shape of the *Curtis LeMay* filled most of the emergency airfield; it was staked down to a dozen heavy steel posts sunk in the earth on either side. The gliders and their launching apparatus were scattered across a wide stretch of sparse pasture around about. Soldiers and ground crew stood about in clumps, their faces grim; many showed the marks of weeping. The air was warm and very still, and smelled of latrines and metal and crude cookery, and under that a chemical taint from the steel gas-generating boxes on a half dozen great six-wheeled wagons.

"The couriers said you were wanted in connection with the president's death," Hanks replied flatly.

The men and women behind him growled slightly, gripping their weapons and staring narrow-eyed.

"We *saved* the president once," Ignatius pointed out. "You know that, and that it makes no sense for us to save him once to kill him a few weeks later. But don't take my word for it."

He urged his horse aside. A gasp broke out as Frederick Thurston's brown face came clear to their sight.

"And here's your own president's son to tell you the truth," Ignatius said, his trained voice rolling out clear.

* * *

"I know this place," Rudi Mackenzie said to himself and his horse, his voice hoarse with thirst.

Mountains rose before him, bare save for a scattering of silvery-gray scrub, up great walls of rock and scree to the glaciers floating far above.

The smell of cold rock and aromatic herbs and old sweat soaked into wool and leather filled his nostrils. The rattle of stone under shod hooves was loud, and far and faint came a baying like wolves that he knew was men. Ahead was the rest of the bare ridge, and over it another huge empty valley. The mountains were very far.

On the slopes of the ridge he could look far behind. Three separate plumes of dust headed towards him; he judged their speed and then ran his hand down Epona's neck. She snorted and tossed her head, weary as she was.

"So, my girl, you've run well, it's splendid and brave and strong you are still," he said.

But there's only one of you, and I'm riding heavier than most of those even with only my helm and brigandine, I think, he mused. *Soon you will be grazing the meads of the Land of Youth.*

High above, black wings cruised through the air. He chuckled. "It's often I've said I'm ready to come when You call me, Lady of the Crows. If this is the time . . . well, I'll harvest a field as a bridal gift for You, so!"

He dismounted and took a careful swallow of his water, then poured the rest of it into his helmet and held that for Epona. She slobbered eagerly and her lips chased every drop into the padded lining.

"Now, don't be greedy, my fair one. That's all there is," he said gently, and put the sallet back on his head.

The raised visor acted as a sunshade; it was six hours past noon, and the long night of pursuit had tired them both.

"Sure, and they're a very determined lot, and have most impolitely kept between me and the rendezvous," he said. "Now let's see if I can break through them eastward and circle about beyond them."

He couldn't; that was obvious. He *might* be able to take some of them with him to the Summerlands, and give them a good talking-to there along with the Guardians, to shame them for serving a bad cause even if they did it bravely.

"And Edain got away," he said. "Now, that's a comfort. If Mother must grieve, at least old Sam is spared that."

Then he laughed, full-bodied. "So much for my grand journey across the continent! Yet I don't regret that as much as never really trying to give Matti a sound kissing."

He mounted again, waiting, and working his sword arm to limber it.

There was no fear now, and he thought he could hear voices singing—a deep humming, perhaps the bees making honey in the flowering clover meads of Tir-na-nog.

"Perhaps my father lingers there yet," he murmured as he drew his sword. "I never knew him as a man. We could talk, eh, and perhaps ride together and hunt and yarn, before we return once more."

The Cutters approached with shocking speed. Their "Cut . . . cut!" sounded triumphant as they saw him, and his answering shout was as joyous. Epona belled challenge, rearing, and he stood in the stirrups to call: "Welcome, brothers, in the name of the Crow Goddess!"

He laughed to see their rage, brought his shield up beneath his eyes as his legs prepared to clamp the horse's barrel one last time. For one long instant he thought the humming and song behind him were *Her* train, and the shadow that suddenly fell *Her* wings.

Then the Cutters were stopping, pulling their horses up so sharply that some of them reared or crashed in a neighing tangle into their neighbors. Bows dropped from nerveless hands. One stood and fired into the air, but a shaft streaked down from behind Rudi's head and went *crack* into his armor, the gray fletching of the Mackenzie clothyard shaft blossoming against the red-brown leather. As he slid from the saddle his mates wheeled and fled, only the cursing of an officer trying in vain to rally them.

Silence filled the air, along with a vast creaking. Slowly, slowly Rudi turned his head to see the *Curtis LeMay* rising further from behind the ridge, a hundred yards in the sky. That was close enough to see the faces—Edain, his half sisters, Frederick Thurston, Father Ignatius.

"Where—" he began.

Two of the crew slid down from the fore and aft of the gondola, planted anchors against solid rock, and winches squealed. Soon his friends and kinfolk were around him.

"What took you so long?" Rudi mock-scolded. Then his face grew serious. "The others?"

"No sign," Ritva said, and her sister nodded somberly. "There were enemy approaching the rendezvous."

Which means someone was captured, and talked, Rudi thought grimly.

He turned to Ignatius. "It's a luck bearer you've been for me, my friend," he said formally, bowing his head a little.

"God's will," the other man said.

"And Hers," Rudi added with a grin. That died as he looked at the others.

"It's a good deal of work we have to do," he said.

"I have to let everyone know how my father died," Frederick Thurston said; his young face looked somber, and more like his father's.

"And we have the others to find," Edain added; Garbh pressed her flank against him and whined, looking up at his head.

Rudi's eyes turned eastward. "And all that's part of something larger," he said softly. "The quest we started on, and that cannot stop either. Because—"

Then he staggered, pressing his hands to his head. *Cold! So cold!*

"Like fire," he muttered aloud, and then: "Lord and Lady!"

It was a matter of minutes before he was aware of hands guiding him to the ground and leaning him back against a boulder; a sharp scent of sagebrush rose as his brigandine crushed the herb against a rock. The mouth of a canteen touched his lips, and he drank eagerly, choked a little, swallowed more. The hard metallic taste of the lukewarm water was delightful as no mountain stream had ever been.

"What is it?" Ritva said sharply, going down on one knee. Blue eyes met gray-green.

She suspects something, he thought. *I wish I could make it clear to her, that I do.*

"What's happened?" her sister repeated.

"I don't know," Rudi said softly. "But it's something terrible."

EPILOGUE

Sethaz screamed and fell to his knees, hammering his fists on the sides of his head. The generals of the Sword of the Prophet stumbled back in horror as the endless wailing shriek grated at their ears; even the unmoving sentries facing outward around the open leaves of the command tent stirred, until an underofficer's bark brought them back to statue-stillness.

Veins stood out in the face of the Prophet's chosen son, and after a moment twin trickles of blood ran down his face from the corners of his eyes. He screamed again, and this time it turned into a howl like a hunting wolf, ending in a squeal and a long panting.

"Water," he croaked at last. "Water."

General Walker sprang forward to offer it, and Sethaz grabbed eagerly, then forced himself to drink more slowly.

"Brandy," he said in a voice like rust flaking off old iron.

The generals looked at one another, and then one produced a silver flask. Sethaz took two swallows, coughed, stood, handed it back, and looked around the circle of hard scarred faces.

"All is well, Light-bearers," he said, and smiled.

A few of them blinked, though none showed obvious fear. Cowards didn't achieve high rank in Corwin's armies.

Sethaz's voice grew stronger, though it might never fully recover from that scream. He could *feel* the strength in it, now, and he marveled as the dark wave of it flowed out through the lifestreams about it.

"Are you all right, my lord?" Walker asked cautiously; thoughts were moving behind his eyes, weighing and considering.

"I am gifted with many bright and fair lifestreams," Sethaz said. "The Prophet has left his mortal shell and Ascended to join the Masters."

This time there were bitten-off exclamations. The news had been expected, but not *this* way. Now several did show fear. Sethaz's lips showed his teeth, and more of them looked afraid.

"I am the Prophet now."

"Ah . . . the enshrining . . ."

His hand moved in a gesture. "The Ascended Ones have made me Prophet; what do I need of men's ceremonies?"

His voice rang in the warm air, cutting through the brabble of camp and siege. Not far away a trebuchet cut loose, the great cage of rocks at the short end of the lever falling, slowly at first, then with gathering speed. The long arm whipped up into the sky; the quarter-ton stone in the sling at its end broke free at the top of the arch, tumbling towards the breach in the walls of Twin Falls.

"But They require action of us."

He drew his shete and pointed it, slicing through their objections: "*Cut! Cut!*"

They looked at one another one more time. Walker drew his weapon as well.

"Cut!" he called, then screamed orders.

Trumpets and drums bellowed, and men scrambled to mass for the assault. Sethaz's banner went forward with them.

"Cut! *Cut! CUT!*"

* * *

The new Prophet climbed slowly to the dais at the front of the Mormon church—they called it a Stake Center. Bright arterial blood spattered the russet plates and scutes of his armor, and his face. It clotted thickly along his right arm, and on the blade of his shete, dropping on the dark polished wood and making the soles of his boots slightly tacky, an iron scent under the growing waft of smoke from the fires outside, and the fear-sweat within. When he rested his elbows on the lectern, more ruby drops fell from the broad curved blade.

The great room was crowded: the Cutters of his personal guard facing in, and a mob of the inhabitants—the more important of them, or the more important ones that were still alive. Some of them were barely so, held up by their families and seeping yet more blood through rough bandages. A few children cried, but mostly the interior of the temple was a gloom through which went silence and rustlings. Firelight flickered through the colored glass of the windows where pioneers dug and angels sang.

A chorus of screams from outside went on and on, like one great shout of terror and agony mixed with bestial triumph; and that was song enough for him.

Sethaz smiled. A woman in the first row screamed at the sight, and the expression grew until teeth showed. When he spoke, his voice echoed clearly to the limits of the crowd.

"*I am the Scourge of God.* If you had not sinned greatly, He would not have delivered you into my hands."

A moan went through them. He pointed with the sword to the woman who'd screamed, and spoke to the guard-commander at the foot of the stairs.

"Set that one aside for me, Captain. And ten men at random to spread the word; let them see the others die, and then take their eyes. Kill the rest."

The blades of the guard troopers rose as one, and firelight broke ruddy off the edged metal. A huge guttural shout of: "*Cut! Cut! Cut!*" almost overrode the screams.

Almost, but not quite.